Evermore

A Saga of Slavery and Deliverance
The Plantation Series, Book III

Gretchen Craig

Pendleton
Press

Evermore

A Saga of Slavery and Deliverance
The Plantation Series, Book III

Chapter One

May 1862

The good citizens of New Orleans slung insults and worse at the Yanks marching up Canal Street, but not Nicolette Chamard. She was elated. At last, these soldiers were going to free every enslaved soul in the South. In an unguarded moment, she forgot herself. Her lips curved and she pressed her hands to her heart.

Without warning, fingers gripped her shoulder, the thumb digging under her collar bone. A filthy man with a red face and glaring eyes loomed over her, his mouth twisted in fury.

"You wipe that smirk off your face, missy, you know what's good for you."

Icy fear shot up her spine. If he denounced her as a Yankee sympathizer, the crowd would stomp her into the ground. She wrenched free and plunged into the mob.

At the edge of the throng, she gripped a light post and told herself to breathe, just breathe.

She'd been careless, letting her feelings show. She knew better. No matter that she was free or that her skin was light, the requisite tignon she wore on her head identified her as a woman of color. And a colored woman in New Orleans better know her place.

Her pulse slowing, Nicolette threaded her way through the fringe of onlookers. Here, where she didn't have to steel herself against the dreaded touching and bumping, she relaxed her hands and shoulders.

Across from Presswood Mercantile, she looked to see if Marcel had come to witness the Yankees claim his city. He leaned against the balcony railing far above the rabble, his steady gaze on the liberators. Invaders, her half-brother would call them, overturning the life of ease and privilege he enjoyed as a rich white planter.

1

She resisted raising her hand to him. He would not welcome the familiarity in front of Miss Presswood, his flaxen-haired fiancé. No matter that they shared a deep affection, and no matter that Nicolette's gray eyes were lighter than his brown ones, her brother lived his life on a different plane. Marcel's mother had been Bertrand Chamard's wife. Nicolette's mother had been a slave on the neighboring plantation.

On a balcony above the hubbub, Marcel gripped the iron railing with white knuckles. His nose twitched at the smell of unwashed soldiers in damp, sweat-soaked wool. He had anticipated the day Union troops would enter his beloved city, but the impact was no less painful for having foreseen it.

A Confederate through and through, Marcel Chamard took a keen interest in the Yankee formations. They were neat enough, though their uniforms were worn and sometimes more gray than blue. He excused them their lack of polish. He even excused them the side they'd chosen. At least these men had rallied to their cause. Too many Southern gentlemen yet lingered in the comforts of home. Though he had not yet put on the uniform, Marcel was no malingerer.

Deborah Ann took his arm and murmured, "Marcel." He glanced at his fiancé and saw the warning on her face. They were amid their enemies. He unfisted his hands and unclenched his jaw.

Marcel spied his little sister down below. Though Nicolette wore an ordinary blue day-dress and a matching tignon, the required cloth folded and tied in intricate fashion over her black hair, she was a bright blue bird among the crows and sparrows of the crowd. Marcel had never wondered that his father fell in love with Nicolette's beautiful mother. His sister, too, was beautiful.

But, as she had been cosseted and adored all her life, she was naïve in her understanding of slavery in the South. No doubt Nicolette believed the Yanks would free the slaves before breakfast and turn the South into some sort of fairy-tale Eden by tomorrow noontime.

He'd done his part in spoiling her, but no one could deny she was an exceptional girl. Sang like an angel, with just enough of the devil in her to seduce an entire audience. And with her coloring, he thought for the hundredth time, Nicolette could pass for white, if she wanted to. But she chose not to. No, Nicolette knew nothing of politics or the real issues of the war.

When Deborah Ann stepped closer to him and wrapped his arm in hers, he patted her hand absently. His attention was still on Nicolette as she made her way through the thinning crowd. So very careful she was not to brush up against anyone. She thought no one knew how she shrank from being touched, but he had watched her withdraw after the ...incident. He hardly let himself think of it in more detail than that. It roiled him and threw him into a rage if he dwelled on what Adam Johnston had done to his baby sister, leaving her unconscious, bleeding and bruised.

Deborah Ann tugged at his arm. Marcel blinked the image away. He took one more look over his shoulder, annoyed with Nicolette for being out again with no protector. What good was the slave he'd given her if she left him at home?

Chapter Two

Three days after the parade marking the Union occupation of the city, Captain Finnian McKee felt he'd arrived in a paradise of blue sky and balmy breezes. Boston had nothing like this lush growth of exotic blooms and fragrant vines. He marched his detachment up Magazine Street, his senses open to the scents and sounds and sights of New Orleans. Particularly the female sights. His gaze followed a fetching belle in laces and ribbons.

"You know anything about foundries, Captain?" Lieutenant Dobbs asked.

"Not a thing. You?"

"No, sir. I was a clerk before the war."

"And I was a book seller." And a poet, but Finn seldom mentioned that. Back in Boston, he belonged to the number one rowing club on the Charles River, and he'd found the lads appreciated his stamina far more than they did his verses.

As a Signal officer, he ought to have been seeing to his flags and code books, but he'd riled old man Butler. When they'd dined with the garrison commander in Key West, Finn had unforgivably monopolized and flirted with the prettiest woman there, who happened to be seated at General Butler's left hand. Butler had cast a bilious, cross-eyed stare at Finn that night. This morning Butler had taken his revenge. Get the foundry going, he'd said.

The responsibility weighed lightly on his shoulders. Though he was no engineer, he imagined he'd figure it out, and the morning was too fine to waste on worry.

Then a lass snapped a carpet on the balcony above, releasing a cascade of dust and ashes on his and Dobbs' freshly brushed blues. Compounding the affront, the girl trilled a mocking laugh.

Rubbing at a cinder in his eye, Dobbs raised a fist to her. "You little wh — "

Finn clapped a hand on his shoulder. "Let it go, Lieutenant. As you well know, it could have been much worse."

4

A couple of blocks back, there had been two ladies who cursed at him and his men, one who'd even spat at them. The spitter, before she spat, had been the picture of decorum, gray haired, the scent of lilacs wafting from her. Finn, who was accustomed to being admired for his tall, dark looks, had accepted the gentle lady's smile as his due. Then she'd hawked at him.

Once the shock wore off, he forgave the old thing. Dressed in a black gown with black lace gloves, she might be a mother who'd lost her son at Bull Run. Plus, he thought with a grin, the crone had missed him and his shiny brass buttons and caught Dobbs instead.

Finn slapped his hat against his thigh to shake off the ashes and hoped they didn't come up on any more sullen ladies. Aware it would take only the smallest spark to inflame the wounded pride and heated resentment of the population, General Butler had sent down strict orders to ignore all insults.

He led his men along the railroad tracks till at last they passed under a wrought iron gateway that read Chamard Foundry. His good spirits evaporated. What once must have been a well-ordered factory was now a morass of rusting machinery. Destructive, but clever, Finn admitted.

"They sabotaged the place," Dobbs said.

"They certainly did."

The sluiceway from the flanking stream had been directed into the yard. Finn eyed the tangled mass of rods and vats and tools stewing in the fetid pond. Well, his small part of the war meant putting this foundry back to work. He blew out a resigned sigh. "Corporal Peach?"

"Yes, sir."

"Take five men and get that channel back into the stream. The rest of you, have a look around. See what you can figure out, what's broken, what's not."

"Captain," Private Scot squeaked, pointing with a shaky hand at a slithering shape in the water.

Finn eyed the inky black snake. They didn't have devils like this back in Boston, but he'd seen one in Mobile. The lad was white-faced, scared to death of the thing. Finn, to tell it true, felt a thrum of fear in his own gut.

"A cottonmouth, I believe, private. Don't play with it."

Finn turned back to survey the tangle of rotting vegetation, the wild growth of vines and weeds all around. This swampy country with its snakes and alligators was as much a threat as a regiment of Rebel soldiers. And by now, the warm morning air was turning into an infernal, sweltering furnace. Finn's unit were Massachusetts and Rhode Island boys, and he feared someone, maybe himself, was going to fall out from the heat. "Take your jackets off, men. You two lads, help me with the cistern."

He got a grip on the fallen tank, two soldiers on the other side, and together they heaved it back into its framework. Corporal Peach succeeded in redirecting the errant sluice back into the stream, then dug a couple of ditches to drain the yard. The task ahead seemed slightly less impossible with the water receding by the moment.

At the end of the day, sweaty and fly bit but revived by the fresh breeze off the river, Finn took his unit back to the garrison through the Vieux Carré. His friend Hursh saw only swamp and pined for Boston's salt wind off the Atlantic. Finn respected the ferocity of the sun down here, suffered from the humidity just like the rest of the New England boys, but there was something primal about the place, a sort of decadence that tickled at his proper Boston senses. He could spend a lifetime exploring these narrow alleys, peeking into the courtyards he glimpsed through ornate iron gates. When people spoke here, in so many tongues and accents, it was like music, like a symphony. And the air, rich with spice and nectar.

Rather than an exotic supper of New Orleans cooking, Finn dined on the mess tent's boiled beef and rice. As twilight fell, he selected half a dozen men to accompany him to a tavern he'd spotted on the levee. He'd ask around, see if some experienced foundry workers could be persuaded to come back to work.

The tavern had unpainted plank walls up to a man's waist, and then was open to mosquitoes and flying roaches, but at least there was a breeze off the river. A breeze smelling of mud flats, foul ships' ballasts, and sewage. Not all of New Orleans charmed him.

Inside, Africans huddled over their beers. Freed men, Finn supposed. Black men were no doubt what he needed. Surely the hot work at a foundry called for African laborers who could better withstand the heat.

Finn's opposition to slavery was abstract and impersonal. His father's bookstore carried all the abolitionist papers and hosted orators espousing their cause, but his life was taken up with the bookstore, a group of poet friends, and the rowing club. What few black men and women he'd seen in the streets of Boston had gone about their business, their paths and his seldom crossing.

Here in New Orleans with a bewildering array of colored people, some black as coal but free, others with *café au lait* skin but bound to a master, he found it easier to recall stereotypes: everyone said Negroes tolerated the sun and the heat. They were bred to it, after all. If you could get them to work. That was the other thing he'd always heard. They didn't want to work. Didn't seem to be true, though. Looked to him like all the work done in New Orleans was done by colored people. And by immigrants, the Irish and Italians crowding into the poor sections of town cheek by jowl with the coloreds.

At the tavern, he positioned his soldiers inside and out, then took a seat at an empty table. The dark eyes of the Africans watched him with guarded curiosity.

The proprietor ambled over, his soiled apron stretched over an impressive belly. "Don't want trouble in here, Yank."

"Neither do I, sir. Do you have wine?"

"Tafia or beer."

"A glass of tafia, then."

Finn had never drunk tafia, but it had to be better than the over-warm beer they served in the South.

When the man brought his glass, Finn spoke up loud enough for everyone to hear. "Would you be knowing anyone who worked at the foundry? Wages are good for men who can get it running again."

The server shrugged. The conversational buzz reasserted itself.

Feigning patience, Finn sipped the rummish drink. Not bad, but rough on the tongue.

Finally a tall, well-built man took the bench across from him. Finn judged him to be in his prime, perhaps his late thirties. As black as any human could be, the man placed his hands on the table. Big hands, with scarred knuckles.

"I help you," the man said in a heavy French accent. "You help me."

Finn stared into eyes black as anthracite and saw a fine intelligence. In coffee house debates back home, the pro-slavery side always asserted that Negroes were dull-minded; another assumption disproved. This man radiated confidence and intellect.

"You worked at the foundry?" Finn asked.

"Not me. I run a cigar store." The man reached in his pocket and passed a cigar across the table. "Welcome to New Orleans."

Finn ran the cigar through his fingers, judging the freshness and quality of the tobacco. A fine smoke. He held it under his nose and breathed in the rich fragrance, then sighed theatrically. "I do enjoy a good cigar."

"I am André Cailloux."

Finn gestured with the cigar. "Thank you, Mr. Cailloux."

"I could help you."

"A man who runs a cigar store? How?"

"Cigars aren't all I do, Captain. I can get you men, skilled men, to run your foundry."

Finn met his steady gaze. "What would you want in return?"

"I want to talk to General Butler."

Finn rolled the cigar between his palms. "What do you have to say to the general?" He heard the condescension in his voice, but with Butler already casting a dyspeptic eye on him, he wasn't about to annoy him with some trivial supplication.

Mr. Cailloux's hard gaze told him to go to blazes, it was none of his business.

Finn waited him out. He put the cigar in his mouth and patted his pockets. Mr. Cailloux produced a match, struck it, and reached the flame across the table, his large hand dwarfing the match. Finn drew on the cigar and then blew smoke toward the ceiling.

He would not yield on this. He'd have to know what he was getting himself into if he escorted this man to headquarters.

Cailloux looked at the table a moment, then raised his head. "The Louisiana Native Guards. We wish to join the Union Army."

"I thought the Native Guards were part of the Confederate Army."

A muscle flexed in Cailloux's jaw. "We are men of Louisiana," he said. "We join the Guards to defend our homes."

Finn studied the man's face. "Something to prove, Mr. Cailloux?"

8

"Oh yes, Captain. We have something to prove." The man's eyes smoldered with determination. "The Confederacy used us like mules, digging ditches and clearing fields. This time, we will be soldiers."

Finn's gaze fell again on the man's big hands, a fighter's hands. "Ever do any boxing?"

Cailloux's mouth slowly curved into a grin. "Yes, I fight. You?"

Finn held his own slender hands up for Cailloux's inspection. They were calloused from rowing, but they were nothing like the hams on the end of Cailloux's wrists. "I hit a boy once when I was fourteen," Finn said. "He hit me back. I didn't like it."

Cailloux grinned at him, a glint of tease in his eye. "You got piano hands, Captain. Not a fighting man's hands."

"Unfortunately, I can't play the piano either." He made his decision. "But I can get you in to see General Butler."

Cailloux's face instantly sobered. "I'll send you eight men. Experienced. And willing."

"They know the foundry?"

"They ran the foundry."

Finn stretched his hand across the table. They shook on it.

Satisfied he'd accomplished something at last, Finn collected his men and strolled through the mild spring night back toward camp. Clouds wisped across the Louisiana moon like some lady's gauzy shawl. Those huge white flowers, each a little moon itself, stayed open after dark, perfuming the air. Magnolias, Corporal Peach had told him. Peach was that rare bird, a Georgia boy in the Union Army.

Reminding himself he and his men were the occupiers of a resentful city, he re-grouped his unit into a sharper, more military formation to march back to camp. As they approached another torch-lit tavern, Finn could make out the words to a raucous ditty. Even though the local wit was at his army's expense, Finn grinned at the new words to an old tune.

Old Man Butler come to town
A blue cape on his shoulders
Took a look at New Orleans
Pissed his pants and hollered!

Yankee Doodle pissed his pants
Yankee Doodle Dandy!

"Keep your heads, lads," Finn told his men. "Stay in formation on the right side of the street. If they stay where they are, there won't be any trouble."

But tafia and hard rum had made the notoriously rough river men quarrelsome and bold. As a deep baritone gusted out with something about a Yankee bull's private parts and a cutting tool, a whore in the doorway pointed her finger and cawed, "Look, there's Yankees right there!"

Damn. A whole platoon's worth of rugged, unshaven drinkers poured into the muddy street ahead of them. Jesus, help us, Finn thought. Must be ten rough drinkers for every one of them. "Steady, boys. Keep going, eyes forward."

Torchlight shone in the puddles of the street as Finn and his men drew nearer. Hard-looking men and a few even harder-looking women stared at them like they were demons rising from the mud.

Finn took the first clod of dung full in the jaw. Jeers and insults he thought his men could handle, but dung in the face was harder to ignore. "It's just muck, boys. Keep going."

From the corner of his eye, Finn caught the gleam of torchlight on steel. Knives then, and no doubt clubs, and only seven green soldiers against this riled up mob. Running for it was not an option. To his right, a windowless warehouse wall. Their backs would be covered.

"Halt," he told his men. "Left face."

The men took their positions and raised their rifles.

"Hang fire," Finn said.

With the soldiers staring at them through rifle sights, the crowd backed off a step, but they could yet attack if a bold fellow showed some leadership. Finn stood just ahead and to the side of his escort, sword in hand. "Gentlemen," he addressed the crowd.

"Go to hell!"

"Damn Yankees!"

Finn gave them their moment before he continued. They would listen to reason, and in a moment they would disperse.

"Presumably, each of you would like to go home to your beds tonight." The shouting picked up again, and Finn raised his voice.

"Perhaps you have a wife or a sweetheart waiting for you. A child who needs you."

They weren't listening at all. They were, in fact, growing more threatening.

"I warn you. These men are the crack rifle unit of our brigade," he bellowed, lying at the top of his voice. Aware how ridiculous he was trying to reason with a mob, Finn straightened under the barrage of hurled clods.

"Watch it, Captain." Corporal Peach gestured to the left with his rifle barrel.

A boy in baggy white canvas britches and a red shirt stepped forward, his mouth a gaping black hole as he shouted scabrous insults. In his fist, a ten-inch blade.

"Hold," Finn told his men, though he raised his sword in readiness to give the signal.

The boy strode toward them, knife held high, his grimacing face orange in the flickering torchlight. He couldn't be more than fourteen.

"Hold!" Finn hissed through his teeth. He'd had no illusions that he could join a great army in wartime and not have to harm, perhaps kill, another human being. But the lad was just a boy. Moreover, if he had to take him down, the crowd would be all over them. His soldiers could shoot a few, and he could cut down a few more. But he and his six men would likely be ground into the mud and the whole river bank would rise up in revolt.

The boy came on, the crowd shouting and cheering, egging him on. Finn held his breath. The roar of the mob threatened to overwhelm him. He couldn't think.

The boy took another step, his fist coming up, brandishing the knife.

Acting on instinct, Finn cut the distance between them in long strides. He grabbed the youth's shoulder in one powerful hand and twirled him round. He seized the back of the boy's collar and with the flat of his sword, clanged the knife out of the river rat's hand.

The crowd stilled, waiting.

The luckless boy, suspended so his toes barely touched the ground, let out a squeaky yelp. A man with a bushy beard nudged his buddy and snickered. Laughter rippled through the crowd, growing as the boy squirmed in Finn's grip.

Finn recognized his opportunity. A cheerful smile disguising his fear, he stepped deliberately on the boy's knife. With a gentle shove, he sent him back toward his friends and tilted his sword in salute to the crowd.

Smartly, he stepped back to his men. "Step lively, boys, but *do not run*," he told them quietly. "Three of you first, then the rest six paces behind. Keep your rifles ready."

Finn hung back while his men moved out. He executed a friendly wave to an imaginary ally among the rest of the mob and forced another smile. Knots of men broke up and moved back toward their tankards of rum.

He lowered his sword and drew in a full breath of heavy moist air. He'd been a fool, bringing these boys down here. He said a quick Thanks be to God for their deliverance and marched his men into darker, emptier streets.

Chapter Three

No matter that the world was on the eve of cataclysmic change, or that New Orleans was in an uproar, Nicolette had a living to earn, and looking glamorous was part of the performance. Squinting through a tendril of smoke from her cigarillo, she tucked and folded a length of lavender silk around her head until she'd fashioned an extravagant flower fastened in the center with an amethyst broach. She dabbed a hint of rouge on her lips, then tilted her head for a critical look in the mirror.

"Need help with your tignon, *chèrie?*" Cleo leaned in the door.

"I've done it, Maman. What do you think?"

"You're going to smell like smoke. And such a pretty dress."

"Maman," Nicolette breathed. She'd heard it all before.

She stabbed her smoke out in the ash tray and grabbed up her shawl. "Don't wait up."

Downstairs, Nicolette called out for William. A burly black man emerged from the kitchen, his left eye milky brown and useless. A wide scar, still pink and angry, scored his face from brow to opposite jaw, cutting across his nose. He had been an intractable presence in the cane fields, continuously defying the overseer in spite of shortened rations and brutal whippings. At last, in frustrated fury, the overseer had raised his whip and slashed it across William's face.

The man had come to Nicolette when Marcel arrived one afternoon and announced he had a surprise for her. Nicolette had expected a packet of hair ribbons or some trinket in a little box. He still treated her as if she were a child. But Marcel had led her and Cleo to the back courtyard where this scarred man waited.

Involuntarily, Nicolette had put a hand to her heart at sight of his face. My God, she'd thought. What had been done to the poor man's face? Then she'd realized: Marcel's gift was this man. No. Surely Marcel would not —

"This is William. He's big, he's strong, and he's intelligent for a black." Marcel handed her a folded document. William's papers.

How could he have eaten at Maman's table countless times, have argued with Nicolette relentlessly about liberty, and still believe she could own another human being? How could he be so thick-headed!

"Now you're performing on your own, you're out late. Alone. And that's madness. You take William with you from now on."

She forced herself to be calm. "Marcel, I don't want a slave." She handed the document back to him.

Maddeningly, Marcel simply handed it to Cleo.

"You aren't expected to work him half to death and then whip him on Sundays, Nikki. Just keep him with you, that's all."

Nicolette fisted her hands, ready to erupt. "I told you — "

"Thank you, Marcel," Cleo interjected. "You're very kind to think of Nicolette's safety." She put her hand on his arm. "You're a good brother."

Nicolette opened her mouth to argue, furious with her mother for taking his side, with Marcel for disregarding her express wishes. But Cleo shot her a look that said hush, and then her mother darted her gaze to the black man standing mutely before them.

Nicolette was as guilty as Marcel, talking about the man as if he were invisible. She looked at him, truly looked, and saw a proud man, his chin up, his gaze straight ahead. A man who deserved a better life than he'd had in the fields.

He would be better off with her. Far better off than being with an owner who saw a black man as God's gift to him for being born white.

She'd been too quick to take offense. She often was these days. Marcel had probably saved the man's life, buying him away from that place.

"All right."

Marcel's grin was insufferable. "Thank you. Now, Nicolette, William is to be your shadow. The war will come to us here in Louisiana, sooner or later, and you're going to need protection."

So Nicolette and William had forged an alliance. He worked during the day doing the jobs a one-eyed man could do, and he pocketed what he made. In the evenings, in exchange for room and board, he kept up the yard, saw to the chickens and escorted Nicolette to and from her engagements. He might have only one eye, but ruffians chose easier marks when they saw the coal black giant marked with the tattoos of an African warrior.

William went into the streets to whistle up a conveyance and returned almost at once. "It been raining, missy. You best let me lift you into the carriage."

"There's the board over the gutter, William. It's not necessary."

Ignoring her protest, he swept her into his arms. Nicolette instantly drew into herself, her body taut and trembling. She'd told him not to, dammit. He'd just grabbed her up. She hadn't had time to prepare herself.

She squeezed her eyes closed against a vision of herself lying on the floor of the cottage at Lake Maurepas, curled into the crumpled heap of skirt and crinolines.

William sat her gently down in the cabriolet. "Now settle down, missy. You just breathe in and out real big and let it go. I ain't hurt you none."

Her voice trembled with anger. "I've told you, don't grab at me."

William drew up to his full height. "Yes'm, missy."

Nicolette's lips pressed into a white line. She knew it was unreasonable to expect never to be touched, but she couldn't help it. She'd felt powerless when William picked her up, powerless and weak. She passed her hand over her eyes. Tomorrow, she would make him a pudding as a peace offering. She'd put coconut in it, the way he liked it. He'd forgive her, again.

The cabriolet moved on through the Vieux Carré, each streetlight casting an island of light in the long dark stretches where brigands waited for the incautious. But she had William and his stout club. She willed herself to relax. New Orleans could be lovely in the evenings. Gas lights from the upper galleries twinkled like yellow stars in the puddles on the street. Jasmine and roses perfumed the air.

Here in the shadowed streets, Nicolette had no need to hold her head at an arrogant angle, to sing and preen for an audience, to pretend to Maman and all her family that she was the same Nikki she had been before Adam came into her life. For now, she could simply be.

At the Presswood mansion, the butler's boy ushered her inside. The cypress pocket doors were open between the two parlors. The upper walls were covered in green damask, the mahogany furniture shone softly. Nicolette took her place at the carved Chickering and spread her music on the piano. Admiring the fine tone and the responsive keys, she began with a soft minuet, something that wouldn't distract the guests. As Nicolette played, she discreetly watched the ladies and gentlemen arrive. Miss Presswood wore an enormous skirt, the latest fashion, so large it made her seem to float across the floor. Her cheeks were feverishly pink with excitement. A fairy-tale princess impatient for her beloved, Nicolette thought.

Ah, the Betrothed. Marcel entered the parlor with a relaxed, confident gait, assured of his welcome wherever he went. It was part of his birthright. White. Male. Wealthy. Why would he not be confident and at ease?

When Miss Deborah Ann rushed to greet him with both hands outstretched, Nicolette switched to a bawdy drinking song about avid young women, but played it softly and slowly as if it were merely a ballad. Only Marcel was likely to notice or to take her meaning. Yes. He raised his head from kissing Miss Presswood's hand to give Nicolette a quick look with an arched brow, an amused glint in his eye.

Knowing that would be the only acknowledgement of his tainted sister tonight, Nicolette yielded to a little streak of meanness imagining the cosseted Miss Presswood's discomfort if she were to grasp the connection. Nicolette had nothing against Miss Presswood herself, other than that she stood for the usual proud, smug, thoughtless girls of her class. But oh, how delicious the revelation would be: Miss Deborah Ann Presswood's debonair fiancé, and the hired colored help, of one family!

Wasn't she in a vinegar mood. She had no cause for it. She loved her brother, and he doted on her. Miss Presswood paid her well, and she had this lovely piano to enjoy. Behave, she told herself. She drew in a deep breath and concentrated on the sweet tones of the Chickering.

The guests mingled, kissing cheeks and admiring gowns as they waited for supper to be called. The room looked as though it were graced with a dozen silk butterflies as the ladies fluttered their fans. According to the code, a fluttering fan indicated the young lady encouraged a gentleman's advances. An ardent gathering, then, Nicolette mused, smiling to herself, and began a more sensual, teasing number. The evening might be entertaining after all. The party's attention would not be on her. She could observe the elite carrying on as though their city had not been overrun by the enemy.

A young woman with sausage curls hanging over each ear fanned away at Alistair Whiteaker. She knew Alistair would rather be in the library with a book than flirting with a belle. Just the same, he'd probably end up proposing to someone very like this girl. She hoped for his sake that he'd choose someone less irritating. The unfortunate girl's voice might have been quite effective at calling chickens, but the over-eager twang did not please in the drawing room. In her rustling taffeta, the girl minced across the parlor to join Marcel. Nicolette noted the fluttering fan as she spoke, gazing up at him with wide eyes.

Marcel stiffened. He said something Nicolette couldn't hear, but she saw his lips form the words *Miss Presswood.*

The girl might have been assaulted by an icy breeze the way she pulled her shawl tightly around her shoulders. She pivoted, and blushing furiously, rejoined her innocent friends seated like a bank of flowers on the sofas. Nicolette was wild to know what the girl said to produce such a cold, dismissive nod from Marcel. She'd weasel it out of him next time she saw him.

The same unlovely, peevish voice cut through the general conversation. "I cannot think why there are any young men left in New Orleans. I could never accept a man who refuses to carry a saber, a man who declines to wear our dear Confederate gray."

Instantly, the room silenced. Several very young men, clad in their black tails and white ties, flushed scarlet and stared at their highly polished shoes.

Nicolette's hands of their own accord fell to her lap. She'd never heard such insulting remarks in fine company. The girl's father stood. No doubt embarrassed by his daughter's remark, he would surely rebuke her and take her home. But when he broke the horrified silence, it was not to chide his daughter.

Righteousness drew him to his full, quite modest height. "Indeed, my dear, you are quite right," he declared. "Every able-bodied son of Louisiana should be defending her against these damned Yankee invaders!"

Mr. Presswood's face bespoke gathering thunder clouds. Ladies whispered to one another behind their fans.

"There are men with traitorous connections in this very room!" the father brayed, stiffening his sanctimonious backbone. He turned directly to Marcel. "Where is your brother, Chamard? Writing anti-Southern tracts as we speak, aiding the enemy?"

Marcel's brows drew together, his face darkening. At sight of his mouth setting into a tight slash, Nicolette rose to her feet, afraid Marcel was going to call the man out. As unfashionable as dueling had become, her brother had certainly not renounced it. The man had no idea how dangerous Marcel was.

Mr. Presswood, a vein pulsing at his temple, attempted to take control of his parlor. "Abelard, that is quite enough. I would ask you to consider you are in my home, insulting my guests — "

"I will answer him, Mr. Presswood, if you please," Marcel said.

Miss Deborah Ann's hand clutched at his arm, her eyes pleading with him. Nicolette hoped she could restrain him, for no man had ever offered such brazen insults to a Chamard and walked away.

Marcel's body seemed relaxed if one did not notice the fire in his eye. In a cool, deadly voice, he addressed the insult. "My brother Yves, Mr. Abelard, has my greatest respect. He had a difficult choice to make. It is not my choice, nor my father's, but he has followed his conscience. I admire a man of integrity, of whatever conviction. Do you not?"

"No, sir, I do not," Abelard declared hotly. "He's a traitor to Louisiana, and there's no white-washing it!"

Mr. Whiteaker, dear gentle Alistair, stepped between the two men. "Perhaps your remarks might be more appropriate, Mr. Abelard," he said, his voice mild and soothing, "if you confined them to those gentlemen who still consider themselves Southerners, and who are here to defend themselves."

"Well, Whiteaker, here you are, you and Chamard, in your coat and tie, by God, when good men in Confederate gray are fighting and dying!"

Mr. Presswood asserted himself. "Abelard, you would do well to know what you are talking about before you open your mouth in another man's home. Monsieur Chamard is not in uniform, but even you would have to admit that raising $20,000 for President Davis' coffers in the last twelve months is a more important service to the Confederacy than adding another uniform to the ranks."

Mr. Presswood pointed a finger at his guest. "Furthermore, sir, the iron foundry which has so patriotically been building ships and machines for our cause belongs to Marcel Chamard. Perhaps you did not know that Marcel personally saw to its being sabotaged before the Union forces confiscated it. A very grand sacrifice, indeed."

Abelard's face looked like a boiled crawdad. Nicolette feared she was about to witness a fit of apoplexy. She looked to the daughter to calm him, but she remained on the edge of the confrontation she had instigated, her posture a curious mix of chin up and eyes down with a slight smirk on her lips.

"You owe these men your most abject apology, Abelard."

Mr. Abelard looked from under his bushy brows at Marcel, at Alistair Whiteaker and the other young men. Then he glared defiance at his old friend Presswood.

"Like hell." He stabbed a finger toward his daughter and then, in a sweeping gesture, toward the door. He stomped from the room without waiting to escort the girl, who followed him with a triumphant glance at her hostess.

Miss Deborah Ann was the first to recover from the stillness following the disgraceful exit. "Mademoiselle," she murmured, and Nicolette resumed playing. She chose a sweet, simple minuet to soothe the party, and the guests began to move about and talk softly. As far as Nicolette could discern, no one discussed the outrageous scene that had just occurred. Of course, once they left the Presswood mansion, these same people would talk of nothing else for days.

A handsomely clad Negro appeared at the door and announced that supper was served. The gentlemen escorted the ladies into the dining room, and the butler closed the high double doors behind them.

"Will you take your supper on the terrace, Mam'selle?" the butler asked with hand outstretched to guide her to her own table.

Moonlight filtered through the scudding clouds, shifting the shadows among the roses and hedges. Nicolette enjoyed the light breeze, the excellent food, and the very good wine the butler poured for her.

"Good evening, Nicolette." Alistair Whiteaker, elegant in white tie and tails, stepped onto the terrace. A little light from the house lay gently on Alistair's pale wavy hair, casting one side of his handsome face in darker shadow.

"Mr. Whiteaker. Have you abandoned the gentlemen with their cigars?"

"I have. Can't abide the reeking things." He smiled at her appreciatively. "I don't believe I've seen that gown before. You look lovely."

Nicolette hoped he would not sit down. It would do neither his reputation nor hers any good to be seen alone together. On Lake Maurepas, at a resort New Orleans society ladies did not attend, it was acceptable for a gentleman to be seen with a mixed race woman. More than a year ago now, Nicolette had in fact been dining with Alistair when Adam Johnston saw them together. Only an hour after that, Adam had pushed his way into her house and lost himself in a jealous rage.

While she recuperated, Alistair had called on her faithfully, reading to her, taking her for drives through the tall pines. His courtship had been sweet and undemanding, like Alistair himself. He would never marry her, of course, no matter how dilute her African heritage. The seven eighths of white blood in her veins were tainted by the one eighth of black, and Alistair was not a man to defy convention. He would never offend his mother, risk his little's sister's happiness, or compromise his position in society. Even his proposal to keep her as his placée had been a struggle for him, a contest of his desire winning out over his straitlaced expectations for himself. Of course Marcel kept a placée, even had two little boys with Lucinda, but Marcel was a Creole. Alistair was only a second generation Louisianan and retained his New England forbears' stiff righteousness.

Fond of Alistair as Nicolette was, she had not consented to being his mistress. Many quadroon women saw being a rich white man's mistress as their fate. Indeed, many of them aspired to it. But Nicolette's mother had supported herself and her children with talent and hard work. With that example, Nicolette could not see herself as a mere appendage, her days only a slice of her protector's life stolen from his wife and legitimate children. Even dear Lucinda, to whom Marcel was genuinely attached, was about to be supplanted by Miss Deborah Ann Presswood.

Still, Alistair was presuming on their friendship now. "Mr. Whiteaker — "

"Don't trouble, Nicolette. The men are reviling the Yankees, and no doubt the ladies are doing the same. They'll be an age yet."

Alistair moved around the table, into the candle glow. "General Mouton is pleading for reinforcements to hold the west. Your brother has collected a unit of soldiers. Did you know?"

Nicolette shoved her wine away. Marcel was going to fight then.

"He's asked me to join him," Alistair said.

"You, Alistair? I didn't think you would put on a uniform."

His smile was part grimace. She'd hurt him, she realized. "I never doubted your courage, Alistair. I only was uncertain of your commitment. You've said nothing about the war, all these months."

"No. I've just wished it would all go away. And yet it hasn't."

"And so you're going to fight?"

"I don't know what I'm going to do."

Alistair walked a few steps into the shadowy darkness, his hands behind his back. "I don't think my courage is so much less than other men's, but I don't want to fight." He leaned his head back to look at the moon. "I have nightmares, Nicolette. Visions. Shoving a bayonet into a man's gut, opening up his chest. Seeing the light in his eyes ... die."

He turned around, his face strained. "How can I do that, Nicolette? How can I take a man's life? And for what? To make rich men richer?"

She'd wondered if Alistair felt anything deeply, had wished at times for more than the restrained, bloodless kisses he'd given her. But here was real feeling. Perhaps he was poised to make the leap to the other side. Yes, Alistair owned slaves, many of them, and like every plantation owner, he worked them through the hot days in the cane and cotton fields. She knew this. For a moment, though, touched that Alistair revealed his feelings to her here in the night, she believed that Alistair needed only a little encouragement and he would do the right thing. He was a good man. He would reject Marcel's call to arms and join the Federals instead. She leaned across the table as if she might reach him.

"If the North wins the war, Alistair, the government will bring justice to Louisiana. Isn't that worth fighting for?"

He made a dismissive sound and gestured with his hand, discounting her.

Stung, Nicolette drew back. So he was more like Marcel than she'd given him credit for. She'd been a fool to think he, a slave-holding planter, cared about justice. Why had she accepted this man's friendship? He was worse than Marcel. At least her brother acted on deep conviction.

"This war's not being fought over slavery, Nicolette, you should know that." His tone was flat, resigned. "We have powerful men in the Southern states, and the North profits from what we do down here. There'll be no end to slavery in our lifetimes."

Anger rolled from her belly and prickled at her scalp. She stood up and tossed her napkin on the table. "Do you even have the capacity for fervor, Mr. Whiteaker? Does nothing rouse you?" She meant for the disgust in her voice to wash over him, to shame him and hurt him. "The complacency of men like you is the very reason slavery endures to this day!"

Nicolette marched away, leaving him to stew in his own lassitude.

Chapter Four

Society habitually fled the city before the heat of summertime, before the Yellow Jack moved into town. May was the very last month it paid the proprietors of the Silver Spoon, one of New Orleans' finest clubs, to stay open.

Finn and his friend Hurshel Farrow read the marquee beside the Silver Spoon's door. New Orleans' finest talents! Avery LaSalle! Cleo Tassine! Pierre Lafitte! Nicolette Chamard!

That afternoon Finn had handed off the foundry to the new engineer from Pennsylvania who, most thankfully, had arrived a month earlier than expected. Tomorrow Finn would return to the Signal Corps, where he belonged, and Hursh would again be his immediate superior. Tonight, though, they were merely old friends, and the night was theirs.

"What do you think, Hursh? Got money in your pocket, itching to get out?"

"We'd be welcome as a banshee at a wake."

"Not so, my friend. Word is, half the general's staff will be here tonight. The owners want their profits rolling in even if it's Yanks filling the seats."

"I'd have to shave." Hursh rubbed the red stubble on his chin.

"End of the season," Finn tempted. "There won't be a damned thing to do but soldier the rest of the summer."

Hursh took a breath as if he were about to plunge into deep waters. "All right, I'm for it if you are."

They marched themselves back to camp and partook of the hard tack and boiled fish their mess cooked up. Bathed and shaved, with coats brushed and linen changed, they pronounced themselves handsome and sweet-smelling.

At the Silver Spoon, the maître d' escorted them into the gas-lit dining room where silver gleamed and gardenias scented every table. A white-jacketed waiter offered them menus. Finn waved him off. Dining here would cost them each a week's wages. He held up two fingers. "Whiskey."

Finn looked around the room at the other patrons who'd come to take a night's pleasure in the midst of war. The gleam of brass buttons revealed that about half the diners were men in the uniform of the U. S. Army, Federal officers like himself. The other half were wealthy planters who had decided it was in their best interest to coexist with the occupying Yanks. Practical men, Finn had to admit.

Amid the fanfare of a drum roll from the stage, the master of ceremonies strode on stage and announced with great fervor, "Mademoiselle Nicolette Chamard!" Immediately the white-tie elements of the audience burst into enthusiastic applause.

A young woman entered from stage right, slowly, demurely, with her eyes cast down. Her gown was ice blue, and she wore the get-up on her head that so many women in New Orleans favored, some sort of turban.

The girl began singing *a capella*, her voice sweet and pitch-perfect, but thin as if she'd used all her breath just getting on stage. Finn figured she'd been applauded for her looks, not her talent. And looks she had, if you liked a perfect, heart-shaped face. Her skin was creamy, not that fish-belly white the young ladies of Boston bragged about. And that lower lip! He leaned forward, his elbows on the table.

The mademoiselle was the picture of innocence, her eyes on the far distance, her hands holding a huge magnolia blossom. Winsomely sweet, she sang her story.

A pretty little maid so neat and gay
To the mill she went one day

Finn took advantage of sitting in the dark to stare at her bosom mounding nicely above her neckline. He paid little attention to the lyrics, no doubt another insipid ballad about love and loss.

Now I think I will make my best way home.
If my mother ask why I've been so long,

The vision in blue suddenly gave her audience a broad wink and a saucy smile. Her voice took on power and depth and an insinuating tone as she finished her number.

I'll say I've been ground by a score or more
But I've never been ground so well before.

Finn, caught unawares, guffawed. Hursh slapped the table. The room erupted in laughter.

Then she assumed a mask of hauteur as she seated herself at the piano. She played a tinkling trill in the high register and then pounded out a few chords in the lower keys with dramatic, body-swaying expression. Suddenly, as if she'd had a thought, she paused with her chin high in the air, her hands poised over the keys.

"I play piano just like Frederic Chopin, you know," she said in a confiding tone.

The men in the audience, and they were nearly all men, chuckled, waiting for it.

"With two hands."

Without waiting for the laughter to die down, Mademoiselle Nicolette launched into a Wagnerian aria in a soaring soprano. Finn's eyes never left her. He gazed, not at her bosom, at least not entirely, but at her face, for she'd dropped the mask altogether now. Her eyes sparkled, her face glowed. The regal elegance she projected, and then the sly humor – she was a chimera, shifting easily from mock-serious to mock-bawdy, from demure to knowing. Her voice flew like a hummingbird soaring and diving.

She was incandescent.

He was smitten.

Applause rolled through the room as Mademoiselle Chamard took her bows.

In Finn's experience, it was true, what they said about show people: women of the stage were likely to be free with their favors.

"I'll square with you later," he said, then bolted, leaving Hursh to pay for the drinks. He wanted to get backstage before the other swains got there.

He found the side door into the performers' area and closed it firmly in the face of a young gentleman following him. He grabbed a nearby chair and wedged it under the knob. He didn't need competition from some rich bloke in top hat and cane.

Here the banjo and flute from the next act barely penetrated. A gas light overhead hissed and dimly caught the gleam of blue silk as Mademoiselle Nicolette strode down the hallway toward the brighter dressing area.

"Mademoiselle," he called.

She turned. He couldn't see her face with the light behind her. He came closer and stood in the doorway with her. He stood too close, he knew he did, but he wanted to inhale her intoxicating perfume. He wanted to inhale her.

Up close, she was even more beautiful. Her gray eyes seemed to see through to the back of his head. The heavy scent of the magnolia blossom in her hand drew him in.

She backed away from him, bumping into the doorjamb.

No welcoming smile? Finn hesitated, puzzled. Back in Boston, he'd often gone backstage to congratulate Coleen after a performance, and if he were the first admirer to reach her dressing room, he left the theater a happy man.

Well, what had he expected? That she would invite a stranger into her dressing room, let him tear her clothes off and make passionate love to her all night? Well, yes. He'd been carried away with the image of himself and this astonishing, spirited woman in a sweaty tangle of sheets. Unfair, of course. She was not a fantasy. Still, was there not even a hint of flirtation about her?

He leaned forward, trying to read those astonishing gray eyes. Her pupils widened, and she raised a hand as if to protect herself. He straightened. He'd blundered, obviously. Yet he was here now. He had to say something.

"I enjoyed your performance, Mademoiselle."

"*Merci.*" The hand at her bodice fisted on a flounce of lace. She glanced toward the door where he'd wedged the chair.

Could this be the same woman, fearless and bold on stage, shrinking from him here in the hallway? Did he detect a faint trembling in her shoulders?

My God, the woman was afraid of him.

Finn stepped back. "Pardon me, mademoiselle. I have alarmed you."

She did not deny it. He felt like a cad. He'd made her feel trapped with the chair under the door knob. She was alone, and he was too close. Heat flushed from his throat to his scalp.

"I do apologize." He bowed, his eyes on her hemline. "Good night to you, Miss Chamard."

Nicolette released the breath she'd been holding. She pressed her hand over her heart, watching *le Américain* retreat down the hallway, his boots loud on the naked boards. In spite of the touch of panic, she'd taken in the thick brows and curling dark hair, the firm jaw. His accent was foreign to her, but his voice had been smooth and soothing, like soft butter on a scorched finger.

His essence lingered, a heady, masculine scent. She breathed, drawing him into her lungs. He'd been so tall, looming over her. And he'd surprised her. That's what had unsettled her. If she'd been prepared, if Pierre had been with her, or Maman, she could have smiled and played the coquette. That's what he wanted, to see the coquette. Not a spiritless gray shadow.

She sat at her dressing table and leaned her forehead against her fist. How long was she going to be like this? A cowardly, timid mouse!

Disgusted with herself, she twisted the lid off the cold cream jar and scoured the makeup off her face. He must have thought her a ninny. She'd managed, what, one word?

Surrounded by the pale cream, her eyes glowed darkly. She dropped her hand, staring into the mirror. I am not a shadow. I am not a mouse. She still had a spine, she just had to stiffen it and get over that awful moment when Adam Johnston had taken her confidence from her. And she would, she was sure she would. Eventually.

She scraped her chair back. To hell with back stage Lotharios.

Nicolette changed her shoes and joined Cleo and Pierre in the other dressing room. They would go home together and have a late supper in the kitchen. Then she would go to bed and forget all about the officer with the dark brown eyes.

Kind eyes, she remembered, once he'd seen she was afraid. Maybe not so easy to forget.

Chapter Five

At the expected, booming knock, Nicolette opened the door to André Cailloux.

"*Chèrie*," he said, stooping to enter, then bending even further to kiss her cheek. "Felicie sends her love."

"*Bonsoir*, André."

Nicolette congratulated herself. She hadn't flinched at all when André towered over her, nor when he leaned even closer to kiss her. But then she'd known André her whole life. Who could not trust this man? "Pierre is in the parlor with Maman."

Nicolette heard her step-father's hurried footsteps in the hall.

"*Mon ami*." Pierre grabbed André's hand. "An historic night! Come in, come in."

In the parlor, Nicolette's mother held her cheek up to be kissed. "Dearest friend, we are ready for you, as you see." Cleo gestured at the table where a kerosene lantern hissed softly, casting a glow over paper, quills, and ink.

"Sit down, my friend," Pierre insisted. "The men at the foundry. How has it gone?"

André lowered himself into Cleo's yellow brocade chair, taking care to sit gently. "The Army pays them good wages, and the men I sent are putting the place to rights."

"Then it's time for the captain to keep his end of the bargain," Pierre said.

André's voice deepened with meaning. "Tomorrow morning. Ten o'clock."

Nicolette shared a proud, amazed smile with her mother. To think that one of their own, a black man, once a slave, would be speaking with a general of the United States Army, in person. What else might be accomplished now that Lincoln's men were actually here, in Louisiana?

Pierre put his hand over Nikki's. "We'll need you at the door, *chére*, to bring the men in as they come to sign their names. André, let's get it written."

Earlier in the day, they had discussed André delivering their message to General Butler orally, but the petition to join the Union forces, in writing, with the signatures of a hundred ready and willing men, would carry enough weight to impress even a Union general.

Proudly, Nicolette let the men in to mark their x's at the bottom of André's petition. Every man who picked up the quill stood tall and spoke in solemn tones, reverent at the opportunity for a Negro to assert his manhood, to declare his courage and determination.

After an hour and a half, Nicolette closed the front door for the last time. André had his hundred signatures and more.

Pierre opened a bottle of port, and the four of them drank to the morrow's good fortune.

When André rose to go home, Nicolette said quickly, "I'll see him out."

At the door, she put her hand on his arm. "André, what I can do to help?"

His handsome black face split into a grin. "You, Nikki? What can you do?" He wrapped his big hand around her upper arm, the fingers easily encircling her biceps, and chuckled. "Don't see you toting a rifle, sugar."

Her blood rising, Nicolette stepped back. She had expected her step-father's dismissal of her desire to be involved. Pierre thought she should have her mind on finding a husband. But she had expected more understanding from André.

She raised her chin at him. "There must be things I could do besides carry arms."

André shook his head, his levity gone. "The things women do for the soldiers, Nikki. These are not things a lady does. You stay home where you belong. You're what we're fighting for, for our right to be men, to keep our women safe."

He chucked her under the chin. "Lock the door after me."

Vacillating between being utterly dispirited and hotly affronted, Nicolette put away the quills, the ink, and the costly paper. Didn't she earn her own way in the world? Didn't André's wife help him run his business? How could he think Nicolette was merely a helpless, useless pet?

An hour later, the house quiet, Nicolette threw a shawl over her nightgown and stepped onto the upstairs gallery. She admired André, she'd even had a mad crush on him when she was twelve. But he did not see how difficult it would be for her to find the same life as his Felicie. Nicolette was educated, even sophisticated. She did not count herself a snob for acknowledging that. And where among the free coloreds was she to find a mate? She knew two other colored men besides André and Pierre who could read. One of them was twelve, the other over sixty. Nicolette had not discovered where she fit into the layers of colored and white people. She was white, and she was not.

What she was sure of was that she wanted the Union to win. Abraham Lincoln would fracture the slave culture, and someday women like her would not have to wonder where she was to find a colored man who could read. But how could she, one woman, do her part?

Maybe André was right. Hadn't women always stood aside, waiting patiently at home while their men risked their lives for principle? Miss Deborah Ann Presswood certainly wouldn't be involving herself in the war. Nor Lucinda, content to be Marcel's lover and the mother of his children.

Nicolette lit a cigarillo and leaned against the railing over the quiet street.

There were women who did not sit passively while men made all the decisions, women who did take life and honor into their own hands. Her white great-grandmother Emmeline had run the Toulouse plantation, and run it well, according to Cleo, just as Tante Josephine did now. And there was Marianne Johnston. She'd helped slaves escape to freedom before she married Nicolette's other half- brother Yves. Women too could make a difference in the world.

She tossed her cigarillo and watched the red tip arc through the darkness into the flooded gutter below. There had to be something else she could do.

There was something else she could do. Barefoot, she padded to her dresser, opened the drawer, and removed a folded document. She slipped her feet into pink slippers and marched down the staircase, her white muslin gown trailing behind her.

The neighborhood had closed their shutters and darkened their lamps. The scent of magnolias and gutters, roses and privies hovered in the damp air. Nicolette picked her way across the courtyard, trying to see the puddles in what little moon light the clouds let through.

At the lean-to in the corner of the yard, she knocked, and then knocked louder. The man had likely been asleep for hours.

William opened the door clad only in his britches. "Missy?" He wiped a hand across his face. "Something wrong?"

"Yes. Very wrong." Nicolette could barely make out his dark features, but the scar caught the filtered moonlight. She held out the thick paper. "You are a free man, William. From this moment on."

William looked at the packet, then at Nicolette. "This true? I's really free?"

"You are really free." She took one of his big hands and placed the document in it. She closed his fingers over the paper and held his hand in both of hers.

"Good night, William."

She crossed the courtyard and climbed the shadowed staircase feeling as powerful as André Cailloux. She had just emancipated a man from his bonds. What more significant act could one human do for another? Let André call her weak and useless now.

All these last months, feeling defeated and diminished. She'd been a fool to let Adam do that to her. She was not defeated. She was not a shadow. She gathered cigarillo and flint, then stepped onto the gallery overlooking the dark street. No one was up, or out, to see her in her nightgown, her hair hanging loose on her shoulders. She settled into the rattan rocker and struck her flint. She drew deeply on the cigarillo, savoring the taste, holding the smoke in her lungs for the full effect. She closed her eyes and listened to the night, felt the velvet air on her skin. She was herself, Nicolette Chamard, a woman with power and the heart to use it.

The gray tabby from next door leapt from its own gallery to hers and pranced to Nicolette to demand a rub behind the ears. Absently, she stroked its silky fur, its purr vibrating against her body. She felt more at peace than she had in a long time. She hadn't just complained. She hadn't just hoped. She'd acted.

The glow of her rosy satisfaction didn't last, however. By the time she ground out the stub under her slipper, she was wondering: Was this enough? To free one man?

She slept late, waking to lingering dreams of the Yankee captain from the Silver Spoon, his lovely mouth whispering across her own. She pushed the hair out of her face. Ridiculous. Pining after a stranger as if she were sixteen again. She'd embarrassed both of them. Just as well she'd never see him again, she thought, an unexpected thorn of regret pricking her.

The aroma of strong coffee lured her downstairs where Cleo and her step-father Pierre were having breakfast. Fried fatback, corn grits, wheat biscuits and molasses graced the table.

"Here she is, our sleeping beauty," Pierre said. He said that most every morning, and smiled with real pleasure every time he said it. Nicolette kissed his creased black cheek and then her mother's before she sat down.

William set a plate in front of her. Nicolette reached for the coffee pot.

"You and William had a night of consequence," Cleo said, setting her cup down.

Nicolette raised her chin. "We did. Do you approve?"

"It isn't for me to approve or disapprove. William's papers were in your name, in your hands. But it was a generous gesture, and I am proud my daughter has a generous soul."

"Pierre?" Nicolette asked.

Pierre nodded at William. "I'm waiting to see if William's going to keep taking care of those damn chickens. I'll gladly pay you for it, William, if you're staying on."

Nicolette gestured at the empty chair. "Sit down, William."

He shook his head. "I cain't do that, Missy."

Nicolette rose from her own chair, pulled his out, and said, "Sit. Please."

William glanced at Cleo. When she nodded toward the chair, he sat.

Pierre poured him a cup of coffee and raised his own. "To freedom!"

Nicolette and Cleo raised their cups. "To freedom."

William cast his eye on each of them in turn. Tentatively, he raised his steaming cup.

"What do you want to do, William, now that you're free?" Nicolette asked.

"I hardly knows. I ain't been free since I was a boy."

"I understand," Pierre said. "I didn't earn my freedom until I was nearly thirty. It'll take a few days to sink in. You don't have to decide anything right away."

"Stay here with us as long as you like," Cleo said.

"Thank you, ma'am. And I'll see to the chickens right on, Monsieur Lafitte."

"That's fine. Now. Let's be practical," Pierre said. "I'm glad to see a slave made freeman, but this is still Louisiana. It requires the consent of the state legislature to free a slave, and they haven't chosen to do so in many, many months. And then only for owners with influence. How much influence do you have, Nicolette?"

"But the Union Army is here now," Nicolette protested.

"Yes, they are. That doesn't mean you can do as you please. You're still a citizen of Louisiana. And a colored one at that."

Nicolette looked from Pierre to her mother, and then finally at William.

"I don't care. William, you're free. Maybe I have to hold on to the papers, but you do not have to answer to anyone but me. And I say you're free."

William studied his big hands. When he raised his face, his cheeks glistened. "I owes you my life, Missy. They'd of killed me, I stayed in the fields."

Finn McKee waited at the front door of Butler's headquarters, the massive Custom House on Canal Street. He rubbed a finger around his collar, the heat already bearing down and it only mid-morning in May. July must be a hell on earth here.

He was still out of favor with General Butler. Going to be a long summer, he thought. No dinner parties for him with fine wine, excellent food, and the occasional charming woman who could be found to grace a Union table. Could be, though, that bringing the offer of a colored regiment would put him back in the general's good graces. General Butler surely needed more men to hold New Orleans.

Finn recognized the unmistakable black skin and imposing figure of André Cailloux from fifty yards away. The man strolled down the street with the bearing of ... a king, McKee decided. And perhaps, in another time, another place, he would have been.

Before the sentries could make an issue of a black man approaching the door, Finn gave them the nod. Inside, Finn led Cailloux to General Butler's office and checked his watch. Ten o'clock precisely.

Finn stood at attention in front of General Butler's desk, Cailloux one step back and two to the side of him. They waited while the general finished reading a document. He placed the pages on the desk, made a notation in the margin, then crossed his hands in front of him.

"McKee," the general said with neither enthusiasm nor pleasure.

"Yes, sir," Finn said. "This is André Cailloux. He is a leader in the town and I believe you will find his proposal useful to you, sir."

An avowed abolitionist, Butler stood, a great gesture of respect, and then placed his hands behind him while he took Cailloux's measure.

Cailloux calmly returned the general's perusal, his hands at his side.

"André Cailloux?" General Butler said.

"Yes, sir."

"What can I do for you?"

Cailloux stepped to the desk and offered his petition. "The Native Guards wish to re-form and serve in the Union Army, General."

Butler grunted. He unrolled the paper and read it through, scanning the scores of names below the text. "You know what's in this document?" he queried, one eyebrow arched.

"General, sir, that document is in my hand," Cailloux replied, no hint of reproach in his voice, but McKee caught the flash in his eye.

General Butler nodded to the table and chairs to the side of the room. "Have a seat, Mr. Cailloux. You might as well stay, McKee." He turned to his adjutant. "Go fetch Colonel Masters. He needs to sit in on this."

And so the discussion began. Finn watched the give and take as André Cailloux, a former slave, negotiated with a general of the United States Army.

Butler needed the Guards, but he gave no indication of it. Cailloux more than held his own. The man could think on his feet, that was clear, and as the Negro outlined his conditions, all in the tones of a gentleman, Finn's respect for him grew.

It was decided. Cailloux would lead the effort among his people to reconstitute the regiment. The officers would themselves be freed black men, up to the rank of captain. The enlistees would be used as soldiers and not as laborers. They would receive monthly payments and a $200 signing bonus.

The men stood, and instead of putting his hands behind his back, this time General Butler held out his right hand. Cailloux took it, and the men shook.

Finn felt the buzz of having just witnessed a momentous event. When had a Negro ever, in this country, in any century, demanded and gained concessions from authority? Never.

Saying good-bye at the entrance to the Custom House, Finn stuck out his hand. "I congratulate you, Mr. Cailloux."

Chapter Six

With the Union Army in town, the Blue Ribbon, the renowned club where gentlemen came to woo and acquire creole mistresses, was one of the few clubs that kept its doors open through the steamy summer. Yanks and Louisianans alike needed some place for their drinking, smoking, and scheming. Nicolette accepted an engagement to sing on a Saturday night.

Once she was coiffed, dressed, and perfumed, she stepped into the parlor to tell Cleo and Pierre goodnight. Nicolette lingered in the doorway a moment, taking in the very picture of contentment. Pierre sat on one end of the sofa. Her mother lay propped against the other end, her feet in Pierre's lap. Cleo had a book, spectacles perched on her nose. Pierre had the newspaper folded, one hand absently rubbing Cleo's bare foot.

Nicolette had yearned, ever since she'd left girlhood behind, for a hot, flaming passionate love. For a man whose kiss would blaze from her mouth to her very toes. But, this, too was love. Would this deep, happy serenity be as hard to find as the passion she longed for?

"*Bonsoir*, Maman. No tickling, Pierre."

Pierre ran his thumb nail up the sole of Cleo's foot, and Nicolette left the two of them playing and scolding.

William saw her to the Blue Ribbon and insisted he would be across the street under a sycamore when she was ready to go home. She went inside to earn her very generous fee.

Waiting for her cue to go on stage, Nicolette's hand stole to her stomach where butterflies fluttered. Stage fright. That was normal. But not the other – not the drained confidence, the weakening fear she'd been carrying this last year and more.

Let it go, she told herself. She closed her eyes and breathed deeply. She could do this, could shrug off all the lingering fears Adam left her with. She was finished with "timid." She was a woman who had freed another human being from bondage. She could certainly do this.

On stage, Nicolette played and sang and sassed her way through her act, inspiring her audience to demand two encores. She left the stage feeling buoyant, feeling like her old self.

At her dressing room door, several gentlemen lined up to declare their admiration. This time, she did not shrink and wilt as she had at the Silver Spoon. She bantered and fluttered her fan and gave her devotees an extra little performance, the personal flirtation they wanted. If the handsome captain came to her now, she would meet his glance unafraid, she'd laugh with him, perhaps let him take her to his table for wine and supper. She glanced down the row of men, wishing he were here, waiting for her.

And there stood Alistair Whiteaker, leaning on the wall under the gas lamp. The light made a halo of his fair hair. Affection and amusement played across his features as she toyed with her admirers.

At last, only Alistair remained. He grinned at her. "Almost as much fun as watching you on stage."

"Come in and sit while I get these shoes off."

"What if instead of coming in I arrange a supper for us? May I entice you with chilled wine and the Blue Ribbon's best Veal Diablo?"

"You may! I'm famished."

Half an hour later, a white-jacketed steward led Nicolette past the main dining room. She hesitated. "This way, mam'selle," the steward said and took her to the third floor.

Alistair had arranged a private dining room? She had been upstairs once before, but that time she'd been in a party of six. This time, she would be alone with a gentleman in the notorious Blue Ribbon.

Yet she felt calm. Ready. Where was the shaking dread that had shuddered through her the last year whenever a man approached her? She'd been fearless on stage tonight. She'd even enjoyed the nonsense with the backstage johnnies. Broken pride, broken jaw, shattered spirit? All healed?

She'd taken her life back. Just like that. When she'd made William a free man, she'd freed herself? She laughed. It couldn't be so simple. She was just full of herself coming off the stage. But it felt good.

With a light step, she followed the steward down the carpeted hallway. He knocked. When Alistair opened the door, Nicolette walked in, ready to enjoy wine, Veal Diablo, and Alistair.

He took both her hands and held them out. "I haven't seen you in this shade of rose. You're even more beautiful than the last time I saw you."

The door closed behind her and they were alone. Actually, truly alone.

"Champagne?"

"Please," she said, removing her gloves, a concession to summer heat.

Alistair wore black tails, a stiff white shirt and immaculate collar. He'd had his fair hair cut short and his beard trimmed close to the jaw. He looked very fine, his blue eyes the same deep shade as the sapphire pin he wore in his cravat. And he wore that tantalizing cologne with the hint of sandalwood she liked so much.

"Supper's on its way." He handed her a flute of champagne and gestured to the red velvet love seat.

He kept her glass filled as he entertained her with society gossip about people they both knew, the Presswoods, the Neys, the Johnstons. Nicolette's attention strayed to the red velvet drapery behind the love seat. She knew what was behind the curtain. She had a friend, now a rich man's placée, who'd told her that after an elegant supper and two bottles of wine, her gentleman had opened the drapes to reveal a plush divan. At that point, after weeks of negotiation between her gentleman and her mother had already taken place, she had sealed the bargain with the gift of her virginity.

"The Presswoods elect to remain in town for the summer. A bit risky, but Mr. Presswood is determined. You might find Miss Deborah Ann flighty, but she's staying with him."

Nicolette remembered Miss Deborah Ann quietly taking control of her parlor after the Abelards' disgraceful exit. She was not a flighty girl, or at least not so silly as Nicolette had first taken her for. "Rather brave of her, with the risk of yellow fever."

Brave, perhaps, but such a virgin, she thought. The American belles seemed unaware of themselves below the waist. When Nicolette and her friends gossiped about the well-to-do whom they entertained, they wondered if the very proper misses even knew where babies came from. Their wedding nights must be a miracle of revelation.

Virginity. Nicolette had guarded her virtue just as every young woman did – every young woman who had the luxury of food and shelter without having to bargain for it with her body.

She had never been in want, never been truly on her own, but she lived with her eyes open. The Quarter abounded with hollow-eyed girls desperate for a man's attention, and for his coins.

She held her flute steady as Alistair poured champagne. His gaze rested on her bare shoulders. He tilted the bottle up as his eyes moved over her lips and finally met hers.

What if I let Alistair take me to the divan behind the curtain? Would the world tip off its axis?

Nicolette was not some cloistered belle whose every act was scrutinized to ensure her reputation was spotless. Those strictures simply did not apply to her, and that was an advantage in her mind. Unfettered by the society ladies' care to appear unrelentingly virtuous, she was freer than a *demoiselle* like Deborah Ann Presswood. Freer than a rich man's mistress. Nicolette's heart, mind, and body did not belong to a father, a brother, a family name, nor to a lover who paid for her affection. She belonged only to herself if she dared take what she wanted.

And what did she want? It wasn't enough to let Alistair love her. She wanted *to love*, to let desire burn away all her fears. She wanted to take and to give, not just accept.

The waiters appeared with covered dishes, the aroma of onion and pepper and veal filling the room.

"Let me help you with your chair." Most properly, Alistair seated her at the round table draped with snowy linen. Most improperly, his ungloved hand caressed her bare arm for the briefest moment.

Awareness blossomed, her skin exquisitely sensitive to his touch. She lowered her eyes at the tightening of her belly, at the jolt of desire.

Alistair opened a second bottle of wine. He was strange tonight, she thought. Gay and amusing, then quiet and even morose until he seemed to catch himself and launched into another story to please her.

Was he thinking of the divan behind the drapery? Was it the same red plush as the drapes? Was it wide enough for a man and a woman to lie side by side? She drank the champagne and felt its bubbling essence tickle through her veins, warming her, loosening her.

If she were truly a white woman, not simply white-skinned, she certainly could not have met Alistair alone, in private. Nor would he have asked it of her. She was not insensible to the interpretation that the invitation itself was an insult. But she chose to see it otherwise. She chose to be here.

Alistair rang the bell to have the table cleared.

"This has been a delightful treat, Mr. Whiteaker. I thank you."

"Are we back to 'Mr. Whiteaker' again?" His mouth quirked in a half-smile, his eyes a little sad. "I thought we'd agreed we might dispense with the Mr. and the Mademoiselle tonight."

She watched his hands on the bottle as he poured her more champagne. His fingers were long and slim, the nails buffed and rounded. She imagined those hands pulling the golden cords of the red drapery, slowly revealing the scene of so many seductions. She took a deep breath and let it out slowly. Might Alistair let go of his famous restraint tonight? Why else had he asked her to this oh so private dining room?

Alistair helped pull her chair from the table and gestured toward the love seat. "Sit with me, Nicolette."

She carried her wine with her and settled against the arm of the little sofa. Alistair sat at an angle to her, his knee pressing into the volume of her skirt. Her gaze slid over his thigh straining the fabric of his trousers. She wanted him to touch her again.

"I told you Marcel had asked me to join him on the Bayou Lafourche," he said.

She could see flecks of yellow in the deep blue of his eyes. He smelled wonderful.

"What have you decided?"

He took a deep breath. "I leave tomorrow. I'll catch up to General Mouton's forces in Houma by Thursday."

Nicolette was unsure whether to commiserate or to congratulate. She knew Alistair didn't want to fight. And he was fighting for the wrong side. But at last he had taken a stand.

"I see."

His fair skin flushed with feeling, he shifted so that he faced her directly. "Nicolette, I know you would have me join the Union. But I cannot." His voice had deepened, roughened as if thorns tore at his throat.

Ah, so he could be roused. He was actually impassioned. But about the war. His mind was not on the red drapery at all.

"My family, my friends ... I am a Southern planter. I am a part of this life. It would be traitorous to join the Union."

Did he expect her to condone his choice, was that what he wanted? They had talked about secession, slavery, Lincoln's election at length in the months before the war actually began. He knew her mind. She knew his.

Nicolette set her champagne on the side table, considering whether she could bring herself to send him off to fight – on the wrong side – with her blessing.

"Nicolette." He took her hand. "I must do this." He knit his brows, his eyes violet with pleading. "Will you forgive me?"

Nicolette withdrew her hand. She stood and walked to the bow window overlooking the street. Carriages were lined up at the front entrance, letting gentlemen off and taking them up. The strains of the orchestra in the main hall came through the floor. "Hear that? It's a waltz," she said.

His voice came to her subdued, flat. "Do you want to dance? We could go downstairs."

She shook her head, still staring at the street. "A dance won't make the war go away."

Nicolette heard his soft footsteps on the carpet. When he took her nearly bare shoulders and turned her to face him, she breathed in his heady scent. This was what she was here for, wasn't it? To be touched? Not to talk about the war.

"Nicolette. My darling." He kept his hands on her shoulders, those lovely graceful fingers on her bare skin. Alistair would never hurt her. She wanted to be rid of the shell she'd erected around herself. She wanted to feel and want and love.

She tilted her head back and closed her eyes, breathing in the scent of sandalwood and lemon. He slid his hand down her arm, a tingle of anticipation following his delicate touch. His other hand slipped round to the back of her waist. He moved her into the waltz, slowly, gently rocking her, then turning her in graceful arcs around the room.

She relished her ungloved hand cradled in his, skin to skin. She floated on the music, Alistair's hand at her waist anchoring her. She felt the warmth of each of his long fingers through her rosy silk, felt his strength as he guided them in effortless, lazy circles.

At the drapery's golden cords, Alistair ceased the waltz. She opened her eyes. At last she saw what she wanted from him. His blue eyes blazed with lust, vital and unveiled, with intensity enough to match her own at last.

His gaze shifted to her mouth. Her lips parted, her breathing quickened. Heat rose through her when his eyes rested on her bosom.

He bent. He pressed his lips into the fullness of her breast above the silk ruffle. Heat flooded her, melting the lonely cold core of her body.

He kissed his way to the bottom of her neck, then her ear. She turned her head, lips parted. They kissed, slowly, hesitantly, then desperation rising, he pressed warm firm lips against hers. He touched her tongue with his, gently, then urgently, driving into her mouth. The taste of wine and desire flamed through her.

She felt transported, wanting, needing more. Alistair leaned her head back, his mouth hot and demanding, one fevered hand on her neck, the other roaming down her back, down, down. He pressed her hips against his hard body, kneading her flesh.

She'd never been kissed like this, with undisguised hunger and need. She burned for him, yearned for more, for skin and muscle, mouth and hands.

His breathing, her breathing, came hot and fast and deep. Glorying in the latent power of his body, she slipped her hands inside his coat, dug her fingers into the lean muscle of his back.

"I love you, Nicolette," he whispered. "You know that, don't you?" He kissed her throat, tasted the hollow at the base of her neck. "Say yes, darling."

"Yes." *Yes, pull the golden cord. Take me to the divan.*

He suddenly enveloped her, tightening his arms around her. "My darling. You've made me the happiest man. You'll have a house, a carriage, servants, everything you want."

Nicolette drew back, her lips, her tongue, still on fire. "What?"

Alistair dropped to his knee in front of her, his blue eyes aglow. He clasped her hands and kissed them.

"I'll take care of you, Nicolette. And the children we'll have together. You'll never want for anything."

She had been thinking of warm bare skin, of caresses and kisses, of an end to virginal aching. That's what she wanted. Alistair's body with hers, in hers, on the red divan.

"Kiss me, Alistair."

"I want you for always, my darling. I want our first time to be perfect, in our own bed, in the house I buy for you. You understand? For evermore."

"Alistair." She put a hand to her head. "No, I … "

"I can wait, Nicolette, if that's what you want. Until after the war. You can continue with your singing, if you like. Continue living in your mother's house. I'll set up an allowance for you before I leave. Then when the war's over, I'll buy you a house. In the Quarter, or in the American sector, wherever you like."

For a moment she gazed into his eyes, bright, joyful, beautiful. She touched his jaw, his ear. Couldn't she and Alistair be lovers, just lovers? She wouldn't have to take his house, or his money.

"I want to take care of you, my darling. You. Our children. We'll build a life together."

He kissed her hands again, his lips hot and fervent. She wanted that kiss on her mouth, on her breasts. She was flushed and heated, but she stepped away. At the loveseat, she lowered herself slowly, her senses still dazed.

All she wanted was to make love. Alistair wanted so much more.

He'd buy her a house, he said. Buy *her*, he meant. He wanted to become her world. She would be idle, bored, impatient, her life revolving around Alistair and his visits to the home he provided. Waiting for him to come to her from his other world, she would be his satellite, no orbit of her own.

Alistair knelt before her, entreating her with his eyes to take what he offered. She didn't doubt Alistair's sincerity. She didn't need a certificate of marriage to be sure of his commitment. What she needed was a love too deep to be dissuaded by convention, a love strong enough to risk what marriage to a colored woman would entail, one that encompassed acceptance as well as commitment. She wanted passion, and she wanted affection that included a man holding his wife's feet while he read the paper.

Alistair's offer paled next to that dream. He could never dismiss the world for her. He wanted to share only a part of his life with her. He would always be a visitor in her house.

"No, Alistair."

His voice carried all his frustration, his yearning, his confusion. "Why, Nicolette?"

When she didn't answer, he turned from her, his hands fisted. "You kissed me!"

Nicolette flushed. She had kissed him, had craved his mouth on hers. Even now, she wanted him. But she'd meant to give him her body, not her self.

"Alistair, you see a colored woman when you look at me. You don't see me. You don't honor me. If I were truly white underneath this white skin, you would not propose this to me."

Alistair winced. "Be reasonable, Nicolette. We are known here."

Losing patience, she spoke in staccato. "Yes, I am known. As a free woman who can take care of herself. I do not need to be kept like a favorite pet."

An earnest, vertical line creased Alistair's forehead. "You don't understand me, Nicolette. I don't want a pet." He captured her hands. "I want you with me, always. Don't you see I love you?

How wonderful. To be loved. She could love Alistair. She nearly did already. But for what? Half a life?

She shook her head. "It's not enough. I want more, Alistair. I want a love strong enough that a man would throw over everything to be with me, strong enough that though my mother was a slave, I'd be worth marrying."

Alistair paced three steps away, rubbing his hand through his hair. He turned back to her, resolute. "Nicolette, I will never marry anyone else," he declared, commitment in every line of his earnest face. "You will be my wife in every way."

"Except that you would be too ashamed to acknowledge me."

She put her hand to her forehead. Was she being unfair, expecting him to give up everything for her? If he married her, they would have to leave New Orleans, never show their faces in Louisiana or even in Mississippi. His mother would suffer, his sister's chances would be ruined.

Even if he made such a sacrifice for her, would she do that for him? Leave Maman, Pierre, Lucinda and the children? Perhaps never see Marcel or Papa again?

"Alistair, I treasure you." She dropped her hand to her lap. "But the sacrifice you would have to make to marry me is one I could not make either. I don't expect you to marry me, truly I don't. I simply don't want ...*less*."

His eyes took on a determined glint. "You don't love me, Nicolette. I know that. But I'll love you constantly, faithfully, until one day you *will* love me."

She shook her head.

He strode to the window, his back to her, frustration radiating from him.

Nicolette stood. She smoothed her dress. She should go. She picked up her reticule and arranged the purse strings over her wrist.

Alistair still stared out the window. She wanted to wrap her arms around him, to comfort him. Even now, she wanted to make love to him, totally and completely. But he would not understand. If she touched him, he would think she had relented.

"Good night, Alistair," she said to his back. "I will pray God keeps you safe."

She let herself out. Downstairs, William spied her coming out and met her at the curb. She hired a cab to take them home, William perched behind on the baggage platform.

She was already in the carriage when Alistair rushed from the Blue Ribbon. He leaned in the open window and thrust a leather bag at her. "Keep this, Nicolette. Please. God knows what the war will bring, or when I will be back."

It was his purse, heavy with coin. He retreated from the window, his face scarlet, his eyes blue fire.

"No, Mr. Whiteaker. Certainly not."

She leaned out, holding the purse toward him. He backed away. "Mr. Whiteaker!" she commanded. Anger heated the back of her neck. She'd said no. She meant no. She did not accept his ... protection, that archaic word ... she would not be bought!

He locked eyes with her, shaking his head.

She reached out further, shoving the purse at him. "Alistair!"

He turned on his heel. The carriage moved into the street.

Her arm still out the window, Nicolette gazed at Alistair standing under the gas globe on the steps of the Blue Ribbon. He raised his hand to her, and her heart lurched. Alistair was going to war. He could be killed.

The carriage turned, and she could no longer see him. Maybe would never again see him.

At home, a lantern had been left on for her. She turned up the flame and lowered herself onto the sofa, the expanse of her rose silk glowing in the lamplight. She set Alistair's fine leather purse on the table. It was heavy. No telling how many gold coins were in it.

He had meant well, giving her his purse. He'd been thinking about the war, that no one could know what was to come. Even after she'd rejected him, he wanted to take care of her. He did love her.

Her feelings bubbled up, confusing her, frightening her. There'd be Yankee sharpshooters, cannons, bayonets. She could lose him. And Marcel. She could lose them both.

The stairs creaked, and Cleo entered the room carrying a candle. "You didn't come upstairs, my love. Everything all right?"

Nicolette's face crumpled. Cleo crossed to her quickly and Nicolette buried her face in her mother's nightgown.

She told Cleo everything. "He might never come back." She wiped her face on Cleo's shawl. "Was I a fool, Maman? Maybe I love him a little."

Cleo's throaty chuckle lightened the moment. "I know you, sweetheart. If you really loved him, it would not be 'a little.'"

In the still night, seated together on the sofa, Nicolette asked her mother what she'd always wanted to know. "Did you love Papa, Maman? Really love him?"

"Oh, yes. I was desperately in love with that man. Bertrand Chamard, the handsomest man on the river. I wanted him with all my heart, Nicolette."

"But you didn't let him make you his placée."

"For a while, sweetheart, I did. When I ran away from Toulouse, Gabriel was a tiny baby, you know. I worried constantly. Did Gabe have enough to eat? Would the mice and the roaches steal him away in the night? When your father found us again, I was glad for the little cottage he took for us."

"But when I was growing up, you didn't take Papa's money. I heard him rant and rave about that over and over. What changed?"

"Your aunt Josie gave me my papers, that's what changed. I was drunk with freedom. I was obsessed with it. I belonged to myself. Not even my Bertrand, my beloved, owned me. And so *I* paid for my children's shoes, *I* paid for the nanny and the tutors, *I* bought this house. That doesn't mean, Nicolette, that I ever stopped loving your father."

"Until Pierre," Nicolette said.

Cleo shook her head. "Your father is in my heart until my dying day, sweetheart. But he had the plantation, his other family, his life in society, and I grew tired of being alone. Seeing your man two or three times a week for a few hours, it's not enough. I wanted a husband."

Quietly, Nicolette asked her, "You don't love Pierre?"

"I most certainly do love Pierre. More now than I did when I married him. Your heart doesn't seal up from loving one man, Nicolette. Lord knows, maybe you can even love three!"

"Maman, you're awful." Nicolette kissed her mother's forehead. "Let's go to bed."

"The purse?"

"I don't want it, Maman."

"Well, tuck it away somewhere." Cleo picked up her candle. "I too will pray for your Mr. Whiteaker."

Chapter Seven

Captain Finnian McKee wished he were back in Boston strolling to an estate sale of some deceased scholar's library instead of staring at a forty foot pole laid out along Canal Street. Charged with repairing the telegraph lines in and around New Orleans, he'd already had the men install the fastening at the top of the pole that would receive the wire and conduct the signals. But he didn't see how four men and a paltry twenty yards of rope were going to get that pole upright in the waiting post hole.

Major Farrow, his excellent friend and drinking buddy, blustered by. "McKee, lad, enough with your moody humors. Do you not know how to raise that pole?"

Finn looked at him hopefully.

"What you do, Captain, is holler, 'Sergeant, get it up.'"

Hursh moved on, leaving a wake of laughing men behind him.

Finn grinned. "You know what to do, Sergeant?"

"Yes, sir."

"Thank God."

Finn turned his attention to Simpson and Wallace, two lads just off the boat. Washington, in all its wisdom, had decreed that telegraph operators were to be civilians. Turned out, however, that Simpson and Wallace knew the Morse code about as well as they new Greek or Latin.

While the sergeant and the men strung wire, Finn took up where he'd left off with the boys earlier in the day. He'd brought a keypad along to drill the code into their thick heads. Though the telegraph lines didn't extend many miles from New Orleans, they'd be ready to transmit by the time Butler routed the enemy from the rest of Louisiana..

"All right, Simpson. Your turn. Transmit: The enemy is on your left flank."

The boy dotted and dashed his way through the message. Wallace covered his mouth, trying to hide his smirk, but Simpson looked up at Finn with a hopeful smile.

"You just told General Butler that the enema was on his left plank, Mr. Simpson. Try again."

With Simpson's key strokes clattering in his ear, Finn glanced down Canal Street where a young woman with a basket on her arm walked toward him. He squinted his eyes. Could that be ... Nicolette Chamard? He felt the heat rise in his face. He'd been an ass that night. If she recognized him, she'd probably cross the street.

She approached, her eyes on the keypad Simpson labored over. Finn swallowed hard, his heart kicking at his ribs. She slowed her steps, her attention still captured by the telegraph.

Not five steps from him, she stopped. She still hadn't noticed him, a blow to his pride, but it gave him a chance for the flush to drain out of his cheeks.

He tipped his hat. "Mademoiselle, good afternoon."

He knew the moment she recognized him. Her pupils widened, her color deepened.

He'd relived that moment at the Silver Slipper a hundred times. His callous assumptions, his bulk looming over her. And now the gods above had sent him a second chance. His hands sweaty, he searched for something to say.

"May I show you the telegraph, Mademoiselle Chamard?"

He stepped aside so that she could move closer to Simpson. "This is not the actual transmitter, you understand. We have a Beardsley machine back at headquarters with the code cycles attached, but if this pad were hooked up to the wires," he gestured toward the pole, "we could send a message all the way to Washington. Theoretically. If the lines didn't need to cross Confederate territory."

She nodded, very still. She wouldn't look at him, but the tiny vein at her temple pulsed. Was that for him? Because she was glad to see him, or because she despised him?

"Simpson, show her how you do it. Transmit — " He'd been about to say, 'The lady's eyes are gray.' He changed his mind. Here in the full light of day, no paint on her face, no soft candle glow, she was so beautiful she sent his heart into his throat, but she did not invite familiarity. Her dress was modest, buttoned to the throat, and the scarf over her head was plain, tied simply compared to what she'd worn on stage. Remembering how unwelcome his advances had been in the dim hallway, he said, "Transmit the quick red fox ran into a hole."

Simpson slowly tapped his way through the sentence. Finn watched her intently follow every key stroke until she seemed to feel his gaze on her. She glanced at him, colored, and quickly returned her attention to Simpson.

Gently, Finn tapped the boy's shoulder. "An x is dash dot dot dash."

"Each letter has a code?"

"Yes, ma'am."

"That's all there is to it?"

"That's all there is to telegraphing, yes, ma'am. But the men have to learn how to code and decode to keep the enemy from deciphering the messages."

She turned her whole body to him and looked him full in the face. "I can do that."

"Ma'am?"

"I could learn to use the telegraph. I could do what these men are doing."

Was she serious? Finn took in the fine cloth, the good leather shoes, the neatly tied scarf. She might not be the same woman on and off the stage, but sassy or timid, whichever was the real Mademoiselle Nicolette, he couldn't see why she'd want to work for the Union army. Southerners who collaborated with the Union Army put themselves in real danger from their neighbors.

"Mademoiselle Chamard, running a telegraph in New Orleans is war work. You understand that, of course." He looked at her closely. Her cheeks had pinked. Her eyes were bright with excitement.

"I am aware of that. Captain? Those bars mean captain?"

"Captain Finnian McKee," he said, and dipped his head.

"Captain McKee. I want the Union to win this war. I want to help it happen."

A passing gentleman halted mid-step. His face turned deep red. His jaw muscles bunched so that his carefully-trimmed whiskers jerked. Finn stepped in front of Miss Chamard to keep the man's hate-filled glare from burning her. She was going to have to learn discretion if she was serious about collaborating with her city's enemy.

"I'm quick. I can learn this code. I can decipher."

Finn turned his head enough to see that the man had moved on. He turned his attention back to the enchanting Miss Chamard. Her soft Southern English, underlaid with a French accent, was music. She was a woman made for singing. For loving. And where had her shyness gone? She didn't quail under his reflective gaze. She didn't avoid his eye. He swallowed, trying to keep his heart where it belonged.

"Captain, do you need telegraphers?"

Simpson volunteered, "Yes, ma'am. We are short-handed. I heard of a lady telegrapher up in Missouri, Captain. You hear about her?"

Finn grimaced at the boy. Shortage of manpower was classified information.

Finn glanced around to ensure no more angry citizens would overhear them and gestured to her to walk a few steps with him. "Mademoiselle." She smelled of flowers. "I'm sure you appreciate there are security issues." Still hoping to read her, he peered into her face. Her eyes were so deeply gray they were nearly blue, the same color as his mother's temperamental Persian cat.

Her lips parted and she tilted her head up to him, the picture of eager excitement. Without thought, he leaned down, closer to that mouth, but remembered in time the street, the people.

He straightened. He'd been about to make an ass of himself, again. She beguiled him, bewitched him. Did she know it? Did she do it on purpose? She was an actress, he reminded himself. Who knew what she was really thinking?

"Sir, I am in earnest."

He couldn't stop staring. Self-consciously, she touched her tongue to her upper lip. His mouth opened.

"Captain?"

He brought his gaze back to her eyes. "Mademoiselle?"

"Will you teach me this code?"

Finn looked off into the distance, searching for the presence of mind to think it through. The Morse code was not secret. She could find it in most any library. He ripped a page from his field notebook and rapidly wrote the code for her.

He handed the paper into her gloved hand. "Learn this. Then come see me."

Her eyes lit up, making them a bluer gray. "Yes, Captain McKee. I certainly will."

The woman strode away with the page clutched in her hand, her shopping basket swinging from her arm. Finn watched her go, memorizing the shape of her shoulders, the way her back tapered down to the tiniest of waists.

When she'd smiled at him, radiant and glowing, it had knocked the breath out of him. But she would come to her senses and toss that paper away. He'd never see her again.

He rubbed his thumb over his moustache. Or maybe he would. Nicolette Chamard seemed to be made of determined stuff.

Chapter Eight

The sun was shining, but at this time of year, the likelihood of rain was close to a certainty. Marcel chose his second best boots to navigate the mired streets.

Today would be a round of goodbyes to family and friends in town. On the morrow, Marcel would take a steamboat upriver to the home place. He'd have the day with his father, and the next morning he'd don his new gray uniform, collect his men at Thibodeaux, and lead them west to join Alfred Mouton's forces.

Marcel took mid-day dinner at Mr. Sherman's for a final counsel with the wealthy, powerful men of New Orleans. This cadre advanced the cause of the Confederacy in finance and industry from the velvet and silk confines of rich men's parlors.

Mr. Sherman excused all the servants and closed the doors and windows. Within minutes, the air grew stale with humidity and cigar smoke. Marcel contemplated opening the French doors so they could breathe, but the men gathered here had information the Union would profit from in countless ways, so the doors remained closed. Over coffee and additional cigars, the gentlemen shared the intelligence their sources provided and discussed the advisories they would pass on to President Davis.

Marcel had other farewell calls to make – to Cleo and Nicolette, then to his fiancé, and finally home to Lucinda and their boys. He left Sherman's mansion with a clear understanding of the South's precarious position. As long as the Confederacy could replenish itself with cotton, wheat, and beef, she'd be able to resist the North indefinitely. However, the Union would put everything it had into gaining control of the Mississippi, cutting the South off from essential supplies. Even more immediately, Butler planned to seize all the cotton and cane crops of Louisiana, enriching the North and deplenishing the South.

Alfred Mouton was already positioning his forces west of New Orleans to hold Bayou Lafourche. The other, equally crucial imperative was to hold the Yanks back from the Red River. God help us, Marcel thought. They had fewer than half the men Butler would send against them. But they knew these swamps, they knew the bayous. They'd outmaneuver the Yanks.

The rain held off, and Marcel decided to walk to Cleo's street. He needed to rid himself of the smoke he'd been inhaling the last two hours and prepare himself for the inevitable scene with Nicolette.

The last year and more, his baby sister had made it clear she thought him a knave or worse for supporting secession. But then she was blind to all nuance in the matter. When she learned he was leaving to join the Rebel forces, she would be mean as an old brood sow.

A vine of red roses arched over the bright blue door of Cleo's house, the scent as welcoming as Cleo herself. Marcel used the boot scraper, then tapped the door with his cane.

A moment later, Cleo answered the door, wiping her hands on her apron. "You've come in good time! Nicolette just made a batch of pralines, and I've been grinding coffee beans."

Marcel kissed her cheek. "I need coffee and pralines, I surely do."

He settled onto the settee and stretched his legs out. Cleo shook out her apron and folded it over a chair back. "We didn't think to see you again this week. What are you up to?"

"Manly things, Cleo." He deepened his voice. "Riding bulls, toting barges, tearing trees up by the roots."

"Ah. I'm glad to see you using that fine education your father paid for."

Marcel sat up and leaned forward. He needed Cleo, his second mother, to understand what he was about to do. To forgive him. "Cleo. Tell me the truth. Do you believe this war is being fought to maintain slavery?"

Cleo looked at her hands a moment. When she raised her eyes to his, Marcel stopped his breath.

"Isn't it?"

A pang darted through his chest. Cleo's eyes were not angry, not even bitter, but she looked at him with such sadness.

"It's so much more complicated than that, Cleo — "

Nicolette's footsteps. They'd talk of it later.

Nicolette smiled, for which Marcel was grateful. When Nikki smiled, the world was a fine place. She played mother, pouring coffee, plopping sugar lumps and dribbling cream into the cups. She was in a fine mood, full of gossip and deviltry.

Marcel balanced a plate of pralines on his knee. The aroma of the strong dark brew, the creamy perfection of the pralines like sugared silk on his tongue – always a pleasure to be in Cleo's house. Such wonderful company, these two, Marcel thought sadly even as he laughed and talked. Such happy times in this parlor. How long would it be before he sat with them again? And would he be welcome, once he'd put on the uniform?

He couldn't put it off any longer. He set the pralines on the table and wiped the sugary crumbs off his pants leg.

"I'm really here to tell you good-bye. For a while," he said.

"You're going home?" Cleo said. "Your father will be pleased."

"Only for a day. The next morning, I'm riding out to join the Confederate forces on the Lafourche."

The room was silent except for the ticking of his pocket watch and the pulse in his ears.

"My dear Marcel." Cleo gazed at him lovingly with her beautiful brown eyes. "I am sorry you will be in harm's way. You know that. But I understand you must do what your conscience dictates."

He let out the breath he'd been holding. "Thank you, Cleo."

Nicolette's clattering cup and saucer interrupted their tender moment. She stood stiffly, her face flushed and angry.

"Marcel, you put on that uniform, and you are lost to me!"

Her vehemence startled him. "Don't be ridiculous, Nicolette."

"I mean it, Marcel. You're turning your back on your own kin. Gabriel and me, Maman, too, we'd be slaves working the fields of Toulouse right now if Tante Josephine had felt like you do."

Marcel stood up too. "You deliberately refuse to understand." His voice was full of righteous rebuke. His determination to accept their condemnation, if it came to that, evaporated. He *was* the older brother. "The abolitionists want you to think this is about slavery, and you're falling for it! This struggle is for autonomy. For sovereignty. You're a child if you think otherwise."

He saw her fist her hands, but he had to try to explain this one more time. Patiently, he said, "When Lincoln won the election — "

Nicolette's eyes flamed at him. She turned on her heel, left him in mid-sentence, and ran up the stairs. He raised his eyes to the ceiling as her angry footsteps tapped across the upper hall. Then the slamming of the door echoed down the staircase.

He'd called her a child. Damn it, he couldn't watch every single word coming out of his mouth. He held his palms out to Cleo. "What can I do?"

"Dearest, Nicolette loves Yves and Gabriel, very much. But you. Maybe she loves you most of all. That's why it hurts her so much that you don't respect her."

"I respect her."

Cleo raised her brows and tipped her head. "Your little sister, the one you still bring ribbons and bonbons? She's a grown woman, Marcel. I don't think you've realized that yet."

Maybe he hadn't. But she was so pig-headed. He could explain the situation to her, the whole war, if she'd just sit still and listen.

"I'll write to her," he said, "if you'll see she doesn't throw my letters in the fire without reading them."

Cleo gave him a sad smile. He knew what she was thinking. She too wanted him to be like his brother Yves, to renounce the South, to renounce his own heritage.

They didn't understand, he told himself yet again.

Marcel bent to kiss Cleo's cheek. "I love you both."

Cleo put her hand to his face. "Be safe, son."

For an understanding of how the world worked, what a young woman's place was in that world, Deborah Ann Presswood had romance novels. She'd escaped from her mother's unrelenting illness, from a house saturated with her mother's misery, by reading. As a girl, she read tales of damsels in frothy pink gowns and heroes rescuing them from dark castles.

Deborah Ann's bookish experience further revealed to her that once a man found the right woman, whatever the obstacles, he made her his and cherished her ever after. Deborah Ann had been found. Marcel had vowed to marry her, and she would be the sunshine of his life.

Happy, and convinced happiness lay before her evermore, she strolled down Rue de Iberville on the way to Madame Celeste's shop, Mammy rolling her great girth along behind her.

At the corner, they waited for a gap in the stream of wagons and horses to cross the street. With an elbow nudge, Mammy whispered, "Look there, Missy," and nodded at a regal young woman waiting on the opposite corner. Her smart linen day gown and the lavender tignon announced she was an exceptionally well-to-do woman of color.

"Who is she?" she said leaning into Mammy's ear.

"I tells you later."

Mid-way across the street, Deborah Ann eyed the woman as they passed. Tall and slim, the woman's manner was unhurried and self-possessed. She had a sensual roll to her walk that made Deborah Ann feel rather cloddish. A true beauty, with the high yellow complexion of a quadroon. If it weren't for the tignon on her head, she wouldn't have been sure she wasn't white. Almost as white as that girl who played and sang, Mademoiselle Nicolette.

Deborah Ann bought her goods and hurried home. Marcel was coming to supper and she had to be rested.

Lying on the daybed in her room, Deborah Ann wondered if he would be in his new uniform. So handsome, those tea-colored eyes, that wide bottom lip. She touched her own lip, remembering the exquisite feathering of his mouth against hers one afternoon in the arbor. She had only a little trepidation of the marriage bed. Marcel would be gentle, of course. She didn't know much about those physical sensations between men and women, not yet, but she already felt something, a heated fluttering, when she was near him.

She loved him. She'd make him happy. She'd be all he ever could want in a wife.

Idly, she watched Mammy tidying the room. Dear Mammy. Since her mother had died so tragically, Mammy had been the only one to help her in those delicate moments of womanhood. Whenever Deborah Ann had one of her spells, female hysteria, Dr. Braun called them, it was Mammy who sat by her bedside, Mammy who cooled her humors. Father of course would not discuss her mother's condition with her, but at such times, Deborah Ann worried that her mother's melancholy had begun just like this, with female pain and nervousness. But Mammy always said, no, you put away that foolishness.

"What about that creole woman you pointed out in the street?" Deborah Ann asked, yawning. Her family were Americans, not Creoles, but even a sheltered young woman like herself was aware that the original Creoles of Spanish and French descent had produced many mixed blood children, the creoles of Louisiana.

Mammy's eyes shifted to the fan overhead. "What woman that be?"

"You know. The one with the lavender tignon."

"Oh, that woman."

"What about her?"

Mammy glanced at Deborah Ann, then shifted her eyes up to the pukha fanning the humid air. "I thought she worth looking at, that's all. Don't see many peoples in the world that pretty."

Deborah Ann knew Mammy through and through. She was avoiding her, and that piqued her interest. "You remember what Mother used to say about you, Mammy?"

Mammy pretended disinterest. "What that, honey?"

"That yours must be a guileless soul because you couldn't tell a lie any better than a hound dog. What about that woman on the street?"

Mammy's resistance seemed to collapse. "Oh, baby, I shouldn't ought to have shown her to you. Young ladies like you oughtn't to know nothing about girls like that. I's sorry, Missy."

Deborah Ann scooted up to sit against the cushions. "You mean she's a prostitute? Mammy, I know what prostitutes are."

Her black eyes rounded in surprise, Mammy said, "How you know such a thing?"

"At the convent. The nuns were always warning us about being too free with ourselves. We'd go straight to hell," she said with a laugh, "but first we'd spend a life in degradation as depraved prostitutes."

"Them nuns told you that?" Mammy shook her head.

"So. That woman was a prostitute? She looked very prosperous."

Mammy again found the fan fascinating. She closed her face, and Deborah Ann realized there was more.

"What, Mammy? What about her?"

"Don't know no more about her. She just a fancy creole gal, that's all I knows."

Deborah Ann wrapped her arms around her knees. This was becoming more intriguing.

"So. Let me guess. She's a prostitute, but she doesn't look depraved or degraded. She's prosperous, in fact. And very beautiful." Deborah Ann paused. "She's one of those rich men's placées, isn't she? I've heard about them."

Mammy humphed. "Seems to me you know more than you ought to then."

"That's it, isn't it? Why wouldn't you say?"

Mammy's chin went up. "I just thought better of telling you 'bout that, but then you already knows it all."

Deborah Ann laughed. "I'm not a child, Mammy. I know gentlemen take up with certain kinds of women until they're married. I'm near to being a married woman myself, after all."

Mammy's face took on a curious expression, but Deborah Ann dismissed it. Old folks just had a hard time believing it when the young ones grew up.

A spring rain suddenly splashed the window sills. Mammy rushed to close the windows, and the subject was dropped.

When Marcel arrived, Deborah Ann was once again the perfect belle, corseted and curled and perfumed. She waited for his knock and ran to meet him in the great hall.

Rain beaded his hat and ran in rivulets from his cape. Jebediah the butler took the wet garments and handed Mr. Chamard a linen towel. Deborah Ann blushed, embarrassed and oddly excited at watching such an intimacy as seeing Marcel wipe the rain from his face and neck. He ignored her, and she thought she must have erred, observing this necessary grooming.

Marcel returned the damp towel to Jebediah. Then, as if only at that instant becoming aware of her, his gaze swept her from hemline to hairline. She stood still, basking in his admiration. This is just how a man should look on his beloved, just how Darcy had looked on Lizzy Bennett.

He escorted her to the drawing room, her hand warmly held on his arm. When he lay his hand over hers, she felt claimed. Owned. Her body actually warmed from physical contact with him.

During supper, Deborah Ann hardly touched her food. All her awareness was on Marcel. On his beautifully buffed nails as he raised his wine glass. On his lips as he brought the glass to his mouth. His hair had just been cut. She could see it by the thin line of white skin behind his ears where the sun hadn't yet bronzed him.

Marcel was quite young, really, far from being thirty, yet he spoke with her father as an equal. Though she did wish he'd spare her a few words. Not when they spoke of the war, of course, but whenever the topic turned to society or the latest novels, he might defer to her. She was, after all, to be his wife.

Why did he not look at her more? She had taken extra pains with her hair. She looked very fine tonight, she knew she did. She was accustomed to being complimented by gentlemen. Marcel, too, when he'd first courted her, had been full of compliments. Lately, he seldom seemed to notice how well she looked.

He was preoccupied with the war, that was all, she thought. When they were married, she'd wake up, and he would be in her bed. He would call her pretty names and touch her hair. And one morning, as they lay in bed together, she'd tell him she was with child.

Deborah's mind skittered away from the subject as soon as she'd thought it. She was fairly sure she knew how child-getting was accomplished, in spite of the veiled warnings and threats she'd heard at the convent. After all, she spent her summers at Evermore, the family plantation, and dogs and cats and horses knew no shame. Even if she didn't fully understand these things, however, Marcel would make it happen.

She'd be a good wife, she thought. Sons ran in her family, after all. She'd had three brothers, before the small pox. Father had four, and Mother had six! Marcel wouldn't be sorry he chose her.

But the talk of the war consumed the men, and she wished they would speak of something else. She might as well be upstairs with her novels.

"I'll take the steamer up to Cherleu tomorrow," Marcel was saying. "The day after, I'll put the uniform on and ride west."

Father nodded. "Mouton will need all the help he can get keeping the Yanks out of Lafourche."

Thank God he was an officer, not one of those poor soldiers Father called cannon fodder. But why didn't he speak to her? She was the one who'd miss him!

She wiped her mouth daintily, the picture of serenity, even if she was boiling with impatience. She pushed her chair back, a little more roughly than propriety demanded.

Abruptly, as if to make amends for his neglect, Marcel rose and held the back of her chair. As she excused herself to leave the men to their port and cigars, Marcel touched her elbow.

"I'll be with you shortly, Miss Deborah Ann."

She smiled sweetly. A lady never showed her displeasure.

"Don't be long, Mr. Chamard," she murmured.

She waited in the parlor, flipping through a magazine of last year's fashions. The longer she waited, the more her doubts surfaced. Maybe he found her dull. The other gentlemen of the last two seasons had admired her and sought her company. But they had been mere boys. Marcel was not a boy. Maybe she was too young for him.

She tossed the magazine aside. She touched her hair. It was a lovely color, everyone said so. Her nose was good, not sharp or stunted or long. She pooched her mouth. That's how it looks when you're going to kiss someone, she thought.

He was going to kiss her good bye, surely. They were engaged, after all. And she was going to kiss him back, this time.

At last, Marcel came to her. For a moment, he simply stared.

"You're lovely, Miss Deborah Ann."

She laughed, a little nervous. He took both her hands in his and looked into her eyes. He does love me, she thought. When he kissed her knuckles, she felt her lips tingle.

He led her to the sofa and sat so his long thigh stretched beside hers. The thought of their legs side by side, only layers of fabric between them, made her breathless.

"Do you understand, dear, why I'm going? Is there something you would like me to explain?"

Of course she understood, but all she cared about was that he look at her as he was right this minute. "No, Mr. Chamard. I admire a man of courage."

Marcel looked at the floor a moment. He's a modest man, she thought, gazing at the dark lashes displayed against his cheek.

"The wedding, Miss Deborah Ann. Considering the present climate, perhaps we need to discuss it. I will do my best to be here on January the twelfth, but we are none of us in control of these events."

He looked at her to see if she understood. She'd never seen eyes so beautiful. Marcel's were somehow richer, clearer than any other brown eyes. And framed by perfect dark brows. She imagined tracing her finger along the arch of those brows.

"What would you think of foregoing a wedding involving musicians, caterers, dressmakers, and all the thousand preparations normally involved? I think only to spare you the disaster of an absent groom on the day of the grand occasion."

A whisper of panic fluttered in her chest. No wedding? He was looking at her, expecting an answer. "An absent groom?"

"Consider, Miss Deborah Ann. If the fighting took me to the Red River. Or if I found myself at Vicksburg come January. I could not leave a battlefield to come home for the ceremony. We could postpone the wedding until it's reasonable to plan a grand event, if you'd prefer. Or we could wed in a modest way, on short notice, when I am able to return in the fall."

Air filled her lungs again. "Of course. A modest wedding." She laughed, her panic melting.

But the occasion should be wonderful! Everyone in New Orleans should be there. Her gowns. The flowers, the banquet. Seven courses, at least, and the ball. How could she make it modest?

But a lady does not argue with a gentleman. Of course, he was correct. They were in the middle of a war. She'd manage it somehow.

"We would be just as married, would we not!" she said gaily.

"Good. That's very sensible of you, Miss Deborah Ann."

He lightly slapped his hands on his knees as if to announce, There, that's done. Then he was leaving?

Impulsively, Deborah reached her hand to touch his arm. Surely he'd kiss her before he left, when he'd be gone so long. Who knew when she would see him again?

He raised her hand and pressed a kiss to it. It wasn't enough. It wasn't what she wanted. She leaned into him, shamelessly. Her balance was off. She caught at his lapel.

He looked at her a moment, questioning. Yes, she told him with her eyes, kiss me. He stood, raising her with him.

Holding her hand at his chest, next to his heart, he bent to her. He brushed his lips over hers, smiling at her.

Did he think she was a child!

She pressed her mouth against his, hard, feeling his teeth behind his lips. That's how she wanted to kiss, with all the fervor in her breast.

He broke away. Her face turned crimson. She had done it wrong.

Then he showed her how, kissing her strongly, but softly.

Oh, God, she thought, struggling to breathe under the tight corset. But she was willing to cease breathing if only Marcel would kiss her again.

Oh bliss. One more real kiss. Please.

He kissed her nose and touched a curl hanging at her ear.

"Be well, my dear. I shall write to your father when I can, and to you if he allows it."

"Do, Mr. Chamard. Do write."

Deborah Ann watched him leave the room, hoping for a last lingering look. When he didn't turn at the door, her doubts rose again. She touched her lips. Why only one kiss? She'd have kissed him from now until forever.

It was simply they were so different. He always cool, she always hot. He calm, she excitable. There would be kisses enough when they were married, she told herself, and pressed her hand to her mouth so as not to cry.

In the hallway, Marcel took his hat from the butler and left the Presswoods'. A sweet girl, he said to himself. She'll make a good wife.

He dashed through the rain to his carriage waiting at the curb. "Elysian Fields," he told the driver.

On Lucinda's street, he hopped eagerly from the carriage at the well-kept yellow cottage with the orange shutters. The new bridge he'd had built to span the rushing gutter still shone of new wood.

He tapped on the door with his cane, then entered, stooping a little for the doorway.

"Lucinda?"

His beloved rushed into his arms. He lifted her off her feet, burying his face in her neck. She smelled of cinnamon and vanilla, of smoke and jasmine all at once. He kissed her, tasting her, loving her, gladness filling his heart. His hand slid up her back to the lavender tignon covering her wealth of wavy black hair. He jerked the silk free and ran his fingers through her tresses, caressing her neck. His other hand pressed her body tight against his.

"Papa!" Charles Armand rushed at him, grabbing his legs.

One hand on his son's head, he gazed into Lucinda's eyes, marveling at the love he saw there. What had he done to deserve her? He kissed her again, then bit at her earlobe. "Later," he whispered.

He hauled Charles Armand upside down and grinned at his cascade of giggles.

The baby, Bertie, slept in his cradle, his mouth a pouty rosebud. Gently, Marcel pushed aside the mosquito net to touch his babe's plump cheek.

"Look, Papa," Charles said. "The gray soldiers have killed all the blue coats."

Marcel adjusted the netting and lowered himself to the floor. "Set them up again, Charles. Show me how you won the battle."

"A glass of wine?" Lucinda asked, her fingers playing with Marcel's hair.

He looked up at his beloved, her smile as open as her heart, as loving as her arms. It was good to be home, one more night.

Chapter Nine

Marcel watched the shoreline for his first sight of Cherleu, the Chamard plantation. Marcel's father had bought the run-down property cheap, invested every cent he could get through mortgage and marriage, then poured his own sweat and brawn into it to develop the place into a model of profit and beauty.

Marcel supposed lots of plantation homes were graced with breezy galleries, moss-draped oaks and dozens of camellia bushes, but only Cherleu was home. He'd grown up here with Mother, dead long ago, Father, and his brother Yves, who'd chosen to embrace the North. He and Yves used to sneak half a mile upriver to Cleo's small country home to play with their half-siblings, Gabriel and Nicolette, swimming, fishing, sharing books and games. Those had been good times, summer on the river.

He tightened his grip on the steamboat railing. It could all go up in smoke if Lincoln's army spread its tentacles north from New Orleans.

The boat stopped at the Cherleu dock long enough for Marcel to disembark with his valet. He and the boy climbed to the top of the levee to survey the old home place. "Glad to be back, Val?"

"Yes, sir. I love it better here than anywhere."

Marcel thought of his boys and Lucinda back in town and couldn't say the same. But he loved the old place. The river breeze freshened the air, the plowed black earth lent its loamy scent. Even from the bank, he could hear the rustle of the cane stalks shifting in the wind.

The sweet voices of the men and women working the fields, singing through their hours of toil, carried across the plantation, reminding him of the peace and plenty of childhood, days without loss, without war. Peace and plenty for him and his family at any rate. Marcel was not blind to the woes of a slave's life, but Papa had at least created a stable home for these people on Cherleu.

Val carried two valises and Marcel picked up the third. Together they walked through the alley of live oaks to the house. Val went around back. Marcel climbed the front steps.

The door opened for him, and there stood Val's father, Valentine. "Mr. Marcel. You here in good time for dinner. Come on in and I'll fix you a cool glass of water."

Marcel gave Valentine his hat. "Water would be good. Papa in the house?"

"He down at the creek fishing. May be we'll have a mess of catfish for dinner."

Marcel shrugged out of his coat. Valentine followed him to his bedroom, carrying the coat. Val was already there unpacking the valises.

"I'll do that, son," Valentine offered. "You go on and get the travel dust off you so you can serve dinner."

Marcel glanced at Valentine as he pulled off his collar. "Time for my report?"

Valentine sat himself on the boot bench. He took such license pretty much whenever he felt like it. He'd been Marcel's father's playmate in childhood and then became his valet when they were both striplings. Marcel had long ago figured his father and Valentine to be half-brothers, like he and Gabriel were.

"What that rascal been up to?" Valentine asked. "He cause you any trouble?"

"Here's the thing," Marcel reported, his face grave with the bad news. "Since you saw him last month, Val managed to get the upstairs girl pregnant, which made the downstairs girl run off with a broken heart. He cracked three of ma mère's Chévres plates. He burned a hole in my best dress shirt. He spent the nights gaming and wandering the town. And then he slept all day. A worthless boy if I ever saw one."

Val's weathered face split into a grin. "Two gals, huh? That's my boy."

Marcel laughed. "He's doing well, Valentine. He's earnest and eager." He tossed his sweaty clothes on the bed. "He did scorch my best shirt though."

"I'll whup him for you. Let me get you that cool water now."

Marcel washed at the pitcher and bowl, then put on a cotton shirt and loose cotton trousers. One of the joys of being home, not having to dress up like a starched linen peacock.

Val clomped into the room with a decanter of water and a big smile. "Daddy says tell you he done whupped me good."

" 'Has whupped me well,'" Marcel corrected. "Good. That saves me the trouble. Listen, I'm going to need extra socks."

"Yes, sir." Val thumped the second valise on the bed to finish unpacking. "I figure, you take your two valises and I take one, my horse can handle all three just fine."

Marcel stared at the boy. "Val, I told you. You're not going. I don't need a valet in the field."

Val's face fell into a pout. "Yassuh," he said.

Marcel shook his head. Every time Val didn't get what he wanted, he lapsed into slave talk, when he knew perfectly well how to speak properly. "Say that again, please, as it should be said."

Val risked a glance at him. "Yes, sir," he articulated.

"Socks," Marcel reminded him, and left him to it.

They'd spoiled him rotten, Marcel reflected. Grew up with everybody fussing over him, petting him. The most privileged kid on the place. Valentine senior was light, but he'd bedded one of the darkest girls on the place. She'd been a beauty, still was, and Val had her darker skin, high forehead, and bottomless black eyes.

"What is he, fourteen?" Marcel muttered. "Not taking him."

Out at the creek, Marcel found his father with his shoes off, his feet in the water, and a straw hat on his head. Biscuit, his favorite hound, lay stretched out beside him.

"They biting?"

"Hey, son. Take your shoes off."

"Think I will." Marcel sat on the bank and started unlacing.

His father handed him the pole and lay back in the grass. "Just going to close my eyes a minute," he said, and settled the straw hat over his face.

Marcel rebaited the hook with a tiny crawdad from his father's bucket. Over the next half hour, all the kinks eased out of his neck and shoulders. The overhanging trees filtered the sunlight right through the clear water to the ripples on the creek bed. Down a ways, blue jays dived and squawked at a hapless squirrel. The war seemed a long way off from this time, this place.

If only a body could stop time, he thought. Could hold on to what's good. Last night, with Lucinda and the boys. This moment, here with Papa.

They could lose it all. Cherleu. Everything.

He felt like a pebble being ground along on the bottom of a mighty river. Helpless to change the course. Helpless to stop the flow. The war was sweeping them all to ruin.

He'd do what he had to. He'd do what he could. That's all any man could do.

When Papa roused from his nap, Marcel gathered the pole and the bucket and the string of catfish. On the way back, they dropped the fish off with Bella at the cook house.

After supper, they took their coffee to the upstairs gallery. While they watched the river roll by, Marcel brought his father up to date. "Word is, Butler plans to target Lafourche next. He wants all that sugar wealth, and if he can't get it, he plans to burn it."

Bertrand scratched behind Biscuit's ears. "Where you joining up with General Mouton? Houma?"

"Thibodeaux. Maybe we can keep the Union from getting as far as Houma."

They talked strategy, trying to outguess Butler. If they lost Lafourche Parish, it would be a heavy blow to The Cause.

Marcel lit one of his father's Cuban cigars. "I saw Cleo yesterday."

Cleo was a delicate subject with Papa. She had been his for so long, he'd been incredulous, and hurt, when she married this Pierre LaFitte. Papa would not ask about her, but he drank in whatever information his sons and daughter would give him.

"She's well." Marcel eyed his father, wondering how much to tell him. He softened his voice. "I think she's happy, Papa."

Bertrand grunted and ground his cigar butt on the railing.

To lighten the moment, Marcel reported on his baby sister. "Nicolette, on the other hand, is ready to horsewhip me for putting on the uniform."

"She's a spitfire, isn't she? Always on the lookout for injustice."

"She's quick to find it, too, Papa."

"Hers is an uncompromising soul. Don't know where she gets it."

After a quiet moment, Bertrand asked, "How many men they got working the foundry?"

They talked till the mosquitoes drove them inside to the study where bouquets of dried tansy deterred the biters. A tansy-loving moth flirted with the lantern.

Marcel opened a leather satchel. "These are the papers. I've already signed them with Monsieur Marchand as witness, but I want to go over them with you."

He laid out the first pages. "This is the ownership papers for the foundry. If the South loses, the matter will be moot. But if we win, the foundry goes to you."

"If we win?"

Marcel met his father's eyes. "You're so confident?"

Bertrand tapped his fingers a moment. "As long as we have Vicksburg, we're strong here in the west. But confident? Hopeful? Not the same as seeing the future, is it?"

Marcel opened another packet. "These pages divide my remaining assets. The race horses, the town house, the carriage, the portfolio, my share of Cherleu. Yves gets a third. Gabe and Nicolette split a third. The last third is for Lucinda and the boys."

"A third?"

"Yes," Marcel said firmly. "A third."

"Very generous."

Marcel stared at his father a moment. Papa had loved Cleo, that had always been apparent, even when Marcel was a boy. He'd provided for her, as much as she would let him. If it had not been for Maman, would Papa not have given Cleo and the children a third of his worldly goods, for love's sake?

"This is important to me, Papa."

Bertrand met his eyes. "I understand."

"And she'll need more than money. I want you to look after her. See about her."

Bertrand's gaze returned to the documents. Was he thinking about Cleo and their babes? The years she wouldn't let him contribute a picayune, so determined was she to be her own woman, not a rich man's placée?

"If Yves were here, or Gabe, I wouldn't ask you — "

"Marcel, I will be honored to take care of Lucinda and your sons."

Marcel stretched his arm across the table to grasp his father's hand. "Thank you, Papa."

"And Miss Presswood?" Bertrand asked.

"Ah." Marcel hadn't thought about it. "I'll gather a few keepsakes for her. Valentine will know where they are."

"Good." Bertrand reached for the bell. "With that grisly business over, let's have a bottle of wine."

Val delivered a bottle of Bordeaux on a silver platter. The cut-class crystal picked up the flickering light as he placed the tray on the desk. Bertrand reached for the bottle, but he stopped at Val's uncharacteristic stance. The boy had pulled himself to attention and stared off into the middle distance like a soldier on report.

Marcel hid his smile. He knew what was coming. Papa doted on Val. When Marcel and Yves had reached their adolescence, they'd been sent to school at St. Charles College south of Opelousas, the best school in the state. Marcel had come home for the summer to find the big eyed toddler ensconced on Papa's knee, Papa shelling boiled peanuts for him.

"You wish to say something, Val?"

"I been talking — "

" 'I have been,'" Marcel interrupted.

"I have been talking to mon père, Monsieur Chamard. He say — "

"'He says.'"

"He says I can go with Monsieur Marcel tomorrow."

"He does, does he?" Bertrand answered. "Your daddy making the decisions around here now?"

In truth, Marcel realized, Valentine did make a lot of the decisions "around here." But Val hadn't yet learned the art of subtlety his father had mastered.

Val shifted his black eyes from Bertrand to Marcel and back. "I only meant, Monsieur, that mon père thinks it's a good idea. For me to take care of Monsieur Marcel when he's in the field."

Bertrand gave Val the eye, but the boy held his gaze. Bertrand puffed up his chest and hollered. "Valentine!"

When Valentine stepped into the room, he said solemnly, "You bellow for me, sir?"

Marcel hid a smirk as his father glared at Valentine.

"What did you tell Val about running off to war?" Bertrand demanded.

"The same as we been telling him. He has to stay here, work on that stack of books he got kicked under the bed."

Marcel watched Val's righteousness override his embarrassment at being caught out.

"Monsieur Marcel needs me. I have to go." He looked at the three stony faces and his courage flared higher. "I'm not a boy!"

"Val." Bertrand skewered him with his eyes. "You ever lie to me again, I will take the whip to you. Personally."

Val's slender jaws worked as he struggled to swallow his anger.

"Val!" Valentine spoke quietly, but the command was there.

Finally Val dipped his head. "Yes, sir. I'm sorry, sir."

Marcel almost felt sorry for the boy. "Go get my kit ready. I'm leaving first light."

Val's bowed head raised enough to look at Marcel with hope in his eyes.

"I'm going alone," Marcel said as firmly as he knew how.

Val slunk away to see to the packing. Each man in the room shook his head. They all saw a scrawny kid, too young to know how young he was. Yet each man remembered how it had burned to be treated like a child when you were not yet a man.

"He get over it," Valentine said.

Marcel drained his glass of very fine wine. "I need to get to bed, Papa. You be up in the morning?"

Bertrand nodded. "Good night, son."

Dark clouds delayed sunrise. By the time Marcel dressed and gathered his gear, the heavens opened. Lightning flashed and thunder rolled down the river. Valentine fetched an oiled slicker for Marcel to wear over the uniform and oiled canvas to wrap his biscuits and bacon. Time to go.

Marcel embraced his father.

"Take care of yourself," Bertrand said.

His papa's eyes were moist, and Marcel worried for him. Yves and Gabe two thousand miles away, and now he was leaving too. But Papa would have Valentine. And Val. And Madame Josephine next door at Toulouse. Their old friendship seemed to be deepening, the best he could tell.

On the gallery, Valentine hugged him hard. "You take care of yourself, Captain. We all wants you back here in one piece."

Marcel entered the onslaught of wind and rain. Val, clad in his own poncho, held Hercule's lines. Rain dripped off Val's nose, over his sullen mouth. There'd be no friendly goodbye coming from him this morning.

Marcel took the reins. "Apply yourself, Val. See how many of those books you get read before I come home. I'll give you a coin for every one you can answer three questions about."

Lightning bleached the air. The live oak thirty feet away burst into flames. Shock waves stunned them into a trembling tableau of horse, boy, and man.

The next instant Hercule reared on his hind legs, pulling the reins from Marcel's hand.

Val lunged for the lines.

The horse came down hard, his hoof catching the instep of Marcel's boot. Marcel went down.

The horse bolted, Val still hanging on to the reins.

Bertrand rushed down the steps into the deluge to help Marcel. Valentine ran after his boy.

Hercule reached the river road and kept going. Val had sense enough to let go the reins before the horse dragged the pants, and the skin, off his legs. He was pulling himself out of the mud when his daddy got to him.

Val and Valentine ran through the downpour back toward their masters. Over the roar of the burning tree and the sheeting rain, Bertrand shouted, "Get him inside. Damned horse stomped his foot."

They set him down on the horsehair sofa, rivulets running off all of them. The wet wouldn't harm the sofa, but Marcel spared a thought for the Parisian rose-patterned carpet they were muddying. If Maman were alive, she'd have palpitations over these muddy streaks, as soon as she'd had her palpitations over his foot.

Bertrand sent for Bella, the cook and also the best nurse they had on the place. Dripping wet, she arrived with clean rags and her needle and thread.

Valentine was unlacing Marcel's boot. "Lemme do dat," Bella said.

Thunder shook the window panes. The flaming oak tree outside crackled. Valentine closed the shutters and lit a lantern before the storm pushed its way right into the house.

"We gone need a fire in here," Bella told him. "M'sieu Marcel gone get a chill, he so wet."

Valentine nodded at Val to get a fire started.

Marcel grit his teeth as Bella worked the boot over his foot. He gripped the sofa arm with one wet hand and a glass of rum with the other. He wouldn't have been surprised if a torrent of blood drained out of the boot, but there was only a red crescent on his stocking.

The hoof had come down so that the outer rim curved with the base of his toes. That's where the blood oozed out. Already the foot was blue and swelling. He'd never get his boot back on.

Bella unrolled the heavy wool sock until his foot was revealed. "Won't need no stitches." Gently she felt of his ankle, his instep, and each toe. "See can you move 'em youself."

Marcel sucked air through his teeth as he flexed his toes. They all worked, at least until the swelling immobilized them. The hoof had pushed his foot into the mud instead of breaking it.

"Dese bones still good then," Bella pronounced. "But you gone have to stay off this foot a spell."

Heedless of the muddied carpet, Bella opened a tin of turpentine and set it down on a wool and silk rose. She stuffed a strip of white linen in the turpentine, then tied that soaked strip over the first clean bandage she'd applied. She bound his foot till it was cushioned top and bottom, and propped it on a tufted leather chair.

That done, the company contemplated the disaster that was Marcel's foot. The storm should have kept him home; the foot certainly would.

"Bella, you make me an oil-cloth boot to go over all this wrapping?"

"Sho, I can do that," she said, raising her voice over the noise of the storm. "Won't take me no time."

"Val, go with her. Take the boot and see if you can seal the cut with wax."

That left Valentine, Bertrand and Marcel in the room, all three silently focused on the bandaged foot.

Finally Marcel said what they were all thinking. "I can't wait on this foot, Papa."

"Don't want me to send word to General Mouton?"

Marcel shook his head. "My men are already in Thibodeaux."

"You cain't get around on you own with that foot like it is," Valentine said.

Marcel looked at his father. Then at Val's father.

"I'll go fix the boy's kit." Valentine left the room with a heavy tread. Papa went to search the closets for a pair of Yves' larger cast off boots that might fit over the swelling in a few days.

Rain beat on the roof and hurled itself against the shutters. Even with the windows closed, the lantern flickered. Marcel sipped the rum judiciously. He'd be a damn fool to ride in this storm half drunk. And where was Hercule? By now, he could have run half way to Donaldsonville.

Bella came in with the oversized canvas bootie over her arm, Val dripping wet behind her.

"Old Ben got Hercule back," Val reported. "You still want to ride him?"

Marcel winced as Bella drew the bootie up over his bandaged foot. "He'll do. Most any horse would bolt with lightning coming down on his head." He stood up tentatively, his nurse hovering. "Thank you, Bella. Your boot will serve very well."

She smiled broadly.

"Go on back to the cabin and get some dry clothes on, crawl under a quilt. You'll catch your death, you don't get warmed up."

She rewarded him with a quick curtsey, something she seldom bothered with.

Alone with Val, Marcel eyed the boy. He was not any more cheerful than he'd been out in the storm holding on to the bay's reins.

Marcel took out his watch. "It is now eight o'clock. I want you back here at quarter past, packed and ready to travel."

One second for the meaning to penetrate Val's grievances. The next second, his face lit. Third second, he was racing through the house to the little room he shared with his father.

Twelve past eight, Val reported to Marcel. "Ready, Michie Marcel!"

"Monsieur, not 'michie.'"

On the gallery, the men said their goodbyes again. Smoke wisped from the ruined tree, the flames extinguished by the downpour. The thunder and lightning had moved upriver, and the rain had reduced itself to a steady, lighter fall.

Marcel paused before he left the porch. "Valentine, I'll do everything under God's blue sky to keep him safe."

"I know you will, Michie. Keep you both safe, hear?"

Chapter Ten

Finn discovered that rain in New Orleans was a mixed blessing. During the actual shower, he'd open his collar a little to feel the coolness on his neck and breathe in the scented air. The magnolias, the jasmine, the very earth perfumed the air. Then the sun reasserted itself. The wet streets steamed. The heavy air smothered him.

He rode out Canal toward the park. Evidently Southern gentlemen still indulged in dueling, and here among the spreading oaks was where they did it. Archaic, he thought, trying to kill each other over slights and misunderstandings. He grunted. War was much more civilized, of course.

His signalmen were paired off, the width of the park between them, waving the big flags in wig wag code. Most of the soldiers took to it right off. Kinda fun, wagging the flags up down and side to side. Finn set them up, unit against unit, to see who deciphered and enciphered the fastest. "Points off for inaccuracies!" he reminded them.

When the hot sun took all the fun out of the exercise, Finn spiced up the messages. "No more 'the enemy is three miles west,' Sergeant. Let's try something else." He thought a minute. "Wag this: 'There was a young lady named Myrtle / Who refused to be bound by a girdle ... ' "

Happy with the morning's work, Finn left his troops in fine spirits. As for himself, he still had the telegraph boys to see about. As busy as they all were maintaining order in an enemy city, Finn had a sense of the war looming like a bank of dark thunder clouds. Preparing for the inevitable, he thought, as his fertile mind latched onto another metaphor, he felt they were poised on the edge of a precipice. Soon they would be plunging over the edge, into battle and chaos and death.

He mounted the fly-tormented horse he'd ridden to the park and headed back to town hoping for a cooling wind closer to the river. The sun beat down on his head and face and shoulders. Sweat trickled into his collar, down his back, his sides, his belly.

He tried to shake the gloom off his shoulders. Was it Horace who said *Carpe diem? For tomorrow we die*? He wished he could seize Nicolette Chamard before he died. He thought he saw her everywhere, getting off the tram, turning a corner. He'd once caught sight of a foamy white petticoat as a young woman descended from a carriage. He'd felt his heart lurch, hoping it was her petticoat. Each time, disappointment cut right through him.

At headquarters, Finn tied his horse in the shade and walked into the Custom House. First step off the street, he began unbuttoning his uniform. To hell with protocol. If he didn't get out of this jacket, he was going to melt.

He took the stairs two at a time. The tapping of telegraph keys, the murmur of voices, a sudden laugh – everything ceased as soon as Finn entered the telegraph room.

Three faces turned to him. Simpson, Wallace, and Nicolette Chamard.

His gaze locked on hers. Then he looked away, acutely aware that his coat hung open, exposing his white shirt, wet, nearly transparent. He probably smelled like a horse.

"Mademoiselle," he said, and dipped his head. Blood roaring in his ears, his fingers worked the buttons to put himself to rights. Decently covered, he could look at her again.

She left her chair and stood in front of him, bold as brass. She had a proud smile on her lovely face, her chin up.

"She's got it, Captain," Wallace bragged. "Miss here can tap it out good as Simpson."

"Well, I like that," Simpson began.

Finn quelled him with a look. "Is that right, Mademoiselle Chamard? You've learned it?"

"I have. And these young men have instructed me in the rhythm required. They've been most generous." She smiled at Wallace and Simpson in turn, and they each radiated a healthy male glow back at her.

He moved to place himself between her and the pups gawking at her. She wasn't here for them. Or himself, either, of course. Whatever her reasons, she wanted to be a telegraph operator, and she wanted it fiercely. He would have to think about her motives, later, when his head cleared. "Perhaps a demonstration?"

"Of course." She turned the full sunshine of her smile on him. He kept his jaw clamped. He didn't want to look like the two grinning idiots at the keypads.

"Take my place," Wallace insisted. He held the chair for her and stood back.

Finn moved closer to the window, hoping for a little air. What was the matter with him? He'd known other beautiful women, had half-heartedly courted a few. But this woman knocked the pins out from under him.

Finn turned. Miss Chamard had situated her skirts and pulled the keypad closer. There was a damp spot between her shoulder blades. He envisioned sweat trickling down her sides, under her corset. When she looked at him in readiness, he blinked guiltily.

"Train arrives at seven o'clock a.m."

With spot-on rhythm, she tapped his message on the practice pad. A little slow, but perfectly accurate.

"This one's longer. Write it down. 'Enemy engaged Red River. Left bank decimated. Right bank holds. Send reinforcements.' Simpson, Wallace, both of you code."

Finn gazed at her freely as she concentrated on what she was doing. Sweat beaded her upper lip and tiny curls stuck to her forehead where they'd escaped from the cloth. It must be hot, that head cloth, he thought. Why doesn't she take it off now she's inside? He imagined unfolding it, imagined a mass of wavy black hair spilling onto his hands.

"Got one run-on. That's all," Wallace reported.

"Yep. Told you she's got it, Captain."

Her eyes shining like a child's on Christmas morning, she turned sideways in her chair. "Do I have a job, Captain?"

She'd be here, in this room, practicing, learning encryption. He could see her every day. But why would a Southern belle help the Federals?

"That'll be up to the major, Mademoiselle."

"It's all right to use the English 'miss,' Captain. I don't mind."

He could listen to that musical accent forever. It was as if, with the slightest adjustment to her lilting, rhythmical speech, she'd be singing. Hoping she couldn't see how far gone he was, he gave her a curt nod. "I'll take it up with Major Farrow, Miss Chamard. Let you know tomorrow."

"Thank you, Captain." She raised her hand in goodbye to Simpson and Wallace. To Finn she curtsied formally. Then she left the room, leaving the scent of lemon verbena in her wake.

Finn closed his eyes and breathed deeply. Tomorrow.

Sleeping, an incessant stream of Morse code scrolled through Nicolette's dreams. Waking, her fingers tapped on her cup as she had coffee and beignets. She read the *Picayune*, and letters transformed themselves into dots and dashes.

When she'd watched Simpson key in "the quick red fox" that day on the street, the thought had zinged through her like a soaring violin: She could do this! She'd found what she needed. She could make a difference.

By the time a week had passed, when she wasn't thinking about the telegraph, she was thinking about the handsome Irish captain. She knew she interested him. He watched her lips as she spoke, he let his gaze wander over her body when he thought she wouldn't notice. Yet he kept a distance. Because she'd stung him that night at the Silver Slipper? Or because he didn't trust her? Either way, she would show him her commitment was genuine. In fact, her commitment was avid.

Walking purposefully, a small basket on one arm, swinging her furled umbrella with the other, she turned left onto Canal on her way to the Custom House. She accepted that the white citizens of New Orleans would despise her as a collaborator if they knew her destination, but the realization made her feel as if eyes followed her through the streets. Should she have asked the large and fierce William to accompany her? She firmed her jaw. William had his own days to live. She would not yield to timidity, certainly not to fear.

As she neared headquarters, a huddle of white boys played at mumblety-peg, taking turns tossing a knife into a circle to see who could make it stick. They were barefoot, their shirts stained and worn. They'd all outgrown their trousers, and their bare ankles were spotted with flea bites.

As she approached, one of the boys nudged the biggest one and the game stopped. Five pairs of eyes watched her, and she made note of which boy now had the knife.

Nicolette took a wide step across the gutter to cross to the other side of the street. The boys moved to intercept her. She fought the tightening in her throat and tried to reason away the thudding in her chest. They were only children.

One boy ran at her, veering at the last instant. Nicolette's knees locked.

"Whore," the boy hissed.

The children surrounded her. "Fucking whore, going in to fuck the fucking Yanks," a child no more than ten declared.

They closed the circle tighter. Where was the knife? A grimy hand reached out and grabbed her skirt. Another knocked her basket to the ground while a third wrenched the umbrella from her hand.

Nicolette shook off the paralysis. They were children!

She seized the boy who yanked at her skirt. Taking him by the shoulders, she twirled him around, used him to shove her way through the circle.

The boy with the knife slashed at the back of her skirt. She whirled around and slapped him, hard. He backed off, but another pair of hands were at her, pulling and snatching. The umbrella lunged toward her. She grabbed it from the boy's hand. Using it as a cudgel, she whirled it around her, not caring if she bloodied their noses. Boys screamed out in pain as the hard wooden handle connected with an ear, then a forehead.

She twirled again, the outstretched umbrella scattering the hoodlums.

A blue-coated soldier rushing toward her was a blur. "Be gone!" the soldier roared. He grabbed hold of the nearest boy and dragged him by the collar while he seized the next child. With a big hand on each head, he knocked their foreheads together. Those two tore away, howling. The other three bolted after them.

"Miss Chamard." He gripped her arms, his face very near to hers. "Are you harmed?"

Nicolette forced herself to focus. Captain McKee's mouth was only inches from hers, his breath warm on her cheek. Her whole body sagged against him. She opened her lips, then blinked.

Suddenly, she stiffened under his hands. She drew back. She had been routing the boys herself. She didn't need a hero. There were no heroes in the world.

"I'm quite all right." She clasped her hands so he couldn't see them trembling. If he hadn't come out, those boys might have ... No. She had been routing them. "They were just children."

"Just children?" he said, shaking his head.

He retrieved her basket and handed it to her. The cloth on top was still neatly tucked in and undisturbed.

"You fought valiantly, Mademoiselle. What a soldier you'd make."

The absurd gratitude, the wonderful relief when he'd grabbed her arms were entirely inappropriate. He'd done no more than any man would for any woman. She took refuge behind the coquette's shield and inclined her head. "A compliment indeed, Captain."

The captain offered his arm. "May I take you inside?"

Nicolette hesitated. She'd imagined touching Captain McKee, imagined the warmth of his skin, but she didn't want his protection. She didn't want to need anyone's protection.

The captain dropped his arm, and gestured toward the back entrance of the headquarters. Silently they walked in together.

Upstairs, Simpson and Wallace already had the windows open. Simpson jumped to his feet. Ignoring the captain, he blurted, "Good morning, Miss Chamard."

"Good morning, Mr. Simpson. Mr. Wallace."

Nicolette needed a moment before she could concentrate on the stack of yellow slips Wallace had for her. She leaned her umbrella behind the door, then set her basket on the table.

"Breakfast, gentlemen?" Nicolette unpacked sugar-dusted beignets from her basket and served the first one to Simpson on a linen napkin. Wallace reached for his and popped the whole bun in his mouth at once.

"You make these yourself?" Wallace asked around his mouthful.

"One of my earliest lessons in life: If I want beignets in the morning, I better get up and light the stove."

Nervous, Nicolette approached Captain McKee with napkin and beignet. "Captain?"

She knew she'd offended him, not accepting his arm. She kept her eyes on the bun as she handed it to him. His hand touched hers under the square of linen. Just a slight grazing of his fingers on the back of her hand. She stepped back, far too aware of him, the heat in his fingers lingering on hers. Probably he had not even meant to do it.

Nicolette brushed the sugar from her hands and turned with a business-like air to Wallace. There was work to be done. "What have you got for me?"

She hadn't been allowed to see anything important yet. She was a Southerner after all, though she couldn't decide why the captain should be more skeptical than Major Farrow. When Captain McKee had introduced her to the major, the big red-haired man had shaken her hand, holding it over long. "Run along, Captain. I believe other duties await you," he'd said.

Finn had scowled, picked up his hat, and left to drill his signalmen.

With courtly manners, Major Farrow had gestured her to a seat near the window and pulled over a chair to join her. "The question, my dear, if you'll forgive my saying so, is one of security."

She had leaned forward to earnestly claim justice for her enslaved people, but Farrow held his palm up. "I believe I may clear up all doubts with one question, if you will allow it, mademoiselle. The cloth you wear on your head, it carries significance a mere bonnet does not?" At her slight nod, he'd added, "I believe it is a signifier of your heritage, if I understand the meaning."

"Yes, Major. You understand perfectly."

Farrow had slapped his hands on his thighs as he rose to his feet. "Well, then, lass. Welcome aboard."

Captain McKee accepted his superior's decision, of course, yet he remained reserved. Curiously so. Sometimes he looked away when she caught him looking at her. Sometimes his eyes held hers, unsmiling, unabashed, and she'd be the first to shift her gaze.

A few minutes ago, however, in the street with those miscreant boys, he'd not been reserved. His gaze had been ... personal. His hands on her arms had been frantic. But, now they were upstairs, he was aloof again. It was just as well. The captain was quite foreign. The captain was white.

She set to work with the slips of paper Wallace passed her. Few messages got through the vulnerable lines from Baton Rouge, and as usual, the first slip was from the fort downriver and had to do with hogsheads of sugar and barrels of pork. She didn't mind the subject was mundane. Decrypting interested her, like playing anagrams.

Nicolette picked up the next message in her pile, one Wallace should have kept for himself, for once she'd decrypted it, it read: "Breckinridge at Camp Moore with better than 13,000. Confederate fleet moving south on M. River. Passed Vidalia two a.m."

The Confederates hoped to re-take Baton Rouge! "Captain!"

Captain McKee took the message from her hand and read it. "Wallace, get this to the general right away."

Finn eyed Nicolette. He hated what had happened to her downstairs, but he hadn't been surprised. Rebel sympathizers, meaning most of New Orleans, could see her any day, morning or afternoon, coming and going from Headquarters. It was a risk she did not seem to have prepared for. Was she so naive? Or perhaps there was a deeper motive to her associating with the Union than simple idealism. She'd had a nasty scare on the street. Those boys could have knocked her off her feet in another moment, and then, he didn't like to think what they might have done to her. Looking at her now, though, the incident might never have happened. When she wanted to, she could hide her feelings very well.

"Sit down, please, Miss Chamard."

She was wearing the blue linen gown he liked with the black tassels, demurely fastened at the neck, but fitted to her figure. She folded her hands on the table, no more than six inches from his own. He liked her hands. Hands that knew how to flutter a fan with perfect comic timing, how to decipher a code, how to make light sugary buns.

"Will you tell me, Miss Chamard, what you understand to be the import of this message?"

She tilted her chin up. "I presume General Breckinridge intends to retake Baton Rouge."

"And if he does so?"

Her eyes darkened. Every emotion seemed to sweep clouds across the grey irises, if she let them.

"If he does so! Then the Confederacy will control the Mississippi from Vicksburg to Baton Rouge. Texas and Arkansas will continue to ship provisions down the Red River, and the war will drag on."

Finn tilted his head to the side, trying to read her. His gaze dropped from her lovely eyes to her mouth, those full lips a torment. She must know her effect on men. What a perfect opportunity here in this office, her superior besotted with her, to glean information for the Confederacy. Hursh might have simply looked into her pretty face and decided no one so lovely could have ulterior motives. And, to be honest, beyond his admittedly slight suspicion, what he really wanted was a moment's conversation with her, something beyond good morning and have a beignet.

"Captain. I don't know what I must do to convince you. I truly want the Union to win this war."

"Why?"

The grey in her eyes lightened. She touched the calico turban on her head in an odd gesture. "Because I want an end to slavery, Captain."

"It's that simple?"

Her tone sharpened, and again her eyes clouded. "Yes. It is that simple." She leaned forward the least bit to make her point, her flowery scent wafting across the table. "Captain McKee, do you think a love of justice can be found only in Northern states?"

Hursh always had been a shrewd judge of character. That was true anger in her eyes, he'd bet on it. Indignation in the set of her jaw. Most convincing, her eyes changed color again, darkening with the vehemence in her voice. He didn't see how she could fake that.

Finn nodded slightly. Without planning to, he reached across the gap between them and touched her hand. He heard her intake of breath, but she did not withdraw. For a moment, he forgot Simpson was in the room. He very nearly hauled her across the table —

He looked up. There were tears in her eyes. Oh God, he'd upset her again. He stood abruptly. "Mr. Simpson, you may allow Miss Chamard full access to the decryption you have yet to do this morning. I'll be back this afternoon."

Finn bowed to Nicolette. "Mademoiselle."

He collected his sword on the way out and tromped down the hallway toward the general's offices.

He'd never met a woman whose eyes and face and body invited touch like hers did, and yet, he couldn't touch her. Why was she so damned skittish? One minute she looked like she could lead the whole Union army by herself, and next minute ... He'd scared her again, and her with two admirers in the room for protection.

Chapter Eleven

Deborah Ann Presswood sat white faced as her father strode up and down the room. "Will I also take the oath?"

Mr. Presswood shook his head. "A girl? Of course not." He paced, puffing on his cigar, rapid little smoke rings rising to the ceiling. He was more agitated than Deborah Ann had ever seen him.

"Father, sit down."

He ignored her. General Butler had declared every man in New Orleans must swear a loyalty oath to the United States government or go into exile. Ignatius Abelard had refused and left the city that morning. Mr. Presswood had taken the oath not an hour ago, and she knew it was eating him alive.

He stopped mid-pace and glared at her. "I had to do it," he declared.

"I know that, Father."

"If I'm to continue funneling monies to The Cause, I have to be here. In the city. And I have to be able to move about."

"I understand."

He stomped to the window and back again. "You hold your head up, Missy. Your father is a patriot! I may be a lying bastard, but I'm no traitor."

"Father!"

He stabbed his cigar toward her. "When this war's over and people talk about what Lionel Presswood did today, you keep your chin in the air, Deborah Ann." His voice quavered, for all his adamance. "You tell them, your father may have besmirched his good name, but he did it for Louisiana!"

Abruptly, he covered his face with his hand, his chest heaving. Deborah Ann knew what to do now. It was his anger she didn't know how to handle.

"Come Father. Let me take your boots off." She rang the bell. Jebediah, dressed in his livery of high starched collar and linen coat, answered. "Lemonade," she said.

She took her father's arm and led him to a chair. "Sit, Father," she said more firmly.

She took his cigar from him, then unlaced his boots and rolled his stockings off. Mr. Presswood submitted, his arm propped on the chair arm, his face hidden by his hand.

Jebediah came in with a pitcher of lemonade and a bottle of whiskey. Deborah Ann hid Father with her body. She didn't want the butler to see him weeping behind his hand.

"Bring a foot basin, Jebediah," she said. "Cool water."

Deborah Ann accepted Jebediah's hint and poured her father a glass of whiskey. By the time Jeb came back with the basin, Father had got hold of himself. He eased his feet into the water and sighed. "Thank you, dear." His voice was nearly normal now. "That feels wonderful."

Jebediah quietly disappeared. Deborah Ann handed her father his whiskey and poured herself a lemonade.

"You should pack up and go home to Evermore, Deborah Ann."

She shook her head. They'd had this conversation twice before in the last weeks. "I don't want to go upriver, Father. I'd die of loneliness. There'd be no news for days at a time." She reached over and patted his knee. "I'd rather be here with you."

He grabbed her hand and squeezed gently. "I'm glad, Deborah Ann. But the first case of yellow fever, I'm packing you off. Jeb can get you home and be back here the next day."

Deborah didn't concern herself with the dreaded yellow fever. She said her prayers, she tried to love her neighbors as the Lord desired, even Eugenia Abelard, and she left her fate in His hands. Besides, she was born and bred in this climate. Everyone knew the lately arrived were the most likely to succumb. They simply had no resistance to the Louisiana miasmas.

Late that afternoon, restless and bored, Deborah Ann decided she must have a new hat. All her bonnets for the summertime were at the home place upriver, and she had no intention of being a freckled bride come January.

Father's horses having been confiscated by Butler's army, she and Mammy took the omnibus to Canal Street and then walked to Madame Celeste's haberdashery. The shop window displayed a yellowing New York magazine open to the fashion page. On a pedestal next to it sat the very same bonnet modeled in the magazine, its green trim faded and mottled. It had been months since anything but war materiel and foodstuffs had unloaded in New Orleans.

The shop had two doors. As they approached, an elegant woman marked as colored by the tignon on her head entered the left.

"Isn't that the same woman?" Deborah Ann said. "The one you showed me last time we were on this street?"

"That her, Missy."

Deborah and Mammy entered the green door on the right.

Inside, the late afternoon sun bore through the windows, revealing dancing dust motes. Bonnets, ribbons, silk flowers, buttons, bolts of cloth – though perhaps a little shopworn, every accessory a woman could want graced the shelves and bins of Madame Celeste's.

Madame bustled from behind the painted screen that divided her shop in two. The colored woman she'd been speaking with on the left side would of course have to wait while she served her white clientele.

"Mademoiselle Presswood! What a delight to see you."

"Good day, Madame. Would you show me the straw hat in the window, please?"

While the proprietress fetched a stool and then leaned into the bow window to retrieve the hat, Deborah Ann wandered to one end of the divider, fingering a bunch of papier maché grapes. Curious, she peeked around the screen.

The woman in the tignon inspected a bolt of brightly patterned cloth Madame Celeste had laid out for her. She was truly beautiful. Smooth, light skin, big dark eyes. She was young, this woman, but not a girl. Her breasts seemed heavy and round under the fabric. Her mouth was full and lightly pink.

Deborah Ann put a finger to her paler, thinner lips. This woman knew how to kiss a man, she thought. How to please him in ways she knew nothing about.

The placée looked up from the bolt of cloth and met Deborah's eyes.

Deborah Ann was embarrassed to be caught staring, but the woman, surprised for only the briefest moment, gave her a polite half-smile. She set the fabric on the counter and left the store, the slight roll of her hips announcing a sensuality without her seeming aware of it.

Deborah Ann's hand went to her throat; her fingers found the bony knobs of bone at the base of her neck. She felt like a stick, bound and cinched. She was a dried corn stalk compared to the lush creature who'd just left. "Who was that woman, Madame Celeste?"

"*Non*, Mademoiselle. You do not know such as she." She lowered her voice to confide a delicate secret. "She is a rich man's kept woman."

"She's quite striking."

"*Oui*. These Creole planters, they have the most beautiful women in New Orleans. But, of course, she is a *femme de couleur*."

Deborah Ann nodded. Some of the old-school Creoles had different notions about what it meant to be a husband. Thank goodness Marcel was a modern man. He'd chosen her, after all, and she was not Creole in any way.

Deborah Ann handed the papier maché grapes to Madame Celeste, then removed her bonnet and handed it to Mammy. In front of the mirror, she tried the straw hat, adjusting the ribbon under her chin just so.

"You can sew the grapes on it, Madame?"

"*Mais oui.*"

As Madame Celeste trimmed the hat, Deborah Ann wondered about the placée. Her father's social circle included a number of Creole gentlemen. Could one of her father's friends possibly be so depraved as to betray his wife with a colored woman? It was none of her business, of course. But no one else was in the shop. "So she belongs to a Creole planter. Who is he?"

Madame Celeste adjusted the small bundle of blue grapes on the bonnet. "One of the Chamards, I believe."

Deborah Ann lost her breath.

Mammy appeared at her side and took her elbow, else Deborah Ann feared she might have fainted to the floor.

Struggling to put air behind the words, she said, "Of the older generation, I suppose."

Madame Celeste turned away to pick up her scissors. She didn't see the distress in Deborah Ann's face. She didn't see Mammy scowling a warning at her to hold her tongue.

"*Non*, I think not. I think it is one of the sons. The good looking one. Here we are," she said, handing Deborah Ann the bonnet.

Deborah Ann's world shifted. The light seemed to dim, the air to thicken. Nothing in life could be what she'd thought it was. She leaned into Mammy, her corset constricting her ribs, cutting off her breath.

"Mademoiselle? Are you ill?"

"I take her home, ma'am," Mammy said, hustling Deborah Ann to the door. "We don't need no hat today."

Deborah Ann clapped her hand over her mouth and closed her eyes. She mustn't throw up here on the street. Surely it wasn't true. There were other Chamards in New Orleans.

Holding on to Mammy, she drew herself up. Of course it wasn't Marcel. He was in love with her. She had only to remember his farewell kiss to know he was in love with her.

"Let's us go home," Mammy said. "I fix you a pot of coffee and cool it off with lots of cream, add a little sugar. You feel better before suppertime."

Mammy hustled her on to an omnibus. The airless bus rocked right and left, forward and back. The cabin reeked of stale cigar smoke, and the odor of manure wafted through the open windows. Nausea threatened to overwhelm her, and Deborah Ann's face was green by the time they arrived home.

Mammy peeled off her sticky dress and unlaced her corset. "You lie there a while and I bring up that coffee."

Deborah Ann lay on the divan in her chemise, staring at the coffered ceiling, breathing deeply while her stomach settled. The shadowed familiarity of her room cooled her and soothed her.

She'd been a goose to let herself get so exercised over the placée. Of course the woman's gentleman was not Marcel. He must have a dozen good-looking cousins in town. She wiggled her bare toes, comfortable and cool.

"Now honey," Mammy said, bustling in with a tray smelling of coffee and toast. "You mamma gone, I sees I got to be the one talk to you about this fancy woman. And I tells you, she ain't nothing at all."

Deborah Ann sat up, looking forward to a cup of coffee. It was all right with her if Mammy wanted to prattle on about the placée. She'd just had a momentary fright that her Marcel might be one of those unfaithful men. Nonsense, of course.

Mammy set the tray on the rosewood table and dissolved sugar in the hot coffee, stirring and stirring. Behind her, Deborah Ann raised her arms over her head, stretching out the tired muscles her corset had pinched.

"Plenty of men loves more than one woman, Missy," Mammy explained. "It don't mean he ain't a good husband. It don't mean he don't love his wife. Mr. Marcel, now, he treat you right. He gone take good care of you. He gone be a good husband."

Only half listening, Deborah Ann smiled. "I know he will be, Mammy." She believed in happy-ever-afters. Her Marcel was as fine a man as any romance hero.

Mammy poured a dollop of cream in the blue china cup and turned to present it to Deborah Ann. "You don't never mind bout his other woman, sugar. She ain't gone mean nothing at all to you."

Deborah Ann lowered her arms slowly. She stared into Mammy's black eyes.

So it was true.

She was Marcel's woman. Mammy had known all along.

The smell of the coffee was bitter, nauseating. She waved the cup away.

She crossed to her dresser on wooden feet and sat down. She picked up her silver hair brush and began the ritual, a hundred strokes, to make it grow longer and thicker. Her hair crackling with energy, over and over she pulled the brush down, staring at the flashing silver in the mirror.

She would not share her husband with a colored woman. She would not.

Chapter Twelve

August 3rd, the action at Baton Rouge began. Nicolette arrived early and stayed late, eager for news, anxious about the outcome. The dispatches came in irregular bursts as the Union tried to keep the lines up while the Rebs just as energetically cut them down. In a broken tide of ups and downs, of high hopes and threatened despair, the news favored or disfavored the Union forces.

Nicolette herself deciphered the news that the Confederate ram boat *Arkansas* was hard aground and useless. She waved the note high over head, announcing the news. Wallace let out a triumphant whoop. Captain McKee snatched the note with a wild grin and dashed down the hall to deliver it to General Butler.

Early afternoon, Simpson was at the key. The message: General Williams, Union commander, felled by a bullet through the chest.

Nicolette feared the worst.

McKee shook his head. "Don't worry. Cahill will take over."

Nicolette tried to imagine the turmoil of battle. The noise must be horrendous, the cannons and rifles and shouting. The horses would be mad with fear. The men would be hot and thirsty. Would they be afraid? Or did their blood rise, their senses shut out everything but what lay in their sights?

She crossed herself and silently began *Hail, Mary, full of grace.* Marcel was not in Baton Rouge. Alistair, too, had gone west to the Lafourche. But all those other young men, so many dying this day. God have mercy on their souls.

At five o'clock, the telegraph fell silent. "It's a wonder there's any telegraph at all, thick as the Rebs are up that way," Wallace said. "Guess cutting wire's not their priority right now or we wouldn't hear a thing."

Nicolette stared at the idle key. McKee wandered the room, hands fisted behind his back. Nicolette knotted her handkerchief, her gaze following the captain's polished black boots in his slow meandering around the room.

At last, the telegraph key leapt to life again: *Breckinridge has withdrawn rebels to the Comite River.*

Simpson and Wallace hallooed. Nicolette jumped to her feet and, in the zeal of the moment, she grabbed the nearest person – Captain McKee. He whirled her around, her skirt billowing behind her, her laughter ringing through the room.

His grin flashed white beneath the black moustache and his eyes shone with the joy of victory. She gazed up at him, nearly delirious with excitement, his hands warm on her waist as they twirled. She wanted him to waltz her around the room, down the hall, into the streets, to never stop waltzing her.

She knew at once when he called himself back. His eyes dulled, his moustache hid the waning smile, and he stopped the dance mid-step. He released her waist. She dropped her hands from his shoulders.

"Forgive me," he muttered. "The excitement. I forgot myself."

He ran his hand through his hair as if he were befuddled a moment. The yellow paper on the desk. He grabbed it up and rushed out of the room to deliver the news to General Butler.

Nicolette swallowed hard. He might have dropped her out the window, she was so let down.

An incoming message clattered on her desk. She sat down and tried to concentrate on something besides the feel of Finnian McKee's hands at her waist.

By the time dusk crept through the street and in the windows, the first flush of exhilaration had faded. A watery wind kicked up, promising a wet night. Nicolette gathered her purse and umbrella. The office seemed very quiet now in the yellow light. She had been part of this great day. She had helped, perhaps, a little.

"*Bonsoir*, Mr. Wallace. Mr. Simpson." Captain McKee? She hadn't seen him since he whirled her around the room. He and Major Farrow were no doubt celebrating with the other officers.

She walked down the dimly-lit stairs to the back door. William wouldn't be meeting her. He'd joined André Cailloux's unit and was to spend the night across the river. She set one foot over the threshold. Captain McKee, in a mad rush to enter, nearly knocked her over.

She let out a little cry. He grabbed her elbows, righting her. Then, swiftly, he stepped away.

Nicolette fingered her tignon to check it was still settled on her head. How many times today had Captain McKee touched her? What did he mean by it?

Of course, this time it was merely an instinctive attempt to keep her upright. But when he'd touched her hand earlier, it had been quite deliberate, she was sure of it. She hadn't quaked inside as she might have a few weeks ago. It had been ... a caress, almost. A gentle, warm connection.

Which he'd clearly regretted immediately, nearly knocking his chair over to get away from her. And the dancing around the office, Finn McKee's bright eyes on her. She'd loved it! Then, she might have turned into a fabled banshee, he'd released her so suddenly.

She came to a sad conclusion: The captain might find her attractive, but in the end, Yankees, too, had their prejudices against her people.

"I was coming for you," he explained. "It's dark."

"Yes."

"Full dark. And it's going to rain."

"Yes, Captain, but there are street lanterns along the way, and I have my umbrella." She moved to step around him.

He blocked her, gesturing over his shoulder at a hack and horse. "I've hired a cab."

She tried to read his eyes, but the lantern over the door cast shadows on his face. What was she to make of him?

"The gangs on the streets," he reasoned, "they're bound to be roused after they've lost Baton Rouge again. I mean only to keep you safe."

The captain's forbidding, distant manner was gone. This was the Finn McKee who'd come to see her backstage, concerned, gentle. The man who'd touched her hand. The man she trusted. But she'd trusted Adam Johnston, too.

It didn't matter. Women did not ride in hired carriages with men they hardly knew. Not even octoroon women. Nicolette shook her head. It was impossible.

"Miss Chamard." McKee took his hat off. "I beg your pardon. Of course it is an impropriety to suggest escorting you home alone. Why don't I find Simpson to accompany us? Would that put you at ease?"

The first raindrops caught the light from the lantern hanging overhead. Earthy scents, roused by the dampness in the air, rose all around them.

"That won't be necessary, but I thank you for your kindness."

Nicolette untied the ribbon around the umbrella. She'd be quite all right. Wet, perhaps. But she'd keep to Decatur Street where so much Union activity took place, and then at Esplanade, she'd be nearly home. And even a woman in hoops could run if she had to.

"Look, Miss Chamard. I do understand it is improper, but I insist. As your employer." Captain McKee stood straighter in the island of light, just enough glow for the two of them, the rest of the world shut out. "As an officer in the United States Army, I give you my word no harm will come to you."

She struggled with the damned umbrella, stuck again. A fat rain drop splashed on her nose, and another on her cheek.

Thunder cracked. The clouds gave way as if someone above had opened a sluice gate. Nicolette stamped her foot, wrestling with the umbrella.

"This is ridiculous," the captain declared over the thunderous downpour.

McKee seized her arm and propelled her through the deluge and into the waiting carriage.

Practically thrown onto the bench seat, Nicolette whirled around to fight her way out, all her fears aflame at being handled. Captain McKee filled the carriage door, coming in right behind her. She prepared to kick, scratch, whatever she had to do – and then the lantern light caught his face.

His emotions seemed to be as confused as hers. Contrition and amusement warred for dominance on his brow, at his mouth. But there was no menace on his face.

Nevertheless, Nicolette scooted to the far corner of the bench with her umbrella, nicely pointed on the end. She had ten fingernails, and a voice to scream. Unnecessary, for Captain McKee took the opposite end of the opposite bench.

The carriage moved on to Canal Street, rain pounding on the roof. He lit the tiny inside lamp next to the door, but he stayed where he was, in his corner.

As Nicolette's blood slowed and her breathing came more easily, she loosened her grip on the umbrella.

The captain tried a smile on her. "You will forgive me, eventually?" He looked like a little boy who knew he'd been naughty but who was also very sure he was too adorable to be punished. "I've saved you from drowning, after all."

Nicolette covered her mouth. He did not deserve a smile.

He let out a noisy breath of relief. "I see that smile, Miss Chamard. Never knew a woman yet who'd rather walk in a downpour than ride with a handsome man in uniform."

"You consider yourself handsome, Captain?"

He settled more comfortably. "I have it on good authority from a number of females." He held up his fingers to count them off. "Grandmother McKee. My Aunt Agatha. Aunt Bess. My mother. And my oldest sister Shannon. Maggie may not be convinced, and my youngest sister, Annette, declares I'm ugly as sin, but the other five testimonials should be enough to convince even a woman whose feathers I've ruffled. Regrettably, I assure you."

"If beauty is in the eye of the beholder, surely handsomeness is as well. I don't find you at all handsome, Captain."

Finn's smile grew into a grin. Here was the Mademoiselle Chamard he'd seen at the Silver Slipper. Sassy. Arch. Beautiful.

"You prefer fat men, then? Or short and wrinkled?"

"Wrinkled, definitely."

"Short, tall?"

She eyed his length in the light of the street light. "Short, I think."

Finn shook his head. "You Southern belles certainly are particular."

All the play left her face. She stared at the rivulets on the window pane. What had he said? "Have I spoken amiss?"

Her eyes were dark smoke. "Sir, I am no belle."

That lovely voice, like warm honey and butter, had gone cold. A crack of thunder split the air. She did not merely flinch. She actually jumped. God, she was tense. And he'd been indelicate.

The woman was an entertainer. A woman who worked for her living. She could not lay claim to the title "lady" or "belle" any more than he, a bookseller's son, could call himself a gentleman, at least not in the archaic sense. But those were mere words.

"Here I am asking your pardon yet again, Miss Chamard. Please forgive me. Louisiana is as foreign to me as Havana."

She at least turned her attention back inside the carriage and gazed at him with those smoky eyes. The elusive Miss Chamard. Assured, timid, warm, distant, tough, vulnerable. How was he to read her? How to appease her?

"I do admire Southern womanhood, Miss Chamard. Pretty as flowers, skin the color of magnolia blossoms. A prodigious feat in this sun."

Though the width of the carriage separated them, he felt a wave of displeasure emanate from her. He'd not meant to be familiar. His sister was forever complaining what the sun did to her complexion. But that was not in company. He was digging himself a deeper hole.

"Tell the driver to turn right onto Rampart, please," she said. "Then right onto Esplanade, left on Pauger. Number 10."

He pulled the little slide that opened to the driver and gave directions, then settled back on his bench.

Should he try again? He had offended her at least twice, but he couldn't just sit here staring at his boots.

"In Boston, on the seaboard ... ?" He hesitated.

"I own an atlas, Captain. I know where Boston is."

"Of course." What a miserable conversation. He'd just keep his mouth shut now.

The carriage turned onto Pauger, the wheels throwing up a heavy spray from the gutter.

"Yes?" she said. He hardly heard her over the rain beating against the roof. "In Boston?"

Air rushed back into his lungs. "I was about to say, Boston's another world." The dim light made shadows under her cheeks, lay mystery over her features. If he were sitting next to her, he would risk it. He would cup her face, run his thumb over that lower lip. "We don't have magnolia trees. Or gumbo."

She wore a polite expression. "I suppose not."

"But if a man takes a nap under a tree, the vines won't grow over him before he wakes up. The bugs won't carry him off."

"Advantages, to be sure."

The carriage came to a stop, one wheel in the gutter on Nicolette's side so that the whole cab tilted.

"Allow me," McKee said. He managed to climb over the bulging skirt without treading on her feet. He opened the door and stepped onto the banquette, which so far remained above the streaming gutter.

Deftly, he pushed the spines of the umbrella open and stood in the rain, blocking the carriage door.

"Miss Chamard. I know I have offended you somehow. I did not intend to."

Her expression gave him hope. She did not glare or avoid his gaze. She merely studied him a moment.

"You have been very kind, Captain. Thank you for the carriage."

She held out her hand to be helped down the step onto the banquette. For a delicious moment, she sheltered under the umbrella with him, no more than inch between them. In fact, his legs were nearly encompassed by her skirt.

He released her hand to brush his fingers across her cheek. She tilted her head up toward him, lips parted. He leaned in.

Abruptly, she took possession of the umbrella. "Good night, Captain."

She quickly strode toward the door of the rain-washed blue house on the corner. Rain rolled down Finn's collar before he remembered to get in the carriage.

At least he knew where she lived now. And tomorrow he'd see her again.

Chapter Thirteen

Across town, with the rain drumming on the roof and running in heavy rivulets across the glass, Deborah Ann curled into her window seat to reread Marcel's letter. It had taken two weeks to reach her, having made its way in fits and starts to the Chamard plantation and then to her father. Her own page, one mere page, had been folded in with the coded account of Taylor's cavalry and the readiness to defend the Lafourche.

The bayou at dusk is magical, Marcel wrote, *filled with the hoots of owls and the cries of white cranes passing overhead. Purple spotted orchids tangle in the vines along the river bank. Trout glitter in the water. A paradise, here on the Lafourche.*

Not one word about his feelings! Did he miss her? Did he not think of her at all? She had expected something personal, not a travelogue. He hadn't even asked her how she did. Whether she dreamed of him as he did of her. He hadn't pleaded for a word from her, hadn't said he yearned to see her, to touch her.

Because that was what she had written to him. That she relived every moment of their last hour together. That she dreamt of his kiss. That she ached to feel his arms around her once more.

Deborah Ann put a hand to her flushed cheek. She had been so forward in her letter. He would think she was foolish. He would think she was *eager.* How very embarrassing. But it was too late now to recall it.

Lightning zigzagged over the river and the thunder boomed. What a terrible night to be camped out. Marcel had probably not slept with a roof overhead since he'd gone into the wilds west of the Mississippi.

If they were married, and he came home to her in a deluge like this, she'd pull his boots off for him, never minding for a moment that she might muddy her hands. She'd pour him a brandy and sit on the needlepoint stool at his feet as he told her how glad he was to be home, with her. He'd touch her face and gaze into her eyes.

They'd have a small supper, then go upstairs to get warm under the covers.

Deborah Ann's imagination allowed for his gentle hands caressing her hair, his soft lips kissing hers, his moustache tickling her. Beyond that, she had never dared envision more than a vague continuation of passion.

She hoped not to be unladylike in her enthusiasm for marriage. And she hoped not to be frightened. Most of all, she hoped to capture Marcel's desire. She would be everything he needed in a woman. He would not need a mistress.

Deborah Ann's feet were cold. Even in August, a rain like this drained all the heat from the house. She folded the letter and blew out the candle, then climbed into bed, lonely and disappointed, resolved to another night of gnawing, indeterminate need.

Water streamed off Marcel's slicker, filling his boots. Steam rose in tendrils from his horse's neck.

Marcel readjusted his collar for the tenth time to stem the flow down his back. If he'd ever been more miserable, he couldn't think when. His injured foot throbbed in the wet boot, and he was saddle sore. When he got home, he'd have a hot bath. And a brandy. Maybe two.

At Algiers, Marcel waited for a ferry to take him across the river into New Orleans. The rain and fog were so thick he could barely see the opposite bank. If it was coming down like this back on the Lafourche, they'd have to move camp to keep from washing down the bayou.

He disembarked at the foot of Canal, slogged his horse up to Royal and turned right. A lantern was lit over the townhouse gate. He dismounted and pounded the door knocker.

The door opened a crack.

"It's me, Baudier."

The butler threw the door open and let him in. "You catch you death out in this mess."

"Have Hercule put up, please, Baudier. Oats, not hay. Then I need a hot bath."

"Yes, sir. You does. I'll get Biddy to boiling water."

"Hercule first."

In the bath, Marcel felt his bones soften in the hot water. Eight weeks of grime ringed the tub. He'd have the second tub set up and take another bath. In a minute. A fire crackled in the grate. His brandy snifter dangled from his fingers.

He eyed the high four poster across the room. He hadn't been in a bed since he left Cherleu, and he ached for a night's rest. But he needed to get over there. If the water had risen into the house, Lucinda would be in a state.

Baudier fed the fire and fixed the second tub. Once Marcel was clean, dry, and warm, the butler brought up a hot supper. "It's just gumbo, Michie Marcel, with half a chicken. Cook didn't know you was coming, but tomorrow she'll do you right."

"Tell her this is a feast. I don't think Val cooked a meal yet that wasn't either burned or half-raw."

Marcel dressed to go out again. He groaned as he tried to stuff his bad foot into a dry pair of shoes. The bones Hercule had ground into the mud back at Cherleu may not have been broken in two, but they were far from healed. Marcel tossed the boot aside and hobbled into the room of his brother Yves, he of the big feet. He rummaged in the wardrobe and found an abandoned pair of boots that were easier on his swollen foot.

Marcel splashed his way the few blocks to Elysian Fields. The gutters either side of the street flowed swiftly, and Marcel was just as glad it was too dark to make out exactly what flotsam the water carried. At Lucinda's, the fine new bridge across the gutter was washed away. He sheltered under the eaves and pounded on the door.

Lucinda peeked out, threw the door open and leapt into his arms. The eaves dripping on his back, the rain curtaining them from the street, he enveloped her. "My darling," he whispered.

Still holding on tight, he moved her inside and kicked the door closed behind him. She tossed his hat away and grasped his head with both hands, then kissed him, her mouth open and demanding. He pushed her against the wall, his fingers gathering the hem of her nightgown. She raised her knee for him, impatient, ready, and they took one another there in the hallway, the rush of blood in their ears as loud as the thundering rain.

By morning the gutters had drained most of the flood from the city, leaving puddles great and small. The air, laden with all the moisture it could hold, was hardly less thick than the mud.

Marcel winced at the beam of light that skewered his eye through the slatted window. Two hard days in the saddle and a bed on pine boards made a man surly in the morning.

The night before, he'd moved his family to the attic so they wouldn't have to slosh around in two inches of water. Lucinda had laid down quilts, and they'd spent a dry night if not a comfortable one. Charles Armand slept amid the dozen toy soldiers surrounding him. Bertie's bow mouth was half open, his thumb wet and ready.

Marcel turned his head away from the stab of light. Lucinda's legs were tangled with his. The sunbeam caught her black hair, streaked across her neck and followed the curve of her breast under the nightdress. Never had he seen another woman to compare to her. Her every move was graceful and sensual. The curve of her lip, the swell of her hips, perfection. As gentle as a doe, Lucinda's heart and soul were as pure as a mere mortal's could be. Yet, thank God above, she loved him.

A stab of pain pierced Marcel's heart. He lifted a tress of Lucinda's hair to his lips, his eyes filling. Anything could happen on a battle field. The thought of Lucinda being lonely, of Lucinda needing him in the dark nights. It nearly undid him.

Marcel closed his eyes and inhaled her scent. Jasmine and something he couldn't name. She turned into his body, her eyes barely open. He stroked her back. Quietly, they made love in their nest of quilts.

Once everyone was up, Marcel took a broom to the remaining water in the house while Charles Armand captured a hoppy toad and a green lizard to escort outside. The front doors were well above street level, but the back doors were flush with the courtyard. He'd have to have the bricks relaid a few inches deeper. When the war was over. By mid-morning, the cottage was put to rights, the sun was shining, and the floors were drying.

Lucinda kept a stash of dry stove wood in a cubby off the floor. While she made coffee, hot grits, and eggs, Marcel rocked Bertie to sleep. Charles Armand sat on a stool next to them with a slate on his lap.

"Let me see your letters," Marcel said.

The boy pinched his chalk and bit his lip as he formed an unsteady A.

"Breakfast," Lucinda called.

Marcel placed his babe in the cradle, grabbed Charles Armand up under his arm like a pig in a poke and tickled him all the way to breakfast.

Deborah Ann despaired of doing anything with her hair as humid as it was. She combed it back and secured it in a severe knot. What difference did it make? She hadn't seen anyone but Father for days, and no one was likely to call today either. Everyone had left the city.

The war news kept Father in a constant state of excitement, elated because Beauregard had routed the Yanks at Manassas, despondent because Breckinridge had failed to re-take Baton Rouge. He raised money furiously, under General Butler's nose, and schemed night and day to finance Jefferson Davis's government.

If Father had not been so intimately involved in gathering information, she'd be blissfully, comfortably ignorant of the fact that her fiancé was about to be engulfed in Yankee violence.

She strode across the long parlor, then paced back. Once Butler's troops moved on Bayou Lafourche, it might take days before they knew anything. How was she to bear not knowing?

She had fretted herself into a stew when the door knocker reverberated through the house. She peered out the front bow window.

Marcel! Her hands flew to her mouth. Then to her hair.

She ran for the stairs as Jebediah reached the door. "Wait!" she hissed. She made it back to her room while the butler obligingly delayed opening the door.

She pulled her hair loose as she ran to her dresser. Her blonde hair was her best feature, that and her blue eyes, and she didn't intend for Marcel to see her with an old granny knot at the back of her neck. She gave it a quick brushing and arranged it loosely around her shoulders. She knew from her novels that men found loose hair appealing, and since his visit was unexpected, she didn't have to justify wearing it down. She spritzed lavender water in a cloud around her head. She pinched her cheeks and bit her lips to make them red. Then she rushed to the staircase leading to the hall where Jebediah was relieving Marcel of his hat and cane.

"Mr. Chamard!" she exclaimed from the top of the stairs, as surprised as she could make it seem.

He smiled up at her, his hands behind his back. Should she appear dignified, or rush into his arms? After the letter she'd sent, she chose dignity, and descended the stairs regally, her eyes on his face.

He had tanned. He had lost a good deal of weight. But her heart rose into her throat at how handsome he was. And he was hers. Was to be hers. Soon.

Her Father emerged from his study at the other end of the hall. "Chamard!" He strode forward, hand outstretched, and she feared he would take Marcel away from her.

"Mr. Presswood."

The men shook hands. Deborah Ann held her breath, waiting for Marcel to turn back to her. Surely he wouldn't leave her to talk war with her father. It had been two months!

This was why she loved him. He disengaged himself from Father and turned his full attention on her. He looked her over, from her flowing blonde hair to the white leather slippers on her feet. "Miss Deborah Ann, you never disappoint."

"All right, all right," Mr. Presswood growled. "We'll talk later, Chamard."

Deborah Ann took possession of Marcel's arm and led him into the front parlor where the little sofa would allow them to sit close together.

"I did not expect to see you yet, Mr. Chamard." The faint scent he wore intrigued her. Jasmine, maybe, with a deeper note as well.

"No. This was a task of opportunity."

A task? He hadn't come expressly to see her then.

"General Mouton had communiqués for the allies here in the city." Marcel smiled sheepishly. "I was homesick. I volunteered."

Ah, so he had chosen to come back to New Orleans. He had wanted to see her.

She discussed with him the hardships of travelling in the rain, thanked him for his letter, tried to speak sensibly all the while watching his eyes, his lips, her heart and mind filled with the scent of him, with the heat of his body next to hers on the sofa. All those lonely nights these past weeks. Lonely nights to come. She yearned to be in his arms.

"Mr. Chamard. Let's not wait." The words tumbled out, uncensored, un-considered. "You are quite right about the folly of a big wedding in these times." She had surprised him, she could see that, but it had been his own idea. When he could get back to New Orleans, he'd said.

"Let's marry this afternoon. When you must leave again, I will at least have the comfort of missing my husband."

Marcel placed a reins-hardened palm over hers. She wrapped his hand in both of hers, eyes lowered, waiting, hardly daring to breathe. What if he said no?

"In such haste? Are you sure?"

"I'm sure." She was a woman grown. What did she need with a fairy-tale wedding?

He looked to the side for a moment, thinking. One shoulder shrugged slightly. "Very well. We'll speak to your father."

Before supper, then, clad in last year's aquamarine silk, Deborah Ann Presswood walked the aisle of the chapel on her father's arm. Candles, lit for the dead and seen through the fine veil over her face, cast a golden glow around the altar. Marcel waited for her in his perfectly creased suit of tails and snowy linen, a white gardenia in his boutonniere.

Father Baptiste began the ritual.

The priest's voice seemed small and far away. Deborah Ann felt herself slide out of her body. As if she hovered in the air above, she looked down on Marcel standing solemn and tall, at herself next to him.

She heard herself murmur "I do."

Marcel slid his mother's beautiful sapphire ring on her finger. He raised her veil and leaned down to kiss her lips. There were tears in his eyes. "I will be a good husband to you, Deborah Ann," he whispered. "I swear it."

Father blew loudly into his handkerchief, abruptly returning Deborah Ann to herself.

"If only your mother could have seen this day," he said through a throat full of tears.

Mrs. Marcel Armand Bertrand Chamard. Married woman.

Deborah Ann took hold of her husband's arm and clasped it tightly to her. He belonged to her now.

Chapter Fourteen

There had been no scores of onlookers at the church, no grand dinner with orchestra and dancing. Yet they were married.

The three of them, Deborah Ann and Marcel and Father, took a fine supper at home. She then endured a decent after-dinner interval, endeavoring to appear patient in spite of the thundering in her chest.

At last, Marcel took her to his carriage, she still in her aquamarine silk, he in his tuxedo.

He held her hand in the privacy of the carriage, but neither of them spoke as they were driven to the Chamard townhouse on Rue Royal. The old butler led them up the staircase by candlelight. Marcel's room was already alight, the gas lamp globes refracted in the crystal decanter on the rosewood table.

In the center of one wall, between the doors onto the gallery, a massive four-poster dominated the room. Deborah turned her head so that the bed was no longer in sight.

She felt cold, as if there were no blood in her fingers and toes.

"Could we have a fire?" she asked. To her own ears, she sounded small, even frightened. What was wrong with her? Mammy had said it might hurt, the first time. But she wasn't worried about that. She wanted to be here, she did. She wanted to know what it felt like when ... when they were in bed together.

Marcel shrugged out of his coat and draped it over the walnut valet as he nodded to Baudier.

"*Oui*, Madame. I'll build you a fire myself."

She shouldn't have asked for a fire. It was August. Marcel would be hot with a fire. She didn't know what to do with herself. She'd never been in a gentleman's chamber before. She stood in the middle of the room, her heart thumping hard enough to make the ruffles on her bosom tremble.

"Deborah Ann, sweetheart," Marcel said. "Sit down." He poured her a glass of claret and handed it to her.

She clasped it in both hands, afraid to drink lest she spill it on her wedding gown. Claret would never come out, not on aquamarine silk. She set it on the little table next to her. Then she had nothing to do with her hands. She clasped them in her lap.

Marcel stood before her until she looked up at him. "Drink it. It'll settle your nerves."

She really didn't like claret. And it certainly wouldn't settle her nerves. Obediently, she picked up the glass and sipped.

Baudier bustled in with a basket of firewood. "Got some of that applewood your maman used to like, Michie Marcel. It gone smell good in here."

She finished her claret as Baudier laid the fire. The old man left the basket with additional wood in it and said good night.

Marcel refilled her glass. Deborah Ann drank this one down as if it were water.

He took the chair opposite her. "Deborah Ann," he said, his voice soft. "We don't have to do anything but sit here and talk tonight, if that's what you want. I can sleep across the hall." He tipped his head to make her look at him. "We'll have the rest of our lives together in that bed you are so studiously ignoring."

Deborah Ann felt the heat flash from her chest, up her neck, to the roots of her hair. Tears spurted from the corners of her eyes, startling her, and she put the back of her hand up to hide the ugliness of her mouth. Gulping between sudden sobs, she was helpless to stop the swirl toward hysteria.

Marcel knelt at her side, stroked her hand, and brought her back. She drew a deep shuddering breath and got hold of herself.

She blew her nose in the handkerchief he proffered. "I'm sorry." She couldn't look at him.

Marcel drew her into his arms. "No need to be sorry, my darling." He wiped his thumb across her wet cheek. "You didn't think I married you just so I could scare you to death on our wedding night, did you?"

"No. Because I'm rich," she blurted.

Marcel barked a laugh. "So am I, Deborah Ann. So am I." He took her chin in his thumb and forefinger. Lightly, as if she were made of spun sugar, he kissed her.

"I don't want to wait," she whispered.

Marcel's smile widened. He had such beautiful teeth, she thought. And he'd be gone for months. She couldn't wait. She had to do this tonight.

"Have another glass of wine," he said.

Marcel untied his cravat and opened his collar. She shouldn't have asked for the fire. Now she'd had this third glass, she didn't feel so cold, and poor Marcel must be sweltering in all that starched linen.

She felt a little light-headed, but she didn't protest when he poured her another glass. They were very little glasses. "Should we put the fire out?"

"We'll let it die down by itself, when you've warmed up."

She drained her glass. She stood up, one hand on the little side table for balance. "All right. I'm ready."

She met her husband's eyes. Such beautiful eyes. His slight smile broadened into a grin.

She tossed her head back and then had to grip the table edge. "Are you enjoying my discomfiture, Mr. Chamard?" She might be drunk.

He laughed. "Yes. I believe I am." Slowly, he closed the gap between them and took her elbows. Once he had her in the chair again, he gave her a look-over. "Let's get this veil off your head, shall we?"

She didn't help him at all, but he seemed quite competent. Once he had her hair loose, he ran his fingers through it. "Like silken champagne," he murmured.

Next he knelt and removed her shoes. "Your feet are still cold." He rubbed each foot and then began to tug at the stockings. They wouldn't come down. "May I?" He reached under her hoop, his hands following her leg up to her garter.

Deborah Ann blessed the wine. She wasn't the least embarrassed. She leaned her head against the chair back, acutely aware of his hands on her thigh. There was that stirring again, down there. Stronger than she'd ever felt it before.

She wondered if he would let her unbutton his shirt.

He did.

When he'd undone her back buttons and taken care of a hook or two where she couldn't reach, he excused himself while she put her nightgown on. When he returned, she was in the bed, he was barefoot and in his nightshirt. He turned the gas lights out so that only the dying fire lit the room.

He crawled in next to her and propped himself on one elbow, so close she could smell the faint lingering scent of jasmine. Was it in his hair?

"We'll do as much as you like, Deborah Ann. It's up to you."

She raised her arms to him and brought him down to kiss her. His hand found her hair, as she'd dreamed, but his kisses were new. Still sweet, still tender, but more insistent. And then not so tender. Urgent.

This. This is what she'd been aching for.

Morning sun woke Deborah Ann in her new bed. Her naked husband lay beside her, the clammy sheet carelessly shoved down to reveal his entire back. She reached out, timidly at first, and traced his backbone down to the hollow at the base of his spine. He stirred, turned and threw a bare arm across her body. Claimed. That's how she felt. Wonderfully claimed.

"Are you one of those men, Mr. Chamard, who can't be sociable until he's had his morning coffee?"

His face half buried in his pillow, Marcel clamped his hand on the curve of her hip, his tanned skin dark against the light cotton of her nightgown. He slid his hand up to her waist and ran his thumb over the soft belly. "I'm sociable."

He lifted his head. His gaze bore into hers with a wicked gleam. "The question, Mrs. Chamard, is how sociable are you?"

He shifted his weight on top of her, capturing her between his elbows. "Hmm? How sociable are you?"

He caught her lower lip in his teeth. His manhood pressed against her thigh. She fought down the nut of fear caught in her throat. She felt powerless with him on her like this.

But he kissed her. He caressed her. She relaxed and ran her fingers over the warm skin of his shoulders.

He touched her down there. She was sore. She hadn't washed.

She squirmed away.

"It's all right," he whispered in her ear. He drew his hand away and slowly readied her, stroking her thighs, her breasts, kissing and nibbling. When he entered her, she pulled all the air in the room into her lungs and wrapped her arms around him.

They lay spent and tangled in the sheets, Deborah Ann cradled in Marcel's arms. She slept again. This time when she woke, she was alone. The sun, rather than the gas lamps, prismed through the crystal on the rosewood table, throwing speckles of colored light on the marble of the fireplace.

Deborah Ann stretched her hand out to admire her new ring. Tiny diamonds circling the deep blue sapphire sparkled in a beam of sunlight. She couldn't have asked for a more beautiful ring. Or a more tender husband.

What they'd done last night, in this bed, seemed more of a promise even than the vows at the altar. At that moment, when he'd cried out, his whole body shuddering over hers, she knew. He was hers now.

After half an hour of drowsy contentment, Deborah Ann determined to get up and find her husband. She rang the bell and presently a mahogany brown girl came in with a cup of coffee.

"Where is Mr. Chamard?"

"He say tell you he got work to do." The girl's eyes were black and huge. She stared at Deborah Ann as if she were some rare porcelain creature.

"What's your name?"

"I's Aisha, Madame. Monsieur, he say tell you, he see you later."

No doubt he was with Father and the others going over the plans for Bayou Lafourche. With the girl's help, Deborah Ann got her corset laced, her hoop tied, the buttons and hooks fastened on the only other dress she'd brought with her, a purple striped morning gown.

She looked into the cheval mirror, smoothing the lace at her throat. Where was the girl who'd been so anxious, so unsure of herself? The obedient child, the subservient daughter? The face staring back at her had the same big blue eyes, clear brow, luxurious golden hair, but she could see a difference even if no one else could. She looked into the eyes of a woman who knew a man's touch.

Downstairs, Baudier escorted her to breakfast. Sunlight poured through the open doors and Deborah Ann stepped into the brick-paved courtyard shaded by banana trees and crepe myrtles. Mine, now, she thought.

"You set here, Madame Chamard, I bring you breakfast out." Baudier pulled a wrought iron chair out for her and seated her at the filigreed table. Last night, slightly intimidated, she'd seen this old man as the keeper of the Chamard household. This morning, she saw him more clearly: he was one of her slaves, and she herself was keeper of the Chamard household.

He returned with a tray laden with eggs, ham, corn cake, honey, bacon, peppers, bananas, grapes, and steaming beignets. Deborah Ann contented herself with the corn cakes and coffee. Chickory. Marcel's people had not kept any of the French roast back, then? She'd have to take a hand in the kitchen here. At her father's house, she'd had the foresight to see to it that cook stockpiled a hundred-weight of good Cuban beans.

After breakfast, she explored the three stories of the Chamard townhouse. It was evident this was a house of men. The drapes, in spite of the family wealth, were outdated and even worn on the hems. The carpets had faded. The unused bedrooms were musty. When had Marcel's mother died? It must have been many years ago, and no one had taken a hand with the house slaves since. The whole place needed a good cleaning before she could even think about bringing in decorators.

On the third floor Deborah Ann found a nursery. Open windows could make it an airy room, but for now it was hot and dusty. She lifted the mosquito netting covering the walnut crib. The wood needed a good oiling. The ivory silk drapery was water stained and brittle. The bare mattress was sprinkled with the dried-out carcasses of black bugs.

The rest of the room was no better. Yellowed wallpaper peeled away from the wainscoting. There were spider webs in every corner.

But this could be a beautiful room, someday.

Why someday? What she and Marcel had done last night, that's how babies were made.

She marched to the landing in the center of the house and called down. "Baudier!" When his grizzled head appeared thirty feet below, she said, "Send Aisha up with some dust rags and a bucket of water. And an apron."

The four large windows had likely not been opened since Marcel and his brother Yves were children. Deborah Ann had to get stubborn about it, but she heaved every one of them up. Morning air wafted in, setting the dust motes dancing.

With her hands on her hips, she surveyed the room. Blue, she decided. She wanted this room to be blue. Not a sky blue. Robin's egg blue with a touch of green in it.

While Aisha attacked the cobwebs, Deborah Ann stripped the old ivory bedding from the crib. The mattress would have to be burned. She looked down into the courtyard to make sure no one stood below and tossed the thing out the window.

She forgot about the war. She forgot to fret about when Marcel would come home to her. This room is where her babies would sleep and play. This room would hold her heart.

The cathedral chimed the hour. Marcel might be home at any moment, and here she was, looking like a woman who'd labored for two hours. Her apron sported streaks of grime like battle scars. Perspiration had spoiled her neckline, and her fingers were actually dirty.

She hurried downstairs to Marcel's bedroom to clean up. She had no other clothes here, there having been no time to prepare, and anyway, she wouldn't live here until the war was over. She would have to make do with the wash basin and endure the sweat-dampened chemise under her gown.

Marcel still did not come.

"Don't you wan' eat, Madame Chamard? Biddy got a nice chicken in the pot, and some of them new potatoes with the skin on 'em."

"No, Baudier. Call the carriage, please. I shall dine at my father's house." Maybe Marcel would be there. And if he wasn't, and he came home to an empty home, well, that might show him she was not to be neglected. He had not married a child.

Marcel had come and gone at the Presswood mansion. Don't fret, her father said over lunch. Chamard's getting married had not been part of his mission to New Orleans, he reminded her. He had a number of people to see, and he had to be discreet. They didn't want Beast Butler sniffing around.

Upstairs Mammy poured a bath for her and helped her out of the soiled purple-striped gown. "That Mister Marcel, he done right by you. You glowing like the moon, honey."

Deborah Ann blushed. He had done right by her, for a fact. "I might at this very moment be with child," she whispered.

Mammy laughed out loud. "You could be at that."

After her bath, Deborah Ann chose a pale green gown of cotton lawn. She pinned her hair up except for a fat sausage curl hanging down over each ear. Tonight, when she and Marcel were alone in his room, he would pull the pins out and let it all fall down.

"You want I should go on over with you tonight?" Mammy asked.

"They have a little pickanniny there who can help me in the morning. And I may not come home until supper time. That house, those servants – Lord knows when the silver has been polished. The chandeliers are positively begrimed."

Mammy put her hands on Deborah Ann's shoulders. "Listen to Mammy now, honey. When Mr. Marcel leave you in the morning, you ain't gone carry on none, y'hear? You send him off to war with a smile on you face."

"Yes'm," Deborah Ann promised.

She took Marcel's carriage back to Rue Royal. At the house across the street, servants were tacking black drapery to the doors and windows. Deborah Ann crossed herself and prayed to Mary Mother of God that there would be no black crepe in her future.

The afternoon passed slowly. Deborah Ann settled into her new parlor and amused herself by mentally redecorating as she embroidered. The deep red wallpaper and upholstery would have to go. The drapes too. She wanted something lighter, maybe cream and blue. But, with the blockades, it might be another year before new fabrics and fashions made it to New Orleans. When the weather broke, she'd survey the attic, see what was worth bringing down. Just as she'd had to be content to marry in an old dress, she'd have to be patient about this fusty old house.

At last, Marcel came in, hot and sweaty from the August sun. She rushed to meet him in the hallway, not caring a whit that he smelled of sweat and horse. He grabbed her up with a smile that showed he remembered what they'd done in the bed upstairs. Though a married woman now, she blushed as he plastered a kiss on her cheek.

"How do you do, Madame Chamard?"

"I've missed you. Come in here and tell me where you've been all day."

Marcel stripped off his broadcloth coat. "Hotter than an oven out there. You don't mind if I loosen my tie?"

A thrill of intimacy tingled up her spine. "Of course not."

Marcel sat down, his fingers working his neckpiece. "First place I went was your father's. Mr. Fowler and Mr. Armstrong joined us." He nodded toward the heavy breast pocket in his jacket. "Very generous men. Colonel Taylor can buy more horses. Then I briefed a gentleman whose name I may not mention. He will get General Mouton's report to President Davis."

Deborah Ann stood before him, her bottom lip caught behind her upper teeth, wondering if she dared.

"Taylor says he has the men to expand the cavalry, but they need more mounts. And Mouton wants mules for the artillery."

"Would you like me take your boots off?"

Marcel seemed taken aback. Was it too familiar? They'd only been married one day.

"Deborah Ann, you do not have to take my boots off."

She shouldn't have asked. Eyes on the floor, she took the sofa across from him, her hooped skirt a barrier between them. She wanted to be closer, to be in the bed upstairs, but he wanted to talk on and on about the war.

He must have read her face. Dear Marcel, he changed the subject.

"I've been to the lawyer," he said. "Frederick Marchand. His office is on Magazine Street. If you should need funds while I'm gone, for anything, he will see to it."

And now business! She'd been yearning for him all day, and he hadn't given her a thought. And he'd be leaving tomorrow. But she was a married woman, now, not a girl. She wouldn't carry on.

"Marcel, please, come sit by me."

Obligingly, he moved her skirt aside and sat close to her on the old red sofa. He draped his arm behind her and teased the curl over her ear. It sprang back, and he smiled. "Pretty as a picture."

She leaned into him and again, that curious hint of jasmine. Not a man's fragrance at all, in her experience.

Understanding seized her. She stiffened and drew back. She leapt to her feet, skirt swaying as if in a fitful wind.

Her husband. With that woman. She'd never been more certain of anything.

"Jasmine! You've been with her."

His eyes, so cold. They looked at her like she was a stranger, not his wife!

"Deborah Ann, sit down."

He didn't deny it! He didn't even pretend not to understand.

She pointed her finger at his heart. "You married me. You made love to me." Her voice rose into a child's shrill wail. "And then you went to her!"

Marcel was on his feet. "Deborah Ann. Calm down."

Her body shook. She couldn't breathe. Betrayed! She yanked the sapphire ring off her finger and threw it at his feet.

"Deborah Ann, you're going to faint if you don't sit down."

She'd never seen him like this, his eyes blazing mad. He grabbed her arms and forced her into a chair.

"Listen to me," he demanded. "I smell like a horse. And maybe I smell like jasmine. Deborah Ann, I have worn the same scent since I was fourteen. My father has it made up especially for us. We all wear it. All the Chamards."

Her fists were pressed against her mouth, but she was listening.

"It's mostly sandalwood. Maybe it has jasmine in it, too. I don't know. Now take a deep breath, Deborah Ann."

A fit of trembles shook her. Why hadn't she ever noticed that note of jasmine before? They'd been close to each other last winter, in the ballrooms, on the verandah. The heat? The August heat brought out the undertones?

Marcel retrieved the ring. He knelt before her and took her hand.

"Deborah Ann, I am going to put this ring on your finger one more time. Do not take it off again. Understand?"

She shook her head. "I won't," she whispered.

He raised her from her chair and took her with him to the sofa. Meekly, she allowed him to sit her down, let him hold her hand.

But it wasn't over. He had not denied the woman.

She had to be calm. She swallowed the tears in her swollen throat. "Marcel, I know about the woman."

"And what of it? Until yesterday, I was a free man."

She looked at him, all the hope in her heart poured into two words. "And now?"

He pushed the curl behind her ear. "And now I am a married man."

"You won't see her again?"

"Of course not."

Chapter Fifteen

Nicolette had almost let Finnian McKee kiss her. She'd wanted to close her eyes, to surrender her mouth, to melt into him. But that would have been bone-headed. He'd nearly fled from her after he'd danced her around the room, then last night he looked as though he'd devour her. She'd be a fool to trust him – he'd half believed she was a rebel spy! And by his own admission he was confused.

With sudden insight, she understood: The captain thought she was white. He'd not meant to be insulting with his remarks about belles and fair complexions. The realization did not lessen her rising irritation. She'd certainly done nothing to indicate she was white. She'd worn the tignon every single day. The man was obtuse, to say the least.

No, there could be nothing between them. She gathered her purse and umbrella, hardly knowing whether she dreaded or yearned to see him again this morning.

"Nicolette?" her mother called.

Nicolette stuck her head in the doorway where Cleo and Pierre lingered over chicory coffee.

"Where's William?"

"He's across the river with André's troops," Nicolette answered.

"No. He came in late last night. They dismissed them because of the storm." Cleo's husband Pierre, mahogany-dark, small and delicate, was a man whose growth had been stunted from malnutrition during his slave boyhood. "I would be happy to walk with you, Nicolette, but William. His size alone scares people off."

"Thank you, Pierre. It isn't necessary. I'll be fine."

"I don't want to frighten you," Pierre said, "but think a moment. You could be taken up. A planter sees you helping the Union, and before we even know you're missing, you're on your way upriver to slave in some rich man's field. Remember Claudette Debousier?"

"Papa would not allow it," Nicolette retorted.

"Of course he would not," Cleo said. "If he found you."

Nicolette's inner eye saw Claudette in chains, in the dark hold of some steam ship going upriver to the plantations. There probably was not a free man or woman of color in all the South who did not fear being enslaved. If a slaver, or an enraged Confederate gentleman, kidnapped a woman, slapped her in chains, removed her from the neighborhood where people knew her and might speak for her, then he could sell her upriver or off-river with no questions asked. Claudette's family, free colored of means, had never found her.

And Nicolette's vaunted light skin would be of no avail. She would be deliberately sunned, but not too much. The slaver would want her white enough to bring a good price but not so white the buyer balked. They'd give her a brothel-bloom, that's what some people called the light skin tones of desirable colored women.

With a weak smile, Nicolette capitulated. "Perhaps William wouldn't mind," she said. "You'll see he gets a good breakfast when he comes back?"

In sodden boots, Captain McKee whistled under his breath as he mounted the stairs to the telegraph office. He repeated her name silently, Nicolette Chamard, letting the French syllables roll in his mouth.

At the door he paused to shake out his rain slicker. He hooked it on the coat rack in the hallway, then ran a hand through his hat-flattened hair. He heard humming. She was humming as she worked.

Finn leaned against the doorjamb, taking in the creamy skin at the back of her neck. A wisp of raven-black hair had wriggled free of the cloth on her head, and she absently wound it around her finger. Finn wondered again why she didn't dispense with the calico head-covering in this heat, at least here inside the building. He'd like to see the rest of that black hair. Did she curl it, even if it was to be worn under the cloth? Back home, his sisters would spend hours curling their hair, and then cover it all up with a bonnet.

"Top o' the morning to you, Captain," Wallace said.

Miss Chamard twisted in her chair to see him. No smile, no twinkle in her eye. "Good morning," she said, her voice flat, her mouth a straight line. She turned back to the table and her yellow slips of paper.

He was disappointed, but not surprised. He knew he had not won her approval the night before, much less her affection. But that didn't mean she couldn't be won. He remembered that long moment under the umbrella when she'd tipped her chin up, almost inviting his kiss. And, this morning, she at least took the trouble to scowl at him.

He hovered near her for a moment, and finally she raised her face.

He bowed slightly. "*Bonjour*, Mademoiselle."

Suddenly, her face flushed. Ha. She *had* nearly let him kiss her.

"Miss Chamard," he said. "I regret I could not see you safely from your home this morning. However, I have arranged for a very trustworthy young man to accompany you in the mornings when I must be at the Park. Corporal Peach. I will see you home this evening, if I may, and Peach will escort you tomorrow morning."

Her face shut him out. "Captain, that is not necessary. Apart from the doubtful wisdom of being seen with a Union soldier on the street, I have an escort, for mornings and evenings."

Who could that be? The able-bodied men had left the city, leaving the halt, the lame, the very young, and the very old.

"Someone who can assure your safety?" he persisted.

Her smile had an amused edge to it. "William more than adequately discourages whatever ruffians cross our path, Captain."

A gentleman friend? "I hope I may meet your protector?"

She studied his face, and he felt the heat rise up his neck. Lord, he felt as transparent as the raindrops on the windowpane.

"He'll come for me at six."

He dipped his head.

Wallace had the office well in hand, and Finn left the three of them to their duties. He had a thousand things to do before he could return here at six o'clock. If her escort was a mere boy of twelve or thirteen, no protection at all, he'd see her home himself.

He left, hoping her champion still had peach fuzz on his cheeks.

Once the North had discovered the Rebels were reading their signals, every effort was put forth to devise more clever ways to thwart them. Finn's unit was trying out a new system for changing the flag codes. His men used a disk with moving outer and inner rings so that the flag signals could be rotated to align with the alphabet in unique combinations. He spent the day drilling the men so they'd be able change code at will, even mid-transmission.

As six o'clock neared, Finn turned the men over to Lieutenant Dobbs. If Miss Chamard's William was some narrow-chested swain too feeble to join the Rebels, he'd send him packing. Finn had a month's pay in his pocket. He'd prefer to walk her home, it would take longer, but if it rained, he'd hire a carriage every day and ride in it with her from Canal all the way to Pauger Street. Only next time he would not sit in the opposite corner.

A block from headquarters, the church bells tolled six o'clock. Finn spurred his horse down Iberville to come at the back of the Custom House. Several knots of soldiers, both officers and enlisted men, stood about on the Union's business, but no elderly gentleman in out-of-fashion knee pants, no pale-faced youth with hat in hand waited at the doorway. No one who looked like a William.

Finn tied his horse to the post, took off his hat and wiped the sweat from his face with a damp handkerchief. It would be another two hours before the sun slipped behind the treetops and roof lines. Another two hours of headache teasing the backs of his eyes, of sweat prickling the skin under his collar.

A black mountain of a man strode up to the back entrance and looked around, then leaned against the building near the door. His calico shirt, mended and patched, had a dry strip at the top of each shoulder and along the top of the sleeves. The rest was stuck to the man's body, dark with sweat. One of the largest men he'd ever seen. Big as André Cailloux. And what an ogre. Face a mass of scar tissue, one eye gone white.

Miss Chamard appeared at the door. Finn stepped toward her at the same time the monster Negro shoved himself off from the building. She saw the black man and bestowed on him an open, freely-given smile of affection.

This was William? Not some fancy suitor, but a ... what? Was the man a slave?

Finn advanced the last yards between them. "Miss Chamard. You're ready to go home."

Nicolette halted, her belled skirt defining the distance between the two men. The captain, his handsome face red from the sun, streaked with sweat, came so close that his legs brushed against her skirt. Had he come back to headquarters just for her?

"Captain McKee. I hope you haven't gone out of your way for me." She gestured toward William on her left. "You see I will not be alone."

"Yes, I see. He is your ... " The captain hesitated.

She had not been in this situation before. One did not introduce slaves to white men, but William was not a slave. William was in fact her friend.

"This is William, Captain McKee."

William kept his eyes on the ground. Of course he would. He'd been a freeman such a short time. "William, this is the officer who taught me to use the telegraph."

"Yes, sir," William said, and returned to studying the ground.

"You see, Captain, I need not fear a few boys in the street with William looking after me."

The captain's gaze flickered over William, head to foot. "As you say. And tomorrow morning? Corporal Peach will wait on you at your home if he may walk you here."

What a generous offer, a white soldier with other duties, directed to protect a colored woman on the street. And the captain himself? Was the offer really as impersonal as he made it seem?

Taking courage from William's presence, Nicolette boldly looked into the captain's attentive face. His eyes, a rich chocolate brown, met hers.

There was nothing impersonal in the depth of those eyes. She would love to walk down the tree-shaded street with this man. Her hand on his arm. His steps matching hers. She would listen to his Boston baritone sliding over the r's and broadening the h's. She would imagine the cool ocean breezes he described coming off the Atlantic.

Moments like these, as they held each other's gaze, she was tempted to forget her ancestors were black Africans, his white Europeans. If he knew, maybe he too could forget. No. Even Alistair Whiteaker, who was in love with her, never forgot for long.

"Thank you, Captain. William will see me safely here in the morning."

The captain took a step back and bowed slightly. "Tomorrow, then."

Nicolette turned toward William, her hooped skirt rotating with her like a twirled dinner bell. William followed her to the far side of Levee where the arching trees created a shady arbor down the length of the street.

Thirty yards down the road, Nicolette yielded to the urge to look back. She turned, expecting the captain would be on horseback by now. Mounted he was, but motionless, watching her.

She raised her hand. He answered with his own.

Nicolette and William stopped at the French market past Jackson Square. Three months ago, before General Butler imposed order and brought in foodstuffs, there had been no corn meal, meat, or rice. By the time Admiral Farragut rammed through the Confederate barriers downriver, flour was sixty dollars a barrel.

New Orleans had been in chaos before the Union arrived. With rumors that liberating Federal forces approached, hundreds, then thousands, of runaway slaves, contraband, General Butler called them, fled from the countryside into the city, starving, sick, half-naked, and desperate. There simply had not been enough food to feed them and the poor white population. People of means barricaded themselves and their provisions behind locked doors as marauding bands prowled the streets. Women wept and sold themselves to feed their children.

Once General Butler took control of the occupation, he put whites and ex-slaves to work, cleaning the streets, draining the ditches, repairing the levee. The "unwashed mob," he called them, but he fed them. He brought in provisions, some of it paid for out of his own deep pockets.

In the market, a hand-lettered sign over the bin of flour read seven and a half cents per pound. A one pound cut of corned beef, ten cents. Fresh bread loaves, five cents. Rice, eight cents a pound. However heavy-handed the general was, he had restored order and sustenance in New Orleans.

Nicolette shooshed the flies away to pick out red-blush peaches, then pulled off green bananas from a hanging stalk. Fat purple grapes went into her string basket on top of the bananas. Across the cobbled floor, the last of the season's watermelons floated in a stock tank like green islands in a pond. Nicolette thumped to find a ripe one.

"This one," she declared, and William hoisted the two-footer to his shoulder.

Two blocks up, they approached the kiosk erected to display the lists of Confederate casualties as they came in. Nicolette's mood darkened. Always, one or two, sometimes a dozen parents, sisters, sweethearts gathered when a new list went up, praying their boy's name did not appear. Always, there were wails as someone discovered her loved one was hurt, maimed, maybe killed.

An elderly man read out the names. "Antoine Henning, captured."

The plump woman next to Nicolette threw her apron over her face and burst into tears. Her husband patted her shoulder. "Now, mother, he ain't killed," he said. "He's just caught."

"Pierre Valjean, killed."

A gray-haired woman, surely Pierre's old grandmother, collapsed into the arms of a big black woman. The slave, maybe the lost soldier's own mammy, wept as she supported her mistress.

The doors of all these people would be draped in black tomorrow, their windows shuttered, their mirrors covered.

Nicolette had forgotten the war, for a moment, as she'd picked out peaches and grapes. But men were dying in Virginia, in Kentucky, in Tennessee. And soon, if she understood General Butler's intentions, they would be dying on the Bayou Lafourche.

Chapter Sixteen

On a routine reconnaissance, Marcel led his half-dozen cavalry down a shady lane, flies buzzing the horses' ears, grasshoppers chirruping in the high grass. About to enter the bright heat of the river road, he spotted a man on a dark bay mule. He raised his fist for the men to hold.

The mule ambled toward them, the man himself the picture of an at-leisure hayseed. He wore butter-colored canvas trousers and an orange and yellow calico shirt open at the throat. Even from fifty yards, Marcel could see a corn cob pipe in his mouth.

Could be the rider was a local farmer with a small parcel of land off the bayou.

Marcel waited, observing, thinking. That was a good looking mule. Prime stock. And the man wore close-fitting boots, not a farmer's heavy brogans. Something about the way the man sat in his saddle didn't seem right either. Farmers didn't put in the riding time to sit a horse, or a mule, with that kind of ease.

Could be he wasn't a farmer. Could be he was a Union scout come to assess the Bayou.

The mule rider pushed his straw hat back on his forehead at a jaunty angle. Curly golden hair caught the sunlight where it grew down over the man's collar. Didn't often see hair as gold as that. Marcel waved away a cloud of gnats and squinted.

I'll be damned. Dix Weber.

Sunshine, they used to call him. Marcel and Yves, Dix and his brother Anton, they'd had good times when they were boys. Dix was the youngest, the one with all the fun in him. It had been his idea to sneak out of the *garconniére* at school up in Opelousas and slip down to the brothel on Orange Street. He'd been the one to finagle their way inside. That was a night to remember, thanks to their fair-haired friend with the face of an angel and the glib tongue of the devil.

A horse behind Marcel snuffled and jangled its bit, giving them away. Abruptly, Weber yanked his mule around and took off, digging his heels into the mule's belly, slapping its butt with his hat.

Hell of a fast mule. But no mule could outrace a good horse. And after weeks of tedious vigilance, Marcel damn well meant to prove it.

"Yeeahhh!" Marcel put his weight in the stirrups and leaned into Hercule's neck. The thunder of the horses' hooves, dirt clods flying – damn, it felt good, his blood scouring the cobwebs from his veins.

Marcel's mount drew even with the mule's right flank. Weber rode hard, his back arched and his seat poised above the saddle. He looked over his shoulder. Marcel grinned at him. Dix's eyes widened in recognition, and the corncob pipe fell out of his mouth.

Dix sat back in his saddle and let the mule slow. The troops had him surrounded by the time the mule decided he was ready to stop.

"Sunshine," Marcel said.

Dix heaved a sigh. "Marcel."

"Last time I saw you, let's see. At the races." Marcel eyed the yellow trousers and the coarse-weave blouse. "I believe you were in a tall beaver hat and a fine black coat that day."

Dix plucked at his loose shirt. "I have to say, Marcel, you'd be more comfortable in this sun if you were wearing calico."

Marcel had heard the Weber brothers had split the family, one sympathizing with the North, the other joining Jeff Davis's forces. Divided, like Yves and himself.

"What on earth are you doing out here on the Lafourche, Dix?"

"Why, I have kinfolks all up and down the bayou, Marcel. You remember Aunt Freda? Her place just down the road a ways?"

"Best coconut cake I ever had was your Aunt Freda's."

Dix's broad German brow was tanned, his curls sun-bleached. He'd been spending a lot of time outdoors.

Marcel took out his canteen, handed it over. "Why did you run, Dix?"

Dix wiped his mouth and passed the canteen back. "All you hear about these days is ruffians, vagabonds, deserters loose on the roads. Figured you for banditos, hiding in the trees like that."

Marcel eyed the familiar, sunburned face. The excitement of chasing his old friend up the road was over. If Dix was out here as a Yankee spy, he was in a world of trouble.

"I heard you knocked your brother's front teeth out, then joined the Union. That right?"

A roguish smile lit Dix's face. "The teeth part's right. Mama's not ever forgiving me for that, spoiling Anton's looks."

"And now Anton's with Lee somewhere in Virginia. And you're here reconnoitering for the Yanks." *Damn it, Dix, deny it.*

Dix shook his head. "Anton's in Virginia, right enough, but I wouldn't make any kind of a soldier, Marcel, you know that."

That familiar half-smile, the amused gleam in his eye caught at Marcel. Dix had been almost another brother to him.

"Mama nigh kicked me out of the house for not joining up," Dix said, "so I'm out here visiting while she cools off. Got kinfolk all the way down the bayou."

God, he hoped Dix was telling the truth.

It was obvious the Yanks would want to seize all the wealth along the Lafourche. Cane, foodstuffs, silver candlesticks, livestock. A lot of resources to fuel the war along this river.

And here was Dix, a son of Louisiana, trying to see how ready they were to defend it? A hanging offense, some might call it.

"And how is Aunt Freda?"

"Getting on in years." Dix's eyes were on the horsefly tormenting his mule. "Complains of the rheumatism."

Marcel nudged his horse closer to the mule. He lowered his voice, forcing his gaze on Dix. "I could drop by, have a visit with Aunt Freda myself. She'd love telling me all about how you've been staying with her."

Dix held his gaze, and Marcel read the truth in his eyes.

"I'm sure Aunt Freda would love to see you. If she weren't laid up with the rheumatiz."

The moment stretched on. The mule's heated scent rose, the horsefly buzzed.

"Sergeant, tie a line to the mule. And bind Mr. Weber's hands to the pommel, please. He'll be joining us back at camp."

Camp was at the back end of the Poitier plantation. The frontages were narrow along the bayou so that every planter had access to the river, and the properties stretched back sometimes more than a mile. That arrangement gave Marcel's encampment, far from the main road on the edge of the swamp, a measure of security from spying eyes. Like Dix's.

Marcel rode beside his prisoner, exchanging gentlemanly pleasantries as if there were no threat of a hanging rope in the future. An observer, Marcel thought, might think they had no more on their minds than how the army conscripted the best horses, ruining the last racing season.

At the Poitier plantation, Marcel and his men turned into the lane. From the lower gallery of the big house, Mrs. Poitier waved her handkerchief. "Captain Chamard!"

Marcel reined in.

"Will you come in for a glass of lemonade?"

Old man Poitier shuffled out to the lane in bedroom slippers and collarless shirt.

"What's he tied up for?" Mr. Poitier put a hand up to shield his eyes and peered at Dix. "This the same man was here a while ago? By damn, it is! Saw him from the upstairs window, sneaking around back toward the quarters."

The old man raised an accusing finger at Dix. "Captain, you got yourself a damn spy! You got him, by God." Mr. Poitier raised his fist and shook it. "Been talking to my Nigras, telling them to run off. Hang the bastard, I say!"

Marcel signaled to the sergeant to take the men and their prisoner on to camp. It was going to take a while to settle these good people. He dismounted and tied Hercule under a catalpa tree.

"You hang that man, Captain. Hang him for a traitorous bastard!"

Marcel took his hat off and mopped his forehead with his sleeve. "There's still some question, sir, about Mr. Weber's intentions. I know the man for a gentleman, Mr. Poitier, and he claims to have been visiting kinsmen." He put his hat back on. "You understand I will proceed with due caution. It wouldn't do to hang an innocent man."

Poitier harrumphed, and Marcel diverted his attention. "Monsieur, have you yet buried your silver?"

A startled look crossed Poitier's face. "Buried the silver?"

"Yes, sir. If I were invading a territory as rich as Lafourche, I'd be taking up the people's silver to pay for horses and ammunition."

"By God, you're right." Poitier wheeled and hurried into the house. His wife watched him go. She hadn't had her say yet. She pulled him along to the shade of the lower gallery.

"If any more of these darkies run off, I don't know what we shall do when it's time to cut cane. Even now, there's hardly enough hands to do the hoeing, and if the hoeing doesn't get done, the weeds choke the cane, and then you have stunted cane come October, and then your profit shrivels right up." Mrs. Poitier drew a sharp breath. "We don't let our overseer lash the darkies, Captain, no, sir, we don't, not unless they need it very badly, but I just don't know. We might have to chain them together and then they get sullen and don't want to work. But if any more of them take it into their heads — " She pressed a hand to her heaving bosom. "Captain, you soldiers have just got to do something about these Nigras running off and leaving their work!"

Marcel framed a diplomatic answer, but Mrs. Poitier clawed at his arm.

"I tell you, I hardly close my eyes at night," she said. "Think of the dozens and dozens of hoes used in the fields every day. It would only take one miscount when the overseer collects the tools at night for some big buck to climb in the window with a hoe and chop us all to death like so many weeds! The machetes are all locked up, I can tell you, but what we shall do at harvest — !"

He reassured her as well as he could. Planters all over the region were facing the same risks, to fortune, and to life. He disentangled himself and road on toward camp. Never did get his lemonade.

He rode the depth of the plantation on his way to camp, passing the pecan orchard, a banana grove, peach and fig trees. At the cane field, Marcel slowed his horse to assess the crop and listen to the slaves' deep-throated work-song. Stalks lush and green were already so close a man could hardly push his way through. Two more months, the cane would be impenetrable, seven or eight feet high, the juice sweeter than molasses.

Nearby, a slave chopped at the weeds down a row of cane. Black as the rich earth, he straightened his back and leaned on his hoe. Two men and a woman did the same. As the slaves further down swung their hoes and bent their backs in time to the song, these four stared right at him.

Never in his life had a slave stared at Marcel. Never. And this stare was hard, cold, and full of acid.

A year ago, maybe even a month ago, these slaves would not have raised their faces to a white man, much less their eyes. Now, silently, they dared him to rebuke them.

Marcel's gaze flickered over the three men's muscled arms. Over the freshly sharpened hoes, the edges of the blades honed to a bright silver. They might have been black statues with the hot eyes of the devil glowing in their faces.

A cold tendril of dread curled into Marcel's belly. In two months, at harvest time, the machetes would come out.

He resisted the impulse to touch the pistol at his thigh.

The slaves out-numbered their owners, but cowed and unarmed and disorganized, they'd had no hope of prevailing. Every revolt, so far, had been put down. But now, the Union offered protection. It made wild promises, put unrealistic, dangerous ideas in their heads. They might actually rise up in numbers too great to resist.

Thank God Deborah Ann had not gone upriver to Evermore. In town, ironically, she'd have the Union army to protect her if the Negroes took up arms against their masters. And at home, on Cherleu? Well, Father was a good master. Even if they rebelled, the Chamard slaves would not hurt Father.

Marcel rode on, feeling the heat of dark eyes boring into his back. He'd have a word with Poitier tomorrow. More locks, at the least, were called for at the house. And loaded guns under their pillows. Dogs in their bedrooms to raise the alarm.

Pray God it would be enough.

Camp was a cluster of tents set up on the strip of land between cane field and swamp. The horses and mules were corralled away from the wetlands in hopes the alligators would leave them alone. The rest of the dry land was taken up with wagons, hay bales, and men in grey moving about.

Marcel dismounted and shucked his jacket off. "Water?"

Val had a bucket and ladle ready. Marcel drank his fill, then raised the bucket and upended it over his head. Val handed him a coarse towel.

"Where's the prisoner?"

Val led him to what the men affectionately referred to as their outdoor parlor under a magnificent spreading oak. The ancient limbs, thick as boles themselves, stretched horizontally and then dipped down nearly to the ground, creating a leafy, elegant shelter. Old crates and a hay bale served as table and chairs.

Dix sat awkwardly on the bare ground. His hands were tied behind his back. His feet stuck out in front of him, trussed up with some intricate rope work.

"You had any water?" Marcel asked him.

"I'd be obliged for another drink of water, long as you're offering."

Marcel raised his chin at Val, who brought a fresh bucket and ladle. While Val held the dipper for Dix, Marcel sat down on an empty ammo box.

"Dix, this is an inhospitable welcome, I confess. But I have to wonder what you're doing out here, dressed like this, idly riding along. I believe Aunt Freda would be dismayed to see you in canvas trousers and calico."

Dix shrugged. "Black broadcloth never suits on the bayou in August, Marcel. You know that."

What if he were to come right out and say it: Dix, you're a traitorous spy. But once the words were said, he couldn't take them back.

"Sunshine, if you'll give me your word not to run off, I can let you out of those ropes."

Dix studied the knots cutting into his ankles and let out a big sigh. "I can't rightly make such a promise, Marcel. A man held against his will, trussed up like a fatted pig, naturally thinks of slipping away from the pit."

"Well, sir, we'll try to keep you comfortable, even in ropes." Marcel skewered Dix with his gaze. "Now tell me what you're doing out here, Dix."

Dix's mouth quirked in a humorless smile. "Visiting Aunt Freda."

Marcel's second in command, Lieutenant Smythe, walked up behind Dix, a noose in his hand. Smythe was a sharp-faced man, yellow-toothed and weasely. His eyes were very blue and very small. A nasty, scraggly blond beard hung down past his top shirt button. Marcel didn't like him and didn't trust him. That went for his sidekick, too. Nelson, an undersized corporal, reminded Marcel of a hungry whupped dog following his master around like he had sausages in his pocket.

Without ceremony, the lieutenant dropped the noose over Dix's head, then turned to Nelson with a smirk on his face.

Poor Dix lost all his color.

"Lieutenant, remove the noose," Marcel said, his voice low but commanding.

Smythe put his weight on one leg, his hip cocked, the other knee bent. "You know he's a damned spy, Captain," he drawled. The blighter checked with Nelson to make sure he was sharing the fun. "You think he's not, you'd let him go. So what are you waiting for?"

His body still but every muscle taut, Marcel stared at the lieutenant. If he had to prove to this man who was in charge, he meant it to be a lasting lesson.

Smythe grinned, but he removed the noose.

"That axle fixed yet?" Marcel asked.

Smythe, not as humbled as Marcel intended to make him, said, "Getting to it."

Marcel pulled out his pocket watch. "Have it done by three o'clock, Lieutenant."

"Yes, sir, Captain." Smythe sauntered off, swinging the noose from his hand, Nelson in his wake.

"Sorry about that, Sunshine."

A little color back in his cheeks, Dix summoned up a weak smile. "Think you could prop me up against the tree trunk? My legs are used to the saddle, not to lying straight out like this."

Marcel and Val hauled Dix to his feet and helped him hobble over to the massive tree trunk. Using his bedroll for a pillow, they left Dix as comfortable as any man bound hand and foot could expect to be.

"Take a siesta, Dix. We'll talk again at supper."

Marcel strode through the camp, seeing that the men were about their business. A terrible weight pressed against his lungs at the thought that Sunshine might have committed a hanging offense. He should relay him on to headquarters, but if he did that – he didn't want to risk sending him to a noose.

Satisfied the camp was in order, Marcel turned back toward the parlor under the arching branches of the live oak. He stretched out not far from Dix, his head and shoulders propped up against his saddle. He didn't want to talk to Sunshine now. He wanted to give him time to think, give himself time to think, too.

With a mockingbird cheerfully trilling over head, he pulled his pocket Shakespeare out of his kit and settled down to the sonnets. He chose one of the happier ones, the last couplet, *Fair, kind, and true, have often liv'd alone, Which three till now never kept seat in one.* That was Lucinda. Fair, kind, and true. He meant to recite it to her some evening when they sat before a fire, she with her knees tucked up the way she liked to sit, her head on his shoulder.

Marcel glanced over at Dix. He had his eyes closed, but his body looked tense. What could he be doing out here if he wasn't spying?

He flipped through the pages, wondering if Deborah Ann liked poetry. Lucinda, not much older than Deborah Ann, was a mature woman. His bride though was still a girl in some ways. Marcel closed the book and pulled his hat down over his eyes. Life would certainly be easier if he'd married a Creole girl. The Americans didn't understand Creole customs, like keeping a placée in town. It didn't make a man a poor husband. To the contrary, in fact.

But Deborah Ann would come around. She had the prettiest smile of any girl in New Orleans. And the bluest eyes.

Drowsiness crept over him. She'd done very well in bed those first two nights. Very well.

When Marcel woke, he left his cap over his eyes and listened to the birdsong. A horse whinnied, and the cane stalks rustled as they reached for the sun. The life of the camp went on around him, soldiers coming and going, talking, working.

What the hell was he going to do with Dix? If he gave him a chance, Dix could slip off in the night. That'd be the easiest thing. But Marcel couldn't have the Yanks knowing how many Confeds were out here waiting for them. Or, more to the point, how few.

He pushed his hat up and looked over at Dix. Dix stared back at him.

Marcel heaved himself up and walked over. He studied the ropes on Dix's ankles.

"Who the hell ties a knot like that?" he asked.

He pulled out his bowie knife and sliced through the rope. "Let's take a walk, Sunshine."

Marcel left the tail ends of rope trailing from Dix's ankles, left his hands bound. They walked up the lane toward the Poitiers's house, the cane shading one side of the rutted road. Sun-warmed dirt and piles of horse shit perfumed the air.

"I appreciate the free legs, Marcel," Dix said. "Hell of it is, I can't slap at the damn skeeters like this."

Marcel flashed him a grin. "Life's tough all over, Sunshine." But he traded places with him so that Dix was in direct sun, which generally discouraged the biters.

"We're in a fix," Marcel said, watching his boots.

Dix didn't answer.

"I don't think I could stand it if they hanged you, Sunshine."

For an instant, Dix lost his bravura. His eyes watered and the muscles in his throat worked. Marcel looked away.

They walked on, avoiding the horse piles with green flies buzzing over them, and came to the garden.

"Want a tomato?" Marcel said.

"Don't think so," Dix said.

Marcel nodded. The two of them stood there, looking at their shoes, at the tomatoes, anywhere but at each other.

"Dix," Marcel said.

Dix raised his head and finally they locked eyes.

"Only way out of this is for you to give me your word you'll leave the war. I could parole you."

Dix's blue eyes hardened.

"You could go home. Find something else to do. Stay out of it."

Dix looked toward the orchard, his gaze focused far off.

A stem of basil grew through the gap between the fence boards. Marcel pinched off a leaf, rolled it in his fingers. He held it to his nose and breathed in.

Still Dix said nothing.

Marcel tossed the leaf onto the packed earth of the lane. "There's nowhere I can send you. No prisoner of war camps in these parts. And I can't let you report to the enemy, giving him information that could cost my men's lives."

Dix stepped over the ropes trailing him, turning back toward camp. Marcel put his hand out to stop him.

"Damn it, Dix."

Dix's eyes blazed at him. "What would you do, Marcel?"

Marcel's hand dropped. He thought of his sons. Of Lucinda. Of Deborah Ann. Was it so dishonorable to accept a parole, to sit out the rest of the war? Was the embarrassment of being caught and sidelined worth a man's life?

"I'd do a lot to keep from being hanged by a good friend."

Dix snorted. "You want me to spare you the honor?"

"Yeah. I do."

Marcel looked into Sunshine's blue eyes, remembering boyhood days, adolescent pranks, and brotherly affection. And now here was Dix, a man's beard bristling on his jaw, a man's honor cloaking his shoulders.

He wasn't going to hang Sunshine, dammit. If he had to, he'd keep him tied up and tethered to his side the rest of the war.

"Think on it, Dix."

A few steps further, Dix answered. "I'll think on it."

Chapter Seventeen

Marcel raised his head at the sound of horses and harness coming down the lane. Alistair Whiteaker was a welcome sight leading his small contingent into camp. Maybe he'd come up with a way out of this mess with Dix.

"Welcome," Marcel said as Alistair dismounted. He gestured to the area under the low-spread limbs of the oak. "Somebody here you'll want to see."

They ducked under the tree canopy. "Dix?" Alistair took in the ropes binding Dix hand and foot, the rough yellow trousers and the calico shirt.

"Dix is out here under suspicious circumstances, Alistair."

"Visiting Aunt Freda," Dix volunteered, his sunburned face the picture of good cheer.

Marcel saw the same sick understanding shadow Alistair's face that he'd felt himself at what Dix was up to. In their set, everyone, even Alistair, had favored Dix, charming, devilish Dix. The look Alistair gave Marcel said surely to God he wouldn't hang Dix Weber.

Marcel gave him the slightest shake of his head. "Can I offer you this fine hay bale for a seat, Captain?" Marcel took the ammo box. The three of them, two Confederate captains and a captured Union spy, settled down to pass the time like the old friends they were, pretending one of them was not bound and caught. Val brought fresh spring water to mix with the bourbon, and by the time he served them gator tail steaks, they were feeling good.

They discussed who among their friends were in which regiments, who had married, who had died. A boy from Opelousas played his harmonica softly and sweetly as orange sunglow silhouetted the black fingers of the cypress trees. An owl on an early foray hooted overhead, and the bass rumble of a bull gator echoed through the swamp.

"Adam Johnston's back," Dix said.

Marcel tightened his grip on tin cup of bourbon. If his brother Yves hadn't knocked him out with laudanum and taken his place at the duel, Marcel would have killed Adam Johnston. Adam was a fool if he'd returned to Louisiana.

"He lost an arm back at Manassas," Dix said, staring into the campfire. "I was there when he got off the boat in New Orleans six weeks back." Dix sipped his whiskey. "Looked like he'd been drunk for a month."

"So Adam's out of it," Alistair said.

Dix shook his head no. "I saw him a week ago, heading upriver on the steamboat. In uniform, his sleeve pinned up. He had that dried-out, pinched look you see on a man who's given up the drink. Going up to Port Hudson, he said, see what he can do with one arm."

Marcel drained his cup. At least Adam had found a little courage, he thought. But if Adam survived the war, he'd better plan to live out his days somewhere besides Louisiana.

"Best be getting on," Alistair said and got to his feet.

Through the flickering fire flies, Marcel walked with him to the horses where Alistair's men were already mounting up.

"What are you going to do with him?" Alistair said, keeping his voice low.

Marcel breathed a heavy sigh. "Head's hard as rock. He won't promise me to go home so I can parole him. I don't know what to do."

"No question he's reconnoitering for the Union?"

"Hell, he's no more out here visiting Aunt Freda than I am."

They listened to the frogs singing to each other for a moment, smelled the coming night.

Alistair ran the leather reins across his palm. "He has courage."

"Honor. Betrayal. It all depends on which side you're on. But, yes, Dix has courage."

"You won't hang him."

"A spy. Out of uniform. War time."

"But you won't."

"I'll give him till tomorrow night. Maybe by then he'll take the oath, I can let him go."

"What if he doesn't?"

"Hell, Alistair. I don't know."

"I'll come by tomorrow evening, see what he's decided. Maybe I can talk to him."

"If you can talk sense into him, God, I'd be grateful."

As dawn painted the swamp in pearls and blues, then added a swath of yellow just over the treetops, Marcel stood at water's edge with his first cup of coffee. A blue heron strutted behind the row of tents, on the lookout for a lazy frog. A trio of roseate spoonbills flew low over the misting swamp to settle into the arms of a bald cypress. This was Eden, back here off the Mississippi, the bayou gently feeding the wetlands.

Back in his tent, Marcel roused Dix with a friendly nudge. "Wake up, lazy. Have breakfast with me."

Over bacon and corn meal mush sweetened with molasses, Marcel tried again to make Dix see sense.

"Here's how it is, Sunshine. If you won't take the oath and go home, I'm willing to make you my bound shadow till the war's over. Everybody says it can't last much longer. I'll keep you tied up, miserable but alive."

Early as it was, Dix managed a cocky smirk. "Always knew you liked me best."

Marcel snorted. "Anton's more fun any day of the week."

Val poured coffee then sat down nearby, openly listening. Marcel let it go. No secrets anyway in a camp with thirty men living on top of one another.

He took in Dix's serene expression and felt his chest fill with lead weights. Did Dix simply not believe he could hang for this? Or was he reconciled? Could a man be as at peace with death as Dix seemed to be?

"Listen to me, Dix. What I'm afraid of, is Colonel Green will hear you refuse to be paroled, and he'll take you."

Marcel left the rest unsaid: Colonel Green would hang him. And Marcel wouldn't be able to stop it. Or, he could knock himself in the head, leave his knife lying out for Dix to cut his own ropes, and by morning, he'd be gone. Course half his men would despise him. Maybe the other half wouldn't.

"Just give me your word you'll go home, sit out the rest of the war."

"Marcel, I thank you. But I can't do that."

Marcel got up, walked a tight circle with his hand rubbing the back of his neck. He stopped in front of Dix, frustration and fear constricting his throat so that his voice came out hoarse and trembling.

"Dammit, Dix. Why not? I would."

Dix shook his head. "Right now, Marcel, this very morning, Anton may be gearing up for battle. He could die, today. I can't go home and watch Mama waiting, praying for news he's safe, and me rocking on the front porch."

Furious, Marcel tossed his empty cup to Val. "Tie him up good, Val. Make sure the rope bites the hell out of him."

Marcel gathered a wagon and the men who'd go with him up the bayou. The horses needed fodder, the men meal and bacon. He had planters to see, lookouts to debrief. He rode out of camp without another look at Dix Weber. Let him play the martyr if that's what he wanted.

Damn him to hell. If Alistair couldn't talk sense into him ...

Maybe he should just let Dix slip away in the night. Keep his cot in his own tent. He could let Dix rough him up, use his knife on the ropes. Slaves all the way up the bayou would help him get to Donaldsonville, and he'd be safe.

Damn him to hell and back.

All the way to Napoleonville, Marcel bought and cajoled stores for his men and for the stock, trying to get enough ahead to see them through the fall, at least until Butler finally began his West Louisiana campaign. When the harvests were in, he'd have a dozen more men join his troops, with horses, and he'd need to feed them all.

At the Rodins', Marcel dickered for corn meal and bacon. Further up the bayou, the Pughs let him have three sacks of corn, a sack of oats, and a bale of hay without gouging him for the price. "I thank you, ma'am. When the war's over, I'll remember your kindness." He shelled out the coins into Mrs. Pugh's hand, knowing she'd have need of the feed for her own animals by wintertime.

Every stop he made, he had to listen to the same tirades. The ungrateful darkies were restless, sneaking off. The planters didn't know if they'd see any profit at all this year, the Union hovering only sixty miles away in New Orleans. This damned war. The damned Yankees. The people seemed to have little sense of their vulnerability.

With a good day's haul in the wagon, Marcel and his men turned around to head down the bayou. All along the river road, Marcel tried to see what Dix must have seen. The growing cane. The complacent planters. The scarcity of Confederate presence. Little to discourage the Yanks, and much to entice them.

The humid, heated, lazy river breeze barely stirred the grass, offering no relief at all. What they needed was a stiff wind off the Gulf, but barring a tropical storm, they'd have to endure another oppressive afternoon of bold flies tormenting them and the horses.

At Poitier's lane, Marcel turned in. Idly, he wondered if Alistair would have refilled his ever-present flask before he came to talk to Dix tonight. Maybe if they poured half of it down Dix's throat, they'd soften up that hard head.

They passed the quarters, the fruit orchards, the garden, the cane fields. Saddle leather creaked and crickets whirred in the undergrowth, the incidental noises emphasizing how quiet the afternoon was, how still the air.

Not a single sound of a busy camp reached him. An uneasiness crept up Marcel's spine. No twittering of birds, no flittering of the brilliant cardinals that usually darted across the lane. A lone buzzard circled overhead in the hot gray sky.

Ahead, a long arm of live oak reached across the far end of the lane. From bright sunlight, Marcel eyed the deep shadow under the tree. What was that?

Slowly, as the horse ambled closer, Marcel made out something hanging down from the limb. Odd, there in the middle of the lane. A flash of yellow, turning. The drying belly of a gator hide?

Pain exploded in Marcel's chest. His heart clenched, his lungs turned to cold hard marble.

He spurred his horse the last fifty yards, a deafening roar in his ears.

He wrenched the reins under the swaying body. The horse reared, wheeling to stop itself.

Marcel reached up, grabbed Dix's legs, pushing with all his strength to relieve the tension in the rope. He screamed for help, struggling to keep his horse in position, to carry Dix's weight.

His men on horseback surrounded him, sharing the weight, steadying his horse.

"A knife," he demanded, "goddammit, a knife."

Someone climbed on his saddle, leapt onto the arching branch, and severed the rope.

As the body fell into his lap, the empurpled face, the bloated lips wisped across Marcel's cheek in a final brother's kiss.

A wordless cry tore from Marcel's chest, scattering the birds, shocking the horses and the men. He clasped Dix to his breast, the body limp and cold. His golden curls smelled of the sun, his stained yellow pants of piss.

Someone led Marcel's horse, Marcel still clutching Dix's body, trembling fingers closing the lids over Sunshine's befogged, vacant blue eyes.

Hands reached up, took Dix away from him.

Marcel slumped in his saddle, lost in a dark mindless grief. Slowly, the marble of his lungs softened, pulling air into his chest. The muscle of his heart, bruised and sore, slowed and the pulsing roar in his ears receded.

Marcel looked around him as a man whose sight is newly restored. Two men were with Dix, laying his body out, putting a handkerchief over his ruined face.

The others watched Marcel, their faces grave and uncertain. Except for two men. Nelson stared at the inert figure on the ground. Smythe pared his nails with a knife.

A terrible silent calm enveloped Marcel. He swung his leg over, slowly, almost trance-like, and dismounted. He felt strangely tall, strangely large, as if his arms were muscled thick as tree trunks, his legs as long and tough as fence rails.

He stood in front of Smythe, aware of the knife, aware of every blond hair on Smythe's knuckles.

"You dishonorable cur. You hanged Dix Weber."

Unresponsive to the insult, Smythe swiped his knife blade against his pant leg, then twisted it into the ready position.

"The man was a spy. You thought so yourself, Captain, else you wouldn't have tied him up. 'Sides, he tried to escape."

"Tied up in the middle of camp, twenty men around him."

"That's right."

Marcel's fist caught Smythe in the center of his chest All the breath in him whooshed out. The knife dropped to the dirt.

Without hurry, Marcel grabbed him by his shirt front and punched him in the jaw. Smythe flailed at him, no air in his lungs, no strength in his arms.

Marcel shoved him against the tree trunk, held him there with his left, flattened Smythe's nose with his right.

Through the red haze of his own fiercely pulsing blood, Marcel dimly saw the man hold his hands up to protect his face, saw the blood gushing over his mouth. He shifted his assault to Smythe's belly, both fists punishing him, striving to burst the liver, the bladder, the gut.

Strong hands pulled at him, men shouted in his ear. He shrugged them off. They persisted, dragging him away. He whirled and threw a fist into his sergeant's face. Two more leapt on him, hauling him down.

They piled on him, forcing him to breathe, to settle.

The weight of his men ground him into the earth. His lungs slowed. The haze cleared. His mind focused. He'd just beat a man half to death. Or maybe he'd killed him. He didn't care, if he'd killed him.

He raised his head. "Let me up."

The men untangled themselves. Someone held a hand out to Marcel and helped him out of the dirt.

Over by the tree, two men tended to Smythe. Blood covered his face, his arms, his shirt front.

Marcel staggered nearer. His legs didn't want to hold his weight, but he stayed upright. "Is he dead?"

"No, sir. He ain't dead. Not yet, leastways."

"Where's Nelson?"

Sergeant French, a bruise forming where Marcel had slugged him, shoved Nelson ahead of him. "Caught him trying to run off."

Marcel stumbled over to where Smythe lay and bent over. He grabbed Smythe by his scraggly bloody beard and forced the man to look at him.

"I ever see you again ... " The world shifted for a moment, and everything turned red. Marcel blinked his eyes and focused on Smythe's misshapen face. "I ever see you again, I'll kill you."

Marcel teetered backward. A man caught him, steadied him.

"Get them out of here."

"Yes, sir."

Marcel took a reeling step and stopped. "Confiscate their horses."

"Yes, sir."

Strange how weak he felt. As if he were the one lying in his own blood, his guts pummeled to mush. He put one foot in front of the other, wavering on the way to his tent.

Sergeant French slung Marcel's arm over his shoulder. "This way, sir. You'll want your cot now."

Marcel held up his hand, warm with Smythe's blood. He didn't like having Smythe's blood on his hand. He wiped it on his pants. "Where's Val? I need a basin of water."

"Your boy's laid up, sir. I'll see you get your water."

Marcel drew himself up. "What's wrong with Val?"

"Val's one of the ones tried to stop Smythe, sir. The lieutenant had him chained to his cot."

The weakness in his legs left him. The steady thumping of blood filled his ears. Val had never known chains. Had never even been whipped.

Marcel stepped away from the sergeant's helping arm. "Where is he?"

Sergeant French took him to the tent Val shared with another slave. The late afternoon sun shone through the white canvas onto Val's curled form, illuminating the iron fetters heavy on his thin wrists. The grizzled Negro dabbing at Val's face with a wet cloth rose and made way for him.

Val's left eye, already purple, was swollen shut. His lip was split, his nose swollen, his jaw blackened. Marcel knelt by the cot, his eyes cataloging the battering Val had taken.

"I'm sorry, Captain. I tried to stop him."

Marcel picked up the cloth and carefully wiped at the blood seeping from Val's lip. "When we see your daddy, I can tell him you were a brave man today." A sudden cough of a laugh erupted from Marcel's throat. "He'd have my hide if he saw you like this."

Val smiled enough to make the blood flow. Marcel touched the cloth to his lip. "I'll get these chains off you. Bring you something soft you can get in your mouth."

Val tried to raise himself, but the chain held him back. "No, sir. I'll bring you your supper, just like always. It's my job."

"Not tonight, Val. I'm taking care of you tonight."

Marcel had Sergeant French move Val's cot into his own tent. The other slave bunked with someone else, leaving a tent free to shelter Dix's body.

Men fixed supper around their campfires, but no one ate much. Some of them looked toward their captain's tent and cursed under their breath. Captain had no right beating a man half to death for doing what he ought to have done in the first place. Others said the captain knew what he was doing. Smythe deserved every fisted blow to the belly. The man never hear of a trial before a hanging?

An hour before twilight, Alistair rode into camp.

Sergeant French told him what happened. Alistair walked along the shoreline remembering Dix Weber. They'd known each other all their lives, might have become old men together, telling tales about the war, Alistair and Marcel and Sunshine.

When he was ready, he went into the tent where Sunshine's body lay. When Alistair was a boy, his father, a rough man, had forced him to watch a hanging. *It'll toughen the boy up, make a man of him,* Father had told his protesting mother. Alistair even yet revisited the scene in his nightmares. He knew what hanging did to a man's face. He didn't lift the handkerchief covering Sunshine's.

He sat a while. A last ray of sun pierced the gloomy tent and lit a golden curl over Sunshine's ear. Alistair's numb reserve crumbled, and he wept.

Spent, Alistair stepped into the dusk, fire flies flitting through the camp. He knocked on Marcel's fence pole and let himself in. A kerosene lantern cast a yellow glow on Marcel's boy sleeping in the second cot, his face a mass of swollen bruises.

Marcel sat in his shirtsleeves, his dark hair wild, his eyes the deepest black. The knuckles on the hand holding his pen were split and raw. He was writing a letter.

"For his mother?"

Marcel nodded.

"You tell her the truth?"

"No."

Alistair took the camp stool. He reached for Marcel's horn cup and poured a dose of healing bourbon from his replenished flask. Together, they drank to Dix Weber.

Chapter Eighteen

Nicolette woke to sunlight slatted through her shutter, setting the rose-washed walls aglow. Another day, the early September morning blessedly cool.

She checked the clock. Plenty of time to make morning mass. The house was quiet, Cleo and Pierre having gone upriver to oversee the small harvest of their gardens.

She dressed, choosing a pale blue tignon to go with her gray dress. William, at her insistence, was with the Guards at their barracks. No one had accosted her in the weeks since the gang of boys had gone after her. She could take care of herself on the way to the Custom House.

Nicolette opened her front door.

The coppery smell hit her before her eyes made sense of the blood and feathers and chicken shit smeared all over her front stoop. She recoiled, one hand at her mouth, the other slamming the door shut.

She fought to keep the bile down, her back pressed against the door.

Just chicken feathers. Just chicken.

Her throat burned. Her heart beat against her ribs. She latched the door, retreated to Maman's parlor, and sank onto the wide-bottomed chair.

Just chicken blood. Like the voodoo queen used in Congo Square.

Nicolette crossed herself. She and her maman were as Catholic as Nicolette's father, as devout as Tante Josie. Still, the voodoo was powerful in New Orleans. She shook her head. This sloppy display on her stoop was not true voodoo. A true voodoyen would acquire a lock of Nicolette's hair and burn it if she wanted to harm her. In spite of herself, Nicolette thought of her hairbrush upstairs on the dresser. She would not rush up there and pull the hair out of that brush. This was not an act of voodoo. This was a white man's warning.

She swiped at the useless tears on her face and calmed herself. This was just meanness. Whoever it was had done no real harm. After the Confederates' great victory at the second Bull Run, the rebels in town were emboldened, that's all. Somebody knew she was a collaborator, and they were punishing her. Scaring her. Well, she was not going to let them scare her into quitting. She'd known there would be risk in working with the "enemy." She was a soldier, in her own way, and she had a job to do.

She tied an apron over her dress. In the courtyard she filled a bucket from the cistern and took it to the front stoop where she sluiced the mess into the gutter. Three buckets and a good scouring with the straw broom and the stoop shone clean. By noon, the feathers would have dried and blown away. The rest of the filth would roll toward the river with the next rainstorm.

She was late now. She strode rapidly down Esplanade and up Levee to arrive at the Custom House at twenty past eight. Determined to put the morning's fright out of her mind, she climbed the stairs with a quick step.

"Good morning, Mr. Wallace, Mr. Simpson," she said.

"Morning, Miss."

"No beignets?" Wallace said.

"No flour, Mr. Wallace. Not until a new shipment comes in."

The day wore on. Nicolette's key clacked out a rapid incoming ratatat and she picked up her pencil. Adept now, she penciled the message on her yellow pad: *Railroad trestle blown up north of Magnolia. No casualties. Train diverted. Need timber to effect repairs.*

Thanks be to God. No tallying of killed, wounded, and missing. As noon approached, she watched the clock. If the captain could get away from his other duties, he'd take her to lunch. Five after twelve, and there in the doorway, Captain Finnian McKee. He leaned in, freshly barbered, a hand on either jamb.

"Hungry?" His voice was low and smooth, like good brandy.

She loved the way he spoke. So direct and to the point. A Southern gentleman would have needed half a dozen sentences to ask her to lunch.

"I am, sir."

He cocked his head toward the hallway in invitation.

Nicolette had to follow the captain's wake through the busy hall and down the stairs. Once outside, she placed her hand in the crook of his elbow. He pressed his arm against his side, capturing her hand.

Everyone on the street must see her heart, if not on her sleeve, on her face. She felt she must glow, walking with him, her hand close against his body, a silly grin on her face.

She no longer bristled at remarks that showed he had no real understanding of a culture stratified by skin color. She no longer withdrew from his casual touches, so inappropriate really. Instead, each time she passed him a slip of paper or handed him a freshly sharpened pencil, she hoped his fingers would brush against hers.

Nicolette knew there could be no future with Finnian McKee, a man too foreign, too preoccupied by the war to see who she really was. In the weeks since he'd driven her home in the downpour, this man from Boston had still not cracked the code: truly white women did not wear the tignon.

She did nothing, nothing at all, to indicate that she was white, but that didn't mean she wasn't guilty of deceit. Her sin was in not telling him. But what harm would it do? Eventually, he would be leaving with his army. After the war, he would go home to Boston and marry some red-headed Irish girl. Surely, for these few weeks, she could be forgiven for simply enjoying the company of a man who didn't look at her and see the taint of African blood.

And so she allowed herself the pleasure of her hand pressed into the wool of his coat, the joy of being on his arm, of looking into his eyes as he inclined his head toward her when she spoke.

The finer restaurants in town would not welcome a woman with a tignon on her head, even on the arm of a Union officer. Instead, through July and August, she'd led Finn to the lunchrooms all through the Quarter, from Dauphine to Dumaine. Open stalls where they ate fresh oysters on the half shell with lemon juice or hot sauce. Small hole-in-the-wall establishments with sawdust on the floor where they ordered red beans and rice across a plank counter. She still hadn't persuaded him that biting off the head and sucking a boiled crawfish was good eating, but he had gamely given it a try.

As they strolled down Rue Condé arm in arm, their steps in rhythm, a September breeze ruffled a climbing wisteria vine, hinting that summer might end at last. Nicolette cast a nervous eye on the other pedestrians, wondering if this was the man, or that one, who'd befouled her doorstep with chicken blood.

This was what the despoiler wanted, that she should be intimidated, looking over her shoulder, afraid. She mentally shook herself. She was not such a coward as that. She was in bright sunshine, on a public thoroughfare with Captain McKee at her side. No reason to be afraid.

Finn took her gloved hand from his arm and held it as they walked, his thumb absently rubbing her knuckles. Entirely inappropriate, surely in Boston as well as in New Orleans. He was quite dense, sometimes. She smiled, loving it.

She refocused her attention on Finn's account of blue water sailing back home. He had a small boat, big enough to sleep two, and in high summer there was nothing finer than a day spent on the ocean. She tried to imagine the exhilaration of salt spray and a fresh wind, the sun glistening on the water. Finn's eyes brightened with the telling. She wished she could see him at the tiller, the wind in his hair, his eyes focused on the horizon. His face would be alight, loving the speed and the challenge of his sailboat.

They arrived at Marie's Mumbo Gumbo, the words painted in uneven red letters over the open doorway, the aroma of hot spicy stew drawing them in.

"Lord, that smells good," Finn said.

Marie, red calico on her head, black eyes flashing over a wide smile, gestured to the shaded plank tables and short stools. No need to order. If you didn't want gumbo, you didn't sit down at Marie's table.

Marie brought them a pitcher of watered wine and then served them each a bowl of okra, chicken, shrimp, sausage, onions, peppers, garlic, and whatever else she'd had handy to chop up and throw in the pot. She placed a straw basket of corn bread on their table and wished them *bon appetite*.

Before Nicolette could warn him, Finn incautiously shoveled a spoonful of gumbo in his mouth. He'd had gumbo before, at a little stand off Canal Street. He loved gumbo. But he hadn't had Marie's gumbo.

Sweat broke out on his upper lip. His eyes watered. He tried to speak, but his voice was gone.

Nicolette quickly poured him a glass of the watered wine and watched him drink it down. "I'm so sorry. I should have warned you."

"Nonsense," he rasped. He drank again, and when his throat had opened, he said, "I only wish she'd added a few peppers to the soup."

He grinned, his eyes still watering, and picked up his spoon.

"I believe I'll make a Creole of you yet, Captain."

Through the open doorway, a mockingbird flew in and fearlessly lit on the table next to them. Instead of scolding them for intruding into his territory, the bird raised its smooth gray head and warbled.

Nicolette put her spoon down to listen. She didn't know which bird's song the mockingbird stole, but it was as lovely a call as she'd ever heard.

She opened her eyes and found Finn staring, the intimacy in his eyes warming her very soul. She felt she could fly, could soar into the sky on the warmth of that look. He seemed to really see her. For a moment, she allowed herself to believe he was in love with her, too.

He couldn't be, though. He didn't really see her, didn't really know who she was. Deflated, she looked away.

Finn was intelligent, sincere, and honorable, but he was not discerning. Gentlemen here were accustomed to the complexities of Southern culture, accustomed to the nuances of a striated society, accustomed to dividing themselves from their vaunted honor. From their earliest years, slave-owning men grew up playing with the black children on the plantation, then sold them off later if they needed funds. They went to mass on Sundays and took the sacrament, and on Monday had the overseer whip those lazy rascals if they didn't hustle to the fields. In town, they smiled at and loved their wives and then strolled a few blocks over to smile at and love their colored mistresses. They were men who lived their lives in layers and partitions.

But this man, this Yankee who described New Orleans as exotic and bewildering, everything was alien to him, the food, the weather, the Spanish architecture, the Creoles, Cajuns, Americans. Slaves and freedmen. Mulattos, quadroons, octoroons, griffones. The captain most certainly remained befuddled about the social subtleties of race. No, he did not really see her.

Sadly, Nicolette met his admiring gaze. The captain's glossy black moustache hid most of his mouth, but her eyes found the curve of his lower lip. Perhaps, some day, before he went away, she might taste that lip.

Smiling a little, she tilted her head to the side. "What are you thinking, Captain?"

He reached across the table and touched her hand. "I'd love to hear you sing again."

Smiling, she closed her eyes. She wouldn't sing here in Marie's Mumbo Gumbo, but she'd whistle. The mockingbird's song slipped from her puckered lips as if he were perched on her shoulder, whispering the melody in her ear. It was absurd, trying to sound like one of God's great vocalists, but it gave her pleasure to try, for him.

Finn put down his spoon. "My God. That's it exactly!"

She laughed. "My maman always said I should have been a mockingbird. I love to mimic." A gleam shone in her eye. With rapid-fire New England delivery, she said, "For instance, Captain McKee, theah is a trumpet flowa abloom in the yahd neahby. Ah've no idear if you would like to see it, but it is on a conna a block noahth of heah."

Finn guffawed. "How did you learn to do that?"

"Why, ah've had a wicket good teacha in you, Captain."

"You know, if you only slowed it down a bit, you don't sound that different here in Newallins."

Nicolette clucked her tongue. "Nobody in Louisiana ever added an "r" to the end of a word, Captain McKee. The very idear."

Finn laughed and talked, a steady, thrumming beat within him. Sitting here in the dappled shade, her prickly defenses down, she was a marvel. He'd never known a more beautiful, more expressive face. That tignon thing on her head kept the hair off her face, revealing a tall, smooth forehead. Her brows arched over thick lashes, her eyes the softest gray, like sunrise over the lake.

Her mouth, he would have that mouth. He held his hand out for her. Docile as a lamb, she allowed him to walk her into a bower of overhanging bougainvillea. Slowly, gently, he turned her to him, cupped her face in his hands and kissed her.

Light flooded his senses like a single bright candle in the dark. She opened her lips, allowing him to deepen his kiss, and the candle light turned into the sun.

This was the kiss she'd dreamed of, hot and soft, demanding, gentle. Harder. Personal. Finn. His tongue glided over her upper lip. On a quick intake of breath, her entire body shuddered. He caught her to him, moved his hand to the back of her neck.

"Finn — "

"Shh." He pressed his lips to her forehead.

"Finn, you don't — "

She closed her eyes and quivered when he ran his thumb over her bottom lip.

"I don't what?"

Three noisy men sat down at the table they'd vacated. Maria bustled out with cornbread.

Nicolette stepped away feeling dazed, swollen, saved. Finn glanced at the newcomers, then gave her a rueful smile.

"Would you like to see the *Essex*?"

"The ironclad? Up close?" Her voice was faint, hoarse, not like her at all.

They walked down Bienville, crossed Levee Street, and were on the built-up banks of the Mississippi. Sailing ships and steam ships moored four and five deep against the wharves, their masts and smoke stacks swaying with the wind like a forest of denuded tree trunks. The rumble of steam engines, the creak of ships' timbers, and the bustle of men and mules filled the air.

Before them sat the *Essex*, aswarm with men bearing sacks of rice and kegs of salt pork. A crane cautiously swung a bundle of shot across the water to deposit on the gunboat's deck.

"Jay!" Finn called.

A crewman dressed in naval uniform looked up and waved. He deftly crossed a plank from the deck to the reinforced bank. "Finn, you old no-account, how are you?" he said, taking Finn's hand in both of his and shaking it vigorously.

"Miss Chamard, my old friend, Jay Zettle, second engineer aboard the *Essex* . Jay, may I introduce Mademoiselle Chamard?"

Jay touched his cap. "Pleased, ma'am." He turned to face his ship, glowing with pride. "What do you think of her?"

"Can you take us aboard, Jay?"

"Sorry. Captain would have my hide. But I can give you her specifics."

Zettle launched into a detailed account of his ship's attributes, so much detail Nicolette could hardly follow him. "... thirty inches of wood, side casemates, sixteen inches. Over all that, one inch of good India rubber. Then your iron plates, one and three fourths inch think at the front — "

"Yet the Reb artillery penetrated through to the woodwork. That's what I heard," Finn said.

Jay frowned. "That should be classified information."

Finn shrugged. "It's all over town, Jay. Story is batteries on the bluff at Port Hudson pounded her good."

"Well, she's better than new now." Jay gestured toward his metallic love and continued his recitation. "Water tight compartments, forty of them ... As for armaments, you have your Dahlgrens, your Howitzers ... "

Nicolette slipped her hand under Finn's arm, and in that way she loved, he bent his elbow and held her hand close to his side. Under the uniform coat, his chest, his ribs, his heart. The *Essex* disappeared from her vision. She saw instead herself with her hair down, wrapped in Finn McKee's bare arms.

Nicolette blinked. The gunboat, huge and gray, reappeared.

Finn held his hand out. "Jay, she's a fine ship."

Jay pumped his hand. "She'll be a wonder up at Port Hudson, harassing the Rebs."

"Good luck, Mr. Zettle," Nicolette said.

On the way back to the street, Finn led her past two gentlemen in black frock coats with arms crossed, eyes on the *Essex*. Nicolette's pulse kicked up. She knew those faces. Red hair stuck out from the taller man's stovepipe hat, his face heavily freckled. The other sported moustaches shaped like the prized rack of a longhorn.

She'd seen the two of them in Jackson Square, haranguing anyone who would listen. "There are traitors in our midst!" the mustached man had shouted, his eyes flashing and his face flushed. "Men, and yes, women, too, stabbing their own people in the back!"

That same man turned a hard gaze on her, tracking her progress across the levee. Was this the man who'd gutted the chicken on her doorstep? No. His broadcloth was immaculate, his hat an expensive felt. He had not dirtied his hands. But he might have inspired the deed. She wished for the shield of a broad-brimmed hat to hide her face, but that not being possible, she raised her chin. Let him see her, then.

Chapter Nineteen

Waiting for Jebediah to serve them a light supper, Deborah Ann sat with her father, each reading the day's mail.

Deborah Ann had a long letter from her cousin Bernadette whose father was a Creole planter on the Cane River. Ever ruled by passion, Bernadette wrote of her fiancé's having at last donned the Confederate uniform. "I would hate him if I saw him flinch for an instant while standing at the mouth of a loaded cannon," she wrote. "Let him die, if necessary; but as to a coward! *Merci! Je n'en veux pas!*"

For the past two years, Deborah Ann had heard similar sentiments from New Orleans belles fluttering their fans and uttering inanities. She considered herself as fervent a patriot as any of the thoughtless sillies, but these over-heated sentiments of glorious death, of foolhardy gestures — standing at the mouth of a loaded canon, indeed. What nonsense.

"We have an invitation, Deborah Ann." Father held up a folded sheet of cream paper. "The General and Mrs. Butler are having an evening of dinner and entertainment, St. Charles Hotel, September the twentieth."

"I shan't go, Father."

He paused in clipping the end off his cigar. "The invitation mentions you specifically, my dear. I'm told Mrs. Butler is a charming woman. You might even like her well enough to ... " He hesitated. "To become her confidant."

"Certainly not!" Instantly, she regretted her tone. "Excuse my rude temper, Father, but you must see, I am the wife of a Confederate officer. It would be unseemly in the greatest degree for me to consort with my husband's enemies."

"Sweetheart, think of what is at stake. Butler's office must, I emphasize to you, my sweet child, must believe they have me in their pockets. If you do not attend, it will look bad, Deborah Ann. Very bad."

Deborah Ann carefully straightened her pen on the desk. She smoothed her hair. She understood Father's dilemma, but she was not merely his child anymore.

"I will not embarrass you, Father, by seeming to decline Mrs. Butler's invitation out of hand." She stood up and crossed the room to ring for Jebediah. "I shall simply not be in New Orleans on the twentieth."

Peeved, Father told her, "I cannot take you elsewhere, now, Deborah Ann. I thought you understood the importance of what I am doing here."

"Oh, Father, I do." She quickly crossed to him and placed her hand on the white linen over his heart. "I am proud to be your daughter."

Jebediah passed by in the hallway. She called him back. "Jeb, I'm going home to Evermore. Tell Mammy to pack."

Mr. Presswood covered his daughter's hand where it lay on his breast. "My sweet girl. You will have your way in this, won't you?"

"Yes, Father."

"I want Jeb with you every churn of the paddlewheel. By your side, understand?"

Deborah Ann kissed her father's cheek. "I promise."

Two days later, she boarded the *Rachel*. She wished she could see her feet under the bell of her skirt, but truly, the gangplank was adequately wide, no real danger of her toppling over into the fetid water as long as she kept her nerve.

Early as it was, the smell of the wharves and the river itself nearly undid her. The public rooms of the steamboat roiled with soldiers, businessmen, and various other travelers who might at any moment spit upon the floor or open up a greased-paper sack of odorous salami for their lunch. Deborah Ann pressed her scented handkerchief to her nose until she and Mammy and Jebediah settled into the private cabin Mr. Presswood had paid a small fortune to procure. Before nightfall, Deborah Ann would be home.

Evermore. Grandmother Meredith had named the new plantation as a bride, sure she had stepped into an abiding paradise. The sun would shine, the fertile soil would nourish the verdant crops, and the darkies would sing as they toiled. Always. Deborah Ann, too, had believed the orderly prosperity of the planter life would last forever when she was growing up. Even now, with the Northern forces threatening to break the South's very backbone, she found it hard to imagine Evermore might not endure.

From the river levee, an alley of poplars drew the eye to a brilliant white edifice. The house staff gathered to welcome Deborah Ann in the grand hallway. Tired as she was, grimy from the grit and soot that seeped into even the forward cabins, she graciously greeted the butler, the second butler, the upstairs and downstairs maids, and the cook. She couldn't remember the name of Clementine's new grandbaby, or whether it was a boy or a girl, but she remembered to ask after it. Clementine, smiling broadly, seemed pleased.

Deborah Ann climbed the wide staircase to her room on the second floor. There were six bedrooms up here, rather unnecessary in the present generation with only Deborah Ann having survived the nursery years. The house had always been quiet during Deborah Ann's growing up. No rowdy brothers running up and down the stairs, no sisters quarreling or playing. Father had spent his days in the study. Mother lay in her darkened room with a vinegar soaked cloth on her forehead. It had been a lonely childhood. No wonder she'd relied on story books for company.

She called over her shoulder. "I'll want a bath, please, Mammy."

"I'll see to it, sugar."

She entered her room in the front of the house. It was just as she'd left it. The aqua tinted canopy on her bed, the blue and green Chinese porcelain on her mantle. Her aqua silk slipper chair still had a small nick in the fabric where she'd once caught a hat pin in it. She ran her finger along the curved mahogany back of the chair. Home.

Next morning, she sent word for Mr. Thompson. She went through her father's questions, listening carefully to the overseer's answers. The cotton yield was good. The cane was high as a horse's ear. They had enough guano to start next year's planting. Yes, there'd been some trouble with the slaves. Laziness, sullenness, unwillingness to work. Nothing he couldn't handle.

"How many have slipped away, Mr. Thompson?"

"Twenty-two men. Four women."

"Where do you suppose they've gone? New Orleans?"

"Some of them probably just hiding out in the woods, but in town, the Yanks will feed them."

"In the morning, while it's still cool, I'd like you to ride the plantation with me, Mr. Thompson."

He shook his head. "No, ma'am."

"I beg your pardon, sir?"

"No, ma'am. I can't let you out on the plantation with the slaves like they are now. This is tense times. You best stay here at the house where you'll be safe. Out in the fields, no ma'am. I can't guarantee it."

A mosquito buzzed. The clock ticked. A child cried out in glee somewhere near the laundry.

"But you'd have your whip, Mr. Thompson."

"And a shotgun. But like I said, Miss. Excuse me, Mrs. Chamard. I can't take you out. These people are riled, and I'm only one man." He stood up and tapped his hat against his knee. "You tell me what you want to know, I'll give you a report. I'm sure Mr. Presswood would agree with me."

Deborah Ann was sure he would, too.

"I'll think about what you've said, Mr. Thompson. I'll let you know in the morning what I decide."

Mr. Thompson showed himself out.

Deborah Ann leaned her elbows on the desk, trying to grasp that she could not ride out on her own land. She'd always freely ridden the plantation, even as a child. The slaves had smiled at her, had fussed over her. In the fall, she had always come back to the house with her pockets full of sweet cane to gnaw on. There had never been the slightest thought that she might not be safe.

She left Father's study to walk down the oyster shell path toward the laundry. Instead of having to chop cotton or cut cane, the laundresses boiled water and stirred pots and made soap. Pearly and Rosa, Maggie, and Anna – they had a good life here on the plantation. Used to, they laughed and sang and told stories while they worked. When she was a child, Deborah Ann would put on a wide-brimmed bonnet in the lonely afternoons while her mother napped, and she'd go down to the laundry to visit her friends. Pearly would put a clean cloth over the chair so the rawhide wouldn't snag Deborah Ann's sprigged muslin. The four women, working amid the sheets hung on cords to whiten in the sun and dry in the wind, would exclaim in delight and amazement as she retold a fairy tale she'd read.

With a ready smile, she turned the corner into the laundry yard, expecting Rosa and Maggie to take her hands, drag her to the best cow hide chair, and sit her down in the shade. "Tell us 'bout them balls in Newallins, darling," they'd say. "You say you a married woman!" And then with mischief in her eye, Pearly would say, "That man know how to do you right?"

Anna had her back to her, stirring a steaming pot of canvas work pants with a big paddle. Maggie was bent over, feeding the fire under another cast iron cauldron. The acrid scent of lye soap filled the yard.

Rosa stepped out of the cabin carrying a wash board and saw her first. She stopped right where she was, her eyes on Deborah Ann.

"Missy's here, ya'll," she said quietly.

Anna wiped her hands on her apron. Maggie pushed a hank of hair off her forehead. No glad smiles. No welcoming hands reaching for her.

The friendly words died in Deborah Ann's throat. "Where's Pearly?"

Anna stirred her pot. Rosa fished a pair of pants out of the hot water and set to scrubbing them against the wavy tin wash board.

Maggie crossed her arms over her chest and looked Deborah Ann right in the eye. "Pearly gone off."

Deborah Ann had never had a Nigra look at her like that, surly, defiant. These dear, dark faces had made her feel loved and important. But they cared nothing for her, after all. Her chest ached with heaviness as it had those dark months after Mother died.

She took a step away, but couldn't help herself. She turned half way back. "I got married."

After a moment, a grudging pity in her voice, Maggie said, "Dat's fine, honey."

Deborah Ann left the laundry yard, her face aflame. She glanced toward the blacksmith shop where Smithy pounded horse shoes, every strike ringing across the yards. Once, when she was a child, Smithy, a gentle man with arms as big as tree trunks, had let her touch the twisted scar on his chest where his first owner had branded him with a hot iron.

Deborah Ann took a step toward him. Smithy lifted his head and saw her. His staring eyes, hot as the furnace, burned her across the yard as he held a red hot shoe up with his tongs as if to show her what fire could do.

Her mouth dried up, her stomach clenched. She hurried back to the house, dark unfriendly eyes scorching her back. She'd heard stories of slave rebellions, but always they'd been in far off places, led by devils like Nat Turner. Could it happen here, on Evermore? Angry slaves marching on the house with torches, machete blades gleaming in the fire light?

She banged open the door into Father's study, slammed it shut, and latched it firmly behind her.

Chapter Twenty

The tinny chime of the clock in the parlor downstairs declared it was two in the morning. Nicolette tensed at every footfall under her balcony until around midnight when the street grew quiet. Now she lay awake listening for a tell-tale scratch at the door or a creak of a window latch.

Those men on the levee had not been observing the *Essex*. They'd been watching her.

She'd known from the beginning she could not go in and out of the Union headquarters unnoticed, but she considered the risk small. There were many people in New Orleans who worked with the occupiers, and after all, the Confederates still in the city could not expect a woman of color to sympathize with their cause. Yet someone had chosen her to make a point.

She tossed under the mosquito netting, the air close and heavy. With William sleeping at the Guards' camp, she was alone. She could leave New Orleans, take a steamer up river to Chateau Chanson where Maman and Pierre were. She wouldn't be frightened there, and no one would harm her.

But that would mean total defeat, and she would be no more than a shadow of the woman she meant to be. She was determined not to be a coward. If someone tried to get in, she'd hear him. She would quietly step into the hall, creep down the stairs, and be ready. With what? She could have the water jug from her dresser in hand. That would crack someone's head open. And if there were two? She snorted. She could take the sheet from her bed, toss it over them, confuse them.

Useless. She couldn't fight one man, much less two. Once she had believed she was invincible, and any attacker who chose to molest her would be very sorry. But Adam Johnston had proved to her just how foolish that illusion was. She'd never hauled a fifty pound sack of cotton behind her, never chopped cane, never bent her back over a row of beans. She was small and weak.

She needed a gun. Nicolette lit her lamp and crossed to the wardrobe. She reached underneath to a hidden drawer and retrieved the lacquered box where she kept her money. Inside were two bags. One was the small leather pouch Alistair Whiteaker had pressed into her hand the night before he left New Orleans. She had not opened the pouch and did not know how much money it contained, nor did she open it now. The other bag was of lavender satin closed with a purple ribbon.

Smoothing her sheet, she emptied her purse, the silver and gold coins glinting in the lantern light.

She'd had a good winter. The well-to-do families who paid to see her perform at the Silver Spoon, or hired her for their private parties, had seemed determined to celebrate regardless of the war. And there was her pay from General Butler. If she were frugal, if she gave her street shoes a proper waxing so they'd last the year, she'd have enough money to buy a pistol.

Feeling calmer, she turned out the lamp and slept.

Just after dawn she woke with a start, her heart thumping. She sat up, listening. A gate squeaked outside. She got up and put her eye to the gap in the shutters. Her gate was ajar.

She looked wildly around the dim room. Her gaze caught on a gleam of light from the dressing table. The scissors. She grasped them in her right hand. In her left, she grabbed a heavy brass candlestick.

At the top of the stairs, she listened. Nothing. She crept down, avoiding the squeaky step third from the bottom. Silently, she stepped into the hallway and listened again. Voices, whispering. They'd got into the courtyard. No one would see them. Maybe no one would hear them. She was on her own.

Nicolette marched toward the back door, pounding her bare feet on the boards. At the top of her voice, she hollered, "Get the shotgun, Papa! There's vermin in the courtyard!"

She scraped a chair across the floor, banged the candlestick against a door jamb, making as much noise as she could. "Jeremy!" she called. "Get that machete you brought from upriver!"

She held her breath and listened again. Rapid footsteps crossed the bricks out back, growing fainter.

Had they really gone? Or were they playing the same game she was? She swallowed bile, determined not to throw up.

She tightened her sweaty grip on the candlestick, its decorative ridge digging into her fingers. She waited, she listened, until sun rays crept through the back window shutters. A mockingbird took up his day's work, trilling in the crape myrtle at the corner of the yard.

They were gone.

With trembling hand, Nicolette put the candlestick down. Carefully, painfully, she unbent her cramped fingers from the holes of the scissors handle. She was fine. Just frightened. Just weak in the knees.

Tonight, she'd have a gun. If they came back, she'd shoot them in the heart.

Dressing for work, Nicolette dabbed concealer on the shadows under her eyes. Then, with a light stroke, she rouged her cheeks. Lastly she applied a dusting of fine powder over all. She wasn't trying to look glamorous; she simply wanted to appear as if she had slept the previous night.

She had her hand on the latch when she paused and ran back up the stairs. She grabbed the brass candlestick off her dressing table and put it in a shopping bag. With the candlestick in hand, ready to wield it through the cloth bag, she opened the back door.

The crape myrtle, the banana tree, the lemon tree, the cistern, the cast iron table. Nothing had changed. Maman's spiky exotic cactus still threatened all comers in its barrel near the outhouse. Everything was as it should be.

Nicolette relaxed her grip on the candlestick and examined the back door, thick cypress boards girded with iron hardware. The blue paint around the latch was scratched and one deeper gouge showed where a chisel must have slipped.

They wouldn't have got in this way even if they'd broken the metal latch. Inside, there were stanchions either side of that door and a stout cypress board for a barricade. But the window would be easy. The shutters, meant to protect the glass window from storm winds, would be little trouble for a man with a chisel. If she'd been the one trying to break in, she'd have chosen the window. Maybe, next time, they would too.

But next time, she'd have a gun.

The candlestick in its bag, Nicolette strode down Pauger Street, alert for watching eyes, for shadowy alleys, for following footsteps. As she neared the Mint on Esplanade, she relaxed. No one would accost her on a busy street filled with soldiers and tradesmen.

After a twenty-minute walk up Decatur, she arrived at the Custom House to find Simpson and Wallace in a dither.

"The mail packet came in an hour ago. Big action going on in Virginia," Wallace said.

"Harper's Ferry," Simpson said. "Ever heard of it?"

"John Brown's raid?"

"The very one. Rebs attacked last week."

"Do we know who won?"

Finn walked in, Major Farrow behind him. "Not yet, we don't."

"Stand aside, lad." Hursh upended the atlas he carried under his arm and spread it open on the desk. As he flipped through, looking for the Virginia pages, he said, "Miss Chamard, should you like to see where the battle rages?"

Finn opened his arm to include her. She stepped into its arc, only a little sure he wouldn't, in his thoughtlessly improper way, lay it over her shoulder. She leaned over the book as the major traced the path of the Baltimore and Ohio Railroad westward to Harper's Ferry where it crossed the Potomac River.

"So the Rebels want to blow up this bridge?"

"Or take it. You may know from Brown's attack in '59, there's a Federal arsenal at Harper's Ferry. Damned near indefensible, too, sitting in a bowl with higher ground all round."

"Who's in command?" Finn asked.

"Miles."

"Dixon Miles?"

"The same."

Finn and the major exchanged grim looks.

"You have no confidence in this commander?" Nicolette asked.

Hurshel Farrow mimed a man tossing back a glass of whiskey.

The three of them looked silently at the brown shading of the map indicating the mountains surrounding the river town. Even Nicolette could see it would be hard for the Federals to withstand attacks from above.

They waited all day, sending Wallace and then Simpson down to the docks on the hope that another mail packet would sail into port. None did, and they were left only with the morning's news that Colonel Miles' rifle volleys had held off a first Confederate assault led by Major General Jackson.

Word had traveled all over New Orleans by mid-day. Hursh Farrow's atlas was not the only one in town. Confederate sympathizers would be assessing the likelihood of Rebel success. They'd be riled up, their favorite ol' Stonewall Jackson sure to be victorious.

At quitting time, Finn leaned over Nicolette, his palm flattened on her desk, creating a sphere of intimacy, an oasis only they two inhabited. His hand was sun-browned. A sprinkling of dark hair adorned each finger. His nails were square cut, probably with his pocket knife, she thought. He had no time for niceties like manicures. And yet, a fine hand. She wanted to bring that hand to her cheek.

"Miss Chamard, sunset's in an hour," Finn said, his voice pitched only for her. She nodded and looked to where Simpson and Wallace manned their keypads, where Major Farrow pored over dispatches.

"Is that big fellow coming for you?"

"William? No. He's with the Guard, miles from here."

"The town's going to be in an uproar again." He straightened, breaking the circle of their familiarity. "Major, I will see Miss Chamard home and be back within the hour."

Hursh raised an eyebrow, then quirked a smile at Finn and nodded toward the door.

Nicolette collected her purse and umbrella. Finn met her at the door with hat and sword and they entered the hallway.

A lieutenant, flushed in the face, barreled toward them. "All officers, Captain. Briefing room. Now." He stuck his head in the door to the communications room and repeated the message to Hursh.

"Damn." Finn took her hand. He rubbed his thumb across her knuckles in that unconscious sensual habit of his. Nicolette drew in a breath and held it. He had no sense of decorum at all, sometimes. No gentleman of Louisiana would ever presume such familiarity. But Finn demolished that barrier of propriety every time he touched her. And she loved that, too.

Hursh strode past them on the way to the briefing. "Sorry, love," he said to her. "Come on, me boy. The General awaits."

"Wallace will take you home." Finn stepped back to the doorway. "Wallace!"

"Finn!" Hursh called from down the hall.

Finn squeezed Nicolette's hand and hurried after the major.

Wallace came to the door. "What?" he called after Finn.

If Finn had been able to take her home, she would have postponed buying the gun to have that half hour with him. But he couldn't, and she needed to buy that gun. She did not want to argue about it nor discuss it with anyone. She would not endanger Lucinda and the children by going to her house, and Cleo and Pierre were still upriver at the farm. She was on her own.

"I believe, Mr. Wallace, the captain means for you to rush any new dispatches directly to the briefing room."

"Right-o," he said.

Nicolette exited the back of the Custom House and walked quickly down the street toward the dusty-windowed gun shop she'd passed a hundred times. She was glad she hadn't told Finn about the chicken blood on her front stoop or the men at her back door. He couldn't stand guard over her every night. It would be impossibly improper, and he had his duties. She would buy this gun, and she would be perfectly safe.

As she approached the shop, her steps faltered. Would the shopkeeper sell her a gun? He would know from her tignon, from her being on the street alone this time of the day, that she was a couleur libre.

She could take off her tignon, but she had no bonnet with her. And if some hard-hearted white man, or woman, saw her uncovering her hair, she'd be called out for violating the law that required the tignon in the first place. She certainly did not want that kind of attention.

She picked up her pace again. She was an actress, wasn't she? She would brazen her way to a gun with sheer force of presence. That, and the shine and jingle of silver coins.

A single lantern glowed inside the shop. Nicolette entered to the tinkling of a bell.

"Mademoiselle," the shrunken, yellow man greeted her. He eyed her from head to toe, assaying the intricacy of her folded headscarf and the quality of her dress, finally lingering on her primly concealed bosom. Nicolette had no doubt he took her for a rich man's placée. She knew from Lucinda's confidences that being a white man's mistress inevitably brought unwelcome advances. Men of a lower sort mistakenly assumed a kept woman's virtue was easier than that of women who were lawfully wedded.

Nicolette smiled at the gunsmith. *"Bonsoir,* monsieur. I wish to buy a gun."

"A pretty thing like you?" He flashed brown teeth at her in a mocking leer. "What you want with a gun?"

As easily as donning a cloak, she wrapped herself in the coquettish persona she assumed on stage. If the ugly little man required her to flirt before he sold her a gun, she'd flirt.

The gunsmith, once she'd assured him with fluttering eyelashes that she was aware of his virile aura, got down to business. He first offered her the smallest Derringer, but she insisted the rats in her courtyard would scoff at such a dainty gun. She wanted a big, powerful weapon.

"How about that one?" she said, pointing to a sixteen inch Colt in the case.

He let her hold it, but he warned her, *"Chère,* that gun weighs near five pounds. She kick you into last week, you try to fire her."

Nicolette was aware guns had a kick. She stretched her arm out and imagined aiming the Colt at an intruder's chest. She could not hold the nine inch barrel steady.

"See? You listen to me, *ma chère.* A Colt Walker, she too much gun for you."

Finally, she settled on a '51 two pound Navy revolver with a five and a half inch barrel. She bought a half box of .44 bullets, assuring the gunsmith she did not require his instruction in firing it. She could load it and she could point it.

Once she was home, Nicolette unwrapped her package and laid the pistol on the parlor table. Lantern light gleamed on the polished walnut grip, on the blue barrel. She gripped her weapon, pointing it at the back window. No man would ever lay a hand on her again without her blowing a hole in his chest.

She loaded the pistol.

Now, let them come. She was ready.

Chapter Twenty-One

"Stonewall Jackson's got them socked in at Harper's Ferry, Deborah Ann." Mr. Presswood rubbed his hands together in satisfaction. "By nightfall, I wager they'll have taken it away from the damned Yanks."

Dutifully, Deborah Ann got out the Virginia map and let Father show her exactly where Harper's Ferry was and explain to her why it was strategically important. She understood, but she simply couldn't bring herself to celebrate, or bemoan, every battle of the entire damned war.

She'd had no word from Marcel in weeks. Not a word. The war had not yet come to the Lafourche country where he played soldier up and down the bayou. Why on earth could he not find a moment to write his wife? He had no regard for how she suffered, waiting, waiting, waiting. Not just for Marcel, but for some nameless something. Something, somewhere, was going to happen to her. It was going to change everything. And it was going to be dreadful.

She'd cut short her stay at Evermore. She couldn't sleep there, not after she saw how the darkies had changed. During the long moonless nights, a candle burning at her bedside, she imagined a horde of blacks climbing in her window, setting fire to the house, committing every kind of atrocity against her. And her blameless. She'd never mistreated a black, not in her entire life.

When she boarded the *Rachel* at the dock that last morning at Evermore, the house slaves again lined up to see her off. Now she could see behind the smiling masks. The lips might curve, but there was no warmth in those black eyes. Not even Clementine had cared that she was leaving, not really.

Father didn't know yet. When she'd arrived home, she reported the numbers of runaways and Mr. Thompson's accounts about the crops. But not what she'd seen in those cold eyes. Even if the South won this hateful war, Evermore could not be the same place, not ever again. Not for her, not for any of them.

She had thought her nerves would settle once she returned to New Orleans, but she was still nervous. Something was wrong with her female parts. She'd had two monthlies in five weeks. Each time, her moods had been mercurial, erratic, irrational. Then she'd feel convalescent, weak and fragile, until the next letting. When the weather broke, she told herself, she'd feel better.

Until then she endured the heat, endured this vague dread of what was to come. She pushed the food around on her plate, perused the Picayune without taking in the words, and counted the hours through the long days, waiting.

After breakfast, Father said, "Come out with me this morning, Deborah Ann."

She pushed a stray lock of hair from her face. "I think not, Father."

Father stepped across the room and stood in the light from the window, shadowing her embroidery hoop.

"Did something happen to upset you at the homeplace, Deborah Ann? Mr. Thompson, the Nigras?"

She shook her head and summoned a smile for him.

"Some river boat ruffian frighten you, insult you?"

"Not at all, Father. It was a perfectly uneventful trip, Jebediah at my side every moment, as I promised."

"Nevertheless, I should like you to come out. You can open your prettiest parasol and ride along with me to the Mint. You like seeing the ships on the river. And afterwards, I'll buy you dinner at The Seasons. How's that?"

Deborah Ann took no care with her toilet. She put on an old straw bonnet, not bothering with the stray hair that escaped from the sides. Mammy thrust the new parasol at her lest she come home with a face full of freckles.

The hired carriage rolled through the pleasant streets of the American sector where the houses were large, the gardens lush, and the war might be a world away. The closer they came to the Union hub on Canal Street, the more the war intruded. Soldiers everywhere. Defensive works abandoned by the Confederates when Admiral Farragut took New Orleans. And Negroes. There must be thousands of them in the city.

Deborah Ann watched them. Negroes on the sidewalk, crossing the street, even on mules. They didn't smile. They didn't bob their heads in passing. Two Negresses dared look her right in the eye.

At her father's side in the carriage, she felt safe enough. It was uncertainty that weighed her down. Nothing was as it should be. No husband. No letters. And now the whole world seemed to be shifting.

Father called her attention to the wharves roiling with people as far down the levee as she could see. There was the famous ironclad the Yankees were so proud of, a graceless, gray hulk of a boat. Flags and pennants waved in the wind. Deborah Ann tightened her grip on the parasol so it wouldn't blow out of her hand. It was, she supposed, a splendid day. But something was coming, something was going to happen to her. She could feel the thump of dread beating down on her.

The Mint, an imposing white structure at the corner of Esplanade and Levee, swarmed with men in the hated blue uniform. They might well be insects, mere bugs, like termites or ants or wasps the way they flitted in and out of their hive. They were the cause of all this. They were the reason the darkies seethed with discontent, the reason old kindnesses were now met with sullen, resentful eyes.

"Here we are, Deborah Ann," Father said, extending a hand to help her from the carriage.

"I shall wait here, Father. Have the driver move us under that chinaberry tree, and I shall be perfectly comfortable until you return."

Father hesitated. He looked around. Federal officers and Southern gentlemen peppered the scene. She would be safe, that was apparent. "Very well. I shall be perhaps an hour, maybe less."

She watched him walk into the building. His stride was less certain, less vigorous, than it had been. The war took its due even from old men.

Under the china tree, it was cool enough. A patch of purple asters bloomed in a garden nearby, and someone's red hibiscus drooped with blooms. The tension in her neck eased as she gazed into the lace of the overhanging leaves.

Women passed among the uniforms, laden with shopping bags they'd filled at the French Market around the corner. In this part of town, many of them were free coloreds, *colour libre* they called themselves, speaking an abysmal French. Here came one with a tignon, as if intricate folds could make up for wearing a mere head rag instead of a proper bonnet.

In idleness, Deborah Ann watched the high-yellow woman stride toward her, a sleeping child on her shoulder, a shopping bag in the other hand. Trailing along beside her was another child. They were breeders, these Negroes, there was no question of that.

In Deborah Ann's despondency, recognition came gradually. When she fully realized who the woman was, she and the children were within mere feet of the carriage. Deborah Ann's breathing ceased. Her entire awareness was focused on the child walking at his mother's side.

Dark silky hair with the suggestion of curl, brown eyes the color of tea. The brow, the tilt of the head. Marcel's child.

The world contracted to a circle around the elegant placée from the hat shop. Marcel had two children with this woman. Two sons.

A cold sweat broke out all over her body. A thunderous buzzing filled her ears. She hardly knew what she did, dismounting from the carriage. With shaky steps, she followed the woman and children as they weaved through the soldiers and businessmen.

The placée turned onto Elysian Fields. There were fewer people on this street, and this was not a neighborhood people like Deborah Ann frequented. She hung back. The little boy kicked at a paving shell, then ran after it and kicked it again, leaving his mother behind.

A mule-pulled wagon rattled toward them. "Charles Armand," the placée called after the child. "Watch the wagon."

Deborah Ann had thought she might name her own child Charles, after her Grandfather Presswood. This child was Charles. Marcel's boy, Charles Armand.

The woman unlatched a gate and went into the side passageway leading to the back of her home. Typically, the house had three doors across the front, but its roof was higher than most. Disconnected thoughts flitted through Deborah Ann's head. Perhaps it had an attic large enough to stand in. Perhaps a banana tree grew in the courtyard.

She stood on the corner, staring, her parasol tilted so that the sun shone full on her face. It was a mere creole cottage. Marcel hadn't bought the woman a proper house, nothing like what he would build for her when she asked him for her own home in the new district, away from all these colored peoples.

Only as she began to turn away did the most salient detail penetrate her senses. A vigorous vine trailed across the doorways, shading and scenting the front of the cottage. Sweet jasmine. Deborah Ann's knees gave way and she swooned in a heap of hoops and petticoats.

When she opened her eyes, she was on the sidewalk, the woman bending over her.

"Come inside out of the sun, mademoiselle," the woman said. "Let me get you some barley water."

The placée's face was smooth as cream, only a hint of a darker tone in her complexion. Her eyes were almond shaped and deep brown, her nose narrow, her lips full.

The little boy stood beside his mother, his hand on her shoulder. Charles Armand. Riveted, Deborah Ann stared at the boy, his eyes big and concerned. Marcel's child.

"Mademoiselle?"

Deborah Ann shifted her gaze to the boy's mother. This woman had no right to bear her husband a son. No right to produce a child whose eyes and chin were the image of her husband's. Hatred flamed through Deborah Ann, conflagrating the very air around her.

The placée recoiled as if she could actually feel the heat on her skin.

"Maman?"

Deborah Ann saw understanding awaken in the woman's dark eyes.

She shrank away. "You're the one," the woman whispered.

Deborah Ann, her jaw clenched, her heart hard as stone, impaled her rival with a malignant eye. "I am his *wife*."

The woman stood up and backed away, the boy clinging to her skirt.

"Mrs. Chamard?" A soldier, a Yankee, pounded up the road toward her. "Your father's worried sick about you, ma'am."

He bent over and as easily as if she were a child, picked her up from the ground. "I'll get you back to the carriage, ma'am. Don't fret."

Deborah Ann might have been a rag doll, unresisting in the man's arms. Whether he lifted her or dragged her, he simply had no importance. Her eyes were on Charles Armand. Marcel's first child should have been hers.

Mr. Presswood raced home with Deborah Ann. Her skin was clammy and her gaze vacant. Scared him half to death, she did. Immediately on reaching home, he had Deborah Ann put to bed.

While Mammy undressed her and bathed her face and hands, Mr. Presswood sent for Dr. Braun. After closeting himself with Deborah Ann for a quarter of an hour, the doctor joined Mr. Presswood in the study.

"Is she ... with child?" Mr. Presswood had asked.

Dr. Braun shook his gray head. "Apparently not, Lionel. She seems a little run down. Beefsteak and eggs will take care of that. But I agree with your earlier assessment. She is not quite herself. Not our bright-eyed girl."

Mr. Presswood handed the doctor a glass of brandy. "The war, I suppose. It wears on us all."

"She might benefit from a course of laudanum. For a day or two only."

"No!" Mr. Presswood set his glass down so hard the brandy sloshed onto the table.

"She is not Malvina, Lionel. She has not her mother's proclivity for melancholy."

"No. I cannot risk it. And you don't know how she's been, Gustav. Irritable. Weepy." Mr. Presswood wiped his mouth with a trembling hand. "I console myself she is more my daughter than her mother's. But she is a woman."

Dr. Braun finished his brandy. "She's a strong girl, old friend. I shouldn't worry. If she's not up and stirring by tomorrow noon time, I'll be surprised."

Deborah Ann was not up and stirring by noontime the next day, nor the next. She didn't complain of headache or any other kind of discomfort. She simply preferred to lie in the bed. She didn't read. She didn't embroider. She would eat only a little of the treats Mammy tempted her with.

Mr. Presswood stopped Mammy in the hallway outside Deborah Ann's door. "What do you think, Mammy?"

"Child acts like she had the life punched out of her, don't she? But she not telling me nothing, neither, Mr. Presswood."

Mr. Presswood sat down to write his son-in-law. With his contacts, he should be able to get a message through to the

Lafourche. True, there was risk involved, but he daily risked everything he had in his surreptitious dealings. Marcel, too, would be at risk if he came to Deborah Ann's side, but his wife needed him.

Chapter Twenty-Two

Captain McKee grabbed a biscuit and a rasher of bacon off his landlady's table and headed out the door. Finn had hollered hallelujah when Major Farrow decided he didn't need to spend every minute baby-sitting the Signal boys in camp. "That's what sergeants are for," Hursh had said, and assigned Finn to the same boarding house he stayed in. Better bed, better bacon, better biscuits.

His horse stabled a block over, Finn strode the quarter mile to headquarters. The night before, he had lingered at the Custom House till ten waiting for news from Virginia, but there'd been no more mail boats. He took the stairs three at a time, thinking Miss Chamard wouldn't be in this early. He was wrong. There she sat, composed, prettier even than yesterday, tapping a pencil on the desk.

"Miss Chamard!"

"Good morning, Captain."

He grabbed a chair and moved close enough to smell the flowery stuff she wore. He wanted to scoop her up and rain kisses over her face, but he wasn't raised in a barn. He sat across from her, the desk between them.

"You're here early, Mademoiselle." He loved the way mademoiselle rolled off his tongue. It suited her, too, exotic, foreign. French. Or French Creole. He hadn't worked all that out yet.

A smile touched her lips and lit her eyes, those mystery eyes, gray and soft and penetrating. "As are you, Captain."

Finn glanced at the quiet telegraph keys. "No news?"

"Nothing."

"Not even a train update?"

"Mr. Wallace is down the hall. He said not a single message all night."

Finn grunted in disgust. "The line's cut somewhere. Damned Rebs."

Nicolette smiled broadly. "Future generations will no doubt think Damned Rebs to be one word, Captain. I never hear one without the other."

"Same with Damned Yanks," Finn countered. He eyed her curiously.

"What is it, Captain?"

"I have a cousin, Colin. Joined the Confederacy. I wondered if you have family on both sides?"

Hell, he'd made her uncomfortable. He could see her swallowing, and she'd turned her head from him. Him and his damned mouth.

"I beg your pardon. I shouldn't have asked."

She raised her head and leveled her gaze on him. She was going to forgive him, again.

"It is a natural question, Captain. I have three brothers. Two are now in New York, one a journalist writing for the abolitionist cause, the other a physician. My eldest brother, however, does indeed wear Confederate gray."

"A split family. It breaks everybody's heart."

"Yes, sir. It does."

"I have only sisters, I think I told you," Finn said. He stroked his moustache. "Though my cousin Colin is like a brother."

Nicolette nodded, her gaze on him.

He drew a breath. "You'd like my sisters. Especially Mags, the middle one. She loves music like you do. Her piano playing may be a little raggedy, but she's enthusiastic, and she sings loud."

That earned him a laugh. He loved to make her laugh.

"Do you sing, Captain?"

"No, ma'am, and be glad of it."

Wallace barged in, ruining the moment. "Morning, Captain. Miss Chamard."

Finn gave her a speculative look. "Miss Chamard, have you had your coffee this morning?"

"I have not, as a matter of fact."

"Then may I invite you to the coffee house up the street? We can do nothing here, and I hear Monsieur Hebert makes the best brew in the Quarter."

"Monsieur Hebert still has real coffee?"

"That is the rumor."

Nicolette inclined her head. "Then I accept."

"Mr. Wallace, you have the con, as our naval friends say."

"If Monsieur Hebert has beignets, Mr. Wallace, I shall bring you one."

On the street, the sun was full up and the city's bustle was well under way. Finn tucked Nicolette's hand under his arm. It was nice, having her close, matching her stride to his. They didn't talk much on the street. That was nice too.

Listen to me, he thought to himself. I'm on air with her by my side, and I'm calling it "nice."

Finn couldn't imagine one of his sisters accompanying a man to the coffee shop without a chaperone. Unheard of. But here was Miss Chamard, propriety itself, and she dared it. He admired the hell out of her for it. Women here had such confidence, such freedom to be out with a man in public and no maiden aunt in tow every minute of the live long day.

If she'd had a chaperone, he'd never have been able to kiss her at the gumbo shop. He meant to find another chance to kiss her before they had to go back.

As they approached Monsieur Hebert's small shop, the intoxicating aroma of roasting coffee beans drew them in. Finn breathed deeply. No parched corn and hickory nuts steeped in tepid water for him this morning.

"*Bonjour*, Jean," Nicolette called as they entered the shop. As far as Finn could tell, Nicolette knew every man, woman, and child in the Vieux Carré. Probably every horse and dog, too.

"*Ah, ma belle!* Come in, come in." Monsieur Hebert, a small man with a halo of white hair, kissed her hands, declared his joy at seeing her, and finally sat them at a cozy table in the corner.

"Is there no place in New Orleans I can take you that you are not acquainted with, Mademoiselle?" Finn complained.

She smiled at his sulky tone. "I don't believe so, Captain."

Finn glanced around the room. Other patrons chatted and read newspapers over their coffee, much like folks did in the Boston cafés. But at home, the coffeehouses leaned toward ashtrays laden with cigar stubs, newspapers strewn about on spotty pine table tops. Here, each marble-topped table boasted a rosebud in a glass. Lacy white curtains at the front window filtered the morning sun. With a squint, Finn deciphered the pattern in the green wallpaper above the wainscoting: leering satyrs pursuing scantily-clad nymphs. No, New Orleans certainly was not Boston.

Finn sighed noisily in contentment. She smiled at him as though he'd said something witty. He felt his heart must be alight in the depths of his chest when she smiled at him like that. He looked away, trying not to show the entire café what she did to him.

He took a sip of rich black coffee, scalding hot, just the way he liked it.

"Strong enough to bend your spoon?" she asked.

"Perfect."

The beignets he left for her and Wallace, but Finn delighted in the dusting of powdered sugar on Nicolette's upper lip. Maybe it'd still be there when he found that quiet place on the way back to headquarters.

"So you have three brothers." He needed to know more about her. His parents would expect a full account of a woman's family if he meant to take her home.

"Actually, one brother, two half-brothers."

"Ah," he said. "Then your father?" he guessed. "Your father, or your mother, was widowed?"

For a moment, it seemed she would not answer him. Had he stumbled again? Maybe her loss was recent.

She wiped her mouth with her handkerchief, then contemplated her hands resting in her lap. At last she said, "My father is a cane planter."

"Then your mother — "

Miss Chamard raised her hand to interrupt him. "Captain McKee, I must explain something to you. Something I believe you have misunderstood about me." She raised her head in a resolute fashion. At last someone was going to explain New Orleans society to him.

"My father is a cane planter. Creole, you may have guessed. We speak French at home, and I know my English is sadly accented. But my mother, Captain, is not — "

She looked at him strangely, her gray eyes darker now.

"Yes, Miss Chamard? She is not French?"

"I ... I am the daughter, you see, of a woman who — "

Monsieur Hebert interrupted, the coffee pot in his hand. "Mademoiselle Nicolette is the daughter of the most wonderful chanteuse in all of New Orleans!" He put a hand on Nicolette's shoulder and squeezed it slightly.

Nicolette shook her head. "No, Jean. He needs to — "

"Do you not agree, Captain, that our French Creoles are the most beautiful women in New Orleans?"

She flushed so red that her eyes teared. Finn had remarked her contradictions before, confident one moment, and vulnerable the next. When she was like this, he wanted to take her in his arms, kiss away whatever fear it was rising in her.

"Mademoiselle Chamard is the most beautiful woman I have ever known," Finn said, putting his heart behind the words.

"*Ma belle Nicolette*, she is beautiful on the inside as well as the outside. And that is all a man needs to know of a woman, I think. Am I right, Monsieur Yankee *Capitaine*?"

Monsieur Hebert leaned over and kissed Miss Chamard's forehead. She bit her lip, apparently fighting tears.

What had set her off? Her mother being a singer? Finn had already accepted that Miss Chamard herself was an entertainer. What did it matter ?

"Captain, truly, I must — "

Mr. Simpson burst into the shop. Wide eyed, he spotted Finn and breathlessly strode through the tables and coffee drinkers. "You got to come on back, Captain. Things is happening."

"The lines are up?" Finn said, rising.

"No, but a mail ship docked twenty minutes ago. There's news from Virginia."

Conversation stopped as every ear in the café turned. Finn raised a cautioning finger for Simpson to hold his tongue and tossed back the rest of his coffee. Nicolette wrapped the remaining beignets in her handkerchief. They left the coffee shop in a whirlwind of curious glances.

The news: the Confederates had renewed the attack on Harper's Ferry at 6:30 a.m. the second day, pushing against the Union breastworks while another Southern unit flanked the Federal right. Col. Miles' men had pushed back, and the Confederates had retreated with heavy losses. Day two to the Union Army.

Feeling optimistic, Finn and his team attended to other messages. Mid-morning, General Butler bustled into the telegraph room, his adjutant trailing behind him.

"No more news from Virginia?" he demanded.

Finn bit back a retort. He couldn't conjure up packet ships no matter how imperiously Butler demanded them.

"No, sir. Not yet."

"Let's hope Miles' counterattack has discouraged the Rebs and they'll back off. But Dixon Miles was an incompetent ass when I knew him ten years ago, and no doubt he's an incompetent ass now."

Butler seemed to realize he had spoken indelicately. He bowed his head to Nicolette. "Excuse me, my dear. I don't believe we've met. Captain?"

"Sir, may I introduce you to Mademoiselle Nicolette Chamard?"

Nicolette had seen the general many times, from a distance. This was the first time she'd been in the same room with him. It was true, what they said. General Butler was indeed cross-eyed.

Nicolette stood and offered her hand. She thought General Butler cast a keen look at her face, though it was difficult to tell the way his eyes strayed from the straight line.

"Of course. Mademoiselle Chamard." The general executed a gallant bow over her hand. "I had the pleasure of hearing you sing last May. At the Silver ... ."

"The Silver Spoon, General," Nicolette said. The general's forehead was an enormous bare dome, the hair hanging dark and scanty on the sides of his head. On the whole he was not an attractive figure, his belly jutting far beyond his boots. But he had bearing, and he exuded confidence. And arrogance. He had not earned the nickname Beast Butler by being charming.

"Exactly. Lovely voice, Mademoiselle, and quite the comic."

Nicolette performed an abbreviated curtsey. "Thank you, sir."

The general eyed her speculatively. "Mrs. Butler and I are having an entertainment at the end of the month. Perhaps you would consent to sing for us, Mademoiselle? I do apologize for the lateness of the invitation. I claim the vicissitudes of war for the *faux pas*."

Nicolette inclined her head in acceptance. "It would be an honor, General."

"Wonderful. Now, McKee, I'm putting her in your hands. Getting her to the party, seeing her home, and so on. Take care of it, Captain. And bring me the news from Harper's Ferry the moment it comes in."

The general and the adjutant bustled out of the room. Nicolette turned to Captain McKee and raised her eyebrows.

The captain seemed very pleased, grinning at her. "It seems I have the onerous duty of escorting you to and from the soirée, Miss Chamard."

Nicolette loved the way he teased, so different from the flowery formality she was familiar with. A Southern gentlemen would have expended great effort to assure her that the honor of escorting her would be all his etcetera etcetera. Forgetting Mr. Wallace and Simpson had nothing better to do for the moment than to watch her and the captain make fools of themselves, she locked eyes with him, the silly grin on her face a match for his.

Hursh Farrow stuck his head in the door. "Finn! Need you downstairs."

Their moment was over. The captain followed the major out. Nicolette sank into her chair. She was going to sing for the Union general! Of course, many of the people of New Orleans would be incensed at her accepting an invitation from Beast Butler. But she had already cast her lot with the occupiers. If society's matrons ostracized her from their gatherings in the coming season, so be it.

As for explaining to Finn that she was a colored woman ... If Monsieur Hebert hadn't interrupted, it'd be over. He would have stared at her, his ready smile gone, his brown eyes suddenly curtained behind courtesy. She couldn't have borne it.

She closed her eyes and pressed her fingers to her mouth. What if she didn't tell him, ever? This was just a passing war-time interlude for him. He'd be leaving with Wetzle's unit soon, and she'd never see him again. Why couldn't she enjoy him until them? Enjoy the lie?

Two days later, they got the final news. On September 15, after four days of battle, the Federals had raised the white flag of surrender over Harper's Ferry.

The defeat was total. Confederate soldiers took possession of 12,419 Northern officers and soldiers, 13,000 small arms, and 73 artillery pieces. Nicolette shook her head. These were not small losses. When were the Union armies going to find their backbone? Why could Lincoln not find a worthy general?

Jubilation flooded the town. Yet another Confederate conquest! Persuaded that total victory was at hand, the Confederate sympathizers, most of the citizenry, would be eager to punish people like her, who had chosen the losing side.

Finn had been called away long before the work day was over, or he'd have not allowed her to leave headquarters alone, nor would Simpson or Wallace, but they were occupied. Feeling confident with the pistol in her shopping bag, she slipped out without saying goodbye.

At Jackson Square, she skirted a crowd gathered around a mustachioed man pontificating with all the fervor of a true believer. Oh God. The speaker — he was the man who'd glared at her with such venom when Finn took her to see the *Essex*. The man's rousing voice carried over the heads of the rabble who were already drunk and shouting out obscenities against Union sympathizers.

The orator was naming names!

"Josiah Everwood! Sold a hundred beeves to fill the Union soldiers' bellies!" The crowd booed. "Ebenezer Rivers! Brought in two dozen horses and four dozen mules from Feliciana and made a king's profit selling to the Union!"

"String him up!"

"Burn the bastard out!"

Nicolette's heart thudded in her chest. She kept her head bent and pushed through the fringe of the mob.

"Nicolette Chamard!"

Nicolette's breath seized in her chest. She forced her feet to keep moving. They don't see her. *Keep moving. Don't run.*

"A Yankee whore! Every single day, Nicolette Chamard slithers into the Custom House to service Beast Butler himself!"

"Strip her and slice her!"

"Whores and witches, throw 'em in the river!"

Nicolette made it to the corner and turned onto Dumaine. Out of sight of the throng drunk on hate and spite, she ran, her petticoats a white spume at the edge of her dark hem, heedless of staring, gaping faces, panic licking at her heels.

At Royal, she veered around the corner, ran to Esplanade, and crossed into the quieter Faubourg Marigny. Her lungs burning, her chest heaving, she slowed her steps, clearing her head.

She passed a tavern where Confederate sympathizers laughed and drank and shouted insults to the Union occupiers. Half this part of town would be roaring drunk in another hour, half of them would have roused themselves into mindless fury.

Nicolette slipped into her house and quickly barred the front door. She judged she had a half hour of daylight to prepare.

Working quickly, an eye on the sinking sun, she retrieved several empty wine bottles from the rubbish box and smashed them against the paving stones behind the house. No one could enter the courtyard without her hearing the crunch of glass.

Her pulse was up. Her heart banged against her ribs. She wished she had a dog. Papa had offered her a shepherd last winter, but she'd declined. She'd still been angry with him for the way he dismissed her opinions, and thereby dismissed her. Papa doted on her, but he showed no respect for her at all. So she had not accepted his dog. In fact, she had not touched the allowance he sent her quarterly either, not since he had told her she was "a little fool" to hope the Union won the war.

Nicolette looked around the courtyard. She pulled Maman's prize cactus under the window. In the dark, it could give an intruder a nasty sting.

One more thing. She smashed another two bottles and gathered the shards in her skirt. Inside, she scattered the broken glass on the window sills.

She locked all the doors downstairs, fastened all the shutters and closed all the windows. She moved the punched-tin pie safe in front of the window nearest the back door.

The gun was already loaded.

Nicolette left the lamps unlit. She ate a cold meat pie and drank a glass of wine. Then she sat in the dark and waited.

With night fall, the celebrations at the tavern in the next block grew louder, drunken sots firing guns into the air. Nicolette wondered if Captain McKee would be one of the officers sent to keep order in the town. He might be only a street or two away from her right now.

She dozed in her chair, the pistol in her lap, the grip loose in her hand. A single crunch of broken glass woke her.

She tiptoed to the back of the house and put her ear to the crack at the door jamb. Nothing. Not a sound. But they were out there.

What did they want? To scare her? They'd succeeded admirably. But they hadn't scared her enough to make her cease going to the Custom House. They hadn't intimidated her into abandoning her principles.

What else would they do? Beat her? Steal her away and sell her? Kill her?

She stood in the darkest shadow, the pistol in both hands, her body tense, her ears alert for every sound. No matter that her pulse raced, that her lungs refused to draw air. She was armed, and she was determined. If someone, even three or four men, tried to get into this house, she would shoot at least one of them. Of that she was certain.

The house remained silent. No footsteps in the courtyard, none at the front steps on Pauger Street. Her lungs pulled in air. She eased her finger off the trigger.

Some wayward current of air, some suggestion of presence drew her eyes toward the staircase where moonlight filtered down from her open bedroom door.

A figure stood at the top of the stairs, silhouetted by the moonlight. A second man moved behind him.

They'd entered from the upstairs balcony. She hadn't heard a thing.

The first man began to descend without a whisper of sound.

From the shadows, she raised the gun, both hands around the butt, extended her arms, and fired.

The blaze from the muzzle blinded her. The kick of the .44 knocked her back, her arms high in the air. She fell to her knees, pointed the barrel, and fired again. And again and again.

One of the men screamed. She'd hit him!

The other one yelled, "Run, you fool!"

She heard them scrambling through her bedroom, heard their panicked steps on the balcony. She imagined a stream of scarlet blood trailing across her bedroom floor and out to the balcony, smearing the balustrade, dripping onto the street below.

She gulped for air, her trembling hands gripping the pistol. She'd done it. She'd defended herself.

Not Adam Johnston, not some degenerate hired thug, no one would ever hurt her again. Fear gave way to euphoria. She swallowed the tears in her throat and wiped her face on her sleeve.

She lit a lantern. With sweaty, unsteady fingers, she struggled to reload the pistol. She shook from her shoulders to her hands, but she felt tall and strong.

This time, despite her fear, she had acted.

If she had understood what she was capable of, had known she could act and not just endure, she would not have succumbed to Adam's fists with only her arms ineffectively raised to shield herself.

She remembered for the ten thousandth time Adam grabbing her by the hair, pounding her face and shoulders. Now? Even without a pistol, she would fight. She would bite, kick, scratch, scream. Now, she knew to act.

She picked the wine bottle up from her supper and raised it to her lips. Never had wine tasted so sweet. The Union had lost at Harper's Ferry, but she claimed her own victory tonight, here, in this house.

Chapter Twenty-Three

Finn absently dodged a reeking drunk sleeping it off on the sidewalk, his mind on what he could say to Nicolette. Hursh Farrow and he were to take their Signal unit north to Donaldsonville on the twenty-first, the day after General Butler's soiree.

He had to speak to her before he left New Orleans.

He couldn't ask her to wait for him. He might end up disfigured, and maybe she wouldn't want him all cut up. Or he might get killed, and she'd have wasted opportunities while he was gone.

With a house full of sisters at home, Finn knew the importance of a girl's having opportunities. Worse thing in the world, for a girl to be an old maid. He'd seen headstones carved with a woman's name, her birth and death dates, and arched above all that, the dreaded words Never Married. As if her time on this earth had had no significance at all other than her failure to find a husband.

Marriage had been something Finn would do sometime, some day. He had been in no hurry. Perhaps when he was thirty or thirty-five. Miss Chamard had changed his mind about that. He had always sneered at that ridiculous fabled experience of being "struck" that his sisters talked about, their heads filled with romantic notions from reading novels. But the first time he'd seen Nicolette Chamard at the Silver Spoon, he'd been struck. In the months since then, his feelings had deepened. He admired her, he desired her. Hell, he even liked her.

Though he had no right to bind Nicolette to him, not now with the war heating up, he had to say something. To at least tell her his intentions. It would be up to her whether she waited for him to come back for her.

He'd tell her at supper, before the performance. With flowers. Hell, flowers were not enough.

His mother probably had a box of pins and brooches and rings he could choose from, but he had nothing here. A brooch, he decided, would be just the thing. Not so promissory as to lock her in if he should be maimed, but a claim on her nonetheless. And that's what he wanted, to stake his claim on her.

He had to see the Signal boys were ready to travel, their equipment, themselves, the wagons, the mules, the horses, the provisions. Somehow, though, he would get to the shops and find something beautiful to give her tomorrow night.

He reached the Custom House and took the steps in doubles as usual, eager to see her. As he approached the telegraph room, he heard General Butler pontificating.

"A noxious symbol," the general was saying in his high-pitched voice. "I believe you make a fine gesture in response to Mr. Lincoln's Emancipation Proclamation, Mademoiselle."

The general's back blocked Finn's view of Miss Chamard while he removed his sword and placed it on his desk. Then the general shifted and Finn could see her. Her hair was uncovered, thick, lustrous dark hair parted in the middle and pulled into a mass at the back of her neck. He'd never seen her without that towering tignon on her head. She was even more beautiful like this, the morning sun catching those dark waves.

General Butler seemed to recall he was a busy man and strode out. Miss Chamard rotated her chair toward him.

"Good morning, Captain."

Finn stepped close and spoke softly, wishing Simpson and Wallace were deaf. "You've uncovered your hair. It's ... you look enchanting."

She flushed. He loved it when she looked haughty and cocksure, a hint of mischief in her eye, the way she looked when she teased him. He loved it even more when she let him glimpse her truer self, a woman unguarded.

He recalled his manners. One didn't stare at a woman and expect to retain his self-respect. "Miss Chamard, will you dine with me before the General's entertainment tomorrow night?"

She met his eyes, smiling. "I would be delighted, sir."

"I'll be occupied today and tomorrow, so I won't see you until then. I'll pick you up at six o'clock?"

He bent and very properly delivered the merest touch of his lips to her hand. Ahh, he thought. She'd done it again. That sudden little intake of breath when he rubbed his thumb between her knuckles.

Finn retrieved his sword and descended the stairs like a school boy flush from his first kiss.

At the quartermaster's store he argued and cajoled an extra wagon load of provisions for his men. At the corrals, he had his mules and horses shod and ready to march. Finally he saw that the signal flags had at last been mended, even the bullet holes from the taking of New Orleans back in May.

At the end of a long and productive day, Finn saw to his own weapon. Cleaning and oiling the gun reminded him that a bullet, whether stray or aimed directly at him, could end his mortal days. In which case, Miss Chamard, Nicolette, would be free to wed another man. What he wanted to spare her was any obligation to a diminished, maimed shell of a man. Head wounds were the worst. There was Tommy Blagoe, caught a piece of shrapnel in his brain when they stormed past Fort Jackson. A drooling half-man, now. *God spare me that*, he prayed. Or what if he lost a leg, or an arm. She might find him disgusting.

It was right not to make it an official engagement. He'd just give her his promise that if he was still whole, he'd be coming back for her.

During the next day, Finn grabbed a half hour to find Nicolette something pretty, something to show her he was serious. In Hyde and Goodrich on Canal, he looked over dozens of lockets, brooches, and pendants and was about to throw up his hands in bewilderment when he spied the perfect piece.

"The cross?" he asked the salesgirl.

She removed a Maltese cross on a black chain from the cabinet and placed it on a velvet cloth for him to examine more closely. "These are particularly fine deepest-red garnets, as you see. Each stone is backed with a tiny sheet of foil so as to enhance its inner glow."

Finn blinked when she told him how much the pendant cost, but hang it, Nicolette would have it the rest of her life, whether he lived through the war or not.

"I'll take it," he said.

He carried the black velvet box in his inner breast pocket throughout the rest of the day, conscious of its weight and its import as he encouraged his lieutenants and inventoried ammo and sacks of beans.

At five o-clock, he reported to the barber to be shaved and bathed. Clad in polished boots and his best uniform coat, he patted the breast pocket where the garnet cross rested and set out for the most important night of his life.

When Nicolette opened the door to his knock, he forgot to breathe. All these months, she'd worn prim day-gowns to the Custom House, only her hands and her face and neck exposed. Now her shoulders were bare right down to the top of her bosom and his breath came back to him in a great inhalation. He forced himself to raise his eyes. Her hair cascaded in glossy ringlets over her ears. And then there was her perfume. He leaned in close, inhaling the scent of her skin. Intoxicating. Gingery.

Pretty compliments were beyond him. He pushed her inside and closed the door behind him, never taking his eyes off her. He advanced a step. She backed up a step. And then she grinned, playing with him. He caught her in his arms and kissed her till he felt her body soften against him. Some day he wouldn't have to stop, he'd push the dress aside, kiss her shoulders. And more. But she wasn't his yet.

He stepped back. "Miss Chamard," he said, and offered her his arm.

Once he had her settled in the cab across from him, his knees brushing against the her deep blue gown, Nicolette attempted to amuse him with the gossip at headquarters.

Finn couldn't take his gaze from her. In an hour, he would give her the garnet cross. In an hour, they would be all but engaged to be married.

"You're distracted this evening, Captain," she said.

The carriage rattled over the stones on Rampart. Already they were turning on to Canal Street. They would soon be at the St. Charles. The hotel would be aswarm with people gathering for General Butler's evening. It'd be crowded and noisy.

He wanted to speak to her now, while they were alone.

Finn leaned forward and took her hands in his. He wished she were bare handed, wished he could feel the warmth of her skin under his fingers.

"Miss Chamard." He looked into her gray eyes, bright in the shadows of the carriage. He should have rehearsed what he would say. If he'd just had time to think the last few days, he could have prepared a proper declaration of his feelings. "Perhaps you have discerned you possess my highest regard," he began. No. That was wrong. She'd think he was a formal, priggish fool.

Her face revealed nothing. She didn't speak. But when he rubbed his thumb across her palm, she closed her hand around his fingers.

"The war has caught up with us. It would be callous of me to extract a promise from you when no man can foresee his fate. But I should like to make you a promise, Nicolette. "

Mary Mother of God. Could he be about to propose to her? She withdrew her hands and held them clasped in front of her breast.

"When the war is over, if am still whole, I will come for you."

Her throat filling with tears, she pressed her hand to her mouth.

"I will ask you to be my wife."

With all her heart, she wanted to be with Finnian McKee. But deep down, in spite of her light skin, she was a Negress, the daughter of a former slave. She would not pretend otherwise. He could never take her home to his family, present her to his mother and his sisters as if she were a white woman.

The carriage slowed, joining the queue in front of the St. Charles. She should have told him before now.

He reached into his pocket and produced a black velvet box. He opened it. Deep red stones caught the long rays of the evening sun. He held the cross up by the chain and presented it to Nicolette.

"I ask for no commitment from you, but I offer my own, with all my heart. Will you do me the honor of wearing my necklace while I am gone?"

Nicolette longed to take the garnet pendant and hold it tight, to never let it out of her hand. But Finn McKee was innocent, untouched by the poison of Louisiana. He didn't understand. No matter that she yearned to hold his face in her palms, to kiss those loving eyes, she shook her head, her eyes brimming.

The captain's body pulled upright as if he were on a string. His brow creased, bewilderment painting his features.

"I cannot," she whispered.

"Cannot?"

She couldn't bear it. She wanted to kiss the puzzlement away, tell him she loved him, anything but see his brown eyes drowning in hurt.

She pushed the door open and nearly fell as she dragged her full skirt out of the carriage. She ran from him. Ran from having to see the disgust in his eyes if she told him the truth. He would look at her like she was some dirty thing if he knew who she really was, and her heart would never mend.

She hurried into the side entrance of the St. Charles, through the familiar back corridors to the room behind the stage. She would perform her piece, then she would go home, close the shutters, and grieve alone in the dark.

The grand room of the St. Charles was filled with chairs lined up in front of the small stage. General Butler and a host of dignitaries sat in the front rows, those New Orleans luminaries who had chosen to cooperate with the Occupation, men like Lionel Presswood, Joshua Engle, and Everett Collins.

His chest feeling strangely hollow, Finn took the seat Major Farrow had saved for him. The gas lights dimmed. The buzzing voices quieted. The evening began.

General Butler gave his speech of welcome, but Finn didn't hear a word. He might have been knocked in the head with a club for all he was able to attend. What could she have meant? She cannot?

A stout gentleman in a black frock coat took the stage and commenced a recitation of Edgar Allan Poe's "The Raven." Briefly, Finn was diverted from his own thoughts, for with each iteration of "Nevermore," Hursh Farrow and perhaps half the audience murmured the famous line along with the orator.

Various performers took the stage, read their poems, sang their songs, and took their bows. Finn saw only a distant pantomime, the voices thin and indistinct. He'd been so sure of her, sure she returned his feelings. All these last weeks, the gumbos they'd shared, the walks to the oyster stand, the kisses. How could he have misunderstood her?

General Butler took special care to introduce the last entertainment himself. "Mademoiselle Nicolette Chamard," he said grandly, his arm outstretched toward the stage.

He couldn't be that stupid, Finn thought. She owed him an explanation!

Nicolette strode from the wings like a woman on her way to a fire sale. She was a vision in her deep blue gown, her black hair, her oval face animated and beautiful. But her demeanor denounced her glamour. She stopped abruptly midway across the stage, seemingly surprised to discover there was a crowd of people out there. A wave of laughter erupted at the arch of her brows and the open O of her mouth.

She put a hand to her forehead as if to shield her eyes from the light and said cheerily, "*Ahh, bonsoir!*" She launched into a chatty familiar dialogue with the audience. "What do you think of these poor Yankees visiting our fair city?" she asked, and then proceeded to answer the question herself.

"I had been told to expect these Northern gentleman to be clumsy and awkward in their manners. But I ask you, What manners?" After the laughter died, she went on. "Let me demonstrate how a Southern gentleman would ask a lady to dine." She affected a stiffened yet gallant pose, her nose high in the air. "My dear Miss Chamard, the sun being near its zenith, and it being that time of day when one most naturally thinks of restoring the bond between flesh and soul, I wonder if you would do me the honor, nay, the very great honor, of dining with me this noon." She finished the invitation by executing a fine bow.

"My friends, how could a mademoiselle resist the suavity and civility of such an offer? Now, I had occasion to witness a Yankee making a similar invitation, and the difference may illuminate why you soldiers are lonely for the company of ladies in New Orleans. May I illustrate?"

She adopted a manly air and cocked her head. "Hungry?"

The audience roared. Heat rushed to Finn's face. The hollowness in his chest filled with hot lead.

She went on, using her talent for mimicry to skewer every type of speech she'd heard in the months since the soldiers from New York, Massachusetts, Maine, Connecticut and all points North had flooded the city. Mixing accents into a crazy quilt, she created a conversation between a belle and a Yank.

What's the name of this lovely pahk? she said in her gruff soldier's voice.

The pahk? said her bewildered mademoiselle.

The pahk across from the hoose.

After playing on "bah-ul" for "bottle" and "earl" for "oil," she dared to beard the general himself. "Peah out the winder yondah," she said, her hand over her eyes as if she strained to see, "and you will espy the Great Beast as he rides by on his chargah." As she smiled wickedly, General and Mrs. Butler raised their hands in applause, the room awash in laughter.

Nicolette closed the evening on a more somber note. "For those of us here in New Orleans who value freedom for all, even for the black man in the field, I welcome you and your men, General Butler, not as invaders but as the angels of liberation."

Singing *a cappella*, Nicolette began the old slave song of yearning for freedom and release.

Swing low, sweet chariot
Comin' for to carry me home.
Swing low, sweet Chariot
Comin' for to carry me home.

Nicolette curtsied deeply, accepting wave after wave of applause.

Finn did not know the song, had no idea of its import beyond the obvious longing to get to heaven. He was too hurt, too angry and confused to match the enthusiastic applause all around him.

Had she really scorned him these last months for his lack of manners? How could he have been so witless? She'd caught him exactly, tilting his head, saying "Hungry?" But she had smiled at him that day like she'd been starved for light and he was the sun itself.

General Butler escorted Nicolette, the star of his brilliant evening, into the crowd to accept the accolades she was due. He had her arm, encouraging her along the aisle where Finn stood rooted to the spot, waves of despair alternating between numbness and turmoil. How could she greet these strangers, her face radiant, her smile wide and gracious, when she'd not two hours ago broken his heart?

She stopped in front of him. She and he might have been alone in the room, her eyes saying again Cannot. Cannot marry you.

An elderly gentleman bent over her hand and the connection was broken.

Immediately to Finn's right, a woman dressed in yards of black lace nudged her husband. Her voice raised to be heard over the din, she let out a disdainful hmf. "Uppity chit. Thinks because she's uncovered her hair, she can pass for white? Everyone in New Orleans knows her nigger mama was Bertrand Chamard's fancy slave girl."

Finn heard. Everyone heard.

Slave girl?

The harpy's husband smirked. A woman nearby tittered.

Finn saw Nicolette stiffen, saw her eyes seek his. Great, grieving eyes.

The General moved her into the press of admirers. Her eyes stayed on his until Butler turned her away.

Nicolette is a Negress?

Everything fell into place at once. The cloth she'd worn on her head, the innocent remarks he'd made that riled her.

He'd thought she was a white woman. She'd never said ...

Major Farrow clapped him on the shoulder. "Nasty piece, that one," he said, nodding at the matron festooned in black lacy flounces.

Farrow looked at Finn more closely. "What, you didn't know our Mademoiselle was a mixed creole?"

The crowd cleared on their side of the room and Farrow gave Finn a small shove toward the exit. In the open, warm fog bathed their faces. Cigar smoke from a cluster of officers nearby scented the heavy air.

After a block of silence, Farrow stopped Finn at the corner. "Look, laddie, if you didn't know, it's your own damn fault. Why else would a proper miss in this town consort with the likes of us to defeat her own people?"

Finn's jaw was stubborn, his eyes on the cobbled street.

Exasperated, Farrow told him, "You can hardly blame her for not announcing her blood line every time she meets a dumb Yank. Besides, you great ass, the girl wore the tignon every single blessed day since we met her."

"I wanted to marry her, Hursh."

Hursh drew up.

"I wanted to marry her, and I didn't even know her."

Finn walked away, then turned back. "You'll see she gets home?"

"Sure I will."

Finn gave Hursh a wave and walked into the fog alone.

She had betrayed him.

Maybe she hadn't actually lied to him. But she hadn't been truthful either. All these weeks. Months, really. She'd never said.

Six blocks into the fog, each street lamp a golden hazy moon, Finn remembered the day in the coffee shop. She'd been going to tell him something about her mother. The old man had stopped her.

She'd been distressed, he thought now, but he'd been too distracted, his mind on the battle back east, to really notice. And then Simpson had rushed in and they'd hurried back to read the news about Harper's Ferry.

So she'd tried to tell him. Once.

He wandered through the Quarter for an hour and more, oblivious to the music and laughter coming from the salons, the siren calls from the brothel doorways. Hardly thinking, he directed his steps to Pauger Street.

The blue cottage was dark and shuttered. He was to have taken her home after the performance. He had planned to kiss her here, at her door. Their first kiss as two people with a future together.

She hadn't really despised him for that ungallant invitation. She'd been happy when he'd said, "Hungry?" It wasn't all a lie. She had been glad when they were together.

But she had not been honest with him.

Finn touched his pocket where the black velvet box lay. Life would never be the same. He would always have this hole where his heart had been.

Finn tried the gate. It was open. He passed into the narrow corridor to the back of the house. With only a little streetlight penetrating the growing fog, Finn saw a cast iron table in the courtyard.

His boots crunched on shattered glass and he paused. It was a common enough security measure in New Orleans. He walked on into the courtyard.

For a moment he clutched the velvet box. Then he set it on the table.

Upstairs in her darkened bedroom, Nicolette heard the gate squeak, heard the footsteps on the bricks. Pistol in hand, she crept down the stairs. Slow heavy footsteps ground the glass against the bricks. Through the crack in the back shutters, she saw Finn's tall form, his captain's bars winking in a stray flicker of light.

He didn't knock on the door. He didn't call to her.

He didn't want to see her.

She watched him place the box on the table. She listened to his footsteps as he left her courtyard.

She could rush out to him. She could call him back. She could tell him she was sorry, she had tried to tell him, but oh God how could she? The way he'd looked at her tonight when he'd finally, at last, understood who she was. How could she bear to see that in his eyes again?

He was gone, swallowed in the fog.

Like a sleepwalker, Nicolette climbed the stairs. She put on her shoes and descended once more to open the door into the courtyard. She crossed the glassy grit with measured tread, the fog thickening now, rolling across the yard.

Nicolette picked up the velvet box and retreated into the house. The door barred once more, she returned to her bedroom.

She lit the candle on her dressing table, opened the box, and withdrew the garnet cross. The stones glowed hearts-blood red. She moved her hair aside and fastened the chain around her neck.

In her looking glass, she saw the unmistakable signs of her ancestry. Deep black hair, the fog making tight curling tendrils around her face. The heavy, curled eyelashes. The full mouth. And the cast of *café au lait* in her skin. But he hadn't seen the taint, hadn't seen her at all.

She touched the garnet cross at her throat. It was all she would ever have of him.

Chapter Twenty-Four

"Mail call!"

Marcel's men dropped whatever they were doing and came on the run. Sergeant French passed out envelopes, some months old, all of them travel-worn and tattered. The men settled down on rain-soaked tree stumps and saddles to read their long-awaited letters.

Marcel retreated to his dank tent to open his envelope from Mr. Presswood, a bit puzzled and disappointed it was not from Deborah Ann. She'd been on his mind. During long lonely nights in his narrow cot, he contemplated the family they would raise, and how much he'd enjoy making that family in the four poster bed on Rue Royale. He cherished Lucinda and the boys, always would. Always. But Deborah Ann was still new to him. He yearned to unpin that golden hair and undress that lovely body.

He unfolded the letter. *Chamard, I write this hastily, without ceremony, for the courier is about to leave with dispatches for the general, which must not be delayed. Deborah Ann is suffering, the cause being somewhat mysterious.*

Mr. Presswood described Deborah Ann's recent trip home to Evermore and her pale reserve after a precipitous return. Then there was the fainting incident on Elysian Fields, a street where Deborah Ann had no reason to be. She was now in the grip of a mysterious case of doldrums.

I do not understand my daughter's melancholy, Mr. Presswood wrote, *and I fear for her. Surely the vicissitudes of war occupy you, Chamard, but a husband's embrace would no doubt put Deborah Ann to rights. If at all possible to leave your duties for a time, I pray you will do so.*

Marcel sat with his elbows on his knees, the letter clutched in his fist. The clue to Deborah Ann's melancholy lay where she suffered her collapse. She'd been on Elysian Fields. Lucinda's street.

Regard for his wife's state of mind mingled with outright anger. Had she intended to confront Lucinda? Upset Charles Armand? What the devil did she think she was about? She might be an American, brought up in the newer sectors of town, but she'd been reared elbow to elbow with New Orleans Creoles. Her husband having a placée should not concern her.

With clenched jaw, Marcel folded the letter and put it back in the envelope. Whether Deborah Ann needed her husband's embrace or not, he could not leave the Lafourche now. At long last, Butler had his men on the move. With October's relief from sweltering nights and blazing days, Butler's man, General Weitzel, was now poised to seize the riches up and down the bayou. Deborah Ann would have to pull herself together without him.

Marcel did not discount the pain of a troubled mind. In the days after Lt. Smythe had hanged Dix Weber, Marcel had suffered a deep melancholy himself. As the men tiptoed around him, he had left the running of the camp to Sgt. French and devoted himself to getting Val well. The boy lost a tooth, but the swelling over his eyes and jaw receded. He was young. He healed.

Marcel's spirits were less resilient than Val's body. Grief over Dix still gripped him hard when, six days after the hanging, Alistair Whiteaker reported they'd found Lt. Smythe's bloated and fly-crusted body.

"Dug a grave on the edge of a cane patch," Alistair said. "Rolled him in."

"Nelson shoot him?"

"No bullet holes. No knife wounds. No snake bite."

Then Smythe died of the beating Marcel gave him. He rubbed his bruised knuckles. "Guess that makes me a murderer."

"The man needed killing."

"That he did." Yet Marcel felt the blight on his soul. God would not excuse him so readily as his friend did.

He'd roused himself over the next weeks to re-establish his authority among the men. Some of his cavalry had resented Marcel's loss of control, beating a man to death like that. What kind of leadership was that? Marcel did not apologize nor explain himself, but with even-handedness and even-temper, he'd gradually won them back. Smythe had not been popular, and even the ones who distrusted Marcel's fitness came round.

He shook his head slightly, trying to dispel the picture of his wife venturing onto Elysian Fields. Had she accosted Lucinda, right there on Lucinda's own street? He would pull Deborah Ann up short if she'd been so brazen. She was his wife, by God, and she would respect the limits he imposed on her.

Marcel pushed his wife, his other family, everything in New Orleans from his mind. The war did not halt for his problems.

"Val," he called. "I want my horse."

It began to drizzle again, weather the swamp creatures appreciated. October rains had ushered in what passed for fall in semi-tropical Louisiana. Mold and mildew coated the tents, cots, shoes, clothes, everything that didn't move on its own. Horses mired in the muddy lanes, mosquitoes rejoiced and bred in stagnant puddles. At first revived by the heat's easing off, the men had grown cross in the unrelenting humidity, restless in the unpunctuated waiting.

Action, that's what Marcel and all the men craved after weeks of mind-numbing tedium. And now action was upon them.

General Butler had acquired a new label these past months. Not only did they call him "Spoons" Butler for confiscating even the ladies' silver, Confederates and Federals alike had taken to calling him "shy Butler" for lingering in the safety of a conquered city.

The lingering was over. Weitzel had marched his men down the Bayou this morning as far as Napoleonville. The only reason there was no engagement was because General Mouton, weighing the fact that the Federals numbered three thousand to the Confederates' thirteen hundred, had ordered his force to slip further down the waterway to a more advantageous position.

Tomorrow, the battle would commence. Perhaps it would not rank as a great event in the prosecution of the larger war, but for the men and women on the Lafourche, waiting and watching in the muggy air, no moment could have greater import. Blood would flow. Men would die.

Before sunset, just as the mosquitoes claimed the night, Marcel and his troops rolled out their oil cloths. To be in position at first light, they were bedding down on wet ground in a crop lane deep in the cane.

Marcel called his young valet to him. Val, surely half a head taller than when they'd left home in the summertime, fell into step with him, his loping gait as gawky as a colt's.

"I can read your mind, you know," Marcel told him, hiding a smile.

Val looked spooked for a moment. Marcel laughed, figuring all those superstitions from Val's childhood afternoons in the quarters had left their mark.

Val recovered with a grin. "Yes, sir?"

"You think you're going to ride in behind the unit, see some action, shoot that musket you've been oiling up." Marcel stopped and put a hand on Val's shoulder. "You are to stay right here tomorrow, Val. Right here behind this plantation."

Val interrupted. "I could — "

"No, you could not. If the Yanks come down the lane, I want you in the cane. Hear me? In the cane."

Val slid his eyes down and to the side. What was the boy thinking now?

Marcel had seen Val watching the darkies along the bayou slipping off by threes and fours these last few weeks. "Val? You thinking of running off now the Federals are here? Plenty of your people doing that."

Val raised his head and looked him in the eye. "No, sir. I don't aim to run off. But that cane is full of snakes."

Marcel clapped him on the shoulder. "They'll hear you coming and scoot out of your way."

Fireflies lit up the twilight like tiny stars come down to hover above the cane. Marcel slapped at a mosquito and turned to walk back to the makeshift camp on the lane. They'd all be a mess of red bites before morning.

"Monsieur?"

Marcel waited.

"I'll be here when you get back. I swear it."

Marcel touched the boy's face. Val carried a lot of hearts on his thin shoulders. If anything should happen to him, Marcel didn't know how any of them would bear it.

"Stay safe, Val. That's what we all want."

At dawn, the world pearled and gray, Marcel quietly roused his men, settling this one with a pat on the shoulder, trading jibes with another. By first light they were primed, their pitch pine torches ready for the match, their rifles and pistols loaded. They had only to wait for the enemy to descend the bayou, and the killing would begin.

The pink and gold streaked sky turned blue. The sun yellowed. The cane greened, and a breeze rustled through the stalks.

Every man, intensely aware of this morning, perhaps the last he would see on this earth, quietly savored the puffed white clouds, the gracefully curving cane leaves, the cardinals flitting across the lane. The morning air was fresh, the dew cool on their faces. Breathing in, breathing out, the blood thrumming in their veins, even the gurgle of empty bellies spoke of the wonders of being alive.

The hours dragged on. Sgt. French labored over a letter with a nub of pencil. A couple of men nearby played mumblety-peg, ruining the edge on their blades as they aimed at a circle drawn in the dirt. None of the men had much to say, their thoughts turned inward, thinking of home, of sweethearts, of making their peace with God.

Marcel contemplated a green beetle as it fumbled with a tattered dead moth. He'd said his rosary the night before as he lay in his bedroll, watching the clouds drift across a half moon. Not a week since, he'd made confession to Father Fortier. He figured he'd done what he could to prepare to meet his maker. He tried to empty his mind of everything but white moths and green beetles, but Lucinda's luminous black eyes, the curve of her neck, even the taste of her skin seemed more present to him than the green beetle.

He had imagined this day, the battle, the killing. He'd seen himself slashing through a horde of enemy soldiers, filled with blood lust and righteousness. Now he felt merely resigned to the blood. It was a job he had to do.

A faint jingling of harness floated over the tops of the cane. Marcel raised his head. The men held their knives suspended.

A cloud of sounds rode the breeze, the low murmuring of thousands of men and horses, boots and hooves, weaponry and wheels, all moving.

"They're here, boys." Marcel checked his watch. Eleven o'clock.

Marcel's scout, a bayou boy, slipped back from the river road through the cane fields to report. Another half mile, the Yanks would be in range of the waiting Confederates.

Marcel grabbed Val and hugged him tight. "Stay here!" he reminded him, then mounted Hercule. As quietly as possible, he led his men behind the shield of the cane fields, riding north as the Federals marched south a hundred yards away on the bayou road.

A single rifle crack split the silence. Then artillery.

Marcel spurred Hercule into a trot, threading through one plantation's crop lane to another. Behind the Petrie's grand mansion, he raced past Mrs. Petrie, blond hair atumble, huddling at the edge of the cane with her four children and an old mammy, hiding from the invaders.

Marcel's mission was to attack the straggling Union support train: the wagons of hay, of flour and beans, of ammunition and tents. Emerging at the river, Marcel led his men in an all-out gallop, unnerving the enemy with the blood-curdling Rebel yell, shooting from the saddle.

"Fire the wagons!" Marcel yelled. His lads lit their torches and touched them to the hay. Almost at once, half a dozen wagons burst into glorious smoky flames. A reserve unit of Union cavalry raced to counter the attack. Marcel and his men wheeled to meet them head on.

The smell of gunpowder, the clash of sabers, the roar of the distant artillery overwhelmed his senses, narrowed his focus to the Yankee arm slashing a saber down across his horse's neck. Marcel's blade intercepted the blow, the scraping metal shrieking and sparking. He rushed the next enemy and cleft his blade down into the Yank's collar bone. The moment seemed to hold, perfect clarity only in this one timeless bubble: the enemy was no more than a boy, his blue eyes full of fear and fury. He spurred Hercule on and saw no more of the Yank with the bright blue eyes.

On the water, more Yanks. Even with his blood up and a terrifying yell in his throat, Marcel knew his Confederates were doomed. They were out-provisioned, out-gunned, and out-manned.

Union artillery peppered the woods and fields, forcing Marcel's men to shelter under the levee and behind the ten foot trunks of ancient oaks. They retreated along the bottoms of drainage ditches, hopeless and scared, some of them dropping mid-stride, their wounds blooming sudden red.

Marcel lost his sword and fought on foot, Hercule having caught a burst of shrapnel in his noble chest. Oblivious to the smoke, to the shouts and screams of wounded men and horses, he coolly sighted his pistol on the charging enemy.

In an instant of mind-numbing noise, a blast lifted him and slammed him to the ground. A wave of pressure shot up his spine, drove into his skull, pushed against the back of his eyes. With a sharp blade of pain, his eardrum ruptured.

Stunned, deafened, Marcel stretched out his hands, searching for his pistol, but black smoke hung over everything. A man trod on his back in a mad dash to escape the fusillade of the Union artillery.

Strong arms pulled him, half blind and deaf, to his feet. Alistair threw Marcel's arm over his shoulder and together the two of them staggered after their comrades, melting into the cane.

Searing pain from his ruined ear befogged his senses, yet Marcel insisted he could walk unaided. Striking off alone, he drove himself through the cane, the ditches, and the lingering smoke to the place they'd camped the night before.

"Val!" he called. "Valentine!"

If the boy called out to him, maybe hurt, maybe lost in the thick, smothering cane, he wouldn't be able to hear him.

"Valentine!"

The boy tapped him on the shoulder. "I'm here, I said."

The good ear received a muffled confusion of sound. Val's words were indistinct, as if the boy spoke through water.

"Thank God." Marcel hugged the boy tight. "You still have your horse?" he said, his voice over-loud.

"Yes, sir."

"Then let's get out of here."

Captain McKee rode the bayou with Weitzel as the general surveyed the battle's aftermath. Throughout the action, Finn had supervised the runners with reports from up and down the bayou, sending flag signals across and down the stream. Now it was over, he was not so battle-worn as the front-line infantry, but the heat, the noise, the bullets whizzing past his head left him feeling flat. Empty. As if he'd swum the length of the bayou pulling three horses behind him.

The Confederates had killed sixty-eight Union soldiers, damn them. What a goddamned waste. But Finn took no satisfaction at the scores of Rebel bodies littering the ground. More than two hundred, he estimated. A fearful toll for this small battle on a back bayou.

Gall rose in his throat. Damn all of them. Hard-headed, misguided, greedy scoundrels, leading men into rebellion, into death. A goddamned waste.

At the back of the line, the green flag flew over the surgeon's tent. Already the groans of men who'd been under the knife rent the smoky air. Finn had not a scratch on him. Only days ago, he'd have expected mighty relief at surviving a battle intact. But that had been when he thought Nicolette would be waiting for his return.

At their campfire the night before, Finn's fitful, gloomy mood had provoked Hursh. "She's a fine woman, and you're a damn fool."

"Yes. I am."

He'd walked off into the dark to punish himself some more for his idiocy. After the performance at the St. Charles hotel, he'd spent a few hours feeling put upon. How could she have not told him?

By the time he had to board the troop carrier at dawn, he'd come to his senses. Why would she tell him? He'd have looked like the idiot ass he was if she'd tried to explain a fact that everyone else in Louisiana found self-evident. If he could relive that night, he wouldn't run away from her like some wounded, ghostly imbecile sneaking away from her foggy courtyard. He'd bang on the door until she came out and explained herself. What did cannot mean?

He put it away. There was work to do. The bayou ran in a straight line from Labadieville to Thibodeaux, and all that was needed were line-of-sight stations to have wig-wag communications in place. Finn got his men to work building signal towers.

Through the remaining daylight hours, Negro men and women, some carrying children, some supporting frail grandmothers, emerged from the plantations. Like ghosts, Finn thought, they moved slowly, their eyes wide, their voices stilled. All along the length of the bayou, they sat down on the banks, waiting and watching.

With the protection of the victorious Union, they would no longer listen for the sound of the overseer's bell nor dread the zing of his whip. They had little idea where to go or what to do next, but the people along Bayou Lafourche were through with slavery.

Chapter Twenty-Five

At Brashear City, west of the Lafourche, Marcel and the other Confederates regrouped.

Everywhere, the survivors walked like men half dead with fatigue, their faces blackened by gunpowder and smoke, dirt in their hair and ground into their palms. Some of them had yet to wash the blood from their wounds. Those who'd sustained serious injuries lay in rows around the surgeon's tent, enduring sun and wind and flies.

The surgeon made quick work of bandaging a gash on Marcel's arm. He peered into the injured ear and announced he would likely never hear from it again. The doctor had no time for sympathy. He was on to the next man.

Marcel tossed his torn coat over the saddle of his new mount. His ruined ear felt like it was stuffed with cotton wool, and he felt oddly lopsided and unsteady. Walking his horse through camp, he kept a hand on its mane to steady him. The dizziness would pass, the doc had said.

Nearby, a mule trembled, a low moan rumbling through its belly. A soldier stroked it's neck, unashamed of the tears on his cheeks.

"You going to put him down?" Marcel asked.

"Yeah." The soldier wiped his face on his sleeve. "Ol' Jack's been this way two days now. Shell shocked, I guess."

When Hercule, the bravest of horses, had been ripped into by hot, tearing shrapnel, he had shrieked a high-pitched scream of terror Marcel would never forget. "I lost my horse," Marcel offered in sympathy, and walked on.

They'd done all they could in their retreat, Marcel and the others, cutting the wires, blowing up bridges. They'd even, here or there, set fire to the cane to keep it out of Union hands.

Everywhere, the displaced Negroes milled in confused uncertainty. They had no money, no tools, no food. They'd soon be the Union Army's problem, Marcel figured. When he and

Mouton's Confederates moved off in the morning, they'd leave these poor people behind for the pursuing Federals to deal with.

Mouton would need months to regroup after this, and Marcel was as close to New Orleans as he was likely to get for the next half year. He should take leave, see about things at home. Lucinda must be sick over Deborah Ann showing up on her street. And Deborah Ann? He'd be as gentle as he could with her, but she had to be made to understand she did not own a husband. He would love her, provide for her, and honor her as the mother of the children they would have together, but he would not allow her to frighten Lucinda. Nor dictate his habits.

He knocked on the pole of Col. Vincent's tent. When he left, he had permission to see to his wife in town and rejoin his unit in Opelousas in ten days. He sent Val over to Alistair, then met with his men and delegated duties for the coming march.

He traded for a pair of patched trousers and a threadbare shirt. He sent his boots on with Val and put on a pair of worn brogans, the insole split, one heel gone. Mid-morning, General Mouton moved his forces out. Marcel stayed behind.

The run-away slaves took shade among a stand of pine near the railway. Marcel pulled an old straw hat down low over his face and settled his back against a tree away from the others. He'd never in his life had a pain like the ache in his ear, as if a thousand crawdads were in there pinching and scratching.

Late in the day, the train arrived with a contingent of Yanks to move the refugees to a camp outside New Orleans where Butler had the resources to feed them. The people gathered their little ones, a bundle of dry corn pone, maybe a few sticks of jerky. The soldiers herded them to one side of the cars to begin loading them aboard.

Marcel felt as conspicuous as if he'd worn the Rebel flag draped over his shoulders. He wore rough clothes and a floppy hat, but he couldn't disguise his hands, nor his features. If a soldier spied him among the slaves, he'd be cried out immediately.

He slipped out of the crowd, under a railway car, and climbed in from the other side where no one watched, no one worried that someone might sneak aboard. Judging from the smell and the floor's dark stains the size of cow pies, the car had once hauled beeves to market. He moved to a corner of the dim interior where he could lean against the wall, away from the open doorway where the soldiers directed people to board.

Men, women, and children climbed into the car, claiming patches of floor for themselves. Their feet, mostly bare, stirred up dust and the smell of unwashed bodies. Marcel counted himself as dirty as everyone else and tried to ignore the stench.

A family surrounded Marcel in his corner. Glints of light through the wall slats revealed a large man, his massive biceps and forearms marking him as a blacksmith. The wife had a babe and a toddler clinging to her spare form. A grandmother, a shriveled little woman, completed the family.

With a sharp screeching of metal on metal and great huffs from the steam engine, the train began to roll. Soon the wheels clacked over the rough rails, the swaying from left to right overlaying the trembling of the undercarriage. The people quieted and slept.

Marcel woke to daylight and the fretful cry of the smith's baby. The throbbing in his ear reverberated through his head and confused the sounds of children and train tracks and engine. In the close and humid air, he put the back of his hand to his nose against the muggy smell of babies and bodies and the open bucket in the center of the car.

Without thinking, he pushed his hat off his forehead and opened his eyes.

The big man, not three feet away, was staring at him.

He'd been stupid with fatigue the day before. All he'd thought about was slipping aboard without the Yanks catching him. This slave, the slaves all around him, could call him out, or worse.

He glanced over the huddled forms, then looked back at the blacksmith. He had his pistol stuck in the back of his waistband, but it would do him no good if there were trouble. Children all around, and far more men than he had bullets. And he didn't want to shoot this man. He didn't want to shoot anyone. He just wanted to go home.

The man's wife looked him over. "You a Cadian?"

Lots of Cadians in this part of the state didn't want any part of the war, neither side's cause having anything to do with them. "*Oui.*"

The big man snorted. "You ain't no Cadian. You a runaway soldier, ain't you?"

"I don't mean you any harm. My wife is sick. I'm going home."

The woman put her hand on her husband's arm. "Let him be, Joseph."

The man eyed him for a moment. "You got any tobacco?"

Marcel's face split in a grin. "I do." He dug into his pants pocket and produced a twist. He handed it over with his pocket knife.

The morning wore on with interminable waits while the soldiers did what they had to to get the train through. The baby cried. "Ear ache," his mama said, and Marcel felt for the little tyke.

The smith, still nursing the chaw of tobacco, tried to entertain the boy. His wife, the babe at her breast, gazed at her man like he was the promised one, delivering them out of bondage. And Marcel supposed he was. It took guts to walk away from all you'd ever known. Even as a slave, the man had privilege and status as the blacksmith. But he'd thrown it away for this, a crowded train bound for a crowded camp. No guarantees there'd be work for him, food for his babies, clothes and shoes for the coming winter.

They crossed over a rough patch of track, the car swaying back and forth and up and down. The grandmother pressed her hand over her mouth, then spewed forth her stomach's sour contents all over Marcel's boots.

"Come here, mammy," he told her, and helped her climb over him to put her face to the cracks where the air blew in.

The toddler grew tired of crawling over his father's lap and launched himself at Marcel as if he were a favorite uncle. The little boy wrapped his arms around Marcel's neck and planted a sloppy open-mouthed kiss on his cheek. Marcel's heart swelled in his chest. Charles Armand used to do that, before he got to be such a big boy.

"Don't bother the man, Sammy," the mother said. She opened her bundle and portioned out her four strips of jerky, handing one to Marcel.

Marcel's mouth watered. He hadn't eaten since yesterday morning. "Thank you, ma'am." He settled Sammy in his lap and bit into the dried beef.

By the time the train pulled into the station at Algiers, Sammy lay across Marcel's lap sound asleep.

What did high-sounding ideals like states' rights mean to a family like this? What difference did it make to them whether the economy would collapse without slavery, whether rich men lost their fortunes? He rubbed his hand on little Sammy's back. So like Charles Armand, bright as a pip, full of energy and the joy of being alive.

The train slowed and they began to see buildings and wagons through the slats.

"I been thinking how you gone get off without the soldiers seeing you. You take Sammy, there, and stick close to us. Keep you hat down. We see can we get you through."

Marcel looked at the man, at his wife. "Why would you do that for me?"

"You sitting here in this stink just like Joseph and me," the woman said. "Got to live best you can, just like us."

The list of Union casualties came in the day after the battle at Lafourche. Before she sent the list on to the new captain, Nicolette scanned for Finn's name. She swallowed back tears. No McKees listed.

Finn was safe, but she haunted the kiosk where Confederate casualties would be listed. Days went by, the bulletin board bare and empty. With the rainy spell, at least the radical orators were not inflaming the citizens against people like her.

Cleo and Pierre returned to New Orleans. After another day with no news about Marcel, about Alistair, Nicolette set aside her tatting. The rain made her want to curl up in bed with a candle and a book. "I'm going to bed, Maman. Good night, Pierre."

At the sound of crunching glass, Nicolette seized the arms of her chair. Cleo turned out the lamp, and Pierre reached for the club leaning in the corner. Nicolette grabbed her pistol.

At three raps on the door, Cleo hissed, "What kind of brigand knocks?"

"Cleo?"

"Who's there?"

"It's Marcel."

Cleo heaved the heavy bar and threw the door open. Marcel stood before them in tattered rags and split-toed, disintegrating boots. His beard was untrimmed and his eyes were hollow. The oiled canvas bag on his shoulder dripped a rivulet of water.

"I saw your light," he said, his sodden hat in his hands, his head canted at an odd angle.

"My God, Marcel," Nicolette cried. Heedless of her gown, she grabbed him in a soggy embrace. A single sob erupted and she laughed in embarrassment.

"It's all right, Nikki. I'm just cold and wet."

She wrapped her arm around her brother's waist, keeping him close in spite of the reek from his smelly wet rags.

"I'm sorry to barge in like this, Cleo, Pierre," he said. "They've all gone to bed at my house and I couldn't rouse a single one of them, the scoundrels."

"You're always welcome here, Monsieur," Pierre said, adding more coal to the grate.

Cleo relit the lamp. "Nicolette, get him a blanket. Marcel, we'll get you warm and dry, and then you must tell us what you're doing here. Surely it's dangerous to be in New Orleans. Why ever would you risk it?"

"My wife ails, Cleo. And to tell you the truth, I had to see the children again before Mouton moves us northward."

Unable to keep the accusation out of her voice, Nicolette told him, "She was on Elysian Fields, your wife."

Marcel nodded. "I know, Nicolette. I'll take care of it."

He wiped his face with his wet sleeve. "Can you allow me the comfort of sleeping on your parlor rug, Cleo? I show up at Lucinda's in the middle of the night looking like a vagabond, I'm afraid I'll frighten her and Charles."

"It'll be warmer in here, Marcel. I'll fix you a pallet."

Once Cleo and Pierre had gone upstairs, Nicolette sat down on the corner of Marcel's bedding near the fire. They turned the gas lamp off and sat together watching the coals glow.

As if there were not a great divide in their sympathies, Nicolette brought Marcel up to date on the war news, the battles won and lost, the news from Washington. She told him what she did, day to day, in the Union headquarters. He offered no criticism, for once.

They sat for a while, watching the embers turn gray on the edges.

"What was it like?" Nicolette asked him.

"The battle? A lot of noise. Smoke. Mostly, it's a blur. Except for one face. A lad, his whiskers hardly out." Marcel wiped his hand over his face. " I will remember him."

"You killed him?"

"I think so. Yes."

After a time, Nicolette said, "I'm sorry."

Marcel released a heavy sigh. "Yes."

"But you're unhurt."

"Some deafness is all."

"You've lost your hearing?"

"Don't fret. Just in one ear."

God how awful, Nicolette thought, to be truly deaf. Never to hear the birds sing or a piano playing.

"And Alistair is all right?"

"The man's a soldier! A brave one, at that. Not what we expected from ol' sissy britches."

"Sissy britches?" Nicolette laughed, feeling a pang on Alistair's behalf. "You called him sissy britches?"

"When we were kids, just one spring. He wouldn't swim the creek with a bunch of us boys at school. It was running high, I have to admit." Marcel paused, remembering. "And a tangled up nest of cottonmouths had just floated by." He laughed. "Maybe he was the smart one."

"I never thought he lacked for courage," Nicolette said. "Just, I don't know. Conviction. He didn't seem to feel anything strongly enough to act on it. Not abolition, not secession. Not me."

A coal crumbled into a red crevasse in the grated mound, the ticking of the clock and the dripping eaves the only sounds in the quiet house.

Marcel lowered his tone. "You ask too much, thinking he could marry you, Nikki. He has his mother, his sister, his estate to think about."

"Of course I understand that," she said hotly. "He can't marry me, and I will not be his placée. Yet he hangs on, as inert as a cabbage, neither giving me up nor claiming me."

Marcel reached for Nicolette's hand. "I've brought my letters for you to keep for me, if you will. You know, in case. One of them is from Alistair. For you."

Nicolette eyed her brother in the last red glow from the fire.

"He gave it to me before the battle, and I forgot to give it back to him."

"So it's for me to read if he's killed in battle?"

"You could keep it here, with my letters, if you like. Or I'll take it back to him."

She did care for Alistair. But what she felt for him was a mere affection compared to the longing ache she felt for Finnian McKee.

"I think it would be best if you returned the letter to him."

"Then I shall. Now, are you going to let me get some sleep?" Nicolette squeezed his hand. "I love you."

"Who doesn't?" His teeth gleamed for a moment in the fire's glow.

She pinched the back of his hand and got up. As she approached the staircase to go to bed, his voice reached her.

"I love you, too, Nikki."

The next morning, Pierre offered to visit the Chamard house on Rue Royale and return with a change of clothes for Marcel.

"Country clothes, please," Marcel said. "Tell Baudier I want to be as inconspicuous as possible. Ask him to loan me his fishing hat."

Marcel kissed Nicolette's cheek good bye as she left for her job at the Custom House. Then he sat down at the table where Cleo plied him with too much breakfast.

Soon Pierre returned with suitably non-descript street clothes and Baudier's own seasoned hat. With warm thanks, Marcel shook Pierre's hand and enveloped Cleo in a bear hug.

The streets were a wet mess, but the sky was scrubbed blue and fresh. Marcel strode through Faubourg Marigny to Elysian Fields where he cut down to the cheerful yellow cottage with the orange shutters. One of the three front doors was open to the sunny street, and there sat Charles Armand with his tin soldiers arrayed on the granite stoop.

"Papa!"

Marcel scooped the boy into his arms and rocked him, his face pressed into Charles Armand's sweet neck.

"Marcel?" Lucinda appeared at the door, the baby on her hip. "Marcel!"

With his free arm, Marcel pulled her and Bertie to him and held on tight.

Bertie snuggled against his maman, wary of the stranger. Marcel released Lucinda and wiped at her wet cheek.

"Bertie's forgotten me," he said, his voice shaky.

"It won't take long," Lucinda said. "Charles Armand will show him who you are."

Inside, the house smelled of early oranges, the rinds drying in bowls near the windows. Marcel folded himself onto the parlor floor, Bertie in his lap, Charles Armand chattering away. Lucinda pulled her rocking chair up close, and Marcel struggled for a moment. His bowed his head to hide the tears threatening to spill and reached for Lucinda's hand.

Marcel spoiled his boys through lunch time until Bertie lapsed into tearful fatigue. He rocked his babe to sleep and then put him in his crib. Charles Armand's eyes were drooping too. They talked awhile about the sailing ships Charles Armand loved to watch from the levee, and then he too fell asleep.

In their room, Marcel sat on the edge of the bed and opened his arms to his beloved. Pressing his face into her belly, he was nearly undone by the feel of her fingers in his hair.

"Lucinda, what am I to do? I'm fighting on the wrong side."

Her loving fingers did not falter. "I know, my darling, I know."

Chapter Twenty-Six

Gray skies, gray mood. Deborah Ann got out her crochet needle and started on what was to have been a purse. What she made instead was a baby's bootie. Soon she'd made three pairs of booties.

Baby booties, but no baby.

That other woman's children were almost white. Idly, Deborah Ann considered that, if they lived in a white family, Marcel's boys would pass.

She put aside her crochet, picked up a book, put it down again. Tales of romance had no appeal for her now. They were all lies.

In the street below, a man in an oilskin coat and a wide-brimmed hat opened the side gate and came in. A tradesman of some sort. Indifferent to the goings on downstairs, Deborah Ann pulled her shawl tighter and wondered if she should embroider for a while. Maybe later. She leaned her head back against the blue cushion and watched the leaves fall from the sycamore outside her window.

At the knock on her door, Deborah Ann barely turned her head. Mammy had probably brought her a pot of tea.

The door opened and there stood a tall man in baggy striped trousers and a flannel shirt. Her immediate thought, absurd as it was, was that here was a poor Cajun come in from the bayous.

Sudden realization had her off the bench, flying across the room into Marcel's arms. Crying and trembling, she clung to him with arms thrown round his neck. When Marcel tried to pull her hands loose, she held on tighter. Finally, he put his arms around her and simply stood in the doorway, rocking her back and forth.

Once she could control herself, she stepped back, red-faced. "I'm sorry," she said, attempting a laugh as she wiped at her face.

"Don't be. Not many husbands get a demonstration like that when they come home." He picked at a lock of hair the tears had plastered to her cheek and pushed it behind her ear.

She captured his hand and didn't let go as he stepped over to the bell pull and gave it a tug.

"You need a cup of tea, I think." He took her elbow, steered her to the window seat and settled her at his side. She clutched his hand in both of hers.

"I got a very worried letter from your father, Deborah Ann."

She was shamed from her hair down to her toes. She hadn't known Father had written him.

"I missed you," she said in way of an explanation.

Marcel twisted on the bench and took her chin in his fingers. Her hair was a mess. It was always a mess these days. She knew there were circles under her eyes. And now her nose was probably swollen and red.

She lowered her face. "Don't look at me."

"Your father says you hardly leave your room. That you don't eat."

"Oh, but I'll be well now you're here. You'll see. I'll eat everything on the table."

Now she really saw him for the first time since he'd entered the room. The hollows under his sun-weathered cheekbones told her how much weight he'd lost. He needed a haircut, and his moustache nearly covered his mouth. Worst of all, though, was the weariness in his eyes.

Alarmed, she said, "Have you been ill, Marcel?"

"No. Not ill. Now tell me what this is all about, Deborah Ann."

What could she tell him? Not the truth. She'd never tell him she'd spied on that woman.

"At Evermore," she said. "I just got scared at Evermore. It was nothing. I'm over it."

"What scared you at Evermore?"

"Oh, just some of the slaves. You know, the ones I knew growing up. They'd turned surly, not friendly the way I remembered them. But it's nothing. Father says all the darkies are riled up with the war and all, thinking they don't have to work anymore."

"Did someone threaten you?"

"Oh my goodness, no." Deborah Ann squeezed his hands. "Really, it was just my imagination running away with me. Now you're home, I'll be fine."

Marcel was gazing at her with such an odd look in his eye.

"Marcel? You're not hurt somewhere?"

"Your father said you fainted. On Elysian Fields."

She pulled her hands back into her lap.

"Oh, was that were I was? I had no idea the name of the street."

"What were you doing on Elysian Fields, Deborah Ann?"

"Just walking. Father had been forever in the Mint that morning, and I just wanted to walk." She glanced at him, wondering if he believed her. "I had a new parasol," she added.

His eyes glittered hard and dark where moments before there had been sympathy. He knew.

"You have no business on that street, Deborah Ann. Ever."

She swallowed at the lump in her throat. He was angry with her.

"You understand me?" he asked.

The floor wheeled. Deborah Ann put a hand over her eyes, wanting to hide from him.

"You get this silliness out of your head. You are my wife. You, and only you, are Mrs. Chamard. You hear me?"

Her face turned away, she reached for him with one hand. "Marcel, do you love me at all?"

When he didn't answer, not even to lie to her, a crawling, shriveling seized her deep in her chest. She drew what strength remained to her and turned to face his contempt.

Not contempt. His gaze had softened. His look was tender.

"My poor girl." Marcel pulled her to him and kissed her hair, her eyes. She clung to his shirt, her face pressed against his heart. "I have hurt you more than I knew. You need never worry, dear one. You are my wife."

Marcel cupped her face, his beautiful eyes gazing at her. He pressed his mouth to hers. Desire surged through her, chasing the grayness out of her mind.

Isn't this love?

After supper, while the men had their port and cigars, Deborah Ann made ready for her husband. She bathed and brushed her hair out. She buffed her nails. She sprinkled lavender water on her nightgown and on the sheets. And still Marcel did not come.

In her bare feet, she crept to the head of the stairs and leaned over the railing. Her father's stentorian voice penetrated his office door, Marcel's lighter tones more muted. Deborah Ann wrapped her shawl around her shoulders to wait on the step.

The grandfather clock in the hall chimed eleven. The study door opened. Deborah Ann rushed back to the room and climbed into bed.

Marcel knocked softly and came in. "You awake?"

"Yes. Did Father talk your ear off?"

"And filled me with port. My head feels big as a melon."

He turned the gas lamp down and pulled the homespun shirt and trousers off. "Hope you don't mind sharing your bed with a Cajun," he said.

"A very handsome Cajun, sir, even in those rags," she said, holding the covers back for him as he climbed into bed.

"Whoa," Marcel said. "How'd you get such cold feet?"

"I waited for you on the stairs."

"Come here, iceberg. Let me rub some life back into you or you'll freeze me out."

He shifted her around as if she had no more weight than a child. First one foot, then the other, he rubbed and kneaded and caressed.

He did love her. She was sure of it. Deborah Ann's blood warmed her from the ankles up her calves, from her heart down into the core of her. She was afire by the time he slid his hand up her thigh.

She twisted in his embrace so that she could see his face in the bit of moon shining through the exhausted clouds. "All I want in this world is you, Marcel," she whispered. "And a baby."

She kissed his ear, then his jaw, and his mouth. "Please, Marcel, give me a baby."

Chapter Twenty-Seven

In December, a frigid wet wind rattled the windows. Tendrils of damp seeped under the doors and threatened to freeze Cleo's lemon tree, now wrapped in burlap.

All of New Orleans felt the strain of war. The men drank to ease their fears; the women frequented the Cathedral. Anxious families gathered at the kiosk where the dreaded lists of dead and missing were posted. Every day, the train brought a few coffins of boys fortunate enough to have been identified and retrieved from the charnel of the battle field. Every day the sounds of weeping and the slow cadence of funeral marches penetrated the window curtains.

Everyone in the city seemed to have lost someone, except Nicolette. Finn was safe, for now, Marcel and Alistair, too. Yet fear breathed down her neck just as it did for every other woman waiting and hoping at home.

Beneath the ordeal of worry, Nicolette struggled to endure her own heartache. Finn McKee's smoldering glare of anger and disappointment, once he realized what she was, tormented her. Yet, bruised and empty, she missed his company. In her mind, she composed countless letters to him. Sometimes she excused herself for deceiving him – hadn't she worn the tignon, always – but she knew he had not understood what that meant. Most often she simply wanted to share her day with him. She wanted to tell him how she'd climbed to the roof of the Custom House to see the ghostly topmasts poking through the blanket of fog over the river. She wanted to tell him about the old horse she saw on the street, its neck lovingly draped in a paisley shawl against the cold wind.

Of course, he could not reply to a letter she composed only in her head. Yet today, as she walked home from the Custom House in the dreary damp, she again envisioned an envelope waiting for her on the hall table. He would have written it weeks ago. It would be worn, the paper collecting chafes and stains as it passed from mail bag to mail bag to make its way to New Orleans and then to Pauger Street.

At her front door, she shook her umbrella and stepped into the house, into the welcoming odor of peppers and onions frying in bacon grease. Before Maman could realize she was home, she sifted through the post on the table.

Of course there was no letter. Of course he did not write to her. There was no reason for him to write.

Throughout dinner, Nicolette stifled her disappointment, but afterwards, with every flick of the crochet needle, her disappointment grew into resentment. She had done nothing wrong. She'd never said she was white.

None of this was her fault! How dare he judge her? How dare he look at her like she had been the one to injure him!

"Nicolette, what ails you, darling?" Cleo asked.

Nicolette yanked the yarn through her crochet needle. "Not a thing, Maman. It's just a little stuffy in here."

"Stuffy! With this draft?"

Nicolette concentrated on reworking the mess she'd made with those angry stitches.

"You have dark circles under your eyes, Nicolette. You stay at headquarters the live-long day. Are they working you too hard?"

"It's war time. Everyone works too hard." She gathered up her yarn. "I'm going to bed." She leant over and kissed Cleo's smooth cheek and then Pierre's. "See you in the morning."

In her room, she hung her brown wool dress in the wardrobe and sat at the dresser to brush her hair out. Only a slight wave in her hair, but it was black, as black as any slave's. Yet that color was the only hint of her Negro ancestors. Truly, her hair was no darker than Marcel's. Her nose was as narrow as his, her skin as fair. Her lips no more full than his bride's lips.

How could Finn have guessed she was not white?

The garnet cross caught the lamp light and winked at her from the mirror, mocking her. Nicolette pressed her eyes against the heels of her hands. Without hope, what was she to do with herself?

At the Presswood home, Deborah Ann's gaiety lasted past Christmas. Father rejoiced over the triumph at Fredericksburg, and surely, Deborah Ann believed, she was pregnant now. She hadn't heard from Marcel since his clandestine visit disguised as a Cajun the first week in November, but she hadn't expected to. The war, of course.

She lightened her father's house with high spirits and entertained his friends with good beef dinners through the holidays. Sitting at her window, she passed happy hours crocheting skein upon skein of cotton and wool, building an entire layette for the baby. Her son would be born the end of the summer, she calculated as she sewed infant gowns in muslin and lawn, every stitch tiny, exact, and even. Her baby would be plump and pink and smiling, a cherub with Marcel's dark hair and her blue eyes, the most handsome coloring of all in her estimation.

And then, in the night, the unmistakable cramping woke her. There was no baby in her womb.

The ache in her belly gnawed through to her back. No baby. Deborah Ann wept hysterically, so heedlessly that Mammy hurried into her room frightened half to death.

"What the matter?" Mammy demanded, her candle held high. She leaned her weight on the bed, and Deborah Ann hid her face from the light. "You having a bad dream?"

With a grasping hand, Deborah Ann reached for Mammy, pulling her down, clutching at her. "I'm barren," she said, sobs shaking the whole bed.

Mammy pulled back the cover to see the tell-tale stain, black in the candle light. "Let me light the lamp," Mammy said. "Then we talk about this."

Deborah Ann heard the match strike, heard the hiss of the gas lamp on the wall next to her bed.

The mattress sank with Mammy's weight. "Now move over, missy, my feets is cold."

Deborah Ann allowed Mammy to roll over close and stroke her back, but she didn't want to talk. What was there to say? She would never have a baby of her own. She was a failure.

"Now, sugar," Mammy said, "I'm gone tell you what's what about getting babies. First off, though, you got to stop this moaning and carrying on." Mammy patted her back, then more gently began to rub between her shoulder blades. "You always was the one to act out with you monthly, but you got to take hold now, Missy, you hear me?"

Deborah Ann felt Mammy's warm hand on her back, rubbing her thumb along the spine just like she'd done whenever Deborah

Ann had the megrims growing up. Slowly, she let the frantic grief go. Crying wouldn't help. Nothing would help.

"That's better. Now you listen to old Mammy. I birthed six chillen, and I reckon I know a thing or two you don't."

Deborah Ann stared into the shadows of the room. What did Mammy know about being barren? Nobody could fix a barren woman.

Marcel would leave her. She'd heard of it once, a man's wife couldn't give him any children, and he divorced her. The woman had had to leave New Orleans, go away where no one knew her and live out her life in shame.

"Count up the days you husband been here to give you a baby," Mammy was saying. "What they come to? Four, maybe five? And say your man some kind of great stallion who put it to you, say what, twenty times in them five days? My stars, honey. That ain't nothing."

Deborah Ann's swollen eyes ached and cramps rolled through her belly. But she counted. Yes, about five days. Maybe ten times. No, nine.

"You ain't a brood mare, honey, gets pregnant first time the stallion gets at her. You gone need your husband here in the bed with you, a month of Sundays, maybe, or maybe just a month. But you ain't got no cause for all this grief, no you ain't."

Deborah Ann shifted to look at Mammy over her shoulder. "I'm not barren?"

"You ain't barren. I bet my best petticoat on it."

She wanted to believe Mammy. Mammy must know. But she'd been so sure Marcel's seed had taken hold inside her. She'd felt it. And yet, there was no baby.

Chapter Twenty-Eight

Daffodils pushed their way through the black earth, their yellow flags waving against blue skies. Spring winds carried the scents of jasmine and honeysuckle.

Deborah Ann dreaded the resumption of fighting now that the roads were passable. She wanted the war to be over. She wanted her husband at home.

Waking or dreaming, her head was filled with babies. Whenever the mammy next door brought the children out to play under the oaks, Deborah Ann paused to watch them from her bedroom window. The curly-haired boy toddled with a toy duck on a string following behind him. The little red-haired girl of four, constrained in a bonnet and long sleeves to protect her complexion, served tea to her dolls. Heart-sick with yearning, she feared there would be no babies in the nursery for her, no little boys with Marcel's chin.

Clinging to the small hope Mammy was right, she threw herself into spring cleaning, supervising the rolling up of the imported wool carpets and the laying down of the heavy straw mats for summer time. When the roses bloomed, she filled the house with sweet-smelling bouquets.

After having neglected the Chamard house on Rue Royale, she attacked it with feverish energy. She had the chandeliers taken down, soaped, and polished. The silver was beyond salvage, she decided, the shine so thin on the teapot she could see hints of the underlying brass. She would order a new silver service, choose a new pattern of tableware. Every day she came back to her father's house on Prytania Street exhausted but gratified. When Marcel came home from the war, he'd be amazed at what she'd accomplished.

As May advanced, the balmy air grew heavy with heat and humidity.

"You best leave off cutting them flowers till the cool of the morning, missy," Mammy fussed.

"Oh, leave me be, Mammy." Deborah Ann dabbed at her neck with a dainty embroidered handkerchief, a basket of red roses in her other hand. She was so irritable today, heavy and listless. The early heat, and Mammy hovering like a bee over clover, no wonder she was vexed.

"Deborah Ann!" Father marched into the garden waving the latest Picayune, his face aglow with excitement.

"We've done it again! Lee's pushed that devil Hooker back across the Rappahannock. We're going to win this war."

"Did you find out where Marcel's unit is?"

"What? Oh, no, dearest. He's with Col. Vincent somewhere. Probably near Jackson if I had to guess, harassing the Union supply lines. Don't fret. He's fine. No news is good news, you know."

Deborah Ann sank onto the cedar bench to read the paper. Even Confederate victories filled her with dread. More than 17,000 Union killed, wounded and lost at Chancellorsville. Thirteen thousand Confederate casualties. She read the line again. Not hundreds. Thousands of men, bleeding and dying.

The numbers confounded her. Thirty thousand men. Were there that many men in all of New Orleans? She tried to imagine thirty thousand white tombstones laid out in rows, stretching as far as the eye could see.

Through supper, Father's elation annoyed her. Had he no thought at all for the dead boys on that field in Virginia? Of course, Marcel was not among them. But what if he had been at Chancellorsville? Or at Fredericksburg, or Murfreesboro?

That night, her body achy and swollen, Deborah Ann tossed on damp sheets, the hair on her neck wet with perspiration. When she roused in the morning, vague images of draped mirrors and widows' weeds, coffins and empty cradles lingered.

"You stay home from over yonder today, Missy," Mammy said. "You looking peaked this morning."

She was light-headed, in fact, though her body felt bloated and heavy. But today, she meant to tackle the nursery on Rue Royale.

"I just need my coffee, Mammy."

She and Mammy, Jebediah along as escort, took the omnibus to Canal and then walked up Rue Royale to the Chamard house. Mammy and old Biddy set to work sorting linens. Deborah Ann climbed the stairs to the nursery. Since she'd cleaned in here before, new spider webs stretched from the walnut crib to the window sill. Not being one of those girls who feigned horror at sight of a spider, she slapped the webs down with a rag.

Even with the windows open, it was stifling up here on the top floor. Deborah Ann wiped the sweat from the back of her neck. The cradle needed oiling before she made the new bedding. Blue satin and cream lace. Her baby would have the most beautiful crib in all of Louisiana.

She pressed her hand to her swollen aching belly.

Unless she was barren. Unless Marcel never came home to her.

Under her too-tight corset, cramps twisted her insides, squeezed her womb until she felt she would faint. Her knees buckled and she ended up on the floor, her forehead resting against the walnut crib.

Those beautiful little boys, only blocks away. The older one, as light a child as she could wish for, his chin carrying the hint of Marcel's dimple.

A sheen of oily sweat covered Deborah Ann's brow. Pain rolled through her in waves, mocking her empty womb.

Marcel wasn't coming back. He was going to die on some God-forsaken field, and she'd never be pregnant. Not ever.

The truth revealed itself with perfect certitude: Marcel's children would be orphaned. He'd want her to see his children had advantages that woman could never give them. He would want her, his wife, to take care of his blood.

On trembling legs, Deborah Ann pulled herself up, steadying herself against the cradle. Blood flowed from her womb with every painful spasm, life's vital force draining from her body just as with all those poor dying soldiers on the battle field. But she would not succumb. She had to go after Marcel's children. Her children. Deborah Ann was his wife, not that other woman.

Holding tight to the banister, she descended the stairs to the second floor, then to the first. She opened the door and closed it quietly behind her. Only three blocks down Royale to Esplanade and then toward the river to Elysian Fields. To the yellow cottage with the orange shutters.

She walked quickly through the Vieux Carré, hardly seeing the shops, the ladies in black, the soldiers. Charles Armand would clap his hands in delight when he saw all the toys she'd buy him. She'd have a swing hung behind Father's house, and he'd yell "higher,

higher, Mama," and she'd push him till his little legs were silhouetted against the sky.

The baby's name. She didn't know what it was. It didn't matter. She'd name him herself.

The front doors of the yellow cottage were open, the gnarled jasmine vine perfuming the air. Deborah Ann stepped onto the stoop and peered into the shadowed rooms. She could see the courtyard through the house, she could hear a child's voice, a baby's hungry cry.

Her children's voices.

Deborah Ann strode through the house, her heels echoing against the hardwood floor. At the doorway into the courtyard, she could see the three of them as if they were frozen in a painting. The woman. The creamy skinned baby at her breast, his dark hair curling at the base of his neck. And the boy, Charles Armand, the image of his father, on a little chair with a red top in his hand.

With perfect clarity and purpose, Deborah Ann stepped into the courtyard. "I've come for the children."

The woman grabbed Charles Armand's arm as she rose from her chair, the baby clutched to her chest. "You get out of here."

Deborah Ann's eyes were on Charles Armand, peeking from around his mother's skirt. "They're Marcel's blood. They belong to me."

"Get out."

Deborah Ann strode across the bricks. She bent over, reaching around the woman to take Charles Armand's hand. "Come with me, Charles," she said.

Charles Armand shrank from her. Why would he do that?

Deborah Ann ignored the shove the woman gave her. "I'm your new mother, Charles. I'm your father's *wife*."

"Maman?"

Deborah Ann seized his wrist and pulled at him, the child still clutching a handful of the woman's skirt.

The woman lunged for Charles, but the woman had to take care not to drop the baby. Deborah Ann yanked hard, and the boy was hers.

Gleeful, flushed with power and triumph, she gripped Charles Armand, oblivious to his twisting and kicking.

"Now give me the baby," she said.

With a great shriek, the woman swung her fist into Deborah Ann's face, knocking her off her feet.

Distantly, Deborah Ann felt the woman's fist smash into her mouth again, banging her head against the paving stone. She raised her arm to block the next blow as the woman, still clutching the baby, punched down with all the force in her body.

The fist smashed into her nose, then into her eye. Deborah Ann tasted blood, salty on her tongue. Dimly, as her mind began to close down, she took in the woman's wild face, the lips pulled back to show her teeth, the eyes black and savage.

When Deborah Ann regained consciousness, her first sensation was of wetness. Her face. Her legs. Her skirt clammy and sticky with the deep, purply scent of menstrual flow. Her tongue, coated with fresh, coppery blood.

One eye swelled nearly shut, she looked around, wondering where she was. In a courtyard. There was a little chair knocked over, a small cradle on its side.

That woman's house –

Shaking, Deborah Ann got to her feet. Dizziness sent her reeling. She bent over and vomited onto the bricks.

She staggered out of the house, lurched across the street, and clutched at an iron fence. She had to get back to Royale Street. Before Marcel found out what she'd done.

Tottering on the undulating cobblestones, Deborah Ann veered from one side of the street to the other.

Esplanade was busy, Yankees coming and going at the Mint, people catching the train for Lake Pontchartrain. No one would notice her amid so many people.

But people did notice. At first, they made way for her, stopping, staring. She put a hand to her face to hide from them and went on.

"What happened to her?"

"Somebody beat the daylights out of her, that's what."

"Call the Guard, somebody."

"Miss? Miss, can I help you?"

A Yankee soldier tried to take her arm, to pull her the wrong way. She had to get back to Royale.

"Leave me alone," she said, jerking away.

A big breathless colored woman rushed up to her in a blur. "Here, here, she my Missy. You let me take her now."

Mammy's strong hands grasped Deborah Ann. "Me and Jebediah, we get you on home."

Deborah Ann clutched at her. Mammy would know what to do about all the blood.

Chapter Twenty-Nine

"Miss Chamard?"

Nicolette raised her head from the message she was encoding. A fresh-faced private stood at the office door.

"If you're Miss Chamard," he said, "there's a nigger fella downstairs come to fetch you."

The word grated, but she knew the private used the word like so many of the Yanks did, without contempt or feeling of any kind. To him, nigger was simply an identifier, like saying there was a man downstairs with long blond hair.

"Did he give you a name?"

"Something Frenchie. Pierre?"

Oh, Lord. She grabbed up her purse and hustled down the staircase, every kind of bad news running through her head. Maman was ill. Or Papa had fallen off his horse. He was a reckless rider, had nearly broken his neck a dozen times.

Or had they had news about Marcel?

Pierre waited for her in the massive shadow of the Custom House.

"What happened?" she said.

"Lucinda's at the house with the boys. That woman Marcel married tried to take the children."

"Take the children?"

"Lucinda's in trouble," Pierre explained as the two of them half walked, half ran back to Pauger Street. "She beat that woman up pretty bad, she says. Likely broke her nose."

"Lucinda did that?"

"That woman was after her children."

At the house, Cleo had little Bertie in her arms, sleeping peacefully. Lucinda, her eyes red and swollen, sat on the sofa clutching Charles Armand to her. He'd given up his thumb months ago, but he sucked it now, his eyes huge and worried.

Nicolette grasped Lucinda's hand and sat beside her. "You did right to come here. Didn't she, Maman?"

"Yes, she did. If they want to arrest Lucinda, they'll have to find her first. She's safe here. At least until tomorrow."

Nicolette nodded her head. "We'll take you and the children to Cherleu. Papa can protect you there."

"But she's white," Lucinda protested. "And she is your papa's daughter-in-law. If the gendarmes come for me, Monsieur Chamard will not resist them."

"He'll throw them out on their ears!" Nicolette said.

"Bertrand Chamard will take care of you and his grandsons," Cleo assured her. "Don't you doubt it for a minute. He can even hide you at my place. It's not half a mile up the river."

Lucinda had probably met Papa only once or twice, when the boys were born. And here she was about to show up at his door unannounced. No wonder she was uneasy.

"You'll need help with the boys, and I haven't seen my papa in too long. It's time I went up there."

Relief washed over Lucinda's face. "Thank you, Nikki."

"That Miss Presswood," Cleo said. "Does Marcel have any idea what kind of girl he's married?"

Nicolette shook her head at the enormity of Deborah Ann's act. "Whatever possessed her?"

When Nicolette knew her before she married Marcel, Deborah Ann appeared to be just another mild, rather dull Southern belle. She seemed an unlikely woman to summon that kind of nerve, much less such brazen cruelty. And yet the deed testified to an ugly selfishness, an indefensible, unshakeable presumption of righteous claim.

Cleo patted Bertie's back as he stirred on her shoulder. "She isn't the first woman to lose her mind since the war started. But to take another woman's children, it passes understanding."

Pierre got his hat. "I'm going to find Beaumont. He owes me five dollars. Ricardo owes me three. If I borrow another ten, maybe that'll be enough for steamship tickets."

"*Non*, Pierre. Wait." Nicolette fetched her enameled box. She opened Alistair's leather pouch. Gold coins spilled out, rolling and winking in the light.

The four of them stared at the hoard. French gold angels, British sovereigns, $50 pieces, Brazilian coins of 20,000 Reis.

"There must be over a thousand dollars here, Nikki. Where did it come from?" Cleo asked.

"Alistair, bless him. Remember? He gave me his purse before he left for the Lafourche."

"I had no idea. So much gold. Did you realize ... ?"

Nicolette shook her head. "I never looked."

Pierre picked up a $50 piece. "We'll get you and Lucinda out of here today. Lock the door behind me."

After Pierre left them, the three women were quiet. No one wanted to say it aloud, but Nicolette thought they surely feared what she did, that the gendarmes would find Lucinda before she could leave town and arrest her for striking a white woman. If Lucinda were a slave, they could execute her for such an offense. But Lucinda was a free woman, and the assault had been in her own home, defending her children. Still, she would be taken up, separated from Bertie and Charles Armand. Perhaps imprisoned, kept in shame, hunger, and filth. Nicolette shuddered at the image of Lucinda, with her delicate bones and gentle nature, being slapped around by some sweaty oaf in the city jail.

Cleo broke the silence. "Let's do something with this money." She scooped the coins back into the pouch and looked for her gardening trowel. In the courtyard, she dug into the soil around her big cactus and buried the purse deep among the roots. "All right?" she said to Nicolette.

"*Merci, Maman.* If I'd had any idea there was so much money there. My heavens."

"We could have been dining out every night!" Cleo laughed. "Now, Lucinda, let's get you ready. You can't go back to Elysian Fields. I'll fetch you a shawl and some linen from my room."

Shortly, Pierre returned, tickets in hand. "You leave within the hour."

Quickly, Nicolette packed her pistol and ammunition in her blue canvas tote bag. Around that she stuffed the diapers she'd made from an old petticoat. Cleo handed her sausage, bread, and a flask of water, and the bag was full.

Together, they made their way toward the docks, Pierre carrying Charles Armand and Cleo holding Bertie in her arms, all of them endeavoring to seem unhurried and unremarkable. Leading the way, Nicolette paused at every cross street to watch for gendarmes before they proceeded. The plan was that if anyone should challenge them, Pierre and Cleo would run with the children. Nicolette and Lucinda would flee into the streets of the Vieux Carré they knew so well. Dozens of shopkeepers would gladly hide them in the warren of courtyards hidden behind the townhouses. But hiding at Cherleu half a day north of the city would be far safer than hiding in New Orleans.

The steamship loomed huge and grand above them, gleaming with fresh white paint, its red gingerbread trim giving it a festive air, as if no one on this sunny day could have a fretful thought. One stack belched white steam, the other black soot from the furnace.

Lucinda kept her face down, hiding behind Cleo's bonnet. Nicolette had Charles Armand by the hand. She too wore a bonnet, not the tignon, and used the shadow of the brim to hide her gaze as she surveyed the crowd for uniformed gendarmes.

Passengers, Union soldiers among them, crowded at the gangplank waiting their turn, thoughts and gazes on the boat. No one showed any interest in them. In two minutes, they'd be safely aboard.

At water's edge, two gentlemen looked on while a nervous, tittering woman was buckled into the hoisting chair. They watched the crane swing her across the gap, the woman shrieking in dismay or delight, Nicolette couldn't tell which.

Then one of the men turned their way. But it was not Lucinda whom he gazed at so intently. It was Nicolette herself.

Red hair straggled beneath the man's stovepipe hat. Even from fifty paces, she could see he was heavily freckled.

The red-headed man nudged his companion, who turned and eyed her with the same lowering expression, his handle-bar moustache framing a thin-lipped mouth. It was the orator from Jackson Square, the man who'd shouted out her name to a mob of drunken thugs.

Nicolette fought the urge to retreat among the mountains of kegs and casks. The blue canvas shopping bag hung from her arm. Buried among the sausage and bread, her pistol nestled, butt up. And it was loaded.

Swallowing hard, she turned her head as if a glimpse of them held no consequence.

In a few minutes, they'd be on the boat. By supper time, she and Lucinda and the boys would disembark at Cherleu. In all the vastness of Papa's plantation, with his good name and Creole connections, they'd be safe.

Nicolette swung Charles Armand up. "Put your legs around my waist and hold on." Surefooted, she followed Lucinda up the gangplank onto the huge steamboat.

This time of year, there were no cotton bales stacked high on the decks, but crates squeezed the passageways eight feet high. Once in the tunnel of the passage, Nicolette breathed easy. No one could see them, and she herself could see nothing but a woman in widow's weeds behind her and Lucinda carrying Bertie ahead of her. She had to put Charles Armand down and lead him sideways through the dim corridor to the day parlor.

She and Lucinda settled the boys on the wooden bench running the length of the chamber. Here poor white people jostled elbows with more prosperous, free people of color. The whistle blew, the paddle wheels churned. They steamed into the middle of the river, leaving danger behind.

"We're safe," Nicolette whispered. "Take heart."

Despite her reassurances, Nicolette remained alert. Of course they were safe, soldiers on board, other free blacks. Nothing could happen now. And yet, a tiny hammer pinged against the taut wire of her spine.

Late in the afternoon, Nicolette calculated how many more stops the ship might make before they hove to at Cherleu's docks. She was blinded by the cargo all around the decks, but she thought only three more and they'd be home.

With a sickening lurch and a piercing screech, the ship staggered and rolled to one side. Lucinda clutched at Bertie with one hand, grasped for Charles Armand with the other. Nicolette threw her arm over all of them.

Silence. Then the rumble of the engines put into reverse. Straining, pumping engine, shouting boat men. Silence. The engines thrown into forward again. Then reverse.

They were stuck on a sandbar.

Soon a crewman strode through the room calling out "All's well. Going to be a few hours. Get her going again directly." Without breaking stride, he took no questions, offered neither details nor comfort.

The room settled down to resigned patience. Lucinda nursed Bertie under her shawl and then walked him up and down the aisle, stepping over thrust-out feet and ankles. Nicolette fed Charles Armand sausage and bread.

If the crew didn't get them off in another hour, they'd be stuck here for the night. As the sun went down, fog would fill the river corridor. Then, even if the boat were freed, they would have to anchor for the night. Only a mad man would try to navigate the shifting hazards of the Mississippi River on a foggy night.

At nightfall, the ship put out anchors, lit the lamps inside and out, and began the continual, intermittent blowing of the whistle to warn away any traffic foolish enough to be on the move in the black fog.

Nicolette leaned over to Lucinda to whisper. "I have to use the necessary."

"I'll go with you."

An elderly mulatto, elegant in her silk tignon, agreed to hold their places on the bench. They gathered the children, Nicolette careful to bring along her bag with the pistol inside. Angling through the narrow corridors, they passed the length of the ship. Fore and aft, huge lanterns glowed like fairy lights in the fog. The engine rumbled quietly, keeping just enough steam to hold the bow into the current.

Abeam of the main deck, the crew maintained a gap in the bales and barrels for disembarkations. A lantern hung at this gateway where a couple of men lingered, the ends of their cigars dimly red in the murk.

The fog was so thick, Nicolette could not even see the river coursing down the boat's side ten feet below the deck. Speaking softly in French with Charles Armand, she led Lucinda and the baby past the ghost-faced smokers.

At the women's necessary, they waited their turn. The only sound that truly penetrated the blanket of fog was the ship's whistle. Aside from the conflagration of an exploded boiler, the most dangerous event on the river was being rammed by another ship running with the current. With that in mind, Nicolette was grateful for the one long, two short warning shrieks.

Leaving the necessaries behind, Nicolette and Charles Armand sidled along the darkened corridor behind Lucinda and the baby. Nicolette anticipated a long night on the hard benches, strangers snoring and belching all around her. But when they arrived at Papa's in the morning, Valentine would see they had a feast of a breakfast with pots and pots of coffee. In the garconniére they would tuck the children into beds with snowy white linens.

Then they would sit with Papa on the gallery and explain what Marcel's wife had tried to do to his grandsons.

Papa had his faults. Too sure of himself where women were concerned. Even Maman, who'd been a fool for Bertrand Chamard most of her life, would agree to that. Always sure only he was right. But as adamant as Papa was about the righteousness of the Confederate cause, he had neither denounced nor renounced his son when Yves declared for the Union. Papa loved his children, colored and white. There never was a moment when she doubted that.

Making her way through the foggy corridor, Nicolette bent to speak to Charles Armand. "Step on my feet."

He loved to do this, to wrap his arms around her legs and let her do the walking for them both. She held on to his little shoulders, leaning to see his face in the foggy dark.

The whistle blew, so loud on the open deck it stunned Nicolette's senses.

A blurred shape came out of the fog. Strong hands jammed a bag over her head.

She screamed, but she couldn't hear her own voice over the second blast of the whistle. The smell of old potatoes filled her nose, the dust choked her. She struggled, trying to breathe, to tear at the musty bag, to hold on to Charles Armand.

He was ripped from her grasp.

Nicolette flailed wildly with both hands. Her fist connected with something, someone.

The gun! Nicolette fumbled for the opening to the canvas bag, then groped blindly for the pistol butt. Her fingers closed on the handle.

A fisted blow knocked her head back. A second blow flattened her against a rough-hewn crate. Splinters dug into her clawing hands as she struggled to keep her feet, to find the pistol butt again.

Lucinda's scream tore into the fog, then the last deafening shriek of the whistle.

The attacker grabbed Nicolette around the waist. She twisted and kicked and scratched. Then a brutal blow, blue fire behind her eyes, pain radiating through her skull.

Consciousness winked in and out, Nicolette dimly registering the smell of tobacco and kerosene, the dryness of her mouth, the ache of her tongue. Finally she wakened, remembering.

Pain seared through her eyes when she opened them, the small kerosene lantern's rays piercing like needles through her brain. A gag dug into her mouth, bruising her tongue, making her wild with fear and anger.

Stay calm. You're not helpless, she reminded herself. She'd taken care of herself before, she would again. She took a long breath through the sour gag. *You're alive. You're going to get away. If you keep your head.*

Rope bit into her wrists, tied behind her back. Rope pinched her ankles. The old injury to her jaw throbbed under the new bruises.

The vibration of the engines told her they were still aboard ship. She opened her eyes with a tight squint. She was on the floor, propped up against a red leather bench.

A stateroom. A lamp suspended from the ceiling. A man at the table, snoring softly in his chair. On the opposite bench, Lucinda, gagged, eyes wide and frightened. Charles Armand lay across her lap, his hands gripping her skirt even in sleep. Bertie slept between her and the back of the bench.

Nicolette returned her gaze to the man. The man with the trailing moustache. The orator. His lean jaw was stubbled, his hair mussed, but he was nicely dressed in good broadcloth.

Where was the red-headed man?

Where's my gun?

Her blue canvas bag lay crumpled in the corner. Empty. Nicolette couldn't see the table top. Maybe her pistol lay next to the man's hand.

She looked into Lucinda's eyes. Hopelessness looked back at her. Nicolette tried to signal her to take courage. They would get out of this. If she had to kill, they would get out of this.

The night dragged on. Nicolette's head and jaw throbbed, her mouth dried out, and her arms and shoulders cramped. If dawn came, she couldn't tell it in the dark cabin. The steam whistle still shrilled every few minutes, bells rang, feet stomped over head.

The orator awoke with a snort. He wiped a long-fingered hand over his face and heaved a great sigh. Then he eyed Nicolette.

A smirk pulled his moustache to one side. "The infamous Miss Chamard. How do you do?"

Nicolette glanced at Lucinda. Bertie was at her breast. Charles Armand sat at her knees, watching the man.

The orator stood up and hawked a gob at the spittoon in the corner. He wiped his mouth with the back of his hand, then ambled across the floor to Nicolette. He stared down at her a moment, his eyes deep sunk and brilliant with the fire of zealotry.

"Not so high and mighty now, are we?" He gestured at the ropes around her ankles.

The man's drawl was thick, but not Louisianan. Mississippi, she guessed. Dressed like a business man, a prosperous one.

He toed the edge of her skirt. "I seen you at the Yankee headquarters, going in and out, in and out." His voice was soft, almost seductive, as if he were shy, talking to a woman he admired. "You likely have a message in that pretty head to deliver to the Yanks in Baton Rouge, don't you, Miss Chamard?"

Nicolette shook her head slowly. She was no spy.

"Oh, I know there is no paper message. While you were sleeping, I took the liberty of examining your clothing and as much of your person as need be." Her stomach heaved. He'd touched her, while she was unconscious and defenseless. She swallowed the bile welling in her throat.

He held a hand up as if to defend himself. "The little mother here can vouch that I did not touch you improperly, Miss Chamard. I am a married man, and a Christian."

She raised her chin and shot a venomous glare at him.

The orator's tone abruptly changed as if he were offended she did not appreciate the delicacy he'd shown her person. "You a mighty fancy whore, you are." He turned back toward the table. "You missing your head rag, but you a nigger, just the same, for all the fine airs you been sporting. Just a nigger whore."

Nicolette pulled her knees up and shoved her feet into the back of the man's knees with all her might. The orator stumbled, catching himself on the table.

He whirled on her, raised his arm, and slapped her so hard it threw her entire body against the wall with a bone-bruising thud.

Charles Armand screamed. Bertie wailed. Blood spilled from Nicolette's busted lips, soaking the rag stuffed into her mouth. The room spun around her as she fought the pain, nausea welling up. The same searing pain as when Adam Johnston had beaten her. The same pain, yes, and the blood. But not the same fear. Nicolette was not afraid. She was angry. And she was dangerous. She would kill him for this.

"Shut that kid up," the man said, fury in his voice, "or I'll do the same to him."

Lucinda groaned from deep in her chest, imploring Charles with her eyes. With shuddering breaths, he hushed.

The man stared at Lucinda a moment, then came close. Ignoring Bertie and his red-faced cries, he rested his gaze on her exposed breast. She kept very still, her eyes turned away.

"Modest, huh? I admire that in a woman. God never meant for womankind to be tempting men with wanton, naked flesh."

He looked at Charles Armand, who had half his fist in his mouth.

"You're a good little lad, boy." His hand smoothed back Charles Armand's hair.

"See?" he said to Lucinda. "I'm a reasonable man. If I take the gag off that pretty mouth, you gone be reasonable, too?"

Lucinda nodded.

He slipped the rag out of her mouth, his hands just inches away from her bare breast. Lucinda shifted Bertie and cooed to him, desperately trying to soothe him. Under the orator's frank ogling, she persuaded Bertie to take the nipple and he quieted.

All around, sounds from the engines, whistles, calling voices, but inside the cabin, silence.

Satisfied the man was not going to touch Lucinda, Nicolette turned her face to the floor so she wouldn't drown in her own blood. The man squatted a few feet away, out of her range.

"You learn anything here, Miss Chamard?" He laughed and returned to his chair.

Nicolette passed out, her face in the puddle of blood.

She woke to the roar of straining engines. The boat shifted and shuddered. Then it lurched free. The fog must have lifted. They were on their way.

Only three stops down from Papa. Who did not even know to expect them. How long would it be before anyone missed them?

The red-headed man came in with a basket. Pale beneath the freckles, he was tall and stoutly built. He eyed the mess of Nicolette's face and dress. "Had some trouble, huh?"

"Hard-headed whore. The other one's a sweetheart, though. What's your name, honey?"

Nicolette thought Lucinda wasn't going to answer, she waited so long. Finally, her voice quiet but strong, she said, "I am Lucinda Benoit."

"You a traitor, too, Lucinda Benoit?"

Lucinda closed her mouth. The man grabbed her chin, squeezing her mouth, twisting her neck. "I asked you a question."

"Leave her alone, Murph," the orator said.

With ill grace, Murph backed off. He eyed the pistol on the table. "Reckon that's the gun she shot me with, don't you?" He glared at Nicolette. "You cost me a inch of muscle off my arm, you damned whore."

These were the men who'd come sneaking into her house!

"Bitch." He kicked at her feet. She kicked back.

"Stop it now, Murph. What'd you bring to eat?"

The men fed Lucinda and Charles Armand. Nicolette's gag remained in place.

"So. Now we got 'em, what are we going to do with them?" Murph said around a mouthful of bread.

"The essential thing, we shall keep the traitor from delivering her messages to the Yanks in Baton Rouge."

Murphy eyed Lucinda over his tankard. "Looks to me like Lucy here's just dark enough we might could sell her in Natchez, Franks. Buy a few more horses for the Rebs with what we'd get for a good looking gal like her."

Franks and Murph. I'll remember them. I'll find them. And I'll kill them.

Franks put his bread aside. "Murph, use your head. A girl that good looking, she's trouble. She'd draw attention. No, I think we'll simply turn them over to the Confeds when we reach Port Hudson. The soldiers can use them as they will." Franks smoothed his long moustaches. "Traitors servicing the very men they meant to betray. There is justice in that, don't you think?"

Nicolette struggled to speak. *Not Lucinda,* she insisted. But her grunted *not her*! came out garbled and incomprehensible.

"What's that you say, Miss Chamard? Unh Unh?"

Murph laughed at his partner's wit. Nicolette fell back, furious.

The boat churned up the river, past Cherleu, past Toulouse, past Chanson. Past Donaldsonville and Plaquemine.

In the darkened dank cabin, Nicolette endured endless hours of helpless rage. Thirst increasingly nagged at her, her swollen tongue trapped by the blood-caked rag in her mouth. She could not think, could not make a plan; as aimless as a butterfly in the breeze, thoughts flitted through her mind.

By the time the second day dawned, she slipped in and out of delirium. Now and then Lucinda's pleading voice penetrated her confusion. "She needs water," Nicolette heard, then slipped back into the fog.

The day passed in silent derangement. Nicolette had long talks with Papa. He sang to her in his wonderful baritone, his eyes full of love and laughter. She walked under an arbor of blooming crape myrtle arm in arm with Captain McKee, his hair shining in the sun. Finn whispered in her ear, *Wake up, Nicolette.*

The release of the gag roused her. Sweet water trickled into her mouth.

"Slow, *chèrie.*" Lucinda's gentle hands held a cup to her cracked lips. "A little at a time."

"Get her cleaned up, too," Murph said.

Nicolette moaned at the pain as Lucinda bathed the blood away.

Franks came into the cabin with bread and a bottle of wine.

"What you want to do about her wrists, Franks?"

"Cut her loose. Ankles too. Got to get the circulation going so she can walk off the gangplank."

Fire seared her veins as the blood rushed back into her hands. Then Murph cut the ropes around her ankles and flames shot through her feet. She heard someone moaning, not aware it was herself.

"Please, monsieur," Lucinda said. "Can you not give her the wine?"

Lucinda rubbed Nicolette's wrists and arms, then helped her hold a cup in her purpled hands.

"How we going to get her off the boat, looking like that?" Murph said.

"Wrap her up good in Lucy's shawl. Pull her bonnet down. Should get us through the crowd."

Murph hauled her to her feet, but her legs wouldn't hold her.

"You're going to have to carry her, Murphy, looks like. You can manage that, can't you?"

"I reckon. She don't smell so good though. I think she peed on herself."

"I never noticed you smelling like a rose, my friend."

Franks took Bertie from Lucinda and cradled him against his shoulder. "I don't have to convince you, Miss Chamard," he said, looking directly at Nicolette, "that if you should cry out, I will drop this baby over the side."

Frantic, Lucinda reached for Bertie. Franks stiff-armed her.

Thick-tongued, Nicolette rasped, "I understand."

"Let's go," Franks said.

Murph tied his soiled handkerchief over Nicolette's bruised and swollen nose. He wrapped the shawl over her blood-stained bodice and jammed her hat down low. Then he picked her up and followed Franks carrying Bertie, Lucinda carrying Charles Armand.

Passengers crowded at the gangplank, intent on disembarking, on waving to friends on the dock, on balancing their way across the plank to shore. Murph handled Nicolette's weight with ease and carried her as if she were his beloved invalid. No one noticed Lucinda's fearful face nor Nicolette's eyes blazing with hate.

Chapter Thirty

The Red River wound its way across north Texas, wet the southwest corner of Arkansas, then flowed across Louisiana. North of Baton Rouge, it dumped its red waters into the muddy brown of the Mississippi. Down this conduit, supporters of the Confederacy shipped foodstuff and livestock to feed the Rebels.

Whoever controlled the junction of the two rivers controlled that flow of goods. The Federals already commanded the Mississippi River from Baton Rouge down to the Gulf of Mexico. Once they took the territory north of Baton Rouge, they would squeeze shut the Red River and slowly strangle the Confederacy.

Twenty-five miles north of Baton Rouge and forty miles south of the Red River, Port Hudson lay at a strategic point on the eastern bank of the Mississippi. Atop an eighty foot bluff, the fort surveyed a sharp bend in the Mississippi. Navigating through that bend involved a slow, meticulous passage, slow enough that Confederate cannon could pick off Union gunboats easy as shooting fish in a barrel.

If the Confederates continued to hold Port Hudson, they might hold the Red River. But if the Union took the bluffs here and further north at Vicksburg, they'd kick the Rebs off the Mississippi entirely.

Port Hudson had another strategic mission as well: tie up Federal soldiers and materiel that would otherwise be sent to aid Ulysses Grant in taking Vicksburg, the other crucial bastion on the Mississippi.

In late May, after weeks of skirmishing, Federal General Nathaniel Banks gathered his forces to encircle Port Hudson. The *Essex* and other gun boats pummeled the Confederate river batteries with arching mortar, trying to get the range. Some of the balls skittered across the ground harmlessly, some struck trees and burst into towering flame. Others exploded in the earth itself, throwing up roots and dirt which coated the soldiers' hats and shoulders like heavy black rain.

For days, Nicolette and Lucinda had endured heat and rain showers from above, bruising and splinters from beneath as they traveled in the back of a buckboard. Franks allowed Lucinda free use of her hands and feet, but Nicolette he kept bound. She could have won some leeway from him had she been willing to disguise the rage that bubbled up every waking hour. She would rather bite the man's nose off.

Nicolette grunted as the buckboard bounced over a pothole, rattling every bone in her body. Murphy drove the mules, Bertie tied to his broad chest with Lucinda's shawl. Insurance, Murphy called it. "You ladies don't behave," he'd told them, "it won't take no trouble at all to pinch the little feller's breath off." They behaved.

She listened to the distant rumble of cannon rolling through the night sky. They were getting close. Charles Armand woke and scrunched up closer to his maman, covering his ears with his hands.

Since leaving the steamboat at Baton Rouge, the zealot kidnappers had surreptitiously bought horses and mules from planters in the outlying regions. By day, they hid from the Yankee patrols. By night, they evaded them, traveling along back lanes and crop roads toward Port Hudson to deliver their much-needed assets.

So close now that they could see the glow of each mortar burst reflected in the overhanging cloud cover, Franks spurred them on, trusting the pre-dawn fog to shield them from Union pickets.

Over the clop of hooves and squeaking of axles, a shout penetrated the night.

"Yo! Who goes there?"

"Friends," Franks called out. "Brought you a remuda."

"Hold right there," the soldier told them. "Be light in a bit. Then we'll let you in. If you ain't Yanks."

Lucinda gripped Nicolette's hand. *She must think this is deliverance,* Nicolette thought. *Maybe it will be, for her and the boys.*

The Confederates would treat Lucinda well enough. But if Franks convinced the commander at Port Hudson she was a Union spy, the Rebels would not treat Nicolette kindly. Nicolette could not muster much concern for her neck. She was numb to every feeling but rage.

The sun rose above the treetops, revealing soldiers peering at them over an embankment. A deep ravine separated the wagon from the newly constructed ramparts.

"Damn, Reb. You got some horses there," a soldier called out.

"Courtesy of the patriots of the city of New Orleans," Franks answered.

"Come on around this way and we'll let you through."

They passed a good mile of raw yellow earth piled into fortified lunettes, ravines filled with felled trees and branches, and curious faces of Rebels staring at them over the breastworks. On the eastern side of the fortress, they passed through the perimeter into Port Hudson.

From here, the mortar rounds from the river sounded distant and harmless, the nearby soldiers too busy to heed the booms and bursts. Murphy pulled the wagon up.

"Going to be a hot one," a sergeant said, accepting a written account of the horses and mules.

"Yep. Mighty damned hot for May. Tell the general Quentin Franks brought him a whole damn remuda."

Murphy turned around on the buckboard seat. "You gals can climb on down from there."

He laughed at Nicolette, bound and helpless. A fresh surge of hatred burned through her.

"Now we're safe in Confederate territory," Murphy said cheerfully, "I reckon I can let you out of them ropes, Miss Sassypants."

He handed Bertie over to Lucinda and walked around to the back. Nicolette's wrists were scabbed and bruised from days of being bound. When Murphy untied her ankles, bearing the same scars, he ran his hand up her skirt and patted her calf. Bitter bile rose in her throat.

"You're done with the ropes, missy," Murphy said conversationally. "Course you got to answer to treason, but that's a different kind of rope, ain't it?"

Behaving as if he were a gallant gentleman, he helped them climb from the wagon. Nicolette's stiffened legs refused to hold her weight. Murphy caught her with a strong arm and leaned her into his chest till she found her feet. She did not protest. She had days ago ceased to imagine spitting in Murphy's face or clawing at Franks' eyes. She intended to do more damage to these two than she could inflict with bare hands.

"See here, lads." Murphy gestured at her and Lucinda like they were livestock. "We brought you Rebs more than horses."

Half a dozen dirty, raggedy soldiers gathered round Lucinda, gawking. "Damn, I bet she's pretty, you cleaned her up."

"She got big titties, see that?"

The third soldier, a skinny boy with pale dirty hair curling over his forehead, stared at Nicolette. Her eyes were drawn to the pistol at his belt.

"Lookit this other one, fellas," he said. "Pretty, but them eyes is scary mean."

Nicolette studied the young man who leered at her. He thought she was some *thing*, a mere object to be used for his pleasure. She had no worth in his eyes, no true identity. This realization did not sting. The last days of contained fury had removed her from herself. She saw clearly, but she hoarded her emotional energy. When the time came, she meant to expend that energy in a blaze of vengeance.

Murphy waxed sociable with the boys. "They is pretty women, that they are. Figured you boys would know what to do with a couple of pretty women."

The young soldiers snickered, red-faced but eager.

"You had 'em yourself?" the skinny blond kid asked.

Franks turned at the insinuation, an indignant frown on his face. "We are Christian gentlemen, sir. Married men, faithful to our wives as we are to our cause."

Murphy winked at the soldiers. "But if you boys is unwed, I don't see no harm to amusing yourselves. But watch out for that one." He cocked his head toward Nicolette. "A hard woman. A traitor. She just as soon kill you as look at you."

The soldiers dropped their eyes when Nicolette ran her gaze over them.

The village was an earthen fortress, there were guns everywhere. If that boy touched her, or Lucinda, she'd blow a hole through the dirty blond ringlet in the center of his forehead.

A one-armed officer in a gray uniform, his hat faded and crumpled, strode across the open ground. Maybe this was the man who would decide whether she was to be treated like a lady, or a traitor. He looked toward the string of horses, then approached the wagon.

"You men," he said, his voice harsh. The soldiers immediately dispersed.

"Mr. Franks?" the officer said with an enquiring look.

"Here, Captain."

"You have just made it in, I believe. The Feds about have us surrounded. This is a fine gesture, sir."

Nicolette edged along the wagon's side, closer to where Franks stood talking to the captain. She knew that voice.

"We are not fighting men, Captain, but we are true sons of the Confederacy nevertheless. We are proud to aid our brothers in arms."

"Let me show you to headquarters. Major General Gardner will welcome you at breakfast." The officer nodded toward Lucinda. "Corporal, show Mrs. Franks and the other lady, Mrs. Murphy, is it? Take the ladies to Mrs. Brickell's house where they can refresh themselves."

"You are suffering from a misapprehension, captain. These women are colored. That one there," Franks said, gesturing to Nicolette, "has consorted with the enemy ever since they invaded New Orleans. At considerable risk to ourselves, we have apprehended her in an attempt to carry messages from the Union headquarters to General Banks in the field. A traitor, Captain."

The captain looked fully at Nicolette for the first time. His face went slack with astonishment. "Nicolette?"

"Ah, you know the woman," Franks said. "Then you understand how dangerous she is. I recommend confinement apart from the other one. My understanding is that the mother, here, is an innocent dupe in the scheme to appear harmless as the Chamard woman carried her invidious missives northward."

"Nicolette," the captain said again.

She hadn't heard Adam Johnston had lost an arm. Even as she held his gaze, giving him neither a smile nor a hint of gratitude to find a familiar figure in this harsh place, she wondered at the hardness of her heart. She felt neither sympathy nor pity for the empty sleeve.

Adam's gaze took in the yellowing bruises on her face. "You've been beaten," he said, his face ashen.

"Quite necessary, I assure you," Franks said.

Adam's sorrowful eyes said more than his whispered words. "Nicolette. I'm so sorry."

Nicolette gave no indication she heard him. "My friend and the children need a roof over their heads, Captain. Food and water. A bed."

Adam drew himself up. "Of course. Corporal, take the ladies to Mrs. Brickell now, please."

Nicolette stepped around Murphy. He'd been enjoying himself, bantering with the soldiers. She shot him a look that killed the merry glint in his eye. Satisfied, for now, she followed Lucinda and the boys.

"Miss Chamard," Adam said. "I will call directly. To see what assistance you require."

"That won't be necessary, Captain. I'm sure the corporal will see to our needs."

The corporal led Nicolette and Lucinda through the fortress. The air crackled with energy as men swarmed over the camp, as quick and purposeful as ants. A group of soldiers sharpened long poles and set them in the ground, slanted outwards. A dozen black men, already shirtless in the morning heat, shoveled dirt, heightening a breastwork. Around an artillery site, men piled sandbags into a protective wall.

A church, a few houses, a barn or two constituted the village. From beyond the settlement, the sound of the gristmill carried through the morning air. Nicolette's teeth ached at the grating of the huge granite millstones against one another, grinding corn into meal. By now, Franks would be telling the commander of Port Hudson that she was a spy. What would the Confederate general do about that?

Tired from the long walk, Charles Armand dragged against Lucinda's outstretched arm, fretting and pulling at her hand. Nicolette caught up to him and swept him on to her hip.

The world was a hard and cruel place. Feelings made a person weak and vulnerable. Nicolette no longer allowed herself that weakness. She felt only this simmering rage that made her chest boil with hot blood. For her nephew, though, for remembrance of how she loved him, she pretended a piece of her heart still lived.

"You hungry as that little bird up there?" She pointed to a nest of robins peeping from a low branch. "He wants a cricket. Maybe that's what you'll have for breakfast. A nice big bowl of crickets with milk and sugar."

That earned her a giggle, and she hoped the sun seemed a little brighter for Charles Armand. For herself, she saw only glare or deepest dark, nothing in between.

On the other side of the battlements, lush forest surrounded the northern edge of Port Hudson. Somewhere beyond those trees, among General Banks' battalions and regiments, it was likely Finnian McKee prepared his Signal Corps boys for the coming assault. Would it matter to him, to know she was here, perhaps a mile away, among his enemies? It was of no consequence. She was not the same Nicolette Chamard he'd known.

Mrs. Brickell, a stubborn soul who'd refused to leave her home as the Federals advanced, fed Nicolette, Lucinda, and Charles Armand corn meal mush and rancid bacon. Then, full of friendly chat, she gathered worn quilts and blankets to make bed pallets. She showed no curiosity about them, whether they were colored or white or something in between.

"It'll all be over in a few days," Mrs. Brickell said. "One way or t'other. Jest rest yerselves here and we'll all make do."

Late in the morning, Nicolette sat on the back stoop shelling hard dry peas. She still had a charge of treason to face. Once she would have thought a woman would be safe from hanging. But once she'd thought a woman would be safe from a beating, too.

She clamped her sore jaw. No one would ever put a rope around her neck. She'd fight them till they'd have to kill her before they could hang her.

Mrs. Brickell stuck her head out the back doorway. "General Gardner hisself wants to talk to you."

Through the house, Nicolette saw three men silhouetted on the front porch. Nicolette met them, confident she appeared calm and unconcerned.

Adam did the introductions. "Miss Chamard, allow me to introduce Major General Franklin Gardner."

Grim faced and red-eyed, the general looked like he hadn't slept and had too many things to do. He nodded his head to Nicolette and she curtsied briefly.

"Good day, General Gardner."

"And Colonel William Miles."

Colonel Miles, bent and white bearded, offered a courtly bow from the waist.

Nicolette dipped into a full curtsey in response.

General Gardner gestured toward the rawhide chairs. "Please, Miss Chamard, won't you take a chair?"

"I prefer to stand, thank you."

Adam took a position at her elbow, a clear declaration of alliance. Nicolette ignored him.

"Now, Miss Chamard," General Gardner began, "we have received a serious accusation against you, which, however reluctantly, we must address."

"Yes, General. I am aware of the accusation."

"Have you indeed messages to General Banks about your person, Miss Chamard?" Col. Miles asked.

"No, sir, I have not."

"Nor perhaps have you committed to memory information which would be advantageous to General Banks were he to receive it?"

"No, sir, I have not."

Miles and Gardner exchanged a look.

There was not a hint of supplication in her voice when she spoke. "I am not a spy."

"There. You see, sir, it is as I told you," Adam interjected.

The general held his hand up to hush him. "Miss Chamard, this man Franks also claims that you were seen entering and exiting the Union headquarters in New Orleans many times. Will you explain your business there, please?"

"Gladly. My mother was once a slave, General. My Uncle Thibault and his children are yet enslaved. I wish the Union to win this war so that slavery is ended forever. To that end, this past year I have aided the Union as a telegrapher on General Butler's, then General Banks' staff."

"A collaborator, then," Colonel Miles said, looking at her over his spectacles.

Nicolette raised her chin proudly. "Yes, sir."

General Gardner motioned with his head to Colonel Miles. They walked a dozen paces across the yard.

Nicolette held her back ramrod straight. She stared at Gardner and Miles, trying to read their bodies. Their heads were bent toward one another in earnest consultation, but she could not see their faces.

"Captain?" Colonel Miles called for Adam to join them.

The General looked back at her once and turned his shoulder toward her again. What could they be talking about for so long? They had no proof! There *was* no proof.

Gardner nodded his head once, twice. He strode back and stood in the grass below the steps. "Miss Chamard, Colonel Miles is acquainted with your father. We regret the unpleasantness. Good day to you."

He bowed reflexively and turned to the colonel. "Very well, Colonel. That's taken care of. Let's have a look at the east rampart, if you please."

Nicolette's fingers uncurled. She took a breath at last. She was not to be hanged. Nor chained to the wall in some dark room. But not because she was innocent. Because Colonel Miles knew her father. And if he hadn't once played cards with Papa, shared a glass of port and a cigar?

"I told them you were not a spy," Adam said.

Nicolette ran her gaze down Adam's length. Former suitor. Former batterer. How often had her dreams been tormented by what this man had done to her? So much smaller than she remembered him. Middling height, sandy brown hair. A bushy moustache. He'd been drunk that day he hit her, blind drunk. She saw no signs of drink now. His eyes, hangdog, appealing to her for some sort of recognition, seemed clear.

"As it happens, Mr. Johnston, I am not a spy. But had the Union general asked it of me, I believe I would have attempted it." She entered the house without another glance at him.

The following day, Nicolette did her best to amuse Charles Armand. Made uneasy by sporadic gunfire several miles beyond the fort's perimeter, he fussed and clung. With every shell whistling from the gunboats and bursting over the river ramparts, he flinched until his shoulders began to shake.

"Look here, Charles Armand." Nicolette stripped a pillow case off its pillow and smoothed the unbleached cotton. "This is a very special pillow case. When it's on your head, the big booms can't hurt you. They're still very annoying, but they are harmless against this special pillowcase. And it is yours, Charles Armand."

Nicolette draped the case over his head. Charles let out a long quiet sigh.

By noon, artillery, musket, and rifle fire rolled across the prairie land east of Port Hudson in a continuous blurred roar. Nicolette gave up trying to divert Charles Armand and held him in her lap. The magic pillowcase at least kept his little body from trembling.

When a soldier passed by, walking double-time with a spade over his shoulder, Nicolette called through the window. "What news?"

"Can't see a thing from the ramparts, Miss. Got no idea who's winning out there."

At last the noise ceased. No cannon, no rifle pop, no mortar shells. Nicolette itched with the need to know what happened. She returned Charles Armand to Lucinda and walked toward the eastern perimeter, out of range from cannon and mortar should the attack resume. The soldiers manning the barrier at the east entrance opened up. Col. Miles rode in with his infantry, retreating in good order, but hot, bedraggled, and defeated. At the end of the column, carts of dead and dying soldiers.

The Union had beaten them back.

One of the casualties, his arm hanging off the side of the cart, cast vacant eyes toward the brilliant sun. The boy from yesterday, the one who asked if Franks had "had" her. Just a boy. And dead. Just one more boy out of so many. A Confederate soldier. An enemy. What did his death mean to her?

In the twilight, she returned to Mrs. Brickell's house where Charles Armand had already gone to sleep. She shooed flies away from him, lay down beside him and closed her eyes.

At dawn, she woke with a start. The mortar fire again. No doubt the *Essex* was among them, Captain McKee's friend Jay Zettle lobbing shells at her. How wonderful, she thought, to be killed by such a friendly, cheerful soul.

The face of the dead soldier on the cart came back to her. A gruesome face, all the blood drained out of it. That boy had been alive yesterday.

That boy had had a pistol.

Nicolette eased off the pallet where Charles Armand slept, sweat beading over his lip. Lucinda and Bertie slept nearby, flies buzzing in and out the window, a slight breeze moving the gauzy curtain.

She slipped on her shoes and crossed the village to the surgeon's tent. The morgue no doubt would be nearby. Closing her ears to cries and moans, her eyes averted from a fly-covered amputated leg, she held a hand over her nose. The large, quiet tent beyond beckoned her with open flaps.

As she drew near, the drone of flies grew loud. Inside, the dead were laid on tarps. Mrs. Brickell and another woman were bathing the faces of the fallen boys. A sergeant was searching pockets for letters, watches, photographs, items to be sent home to mothers and fathers and sweethearts.

Nicolette looked for the face she knew. Somehow, it had to be his gun she took. She found the boy, his face the color of magnolia blooms. A wound in his thigh gaped right down to the bone. A sword slash? However the gash was made, it had drained the blood from his body, his entire pants leg thick and stiff with it. He would not suffer amputation or fever or years of pain and debilitation. It was over, for this boy. Louisiana Legion, the patch on his sleeve said. A boy from home.

His weapons were gone. Nicolette looked around. All the bodies were disarmed. In the corner of the tent, the sergeant had made a tepee of the muskets and rifles. At the base of the pyramid, one pistol, still in its holster and ammunition belt.

Nicolette checked that the women and the sergeant bent to their tasks. They paid no mind to her. She moved down the row of bodies to the pile of arms, picked up the pistol and belt, and slipped out of the tent.

She crossed open ground and hid behind a shed. The wounds on her wrists had bled through the gauze bandages again. Ignoring the stains, she loaded the pistol. All she needed now was a clear line of sight to take down Franks and Murphy. The fort might be a mile wide and two or three miles long, but she'd find them.

The Nicolette who sang ballads, who made up funny ditties, who once fell in love – she didn't know that Nicolette any more. She was merely an instrument now, the hand behind the gun that would send Murphy and Quentin Franks to hell.

Chapter Thirty-One

Before dawn, his eyes gritty and red, Finn McKee climbed a crude ladder to a tree-top platform. He hadn't slept. Mortar fire meant to soften up the Rebs before this morning's attack had kept him and the other 30,000 Union soldiers on edge all night. Now, with the sun about to rise, the land batteries chimed in, blindly bombarding the Confederate stronghold.

Two signal corpsmen climbed up and squeezed onto the platform. "Keep your heads down, lads," Finn told them. "First sunray to catch your pearly whites, those Mississippi sharpshooters will get you."

At first light, Finn trained his telescope toward the Rebel fortifications. He'd been studying this terrain for days. What a mess. The Mississippi was in full flood, backing up the creeks and filling the swamp on the Federal right. Hursh had made a sport of killing the rattlers that wanted a share of dry land. Got himself eight the day before, and another fellow fired a shotgun blast into a nest of cottonmouths.

Finn surveyed the pontoon bridge the Union engineers had built across swollen Little Sandy Creek, which would be helpful until the Rebel artillery took it out. On the other side of the creek were deep ravines choked with timber that the Rebs had deliberately felled every which way, then an open killing field. Beyond that, Confederate earthworks shielded the Rebs and their artillery for several hundred yards outside the actual fort.

Finn shook his head at the intricacy of natural defenses around Port Hudson. Thank heavens for the Union's artillery. Without cover from mortar and cannon, it'd be a slaughter to advance across the creek, over the hillocks, down the gullies, through the branches and logs, all under fire from Rebel guns.

Before full light, Finn heard the jingle of harness, the rattle of canteens and weaponry. General Weitzel had begun his advance.

"This is it, boys," Finn said. "We take Port Hudson today, we'll be at Vicksburg within the week. You got a brother up there with Grant, don't you, Dudley?"

"No, sir. I got two."

Federal soldiers ghosted under their tree, wisps of fog deadening the sound of their passage through the deeper dark under the tree canopy.

Without warning, the Rebs opened fire. Through the gray fog, Finn saw the yellow flashes of rifle and musket fire, the puffs of smoke, then heard the pop pop pop and the cries of men caught by minié balls.

The Federals raised their battle cry and rushed the Rebs' advance positions, firing as they ran.

Muskets, rifles, and artillery blazed. Tree limbs crashed down, men cried out, red flames burst from the mouths of cannon.

"All right, boys," Finn shouted.

Privates Dunston and Dudley raised their signal flags, ready to send a wig wag message to pin point the action. Finn bit back the urge to warn them, *Keep behind the flags!* As if a strip of cloth could stop a minié ball.

The Union's greater numbers at last pushed the Rebs back until they made a run to shelter behind their forward earthworks. The Federals had prevailed, thank God, but Finn's telescope revealed Union infantrymen in disarray, confused and stalled, their line broken by the steep ravines and the thick virgin forest.

Stinging sweat trickled down Finn's stubbled face. The soldiers below him, laden with weapons and ammunition, must feel themselves in the heat of hell. Yet go on they must despite the maze of obstacles before them — dense stands of pine, magnolia and willow, the creek itself, hillocks, deep snake-infested gorges, and the Rebel's abatis of trees and branches felled into a massive tangle. Rifle shots from both sides rang out as sharpshooters took aim.

To Finn's left, an officer shouted out "Come on!" Finn searched the battlefield and found Colonel Babcock in his lens. His spirits soared as the colonel raised his sword and dashed ahead of his regiment in pursuit of the enemy. In ragged form, men followed him into steady fire from Confederate musketry. Then the Rebel gunners found their range. Twelve-pounders exploded over and among the blue-clads.

Finn focused on a file of soldiers, running one behind the other into the fight. In freakish carnage, a Rebel artillery shell tore through the whole row, killing every man. He dropped the telescope, Dudley catching it before it rolled off the platform. Finn leaned over the side and vomited, the image of those mangled men forever imprinted in his mind.

He wiped his mouth and held his hand out to Dudley for the telescope. The battle had not halted for his lapse of attention.

The noise of cannon and rifle, of the terrified shrieking of bullet riddled horses and exploding grenades stunned him. The assault force, diminished but determined, continued through the killing artillery fire, closing on the Rebel position.

Finn focused his lens on the Confederate line under the 1st Alabama flag. They carried outdated flintlocks. They'd be no match for the Federals' Springfields and Enfields. Finn's confidence evaporated as the Federals got within forty yards of the Confederate's forward breastworks. As one, the Rebels rose from behind their cover and blazed a volley of musketry directly into the Union line.

With no time to reload, the Confederates ran full tilt to the fortifications behind them. The Federals rallied and pursued.

Everywhere Finn trained his telescope, some valiant action, some deadly event filled his lens. A youth carried the 75th New York's flag, running and leaping over fallen comrades. A ball took him and he dropped, the flag clasped to his chest. Immediately a soldier rescued the flag and charged ahead. Further on, a shell cut a soldier in two. Near him, a minié caught another in the throat, the spray of blood visible through Finn's eye piece. He closed his eyes, just for a moment, wishing the vision could be washed from his mind.

But he had his part to play. In the confusion of smoke and movement and deafening noise, Finn tried to make sense of the battle scene to signal the next tower and the next, on to General Banks himself: the 1st Maine battery took a direct hit, men and horses blasted and dead; an overheated cannon at Battery F exploded, the installation simply gone; Rebel cannon dismounted two guns at Battery A leaving the bodies of men and horses strewn about in bloody heaps.

Unbelievably, the Confederate resistance quelled the advance of the greater Union force. The Rebs didn't seem to care how outnumbered they were, they fought like Titans. In frustration,

Finn pounded his fist against the deck of the platform as, by platoon and squad, the Federals' fragmented attacks failed.

A trumpeting bugle announced the stirring of another regiment to Finn's rear. He trained his glass behind him, northward. From this angle, Finn spotted the white crosses Rebs had nailed to the trees to mark their artillery range. The enemy had had weeks and weeks to prepare for this day.

Peering over and through the trees, Finn caught the waving flag of the Louisiana Native Guards, anchoring the far right of the Union line. With dread, Finn realized the colored regiments were about to draw fire. André Cailloux was to have his wish.

The most rugged and treacherous terrain along the whole front lay before the Guards. Beyond the swamp and gullies and abatis-filled ravines lay rifle pits and sharp-eyed Rebs. Beyond them, a heavily fortified redoubt of Confederate cannon filled with grape aimed right at the ground the Guards were to cross.

Hundreds of black troops crossed the pontoon bridge, marched through thick stands of willow knee deep in water, and emerged from the trees to advance at quick time, then double-quick. They formed a long line, two men deep, rushing toward the Rebels, screaming the battle yell of defiance and blood-lust.

Confederate fire tore into their line. Men fell, arms stretched to the sky.

Unbelievably, the line pushed on.

Finn scoured the ranks for Captain Cailloux. He found him in the forefront, sword raised, exhorting his men onward.

The Guard dove into deep gullies full of brambles and a confusion of limbs and vines. Some made it through, crawling once more into the barrage from rifles, muskets, and howitzers.

Finn found André in his lens again.

"Jesus," he breathed. André's left arm dangled from a hit above the elbow, the odd angle sickening to behold. But André pressed on, his mouth open in a shout. *En avant, mes enfants! Follow me!* Men dropping all around, his troops rallied behind him.

My God, what courage!

Finn's hands trembled, the telescope wavering. Courage would not be enough. No force on earth could cross that fearful terrain under the constant, deadly fusillade from the Confederates. Banks had thrown those men into hell.

Finn forgot the snipers, the whizzing artillery. He stood his full height and screamed "Turn back!"

Private Dudley pulled him down.

Finn fumbled with his telescope, searching for the giant of a man leading the Native Guards.

Found him. Focused.

André's big body suddenly whirled round like a doll on a string.

"Get up, André! Get up," Finn shouted, his voice breaking. "Get them out of there!"

André Cailloux lay motionless.

Men nearby stopped, stunned. How could this man die? Not this man!

Their uncertainty spread. Confusion and fear seized those brave soldiers. They ran for the line of willows if they could, sheltered in the snaky abatis if they could not. Even fleeing through the willows, the Native Guards fell as Rebel artillery rained down on them, shattering trees and hurling killer splinters through the ranks.

Some heroic soldiers tried to wade through the swamp water to launch another attack, some joined them, scaling a ridge. All were cut down.

Finn bent over his knees, the telescope forgotten.

Inside the Rebel fortifications, Nicolette lived with two intentions. Killing Murphy and Franks never left her mind, but in a camp of thousands spread over a large area, she had not yet found either of them. Her other intent, to live through these days with purpose. She showed up at the surgeon's tent at dawn every morning.

Another skirmish at the battlements had sent a fresh surge of wounded to the tent. Nicolette dripped chloroform onto a paper cone, then lowered it toward an ashen faced boy. The boy panicked, struck at her hands, his eyes on the surgeon's looming scalpel.

"Dammit!" the surgeon roared, holding the man down with the weight of his body. "Get that mask on him!"

Nicolette jammed the cone over the soldier's face and in seconds he was out. She turned her head to the side, anticipating the surgeon's quick slice into the man's thigh above the shattered bone.

Ten minutes or less, that was the goal. Put him out, pick out the lint the man's fellows had packed into the wound, cut through bone and sinew, sew the wound closed, and say a quick prayer the man would fight off the inevitable infection.

Odd, she thought, all this pain, suffering, horror taking place in such quiet. After hours of deafening cannon, her head felt like it was stuffed with straw. Sounds seemed distant and muffled, even the scrape of saw on bone. The surgeons used hand signals to indicate they were ready for the next man. The men, quieted by shock and chloroform, hardly groaned.

Nicolette pushed sweat-soaked hair off her face, the other hand holding the chloroform cone in place. Flies flitted above the surgeon's hands, hovering, then lighting on a bit of raw flesh. A drop of sweat fell from the doctor's nose into the open wound.

The smell of burnt powder and blood and fear hung in the air. If only there were a breeze, Nicolette thought. A little air stirring so she could breathe.

"I said, You from New Orleans, ain't you?" Mrs. Brickell shouted into her ear.

Mrs. Brickell carried a basin on her way to the growing pile of limbs outside the tent. Nicolette knew better than to look into that basin, but she couldn't stop herself in time. A hand, grimy, with close-bit nails, nestled in a puddle of watery blood.

She closed her eyes. Mrs. Brickell shouted into her ear. "Fella from the front line says the Federals are sending them black troops from New Orleans into the fight. They's getting desperate, you ask me." Mrs. Brickell hurried on her with her basin to be ready for the next separated appendage.

André's regiment. And William with him. Not quite aware she was doing it, Nicolette untied the bloody apron that covered the pistol at her waist, and left the tent. She quickened her steps, walking faster, trotting, then running to the barricades north of the surgeons' tent.

At the earthworks, men shot and loaded, aimed, shot and loaded. Nicolette climbed over a fallen mule, deaf, a little crazed. She stepped onto a bale of hay, about to hoist herself up so that she could see over the barricade. If she could see them, she could keep André and William safe through the force of her will.

Gretchen Craig

A lad elbowed her aside, raised his musket, and fired. Some other man grabbed her by the arm and whirled her around.

Adam Johnston. His face was red and contorted. He shouted at her, but she couldn't hear him. With his one hand, he pulled her off the rampart, hustled her past the mule, and nearly dragged her across the field toward the village.

He shoved her into the front door of Mrs. Brickell's house. "What the hell you think you were doing?"

His voice came through thin and reedy. Her own voice seemed as distant as his. "Did you see? The Native Guard?"

"The colored troops? It's over, Nicolette. They're finished."

Adam still had hold of her arm, squeezing it. It hurt, vaguely.

"André Cailloux," Nicolette said. "He led the Native Guards."

Adam strained to hear her. "The cigar store man? I saw him. He's dead."

Nicolette sank onto the chair, Adam still holding on to her.

"You want a glass of water?"

Her gaze on the floor, Nicolette focused on a vision of André Cailloux, his boy perched on his broad shoulders, a grin on his handsome black face.

"William was with him," she muttered.

"Who?"

"William."

"I don't know him. Listen, Nicolette." He shook her shoulder. "Nicolette, you hear me?"

She looked at him, wondering why he didn't wipe the blood off his cheek. Was it his blood?

Lucinda appeared at the doorway, carrying both her boys. "What's happened?" she yelled over a cannon blast.

"I found her at the barricade about to get her head shot off. Keep her here."

Lucinda sank to the floor next to the chair and freed her hand from around Charles Armand to take hold of Nicolette's.

"I'll keep her here, Captain."

"Stay here," Adam shouted. "You understand?"

Nicolette felt the floorboards vibrate as Adam ran from the house back to the battle.

"You just lost yourself for a few minutes, honey," Lucinda said, her voice distant. "You're going to be fine."

252

Gradually, Nicolette regained a sense of where she was, of what she'd done. She felt no regret for having rushed into the whizzing bullets. She didn't even feel grief for André and William. That was a deep pool waiting to drown her, but not now. Not yet.

Nicolette drank the glass of water Lucinda handed her, Charles Armand watching her with big frightened eyes, the special pillow case draped over his head. He clung to Lucinda's skirt, his thumb in his mouth.

Nicolette opened her arms to him and he climbed into her lap. She adjusted the pillowcase so it covered his face and rocked him back and forth on the rawhide chair for a while. She held his bare foot in her hand, the weight of him against her heart anchoring her. If she couldn't feel fear, or grief, she could feel this. She loved this child, and he needed her.

Charles Armand's body slowly softened and he slept, bombs bursting not a quarter of a mile away.

"Thank God," Lucinda said. "He didn't sleep the whole night through, nor yesterday."

"I'm going back." Nicolette shifted Charles Armand's weight so she could stand.

"You are not going anywhere near those barricades!"

"No. To the surgeons' tent."

She carried Charles Armand into the bedroom and lay him down. Gently, she surrounded him with pillows and made sure the pillow case covered his head. In the still room amid the tumult and din, Nicolette recited the *memorare. Remember O Most Gracious Virgin Mary*, she prayed, and asked her protection for this house and its inhabitants.

In the hospital tent, Nicolette stood at the head of the operating table. With steady hands, she took the chloroform cone from the doctor's hands.

Chapter Thirty-Two

As night fell, Finn peered through the drifting smoke and fog. He couldn't bring himself to leave while soldiers were still stranded in the killing fields.

The gloaming deepened. A Yankee crawled from under a fallen tree, cautious and quiet. A dirty youth, parched and sunburned, climbed out of a gully.

Nearby a man heaved off his comrade's dead body. He'd lain in the line of fire since morning, the sun pounding down on him. Finn imagined the stink and thirst must have driven him nearly mad, too scared even to brush away the ants that stung him. But he hadn't given the Rebs any reason to shoot at him, and he'd lived through the day.

The survivors crept through the field, keeping low and making for the pontoon spanning Little Sandy Creek. Once across, they broke into a run through the Union defenses, shreds of cotton gleaming on the ground from the blasted cotton bales used as bulwarks. Finn climbed down and followed them through the dark.

Safely in camp, he leaned his back against a pine tree, hoping if he were still the pain in his head would stop throbbing. Earlier, he'd drunk a canteen full of bad water and paid the price. Now, feeling limp and empty, he simply sat, watching his signal lads gathered around a fire.

Finn had seen men die. He'd been with General Weitzel since September, near nine months now. They'd mopped up the Lafourche, then moved over to the Teche, up to Alexandria, and back over to the Mississippi. He'd twice been swept into the action as Rebels advanced on his observation post. He'd shot men and been shot at. He'd seen men's throats torn out by minié ball, seen them holding their guts with their own hands, seen them take a bullet in the eye.

But he'd seen nothing on this scale. Seen nothing as wrong-headed and pointless as sending all those good men into the enemy's maw. Had the generals no idea what they asked, sending soldiers across swamp and abatis and gullies and open ground? Had they not scouted the terrain? Finn burned at the waste of all those men. How could they excuse such a blunder?

André Cailloux's body still lay out there in the dark. Under a white flag, the Union had removed some of their dead for burial, but not all of them. The one's who'd braved the fire the longest and got closest to the ramparts were the men left on the field. Finn wiped a hand over his stubbled jaw, unable to fight the thought of rodents out there in the night, among the dead.

Hursh Farrow lowered himself next to Finn and shared the tree trunk.

For a while, they watched the fire together, too exhausted to talk.

Hursh pulled out a twist of tobacco and offered a chaw.

Finn shook his head. "Anything I put in my mouth is coming right back up."

When Hursh had his chaw under control, he tucked it in his cheek.

"Over at headquarters, they're saying it's going to be a siege, we don't take 'em in the next few days."

"Guess it'll be a siege, then."

After a time, Hursh hauled himself up. "Think I'll add to my letter before I go to sleep."

"Good night, Hursh."

The men sat around their campfires, exhausted, but too nerved up to sleep. Dudley and Dunston played checkers. Charley Beam whittled. Sandy White played his jew's harp. No one said anything about Pete Poteet whose body lay in a line of other casualties waiting for morning burial.

Finn pulled out his packet of letters. The ones that would be sent home if he were killed as well as the ones he'd received in the last year. He opened Da's letter and read it again. There was barely firelight enough to see the elegant script, but he knew the core of it by heart.

I admit your avowal to marry this young woman, whether you have my and Mother's blessing or not, disconcerted me, son. A Father likes to believe he is the absolute authority in his little kingdom. However, now that I am recovered, I wonder at your

rather wild proclamation – did you think you were spawned by
savages? have I not subscribed to the abolitionist journals for
years? – I have to acknowledge that I would think less of a man
who did not choose the woman he loves over the approval of a
cantankerous father. The issue, however, is moot, Finnian.
Mother and I have discussed this at length, as you can imagine,
for as you know, your mother will discuss the price of laundry
starch — at length. Our hearts and heads are as one in this
matter. If your mademoiselle is black or brown or white, if she
comes home on your arm, she is welcome in our family. If she
chooses to "pass," as they call it, we will honor her wish. If she
chooses to proclaim her mixed heritage, we will abide by that
decision. A few friends may decide to cut us, but as Mother says,
who needs "snippy" friends? There. Who could be more
reasonable than your wise and loving parents, Finnian? As I
have told you before, you are a lucky son of a gun. Bring your
girl home, and yourself. Your loving Da.

Even now, after all these months, Finn flushed, tormented by
shame that he'd walked away from Nicolette. He'd been too proud
to see the truth of it at first. Once he kicked his pride aside,
though, he'd found a trace of the devil buried deep in his heart.
There had been a tiny ember within himself that flared at thought
her veins ran with tainted blood. He, an abolitionist, and he'd
harbored a seed of racism. He'd burned that ugliness out of
himself. Now, filled with remorse and self-recrimination, he would
crawl on his knees to ask her to have him.

Back in New Orleans, Nicolette would read the casualty lists
coming in to headquarters. If Finn fell tomorrow or the next day,
she might read his name. He wondered if she'd care.

In relentless sun or drenching rain, through the onslaught of
random artillery fire and ravenous mosquitoes, the men kept to
the barricades. After the onslaught of May 27th, however, the
furious pace of cutting and stitching slowed in the surgeons' tents.
Inevitably, those who survived the knife developed raging fevers.
Nicolette held a tin cup to her patients' lips, urging them to drink
the bitter tea she made from Indian sage. Some would survive,
some would not.

Two weeks had passed since André was snapped like a brittle cog in the great war machine, as if he were not a man who sang with gusto over a pint of beer, who rocked his babes to sleep, loved his wife and his friends. Once Nicolette would have said her rosary when she woke, praying for André's soul, beseeching Mother Mary to protect Bertie and Charles Armand. But now she stared unblinking at the ceiling, unable to pray.

Was William still out there, alive, or did his body rot next to André's?

The hospital tent filled with men dehydrated from diarrhea, delirious with sun stroke, or trembling with malarial ague. Nicolette became a ministering angel, that's what some of the boys called her, in spite of the menacing pistol she wore on her hip. She no longer gagged at the sight of maggots and pus. The stench of putrefaction and unwashed bodies, the hot heavy air under the tents, the constant droning of flies – all of it achieved a state of normalcy.

The constant gunfire nevertheless took its toll. Lucinda wore great circles under her eyes. Bertie turned from a placid easy-going sweetheart into a tense, fussy baby. Charles Armand never took the pillow case off his head. He slept little and seldom spoke, growing quieter with every day's tension. Lucinda fed him the sweet potato pone Mrs. Brickell made, and the concoction of boiled rice and molasses the whole camp ate, but neither she nor Nicolette would countenance the blue-scummed beef the quartermaster doled out.

Through the scorching summer days, Nicolette functioned like an automaton, her mind distanced from the work of her hands. Somewhere in this camp, perhaps only half a mile from her, Murphy and Franks lay on their hard pallets or took their turns at the barricades. During the day, she watched for them, but the fortifications ran several miles around. At night, sleepless in the heat, edgy from the blasts of cannon and musket, she planned how she would kill them when she had the chance. No man would ever again take her strength, take control of her body or her will, and live. She kept the pistol on her hip loaded.

Nicolette tolerated Adam Johnston as an annoyance of little account. He habitually appeared at the porch door late in the evenings, assuming a mantle of protection. "Do you have everything you need?" he'd ask. "Did you get enough to eat? And the babies?"

Generally she responded with a curt yes and turned back into the house without summoning a kind word. At last, however, after a day of infernal heat and plaguing mosquitoes, she turned on him with the force of an icy gale.

"Mr. Johnston. We are not friends. I do not require your solicitude. Please do not again trouble yourself on my account."

Adam blanched as if she'd spat at him, but he held his ground. "That man Franks." He looked to be sure she knew who he meant. She knew. "He lit out last night. Gone. Two other fellows from Mississippi went with him."

Nicolette ground her teeth. The damnable coward.

"And Murphy?" she asked.

"I don't know."

Nicolette turned on her heel and walked straight-backed into the house.

Adam did not appear again, though she often saw him watching her from across the village if there were no skirmish to keep him away.

June the tenth, rain poured down as if to provide the flood that would float Noah's ark off the mountain. Surely for this day the war would cease, Nicolette thought. But the storm did not dissuade General Banks from launching his second major assault. In spite of the deluge, howitzers, parrots, and mortar tore through the downpour with deadly effect. Men shivered and fired their weapons blindly, unable to see through the heavy rain.

In the hospital tent, Nicolette stood in a running puddle, dripping chloroform or winding gauze around stumps, answering this doctor's call or that surgeon's demands. The next victim was heaved onto the operating table in front of her to await the surgeon's rotation, the man's neck opened by an errant fragment of shell.

Nicolette's hands stilled. Her spine turned to ice. Murphy. Kidnapper. Tormentor. He had not raped her, but in every other way he had violated her. He had bound her limbs with rope, bound her will with fear for the children. And now he was helpless. She touched the gun at her waist.

"Just fainted, miss," the orderly said. "This one's got a chance yet."

She stared at Murphy's tangled filthy red beard. Franks had said they were married men. Murphy might have a houseful of children at home. A mother who waited for him. But he was about to die on this table.

As if in a dream, Nicolette slowly pulled at the lint stuffed into the wound. Under the flap of raw flesh, a red vein pulsed. She touched her fingertip to it. She pressed a little harder, felt the blood coursing beneath her finger.

She didn't need the gun on her hip. Just a flick of her fingernail, the artery would open. Blood would spray all over her, but she was used to blood. She stroked the quarter inch of exposed artery. So easy.

Franks had escaped her, but she could kill Murphy. Right now. But he wouldn't know who killed him. She wanted his eyes open. She wanted to see his fear as he realized she was about to kill him. And then, she'd see him die.

She pinched his ear lobe, gouging the tender flesh with her thumb nail. She leaned over him so he could see her clearly.

Murphy stirred and blinked.

"You know who I am, Mr. Murphy? You remember me?"

Murphy let out a sigh. "Miss Sassypants." He said it as if it were a pet name for a favorite child. "Thank God," he said. "How bad am I hurt?"

Nicolette pulled back abruptly. *Thank God?* She took a step away. Thank God? He thought she was going to save him?

What did he mean, calling her Miss Sassypants, like they were friends?

Did he have no understanding how much she hated him? How could he not know? Where was the fear in his eyes?

Thank God?

The shaking started at her fingertips, ran up her arms, down to her knees. He thought she would save him?

Nicolette ran from the tent into the driving rain. Thunder vied with heavy mortar, the rain drops pounded against the trees, the roofs, the ground. Water streamed through her hair, between her breasts. Mud oozed over her boot tops. She shuddered, cold to the bone, cold to the heart.

Instead of Murphy's trusting face, what haunted Nicolette was the serene, alabaster countenance of the Virgin Mary, tranquil but watchful in her niche at the cathedral.

Murphy had looked at her as one living soul to another, seeing no difference between them, sensing only their common humanity. A look that Mary, Mother of God, would expect her to understand.

And she'd been about to kill him. Under God's own eye, she'd been about to bleed the life out of one of His children.

What had she become?

She raised her face, the rain spattering against her cheeks and eyelids. *Mother of God. Help me.*

She didn't know how long she punished herself in the rain. By the time she climbed onto Mrs. Brickell's porch, her legs barely held her up. She opened the door, shaking so hard her teeth clicked together.

Lucinda leapt from her chair, spilling Charles Armand to his feet. "My God, Nikki. You're blue."

Lucinda dragged her to the fire, started at the buttons of her wet dress. "Charles Armand, get that quilt off the bed. Hurry."

Lucinda stripped her to the skin and wrapped her in the quilt. Nicolette couldn't stop trembling.

"Sit in Nikki's lap, Charles. Warm her up." Charles Armand climbed into Nicolette's lap and wrapped his arms around her neck.

"I nearly killed a man, Lucinda." Nicolette told her, tears of shame rolling down her face.

"Blessed Mother, thank you." Lucinda wrapped her arms around Nicolette and Charles Armand together. "My dear Nikki, I feared you'd gone to stone. You cry it out."

The sun set behind a curtain of rain. Warm now, Nicolette sat inert before the fire. She felt weak and strangely light. Her head ached from crying.

Mrs. Brickell warmed up the rest of the soup, bits of carrot and parsnip and bacon floating in it. Nicolette managed a bowl, but the fatback, moldy peas, and biscuits repulsed her.

"Them boys at the ramparts would give a sight to sit here tonight and eat this sorry dinner," Mrs. Brickell declared. "You eat up, hear?"

The back door into the room banged open and a tall figure in dripping rain slicker loomed, his face hidden by the floppy hat. Charles Armand screamed as if the devil himself had stepped in the door.

Marcel threw his hat off and reached for his son. "Here, little man. It's me. It's just Papa."

Charles Armand clawed to get away, grabbing at Lucinda, heedless of the pillow case falling off his head.

"I'll take him, Lucinda," Nicolette said over the panicked wailing. "Here, Charles, come with me. I'll take you to bed and we'll crawl under the covers together. Come on," she coaxed, grabbing up the pillow case. "We'll cover our heads and we'll be safe under the quilt."

Charles Armand leapt into Nicolette's arms and buried his face in her shoulder.

All her long-banished emotions welled up, threatening to overcome her again, as they had in the rain. Her voice scratchy, she whispered "Hello, Marcel" and took Charles Armand to burrow into safety.

Lucinda threw herself into Marcel's wet embrace. He rocked her in his arms, inhaling the scent of smoke and fear.

"I'm getting you wet," he said into her hair.

She clung to his neck. "I don't care."

"Give me that slicker, mister," Mrs. Brickell said, "before you wet up the whole house. I reckon you're staying a while."

Lucinda led him to the parlor fire where Bertie slept in a drawer. Marcel lifted him into his arms and gazed at him in the candle light. "There were times ... ," he said, a catch in his throat.

"Sit down," Lucinda said. "Tell me how you got here."

He and Alistair Whiteaker had ridden through the rain retreating from Grierson's cavalry on the Clinton road. "We brought in about forty men a piece. I figure we're welcome. Adam Johnston was at the barricade. He told me you and Nikki were here, with the children."

Marcel reached for Lucinda's hands. "Now, my darling. Why are you here?"

She told him about that day. She even told him she had beaten Mrs. Chamard and left her bleeding on the bricks.

Marcel listened, his eyes growing darker. He shook his head, gazing at her lovely hands, rubbing his thumb over the smooth skin. "Come here," he said, and took her into his lap. "Tomorrow, my first task will be to find these men, Franks and Murphy. They will never cross your path again."

"Marcel, you won't kill them? Please, they will be armed, they'll ... ."

"Hush." If he killed them, he would do it so that she would never know of it. "I will begin with General Gardner. If he will undertake a prison term, he may save them."

"Please, Marcel. God will not forgive a murder."

He placed a finger over her lips. "The next thing I will do is write to my wife. To her father, and to my father. And lastly, to my solicitor. The children will be yours, always. Whatever happens to me. You understand? You need never worry this will happen again."

Lucinda stroked his scraggly beard, pushed the hair off his face, trying to hold in the sobs building up.

Marcel pulled her to his shoulder and held her while she cried.

At sunrise, there was a lull in the fighting. The only sound was a single bird singing in the chinaberry tree at the front of the house. Marcel tiptoed into the room where Nicolette had taken Charles Armand to bed. Gently, he touched her shoulder.

She sat up and Marcel leaned down to hug her.

"Thank you, Nikki. For taking care of my family."

"We took care of each other."

He sat down on the bed. "These men, who are they?"

"Fanatics. Franks fancies himself an orator. Murphy, just a thug."

He eyed her suspiciously. "You seem very cool about having been abducted, bound, and accused of treason."

She nodded toward the gun on the bedside table, the cartridges emptied beside it lest Charles Armand pick the pistol up. "I meant to kill them both. But Franks slipped out a fortnight ago like the coward he is. And Murphy." Nicolette reached for her brother's hand. "Marcel, I nearly killed Murphy."

She told him about the gaping wound, and how blessed she was not to have lost her soul to vengeance.

Marcel gazed at her in wonder. He believed she could have killed those men. She had a spine in her, and an uncompromising spirit. And perhaps she had saved his soul, too. He didn't see how he could in conscience and honor not have killed those men. And now this Murphy lay in the hospital with a fist-sized hole in his neck.

He took Nicolette's hand, and together they said a short prayer of thanks. Killing all around them, day after day, but they had neither of them committed Cain's sin.

He looked at her a long moment. "You're really all right?"

She nodded. "Now that I can pray again. And feel again."

"All right. Where's my boy?"

Nicolette pulled the covers back to reveal Charles Armand snuggled up to her, the pillow case around his head.

"Charles," she said quietly, rubbing his back. "Charles, your Papa has come to see you."

Charles Armand raised his head. He began to cry, but this time he reached his arms up for his Papa.

Marcel held him close, waiting for the sniffles to stop. After a time, he picked at the pillow case covering his boy's head. One corner lifted so he could see Charles Armand's face, he said, "Do we need this?"

Charles Armand gripped the cloth in his fist. "Yes, Papa."

Marcel dropped the corner, covering his face again, and walked his son out to the porch. He sat down in the rawhide chair and settled Charles Armand on his lap. Peeking underneath the pillow case again, he said, "If we pull back a corner here, you can watch the sunrise with me. Want to do that?"

"Just a corner," Charles Armand said.

Alistair Whiteaker showed himself as early as it was decent to come calling. Waiving propriety, Marcel took his boys and Lucinda to the back porch to give him and Nicolette a little privacy.

Nicolette wouldn't have known him. His beard bushed out all around his face, and there were lines in his forehead that were not there before. His sapphire eyes bored into her.

Tears wet Nicolette's cheeks. "I'm sorry," she said, trying to laugh. "I seem to cry at everything the last few hours."

Alistair tossed his hat aside and swept Nicolette into his arms. He kissed her hard, without relent. Nicolette's first resistance melted. For a moment, the loneliness lifted. For a moment, she felt safe. She held his kiss, gloried in the sweetness of his lips.

Rifle fire cracked through the fort. Marcel marched onto the porch putting his hat on.

"Let's go," he said.

Alistair touched her cheek. "I'll come tonight."

Day and night, the siege continued. Great numbers of dead Union soldiers lay outside the ramparts in the mud, broiling in the summer sun.

Surely to God the Yanks would wave a flag of truce so they could collect their dead and wounded, but none came. The bodies lying in the sun swelled and turned black. The Rebs manning the barricades gagged and tied kerchiefs over their noses against the fearsome reek.

"They can't shoot us out of here, they aim to stench us out," Mrs. Brickell declared.

The Union's callous disregard of their fallen soldiers shamed Nicolette. These were the heroes who were to set her people free? Lincoln's toothless Emancipation Proclamation, the inept Union siege around Port Hudson, and now this?

In the hospital tent, the quinine ran out. Nicolette mixed poppy head elixirs and even made a weak tea from the deadly night shade for men who were out of their heads with pain and fever. She learned to be alert for the dreaded smell of gangrene that sent a man back to the operating table for amputation, or sent him to his grave.

Murphy's wound suppurated, as she expected. His neck grew hugely swollen. Nicolette herself mopped the angry red stitches. Now, at last, she saw fear in his eyes.

She did not feel the satisfaction she'd once imagined. Instead, out of pity, she allowed him to grip her hand, begging her for reassurance he would yet be well. But there was nothing more the doctors could do for him. "Shh," she said. "Don't fret. It's a small wound, Mr. Murphy."

She peeled the soiled shirt off him to cool the fever. There was the gouge in his upper arm, healed but deep and red. She had made that wound. Opening Murphy's vein with her fingernail, him no threat to her any longer, that would have been cold blooded murderer. She thanked the Blessed Virgin she had not done it, but defense was not vengeance. She was glad the shot up her dark stairs had got him. She hoped it had pained him and scared him.

The next morning, Nicolette again made the rounds of the men laid out under the shade of a spreading oak. Six feet away, she smelled the gangrene in Murphy's neck. Her gorge rose at the putrid odor. The bandage around his neck was slick with exuded pus.

Steeling herself, she knelt to tend to him, but what could she do? She didn't dare open the gauze over his neck. His breathing was shallow and rapid, and his eyes were closed tight. The pain had to be awful. Pity, blessed pity sent from Mother Mary herself, washed through her.

Murphy opened bulging, blood-shot eyes. It took him a moment to focus on her. He gasped. His pupils widened as if he looked on a terrible avenging angel come to claim him and take him to hell.

His eyes bugged out. "Get away!" he screeched. "Don't touch me!"

The doctor hurried over. "Gad," he said. "I'll never get used to the smell. Get the chloroform."

Nicolette quickly fetched a cone and the brown bottle of precious anesthesia. The doctor held Murphy down, wild now, and she administered the requisite four drops. Murphy still struggled.

"Two more," the doctor said.

Murphy's body slackened and went limp.

"Nothing else we can do for him now. If he wakes up, we'll fill him full of whiskey."

Murphy never woke. By mid-day, he was gone.

Nicolette herself closed his eyes and made the sign of the cross over his dead body.

Sustained by hope and extraordinary courage, the Rebels endured days of heat, bombardment, and death. Rations grew shorter, and shorter yet inside Port Hudson, but they still had a few ears of hard corn every day and plenty of rats for meat. Nicolette and Mrs. Brickell colluded to keep the identity of the stew meat from Lucinda else she would have starved herself. Occasionally, Marcel or Alistair would bring a squirrel for Mrs. Brickell to cook, but with near five thousand men within the fort, every edible creature was soon taken.

Then there were not even enough rats. Men who had learned to eat every rodent they could catch balked at eating their mules and horses. These animals had names, they had eccentricities and loyalty and heart.

To encourage the men, General Gardner ordered up a mess of thoroughly boiled horse meat and ate it out in the open air where the troops could see him. His example, and the pain of empty bellies, persuaded them, though many cried without shame when it came time to slaughter their own mounts.

Their weakened bodies quickly revived with the infusion of fresh meat, and their morale soared. Some of the high-spirited soldiers, aware they were now part-horse after eating their flesh, kicked their heels at mess time and hollered "ye haw!"

On the other side of Little Sandy Creek, General Banks busily indulged in oratory and declared a hiatus in the attack. If the Union were going to take Port Hudson, they'd have to dig saps to reach the ramparts. Banks put his soldiers and the hundreds of non-soldier blacks to work in the June sun.

During this relative peace, for skirmishes still erupted along the perimeter, Alistair arrived at the Brickell house every evening, shaved and washed. Marcel did not allow an opportunity for another kiss like he'd seen his friend bestow on Nicolette, but he did allow the courtship, if that's what it was, to continue on Mrs. Brickell's front porch.

Marcel sat on the porch, leaning against a roof post, Charles Armand in his lap. He had persuaded Charles Armand to let him tie the pillow case so it looked like an Arabian prince's turban. Lucinda, close enough her skirts brushed against Marcel's shoulder, rocked and hummed to Bertie.

Val stretched out in a patch of shade. All gangly arms and legs, his body trying to grow past the six foot mark on half rations, he was skinny as a rail. A dark fuzz proudly shadowed his upper lip else he would have been too pretty for a young man. When Val wasn't in motion, he was asleep, and he snored softly beneath his straw hat.

Nicolette sat on the top step next to Alistair. No longer diffident or hesitant, he seemed a different man. He laughed more easily. He looked at her more boldly, took her hand more confidently. She liked him the better for it.

"Why this show of mercy? Why has Banks ceased the attack?" Lucinda asked.

"No mercy in it," Alistair said. "Banks has his men digging rifle pits and tunnels and ditches to finagle a few hundred yards closer."

"So they are going to breach the barricades?" Nicolette asked.

This new Alistair gave her a sly grin. "Don't think so. We're going to let them invest a little more time and energy in their pretty zig zag trenches, then a few of the lads and I will go out and blow them up."

Nicolette gazed toward the Northern garrisons outside the fort. Finn wouldn't be in a tunnel. He'd be in the rear, running messengers, sending coded wig wags.

Unless he had to be in a signal tower. Nicolette heard the snipers boasting about their body counts. A sharp-eyed lad with a Springfield, one he'd confiscated from a fallen Yank, could hit his target at 900 yards. The Yank would fall and never hear the rifle crack.

Finn would know that though. Surely they built some sort of barrier in the towers, a stout plank of oak to protect themselves.

Finn had told her all about wig wag signaling one day over a cup of chicory coffee. They'd sat under a sweet gum tree in a courtyard café off Rue Royale, someone nearby playing a harmonica. Finn had poured salt on the polished pine table and showed her the flag combinations. Miss Chamard he'd spelled out. And then that six feet of manly tanned confidence had blushed.

Alistair touched her hand. "Don't be frightened. We'll beat them back."

She fingered the garnet cross at her throat. Here, in a besieged fortress where there was no water for bathing, where the temperature reached 100 degrees in the afternoons, it seemed reasonable to leave the top two or three buttons undone. Alistair's eyes followed her hand to the cross.

"I was just imagining those poor boys in the trenches."

"You want the Yanks to beat us out."

It wasn't a question, she noted. "I just want it to be over."

A hundred yards away, Adam Johnston rode by in the last light of the day. He generally found occasion to direct his horse this way every evening, making no show of disguising his steady stare.

Alistair stared back. Disgust in his voice, he said, "I'll speak to him. He's got no cause to be riding by here."

Nicolette shrugged. It didn't matter to her what Adam Johnston did.

In fact, she realized, the first flush of joy she'd felt when Alistair arrived had passed. She liked being courted. She liked being kissed. The awful numbness of heart had left her, but if she should not see Alistair again after the siege, she would not pine for him, would not ache for him in the night like she did for Finn.

Alistair regarded her in the failing light. She had changed. Not just from the strain and poor rations. There was a sadness about her eyes now that he had not seen before, not even after she'd been so badly hurt. Had she lost someone to the war? Someone had given her that stunning cross. The idea that she'd been attached to a man he knew nothing about burned like a hot knife in his gut. And yet, in spite of the hint of sorrow around her eyes, she was cheerful. She was, almost, serene.

"How is it, Nicolette, you can be so composed in the middle of a battlefield?"

"It is hard won, I assure you. And you? You seem quite imperturbable. Where is the man I knew in New Orleans, full of doubt and conflict?"

Alistair fiddled with a piece of grass. "Left him on the Lafourche, I guess. Living through your first battle, and the next, and the next. Finding you can face death as well as the next fella. That'll change a man."

He tossed the blade of grass away and openly took her hand.

"Let's take a walk."

He put her hand on his arm and strolled through the rare quiet hour toward Foster's Creek running through the middle of the enclosure. A posse of soldiers scoured the ground for Union minié balls they could melt and reform into ammunition for their own guns. Others collected shell debris to pack into hand grenades and canister.

Alistair led her through the shade of a tattered oak grove. He lost the easy manners he'd shown the last days and resumed the formality Nicolette had known in New Orleans. He suddenly held his arm out the requisite three inches so as not to entrap the lady's hand. His neck had gone stiff as a statue's.

"Nicolette," he said, a frown line deep between his brows, "after the war, the plantations will be in a bad way, whoever wins. But if the Yanks win and all the slaves walk off, the cane and cotton growers will be ruined."

Nicolette merely nodded. She knew this.

"However," Alistair went on, "I own part-interest in a silver mine in Colorado. Two steam boats. And I've invested in the railroad they're building through Texas."

He parted the hanging branches of a willow tree and led her into a leafy bower. "Whatever happens after the war, I will still be a wealthy man."

Nicolette murmured something congratulatory, not paying much mind. Why did he think she'd be interested in his finances? Unless ... . Oh no.

"Alistair — "

"Please, Nicolette. Let me say this. I know I've been a fool. I let propriety and tradition and all that nonsense rule me, when all I've wanted since the day I met you was to make you mine."

"Alistair — "

He touched his finger to her lips.

"Not as my placée, Nicolette. As my wife."

Alistair bent to his knee and took her hand. "Nicolette, will you marry me?"

Sadness descended on her like a cold heavy dew. Once, maybe, she would have said yes. But not now.

"Dear Alistair." She shook her head. "I am not in love with you."

Alistair remained on his knee, his hold on her hand unwavering. "I know you don't love me the way I love you. I know it. But I can take care of you, Nicolette. We'll live anywhere you like. New Orleans. Baton Rouge. New York. I'll make you happy, I know it."

She shook her head. He could make her secure. Give her children. Give her his love. But she had nothing to give in return. Her heart remained tied to a dream, a fantasy of loving Finnian McKee. She was not ready to let go of that longing. Yearning, if not hope, was what sustained her.

She looked into his eyes, so full of hope. But again she shook her head.

Alistair raised himself. After a moment, he faced her again. "Is there someone else?"

Nicolette's gaze penetrated through the willow branches to the treetops beyond the barricades. Finn was over there, in the Union camp.

"Not anymore."

Finn trudged through the heat back to his preferred observation post. He and his signal men did not have to wield shovel and pick digging the trenches that would protect the soldiers in their next assault against Port Hudson. He had time on his hands. He climbed the tree to the tallest platform on the north side of the ramparts. From there, on a quiet day like this, he could see a patch of the village itself.

He checked first, as he did every day, that André Cailloux's body still lay where he fell. He didn't know why he tormented himself like this. Of course the body had not moved. But this vigil was all he could do for a brave soldier. By now, after heavy rains, the body had begun to sink into the ground. If Banks wouldn't arrange a truce flag for burials, the earth itself would accomplish the task.

At his leisure, no skirmish ripping the quiet air, he trained his scope into Port Hudson. Two women and a small boy walked across the field outside the village proper. He knew there were a few women and children inside. Must be hell for them, he thought. He adjusted his scope and focused on the woman on the left.

Can't be! He stood up and squinted into the eyepiece again. *What the hell is she doing here?*

Finn scrambled down from the platform and raced back toward headquarters. Since the Rebs had wounded and captured so many Yanks, Banks was sending a wagon load of medicine and bandages into Port Hudson. He'd go with the wagon. She must be desperate to get out of there. He'd bring her back with him. She could stay in his tent. He'd bunk with Hursh. She'd be safe behind the lines.

He tore into Weitzel's tent where the adjutant pored over dispatches.

"That medicine wagon. Where is it?"

"Just left, I believe."

Finn whirled. He'd catch up and go along as escort.

"Captain McKee." General Weitzel himself hailed him from across the lane of tents, Hursh Farrow at his side. "Just the man we need."

"General. Request permission to escort the medicine wagon."

Weitzel frowned. "That's hardly necessary. I want you and Major Farrow to go over this new scheme from headquarters with me. They're proposing taller towers, and I have to say, I don't see the benefits outweigh the risks. Come inside, Captain."

The wagon got further ahead with every minute. "General?"

Weitzel looked at him, one eyebrow raised.

Finn felt his chest might explode. "Sir, five minutes please?"

"Make it quick."

Finn ran toward the signal men's enclave. "Corporal Peach!"

Finn tore a leaf from the code book, hell they all knew it by heart now anyway. "Sir?" Peach said.

Finn scrawled a message on the page. He hesitated, then added another line.

"Do you remember Miss Chamard, from the Custom House?"

"Yes, sir," Corporal Peach said, smiling wide.

"Catch up with the wagon we're sending into Port Hudson. Go in with them. Bring Miss Chamard back with you."

"What's she doing in Port Hudson?"

"I don't know, Peach. Just bring her back."

"Yes, sir."

"Take my horse. Don't fail me in this, Corporal."

"No, sir!"

Finn spent the rest of the day performing the minutia of camp duties required of him. He took out his watch every ten minutes, then every five. Where the hell was Peach?

The men were building cook fires by the time Peach rode up on Finn's horse. Alone.

"What happened?" Finn called, on the march to intercept him. "You didn't find her?"

"Yeah, Captain. I found her." He slid off the horse and handed the reins to Finn.

"Then where is she?"

Corporal Peach shook his head. "She wouldn't come. I give her the note, like you said, but she had a little feller pulling at her skirt, she said she couldn't leave him."

Finn's chest went hollow on him. "Well, what did she say when she read my note? Did she look mad?"

"She warn't mad. She was all smiley. Oh, I recollect what she said. She showed me this pretty cross made out of red stones. Said tell you she's wearing it."

The air rushed back into Finn's chest. "Thank you, Corporal," he said, pumping Peach's hand. "You are relieved of your duties for the rest of the day."

Finn swung himself onto his horse and trotted into the woods. At the creek, he tied his horse, stripped off his clothes, and plunged into the cool water.

She was wearing his garnet cross!

Chapter Thirty-Three

Nicolette read Finn's note and pressed it to her breast. Heavy, humid air turned to tiny bubbles of cool, sparkling champagne tingling on her skin. She wanted to dance! She wanted to whisper, to shout, to sing.

Captain McKee's corporal turned and waved to her as he followed the wagon back to the barricades. Nicolette blew him a kiss and the boy grinned back red-faced.

Charles Armand stood close, the hand holding on to Nicolette's skirt keeping him safe. She whisked him into her arms and covered his face with kisses. "I love you to pieces, Charles Armand."

He was more interested in keeping his turban in place than in kisses, but she finally won a smile from him, the first in days.

"Let me take you to Maman. I have to go to work." She carried him to Mrs. Brickell's house, nibbling at his earlobe and tickling his ribs. When he gave in and giggled, she felt the sun relieve the last dark corner in her soul.

At the open air hospital, Nicolette flitted from one soldier to another with cool water, tender hands, kind words. The doctor unpacked a case of quinine from the Union supplies and she dosed the malarial patients with assurances they would soon feel better.

"You're all sunshiney, Miss," a soldier with a mending arm teased her. "You got yourself a feller?"

"Yes, sergeant, I have indeed."

"Is it me?" the soldier next to him called out.

"Nah, it's me, you jackass," a third said.

"You all a bunch of fools. She's been in love with me ever since I got dragged in here. Ain't you, Missy?"

Laughing, Nicolette leaned over and kissed the top of the soldier's head. "I am in love with every single one of you, and that's the truth."

Nicolette spent the day tending sick and broken men, but a waltz buzzed in her head as she soothed and cleaned and cheered her patients.

At sunset, Mrs. Brickell relieved her. "I left supper setting out for you, honey. You go on back to the house and sit with your beaux."

She meant Alistair. He'd accepted her rejection as if it were merely a temporary setback. He would appear at Mrs. Brickell's front porch as usual tonight, if the lull in the fighting lasted. She had let him to continue to call, out of loneliness, out of indifference. She shouldn't have allowed it. Now she would have to hurt him all over again.

When Alistair arrived, the fireflies and the mosquitoes animated the night air. Nicolette met him at the porch steps. "Will you walk with me?"

They were nearly to the creek, their way lit by a half moon. "If you've changed your mind, Nicolette, you've only to say the word."

"Alistair, you are my dear friend, and I don't want to hurt you. But you must let me go."

He stopped and turned her to face him. "This is what you brought me out here to say? Give you up? Nicolette, I can wait. After the war, when you've — "

"I've heard from him. The man I knew. A letter."

"A letter," he said dully. "How did you get a letter?"

Nicolette drew a deep breath. "Alistair, he still loves me. And I'm in love with him."

Alistair looked up at the moon, shriveling inside. He was going to lose her.

"Will he marry you?"

Words do hurt, she thought. All the joy from Finn's scrawled note across the torn page — "Come out with Corporal Peach. Finn. I love you" – had hid a small nagging, niggling doubt.

"I don't know," she said, her voice just above a whisper.

"I will marry you, Nicolette. Tomorrow. Tonight."

"No," she said.

Under cover of dark, braving rifle and artillery fire, Alistair led his men in a sneaking approach to the enemy sap, the trench dug to shield the Federals from Rebel fire as they ran in closer to the barricades. His heart was a dead thing in his chest, but his mind was alert to every cricket chirp or clink of a canteen. He saw his men, dark forms against black earth, crawling over hummocks of dirt with great clarity, as if the starlight illuminated the shadows as brightly as mid-day sun.

Alistair meant to die this night. But he would damage the enemy, destroy and devastate and kill, until the moment arrived.

Alistair signaled four men to creep further to the right. He motioned for another three to maneuver to the left.

At Alistair's short sharp whistle, his men erupted into their terrifying, stunning Rebel cry and swarmed into the sap. The Federals, senses dulled by the noise and lulled into security by their own punishing artillery, were completely unprepared for a reckless midnight raid outside the fort.

Five minutes of close combat, and Alistair's Rebels had the sap. They cleared the trench of captives, then threw grenades up and down its length, destroying a week's worth of digging. Alistair retreated to the fort with all of his men and half a dozen prisoners with their rifles.

He grabbed a few hours of fitful sleep, mosquitoes and heat plaguing him less than Nicolette's painful, final no. At dawn he woke to the furious roar of artillery. He didn't wait for orders. He roused his troops and joined the rush of reinforcements heading toward the noise and flash at the southwest corner of the fortifications.

As Alistair arrived, the Federals rushed through an intact sap right up to the barricades.

A strong-armed Yank lobbed a grenade over the parapet. A quick-witted Reb grabbed it up and heaved it back, the too-long fuse exploding amid the attackers, shooting dirt into the air, hurling a man's arm across the embattled ground.

Adam Johnston and his unit rushed in at Alistair's left, their musketry loaded and ready. Adam slashed the air with his sword, the early sun gleaming on the blade. "Onward!" he shouted. At the brink of the parapet, his front line fired. Shouting, he directed the next row to fire into the enemy, the front row kneeling to reload.

Across the yards of open ground, a second platoon of blue-coats leapt out of the trenches and charged, bayonets at the ready. Alistair plunged his bayonet into a Yankee's ribs, snapping the blade off. Heedless and fierce, he raised his rifle stock as a club and rushed into the oncoming enemy.

All around, men lunged, stabbed, clubbed. The rhythm and the abandonment of all but the killing seized Alistair in a kind of crazed joy as he thrust, dodged, parried, and struck. He knew only the scent of cordite and blood, the sight of grimaced faces, and the thud of his rifle stock smashing into an enemy's head.

"Fall back!" a Yankee captain yelled.

Alistair pursued, his long legs overtaking another soldier, his rifle butt raised to bash at his head.

"Captain!" Alistair heard the word, but he dwelt only in the moment, only in the blur of blue coats and the mindless heat of battle. "Whiteaker!"

Club upraised, Alistair ran down a retreating foe, fear on the Yank's face as if he were pursued by a mad man. The Yankee twisted to avoid Alistair's rifle butt, brought his bayonet up and lunged for Alistair's gut.

Before the bayonet connected, Alistair hit the ground hard. The breath knocked out of him, he lay stunned. Then a gray-coat body fell on top of him. Blood. So hot. Blood pouring from the man's chest.

The fool! The man had taken the bayonet he'd wanted for himself.

Air rushed back into Alistair's lungs. He had to fight. He had to kill. He had to end it now.

He shoved the body off and crawled out from under the man pouring his life's blood into the Mississippi soil.

Around him, open ground. The Yanks had retreated. There was no one to fight.

His body slow and heavy, he looked down at the thief who'd robbed him of the Yankee's bayonet thrust. He bent to roll the wounded man over. A man's last sight should be of the sky, not the dirt.

Adam Johnston.

Alistair dropped to his knees. Blood dribbled from Adam's mouth and drained from the wound in his chest.

"Johnston, what the hell have you done?"

Adam gasped for breath, but he could smile. He held his hand out and Alistair clasped it. "For her," he said. "So she can be happy."

He blinked, and in that blink, the light in his eyes dimmed out. Alistair closed the lids with shaking fingers.

"I wish you hadn't done it, Johnston. I wish you hadn't."

At the opposite side of Port Hudson, Marcel grabbed a cold torch from the night's watch, lit it, and hurled it into the Yanks' moving shield of cotton bales. Other Rebs did the same and the cotton turned into a wall of flame.

The firing on this front ceased as the Rebels watched the conflagration, horrified at the screams of men caught in the flames.

"Jesus. Look what we done," a man said.

"God help 'em."

Marcel rushed along the barricade, checking his men. "How's your ammo? Be ready. They're coming back."

Among the defenders, one skinny lad stood out. Val sighted along his rifle barrel, ready to fire into the enemy.

"Val!" Marcel's hands fisted. He'd beat the shit out of Val for being up here in the line of fire. "Get down from there!"

"No, sir. I been doing ... I have done what you said ever since we left New Orleans." Val's voice still wavered in adolescent transition, but he raised his chin and looked his master in the eye. "I'm a man now, Mister Marcel. I'm a soldier."

"The hell you are. You're not here to fight."

The Yanks renewed the assault. Bullets whirred through the air, zinging against a rifle barrel, slicing through a Reb's hat.

"I am here to fight."

The men around him aimed and shot double time, their fire deafening. Val shouted over the din, "I'm a Louisiana man, just like you."

Marcel grabbed at Val's collar, dragging him.

Val struck at Marcel's hands, fighting at him for every step.

Marcel raised his fist to punch Val in the face so he could get him out of there, out of the deadly onslaught.

Val's head dropped forward. His hands opened.

The back of his skull was blown away.

Stupid with shock, Marcel's mouth gaped. He collapsed, gathering Val into his arms, no air in him to wail or shriek.

Another moment, he'd have had him out of there.

The fight raged on. Marcel lifted Val and carried him from the battlements and through the pitted landscape. Val. The brightest, most beautiful boy.

Marcel bore his burden through Port Hudson to the hospital tent. Nicolette bent among the wounded soldiers, feeding someone a dose from a cup.

When she saw him, she came running. Marcel sank to his knees, Val draped across his body.

"Oh, God, Marcel. Not Val."

Marcel wiped a smear of dirt off Val's chin. "He's dead."

"Yes," Nicolette said.

Marcel smoothed the closed eye, brushed off a lilac petal that floated onto Val's cheek.

"We'll take him to the house and I'll lay him out there," Nicolette said. She signaled to an orderly to help Marcel carry the body, but when the soldier bent to take Val under the arms, Marcel waved him off.

"I'll carry him."

In the house, Marcel laid Val on the plank table.

Nicolette sent him into the parlor where Lucinda poured him the last of Mrs. Brickell's brandy. Back at the battle line, bombs burst and cannon boomed, but here in the parlor it was quiet enough to hear the rocker squeak on the floor boards. Charles Armand climbed into his father's lap and sucked his thumb as Marcel rocked back and forth.

Nicolette washed and dressed the body. Lucinda sewed a shroud.

Marcel thought of all the plans they'd made for Val, he and Papa and Valentine. He was to go to Paris to study at the Sorbonne, maybe become a doctor, or a scholar who wrote history books.

Val was meant to be a great man. Not a corpse lying on a pine board table.

Marcel lay his sleeping son on the settee, carefully adjusting the pillow case turban so that it wouldn't fall off.

At the dining table, he found Lucinda sewing the shroud up the center of Val's body. Val's face was bathed and serene. Lying face up, there was no sign of the damage the Yankee bullet had done. Only the hint of gray around his mouth suggested his heart had ceased to beat.

Marcel caressed the boy's forehead. "I have to go back," he said.

"We'll take care of him," Lucinda said.

She opened her arms and held Marcel tight. "Be safe," she said.

Marcel kissed Val's forehead, then held on to Lucinda's hand as he walked through the house. At the open doorway, he turned and tilted her face to the light, studying her.

"I love you," he said. He enfolded her in his arms and spoke into her ear. "You won't forget, Lucinda? I love you."

She wiped at the tears on his face. "I'll never forget."

Nicolette returned to the hospital. Casualties were coming in fast now, shattered limbs, missing limbs, cracked heads.

Late in the day, nauseous from the chloroform fumes, Nicolette yielded her post to a medic and escaped to the open air. Out here, men needed water and bandaging, pain medicine and quinine. She moved to the next man, propped up against a tree stump waiting his turn, his hat pulled down to keep the sun out of his eyes. He had a handkerchief tied around his bare arm, a smear of dried blood underneath. Not too bad. He'd just need a good bandage to keep it clean and he could go back to the lines if he wanted to.

She gripped one edge of a piece of gauze in her teeth so she could rip the end off.

Alistair shoved the hat off his forehead. "Nicolette." He'd been watching her from beneath his hat brim, glad he was alive to see her in the morning light. After the roar and frantic hours of sword and rifle, he felt calm. He hadn't died like he'd wanted to, but a tranquil resignation lay easy on his heart.

"Alistair!"

"Now don't fret," he said. Nicolette looked a sight, her hair uncombed and her face sunburned and sweaty. And more beautiful than he'd ever seen her, in spite of the crease of distress on her forehead. "It's just a scratch."

"Let me see."

Her fingers fumbled at the knot stiffened with dried blood. Alistair took his knife out of the sheaf on his thigh and handed it to her.

"Been a long day?" he said gently.

"Val died this morning," she said. He could see her throat working so as not to cry.

"I'm sorry. He was a likely boy. I guess Marcel knows."

"He knows."

Alistair winced as she peeled the bandage away from the wound. He looked at it now he had the time. A chunk of muscle about the length of his thumb was gouged away, but it was superficial. It'd heal.

"Nicolette," Alistair said, watching her. "Adam Johnston died this morning, too."

As quick as he'd said it, Nicolette's face crumpled and tears spilled over her cheeks. She put the back of her hand to her mouth, trying to hold the grief in.

He hadn't expected this. Alistair had been there right after Adam had assaulted Nicolette. He saw what he did to her face. He guessed what he'd done to her spirit. And now she cried for this man?

"Come here," he said and held his good arm out. It was just too much for her, he thought, death all around, the noise, the heat. The boy Val. And he remembered that once, it seemed like a long time ago, she'd been fond of Adam Johnston, before he'd turned into a drunken, raging beast.

She sobbed into his shoulder. Alistair cradled her head in his hand, his breath shuddering with the pain of loving her. He would never again hold her like this. The deep pleasure of her head under his chin, of her just for this once allowing herself to need him – it would never come again.

He bent his head and pressed his lips into her hair.

Chapter Thirty-Four

The Rebels rightly regarded themselves as the best damned soldiers in the world. Out of food, nearly out of ammunition, they repulsed attacks all along the perimeter. They built land mines from the Union's own unexploded ordnance, they raked the enemy with every shell and rebuilt ball they had, and they rolled homemade bombs into the Federals' advance trenches.

They braced themselves for a final, decisive assault from the Federals, but before the onslaught began, the gunboat General Price steamed down the Mississippi, its flag signaling it bore urgent news: Three days before, on July the fourth, the Confederates had surrendered Vicksburg.

General Grant now had no need for Banks to keep these Confederates confined to Louisiana. The Rebels no longer had any need to keep Banks from reinforcing Grant at Vicksburg.

The siege of Port Hudson was over.

Finn raced to the signal towers and had his men wig wag the news down the line all the way to the far end of Port Hudson. The Federal soldiers hunkering down in the trenches erupted in cheers and jubilations.

They shouted across the barricades to their Southern brethren. "It's over! Lay down your arms, you damned Rebs. It's over!"

"Damned lying Yanks," the Rebels yelled back.

At noon, a hundred guns fired into the air in unison. The Nineteenth Army Corp's band started up, their brass notes penetrating the length of the fort in stirring renditions of Yankee Doodle.

Nicolette dropped the basin of water she was carrying and ran all the way to Mrs. Brickell's house. "Lucinda!"

Lucinda rushed from the bedroom holding Bertie, Charles Armand behind her.

"Listen! What do you hear?"

Lucinda cocked an ear. "A band? What does it mean?"

"It's over! It must mean it's over."

"Charles Armand, uncover your ears. You hear that?"

Lucinda clenched her hands together as Marcel rushed through Mrs. Brickell's house gathering his few things, talking as he loaded his pistol and rifle.

"Gardner's going to stall the surrender a day," he told Lucinda. "That'll give some of us a chance to slip out tonight."

Struggling to keep the quaver out of her voice, she said, "You let them take you captive, Marcel, you'll be out of it. You'll be safe."

Marcel stuffed four precious bullets deep into his pocket. "I can't do that. I took an oath."

"But you said — " It would hurt him, to throw his words back at him, but she had to try. She could hardly find air to speak. "You said, you were on the wrong side."

Marcel gripped her by both her arms. "Lucinda, I said it. But there's more to this than sentiment. If the South goes under, we'll lose everything. Cherleu will be ruined. My fortune, Papa's, gone. Lucinda, we're defending our home!"

She covered her face, her shoulders shaking.

"Lucinda, darling. Listen to me." Marcel pulled her hands down and kissed her fingers. "Go to Cherleu. Papa will take care of you and the boys. If you want to go back to New Orleans, he'll make sure you're safe."

"I'd die, Marcel, if your wife came back, if she — "

"You have the letters, sweetheart. No one can take the children away from you. I promise. Papa will never let that happen, and I'll be home as soon as I can."

She leaned into him and wrapped her arms around his waist. When would she ever feel safe again?

Marcel stroked her back, soothing her. "Your allowance is protected, Lucinda. It'll go on whatever happens to me. Understand? Papa will look after you, and you and the boys will always have money."

"I don't want money," she whispered.

"I'm coming home, Lucinda. Believe it. I'm coming home. All right?"

Unable to speak, she nodded again.

They heard quick footsteps crossing the porch.

He grabbed Lucinda in a fierce hug, then strode out of the room.

He pushed by Alistair on the porch. "Let's go," he said.

Alistair lingered. "Miss Lucinda?"

She stepped out onto the porch.

"Tell her I'm going to make it through this. I am. And whatever she needs, after the war, anytime ... tell her, please, she can come to me."

"You're a good man, Mr. Whiteaker. I'll tell her."

Alistair mounted his horse and caught up to Marcel. They rode through the fort to the southern-most point of the battlements and waited for dark.

A few infantrymen created a diversion for them, inviting the opposite Yanks to sit with them around their campfire and drink Yankee coffee. Marcel and Alistair slipped out, eased their horses in the river below the cliffs and swam them downstream. Once they were clear of the Union lines and the high bluffs, they climbed onto the river bank.

They headed south and east, free to carry the fight onward.

Everyone in Port Hudson slept the night through, no artillery or musket fire rousing them, threatening them with annihilation as they lay in their beds. They woke tired, though, depleted from lack of food and rest, burned out from fear and worry.

Nicolette, lying abed on her pallet past dawn like a lady of leisure, prolonged the luxury of quiet and ease. There would be no new casualties coming in. No need to rush to the hospital.

Today. She would see him again today. After all these months, hopeless months, her life was about to begin anew. What had he become, soldiering? Had he killed? Been wounded? Had he grieved for her as she had for him?

I love you. That's what he wrote.

His face was as vivid to her as if she'd seen him yesterday. The heavy black moustache. The fine eyes.

What did Finnian McKee mean when he wrote those three words? There had been many lonely nights when Nicolette wished she'd given herself to him, no expectations, no demands. But he hadn't asked of her merely sensual love. He'd offered her marriage. Until he understood whom it was he'd proposed to.

What now? What if he dashed off I love you unthinkingly, in the excitement of the moment? What if he meant it, but like Alistair, could not imagine she would expect more from him than love?

Could she bear it again? Lose him because she insisted on more? Go through the heartache of seeing rejection in his eyes because she would not accept love without total commitment? She wanted passion, yes, but she wanted a shared sofa, reading glasses, and bare feet in her husband's lap. But she had suffered loneliness and loss for so long. Would she let him go, just for some impossible ideal?

There was to be a ceremony on the central plain, Union officers formally accepting arms from the Rebels. Finnian McKee would be among those officers.

Nicolette feared he would think she'd turned into a scarecrow. She'd lost weight. Everyone in Port Hudson had lost weight. She smoothed her hand over her skirt. The dress was too big now. Her petticoats had long ago been ripped into bandages, and the fabric hung limply, dragging the ground. This was the same gown she'd worn, day and night, since she arrived in Port Hudson. She'd managed to wash it once, but it was torn and stained. It smelled.

Nicolette held her hand up. She'd always been vain about her long fingers, about the smooth pale skin of her hands. Now her nails were chipped and dirty. And her skin was brown. With a pang, she realized her face must be as tanned as her hands. Mrs. Brickell didn't own a mirror, but Nicolette knew she was not the creamy-skinned girl Finn had last seen.

He'd never seen her dirty as a mud hen, either. She could do something about that. "Mrs. Brickell, is that a soapberry bush back of the house?"

Nicolette washed her hair and her dress. She crushed mint leaves into the rinse water. It was the best she could do.

Before her hair was dry, she heard the Union cavalry marching into the fort, heard the wagons and shouted commands to line up. In her damp dress and cracked boots, she hurried toward the parade grounds.

Nicolette stood to the side, straining to see the length of the Union line. Her heart thudded so hard it rivaled the beat of the snare drums. The soldiers marched into position.

How could she find him among so many soldiers, all standing at attention in the same blue hat and coat? What if he was sorry he'd scrawled that note?

Gardner was offering his sword to General Andrews, who, after a few diplomatic words, returned it to him.

Was that Finn over there, standing at attention at the far left of the Union line? No. He was too short. That one? Impossible. Finn would have to find her. She kicked an empty ammo box over and stood on it so she would be conspicuous. Then she waited, the echoing drum beats loud and insistent.

"Attention!" General Beall called to his soldiers. "Ground Arms!

The jangle of weapons being placed on the ground carried through the air. Even from her perch, Nicolette could hear the disarmed Southerners muttering loudly up and down the line. They were defeated, for now, and they'd accepted friendships around campfires the night before, but the stony glares they cast toward their foes across the field announced they were not finished.

Today, though, in this place, there was peace. The ceremony concluded with Union and Confederate officers saluting one another smartly. Federal soldiers commandeered the weapons and the opposing lines broke up.

Nicolette stretched her neck to see the length of the field. If he could see her, if he were here in the fort, he'd come to her.

There he was! Marching through the intermingling soldiers, striding around a knot of men, pacing through another, straight for her.

Nicolette stepped off the box. With no thought of propriety or pride, she ran for him.

Ten feet away, she halted.

Finn slowed his steps and stopped an arm's length away from her.

He gazed into those gray eyes. She still looked at him as if he were the handsomest of men. As if he deserved her admiration.

"Miss Chamard," he breathed.

"Captain."

How did he begin? Did he tell her he loved her? She knew that. Should he simply apologize? That's what he should do. Simply say, I'm sorry, I'm an ass. See if she would forgive him.

"My mother wants to meet you," he said.

Thank God, he'd said the right thing. Those beautiful gray eyes filled. A brilliant smile lit her face.

Finn stepped closer, forgetting all the people around them. "Do you forgive me, Nicolette?"

"Finn, I — "

"Nicolette, will you marry me?"

A sob erupted from her chest. Her nose running, her eyes streaming, she pressed the back of her hand to her mouth.

"I think that's a yes." He thumbed a tear from her cheek, and then, in front of privates, sergeants, generals and God, he kissed her.

Finn allowed a four hour engagement. He walked her under the shade trees along the creek. They talked until they were in the thicket of willows. Then he tipped her chin up, gazing at that mouth he'd dreamt about all these months.

He kissed her gently, softly. And then more firmly until he felt her body sink into his. He grinned at her and walked her further along the stream until another tree offered them a little privacy.

Finn enlisted Port Hudson's chaplain, Father Simon. Mrs. Brickell polished up her grandmother's marcasite ring. Lucinda and Charles Armand picked wild flowers. For their chapel, they stood among the willows.

Lucinda and the boys and Mrs. Brickell attended. Hursh Farrow walked Nicolette up the grassy path.

Finn's eyes never left hers as she turned to him, a bouquet of daisies in her hand. "I love you," he whispered, the words not nearly enough to tell her what he felt.

Father Simon began. "In the name of the Father, and of the Son, and of the Holy Spirit. The grace of our Lord Jesus Christ and the love of God and the fellowship of the Holy Spirit be with you all."

"And also with you."

"I will love you and honor you all the days of my life," Nicolette promised, gazing into the dark eyes she loved.

"I will love you and honor you all the days of my life," Finn responded. He slipped the ring on her finger, his heart beating the steady thrum of deep content. "With this ring, I thee wed."

"Lord, Bless this union we pray, and walk beside Finnian and Nicolette throughout all their lives together. Amen."

Chapter Thirty-Five

The Union claimed Port Hudson, but the Confederates argued they won the siege. The Rebels lost 700 men holding off the attackers. General Banks lost upwards of 5,000. With added losses from Louisiana's harsh climate, disease, desertion, wounding and death, the Union paid a very high price for this bluff over the Mississippi River.

André Cailloux, identified on the battlefield only by the ring he wore, was taken home. His body lay in state for four days, the flag of the United States of America draped over his sealed coffin. Candles and the scented flowers of late summer perfumed the stifling, heavy air. On the fifth day, the coffin was placed on a black, horse-drawn caisson adorned with drapery and tassels befitting a great hero. A brass band paced alongside him playing solemn music as the procession marched slowly through the city. Thousands of mourners, former friends, former slaves, and Union sympathizers, lined the streets.

Lucinda and Nicolette trudged home after André's funeral. They shared the yellow cottage, now, in a limbo of waiting for their men, praying for an end to the war.

Across town, Deborah Ann did what all the other women did whose husbands and sons might lie dying on some far-off battlefield. She too waited.

She'd had a long convalescence after the incident on Elysian Fields. She was still fragile, still brittle. But she was no longer confused.

Dr. Braun prescribed long walks twice a day. She spent hours knitting socks and rolling bandages for the troops. She often thought of writing to Marcel's other woman, telling her how sorry she was to have frightened her, promising her she would never bother her again. But she never wrote the letter.

In late summer, Deborah Ann insisted on accompanying Father to Evermore to see just how much damage the Yankees, and the slaves, had done. Along with Mammy and Jebediah, they rode the steamer Annabelle up river. As ever, there stood the massive oaks, furred with resurrection fern, dripping with moss. The grass along the levee grew as lush and green as ever.

But Evermore – the eastern half of the house gleamed white under the bright sun. But the western half – black, skeletal, and open to the sky. Deborah knotted her handkerchief, gazing on the ruins. Mr. Thompson had written to tell them the news, but to actually see it was far more painful than the letter had been.

Silently, Deborah walked up the path between the poplars, worried at the slump of Father's shoulders. They climbed the brick steps. Father pressed the brass handle and shoved the door open.

The hallway was dim. The house smelled of smoke. Dust and ash covered every surface. Their leaden footsteps echoed on the hard cypress floor.

Old Clementine shuffled into the great hall from the back rooms, the shotgun in her arms too heavy to hold steady.

"Dat you?" she called. "Lawd, Mr. Presswood, I's glad yo's not dem Yanks again. Dey done made off wit all our stuff already."

"Clementine, go get Mr. Thompson for me, that's a good girl." Father still had his hat in his hands. Clementine had forgotten to take it from him.

"Deborah Ann, dear, can you see what we have to offer Mr. Thompson?"

Deborah found not a single bottle of wine nor brandy nor port left in the house. She brought in a pitcher of well water, then sat down in the third leather chair in Father's study.

"I got six darkies left, Mr. Presswood," Mr. Thompson reported. "We're working the garden to have enough stores to see us through the year. There'll be enough for you to take back to town with you when we get through with the harvest. Course you know there'll be no cane crop this year."

"What'd the Yankees take?"

"Every horse, mule, cow, pig, and chicken on the place. The silver, and anything that looked valuable and small enough to go in a saddlebag. Same up and down this part of the river. They came through like locusts, I swear, eating everything they could get. I showed them the letter you sent on from General Butler.

They read it. Kept them from burning the place, I guess. But then, the darkies took care of that."

Deborah Ann listened to the quiet, inside the house and out. Anna and Rosa, Pearly and Maggie, so many others, gone. And now the place felt like a land asleep with no clang of metal tools, no voices raised, no children laughing. Evermore was finished, merely a ghost of what she'd been. There was nothing to be done about it.

At supper, Clementine served boiled sweet potatoes, fried squirrel, and huckleberries heavy with seeds. Deborah Ann and her father picked at their food, silent and grieving.

After supper, Deborah Ann found a candle stub and retired to her room. This part of the house was intact, but it was stuffy and hot upstairs. No one had aired her room nor swept up the dead flies on the window sills. The smell of smoke was strong. Dust lay thick on her writing table.

She sank on to her aqua silk slipper chair and pulled out the letter she'd had from Marcel. She opened the paper and smoothed the creases. It was a painful letter, but she had nothing else from him except the ring on her finger.

When the letter had reached her at last, she'd been thrilled. But her first flush of relief that he was alive, that he had thought to write to her even as he escaped from Port Hudson, drained away as she read.

You have broken my heart, he wrote. *To tear my children from their mother is a cruelty which I would not have believed of you. In order for me to excuse such an act, I must imagine that you suffered a temporary madness. I have sent documents to my attorney, to my father, and to yours detailing my express wish that the children never leave their mother's care. Do not embarrass yourself by further attempts to interfere.*

I hope and pray that you reconcile yourself to reason and that I may one day call you Dearest Wife once again. Be well. The war cannot last forever. Your most devoted husband, Marcel.

She lay down on the bed where she had hoped to lie with her husband. She did not weep nor brood. The pain of that brutal letter was an old familiar by now, and she had interred the episode of madness, for that is what it was, in a dark chamber of her mind.

Deborah Ann's entire existence now was focused on enduring. Holding on, with as little feeling as she could manage. She knew now how to accept what she could not change. She could not undo what she had done in New Orleans. She could not bring the darkies back to Evermore. She could not hasten the war's end. But it would end. And life would go on. Had he not signed his letter "your devoted husband?" Had he not hoped to call her "Dearest Wife?" His words whispered of a future, and that would have to sustain her.

Tomorrow, she and Mammy would sweep away the cobwebs. She would keep a good house, here and in town, for when Marcel came home. She would prove to him she was ready to be a good wife, and, someday, he would forgive her. He might even love her.

She had been naïve. She had been trusting. Cruelly, he had violated her faith in him. She still loved him. Someday, maybe, she would forgive him.

In April, 1865, General Lee surrendered to General Grant at the Appomattox Courthouse.

Marcel was among the first Confederates to return to Louisiana. He'd turned in his arms on the fields above Richmond, still in uniform. So many others had died before the armistice, so many had, like Alistair, been captured. He counted himself among the fortunate.

He stopped first at Cherleu where his father and Valentine were rediscovering unused muscles. The plantation was in a shambles, but the former slaves who chose to remain for wages worked alongside Bertrand Chamard and Valentine to put in a subsistence crop.

In the cool of the evening, Marcel walked the fields with his father, Biscuit following along, flushing doves out of the tall grass. Marcel eyed the neighboring plantation through the row of sycamores. "How is Toulouse?"

"Better than this," Bertrand answered, mindful of which ear Marcel could hear from. "Probably half her blacks stayed on the place. They love their Madame Josie."

"They stayed for wages, I presume."

"Yes, for wages." Bertrand eyed his son. "I'm thinking of marrying her."

"Josephine DeBlieux?" She was a handsome woman, but she had to be close to fifty. "I suppose it makes sense, financially."

Bertrand made a disgusted face. "Not for the money, Marcel. I married for money before." He seemed to remember he spoke of

Marcel's mother. "Not that I regretted marrying your mother, son. She was a faithful wife and she gave me you. But before Abigail, Josie and I ... Well."

Marcel grinned. "You old rascal."

Bertrand, his home and his livelihood in ruins around him, smiled contentedly.

Marcel worked the fields with his father, fished in the creek, and tried to put the last years behind him. So good to be home. So good to put the rifle away, to wake up every morning without having to kill some other poor fool in a uniform.

He loved it here on the plantation, but he had to begin anew. His livelihood, his children, and his women were in New Orleans.

He packed a set of old but respectable clothes from his closet and sat with his father on the gallery waiting for the steam boat.

"Papa, how did you do it?"

Bertrand cast a glance at him, waiting.

"You had two women. I don't know if I can."

Bertrand flicked ash off his cigar. "Son, you give one up, it has to be Lucinda. You married Deborah Ann in the church. You divorce her, she's ruined. The war's changed things here in Louisiana, but it didn't change that."

"Lucinda is my heart, Papa. There's no record in the church books, no piece of paper to prove it. But she is my wife."

"I know, son."

Marcel bowed his head. "I shouldn't have married Deborah Ann."

"But you did, son. You did."

They smoked their cigars until the steamboat whistle blew, acknowledging the flag on the dock.

Biscuit followed him down to the river, his tail wagging. Marcel gave him a scratch behind the ears and stepped aboard the boat. His life, and his wives, awaited him.

Alistair Whiteaker, his proud gray uniform now tattered and threadbare, walked out of the disease-ridden prison camp at Point Lookout. Tired, sick, but determined, he trudged five days to Washington with a broken band of Confederates.

At the biggest bank in town, he marched in, infested with lice, barefoot and ragged, but with the bearing of a gentleman. He introduced himself. The chief teller escorted him to the president's office.

Alistair left the bank with a packet of money. He handed each of his friends a U. S. hundred dollar bill. They hugged their good-byes and resumed their journeys home.

On sore feet, Alistair hobbled across Pennsylvania avenue to the best hotel in town and convinced them to rent him a suite by flashing a peek at his wallet. In his rooms, he called the barber in and had a bath for the first time in two years. Then he climbed into a bed free of vermin, free of other men's elbows and filth and sickness. The snowy sheets smelled of lavender and sun-dried linen. They smelled like home. Alistair closed his eyes and slept round the clock.

By the time his ship sailed up the Mississippi to dock at the Bienville pier, Alistair had gained twenty pounds. His health was adequate and his bank account was fat. The loss of the war had clarified his thinking as well as his feelings. The rightness of freeing the slaves, now, not in two or three generations, settled on him with a deep certainty. Nicolette had been right in her impatience.

His plantation was ruined, the Union troops having provisioned themselves from his stores and then burned the house down. But his goal was not a re-creation of the old plantation. He built a modest house for his mother's use in the summers. Then he invited former slaves to return to the old place, this time to work for money. He allotted ground for vegetable plots. He built a dispensary and hired a doctor to attend it three days a week. And, alone among his planter acquaintances, Alistair built a school for the Negro children.

In town, Alistair let it be known that his sister, now nineteen and dangerously close to spinsterhood, was inclined to accept the attention of eligible bachelors. So many men had died, she wailed, there would be no one to court her, but Alistair assured her that her charm, and his purse, would bring many suitors to her door.

His business and family obligations underway, Alistair sought out a man who did investigations for his friends in law. "I wish to make inquiries of a lady, Mr. Dickens. Discreetly, if you please. This is her last known address."

The following day, Mr. Dickens returned. "A married woman," the investigator reported. "Married a damn Yank. Mrs. Finnian McKee, she is now."

Then finding her was pointless.

Alistair dismissed Mr. Dickens and closed his study door. He poured himself a whiskey, a rare indulgence in the afternoon. He tried these days to always be honest with himself. He wanted to know the truth of the man he was. He was strong enough for that now.

Was there perhaps a whiff of relief in Dickens' news? Alistair would not have to grapple with the difficulties of following his heart. He would not have to choose Nicolette over his mother's disgrace, his sister's marriage hopes, his own standing amongst other Southern gentlemen if he should marry a woman of color. The war had devastated the South, had ended the plantation system, freed the slaves. But Alistair's people had not relinquished their notions of white and black.

And yet, the dream. Nicolette would never share his bed. Bear his children. Smile at him over morning coffee.

Alistair tossed back his drink and poured another.

Deborah Ann waited for her husband to return from his day's work at the foundry. The Union had long ago confiscated it as rebel contraband, and Marcel now managed it, not owned it. That did not concern Deborah Ann. Father had plenty of money coming in from his City interests. Some even whispered he had profited over-much from his association with the Occupiers. Father ranted about that, but he would get over it. He would probably buy the foundry from the government in a few months and give it to Marcel.

In the New Year. That would be an occasion for gift giving, when their first child was to be born. Perhaps Marcel would find it easier to accept Father's charity if it were tied to the birth of their son.

Deborah Ann thanked God every day for her blessings. She had endured. She'd grown a little older, a little less pretty, but she had survived the war. And God had blessed her: her husband had come home to her, his only wound one deafened ear. If he were not the dashing, self-assured figure he'd been before the war, he was perhaps a little kinder, a little more thoughtful of her needs. He never reproached her for that dreadful incident with his children, never mentioned that he harbored any resentment of her rash, mad deed. He'd forgiven her, she was sure of it.

Though Marcel would never know by her words or deeds, she had not yet forgiven him for his transgressions. She had, however, come to an acceptance. One had to live with disappointments in this life.

As her belly grew, so did her sense of well-being. The storms and confusions that came with her monthlies yielded to an abiding serenity. That other woman, those other children — she blocked them from her mind.

Marcel came home to her for noon dinner and then went back to his work. He returned to her for supper. In the evenings, he went out. To his club, he said. To play cards, to talk with other soldiers about the battles they'd fought. Deborah Ann knew better. Sometimes, in season, she smelled jasmine on her husband, but she said nothing. She chose not to think about his other life.

After all, the world was much changed. Deborah Ann was no longer a dewy-eyed innocent full of romantic ideals. The war was lost. There was no Evermore. And there was no perfect love. Only this, her husband in the bed beside her when she awoke, and a child on the way. It was enough.

Nicolette woke to a mockingbird trilling to his mate in the bougainvillea vine outside her window. Finn's arm lay draped across her belly, a warm and welcome weight. She smoothed the dark hair of his forearm, careful not to wake him. He'd worked from early yesterday to late last night rebuilding the front entrance to his book store on Rue Dauphine. He'd come to bed exhausted, but not too exhausted to remind her how much he loved her. Smiling, she slipped from under his arm and eased out of the bed.

With her matches and a pack of cigarillos, she stepped onto the balcony to a blue and yellow sky. The scent of gardenias mingled with the smell of frying bacon from next door. A ship's bell dinged through the wisps of fog over the river. It was good to be home.

Finn had taken her home to his big Irish family. Finn's mother and sisters and father had been wonderfully welcoming and she'd grown to love them the six months she stayed there. But they were bees, constantly busy with some task, seldom stopping to notice the color of the sky or the scent of the roses in the garden. Nicolette decided she was more like the lazy pigeons on the balcony railing, content to just be.

She drew on her smoke. The war was over. Slavery was over. She reveled in that, that every soul in the country was as free as she. André Cailloux's death had not been for nothing.

Nicolette turned back into the room to drink in the sight of Finnian McKee, his hair tousled, his arm thrown across her side of the bed. On the little table next to the bed were his notebook and pen, the pages open to his latest poem.

What more could she ever want or need than her husband sleeping peacefully, and this lovely morning of warm, scented air?

"Come back to bed," Finn growled, his voice sensual with sleepy promise. His bare arm stretched toward her, inviting her. She went to him, the familiarity of his arms around her as heady as wine. Afterwards, they lay entangled, drowsy and sated.

"I'm not getting out of this bed. Ever," Finn said.

Nicolette rubbed her nose against his chest. "Then I'm not either."

A few minutes later, coffee smells began to drift under the door. Real coffee, strong enough to bend your spoon.

"Smell that?" Finn said.

"Ah, how easily you forsake me. Go have your coffee. I'll be down in a minute."

After breakfast with Cleo and Pierre, they walked side by side to the new store. On every street in New Orleans, the bzzt of saws and the thomp of hammers foretold a vigorous future. The city, stunned and grieved by the war, was wakening to a new era. Men and women from the north with new ideas were battering at old assumptions, bringing with them cash and energy. Men like Finn McKee.

Mid-morning, Alistair referred to a slip of paper and checked the numbers over the shops on Rue Dauphine. He paused outside No. 12. The freshly painted sign in green and gold read Books.

Alistair cocked an eyebrow. An understated man, Nicolette's husband.

Alistair had delayed this day. So much to do, rebuilding a city, a life. He wanted to see her, but he had not been sure how much pain it would cost him. Surely, he thought, the loss of her was an old hurt now. After all he'd been through since the siege at Port

Hudson, what remained to him was the love, no longer ardent, but steady and comforting.

He'd been undecided whether he would call on her or simply hope for a chance glimpse of her. Now he crossed the cobbled street. When he opened the door, the scent of sawdust and paint, paper and glue greeted him. The sun shining through the front window cast a golden glow over the empty bookcases.

A tall Negro with a horrible scar slashed across his face turned to him, one eye ruined, the other curious. He took a nail from his mouth and set his hammer down. "We not ready to open yet, mister."

Beyond the Negro, a tall man with dark hair and moustache looked up from the shelf he was painting. "Good morning to you. William is correct, we are not yet open for business. However, you are welcome to look through the boxes of books if you like."

An Irish name. A Boston accent, of course.

"Mr. McKee, I presume. Sir, I wonder if you would permit me to enquire after your wife?"

Alistair noted the speculative gleam in McKee's eye — a husband aware his wife was a treasure to be guarded.

"Forgive me. I am Alistair Whiteaker, an old friend. Might I see her?"

McKee hesitated a moment, his dark eyes flickering over Alistair, measuring him. "Of course. I'll call her."

McKee climbed the stairs and disappeared. Almost immediately, Nicolette rushed down the steps. Her face was flushed with pleasure, and Alistair drank in that pleasure as belonging to himself. The deeper glow of a happy woman, that he could not claim.

"Alistair!"

She crossed the floor hands outstretched. He took them, a foolish grin spreading across his face.

"You look wonderful, Alistair. You're well?"

"Perfectly."

McKee joined them with a friendly but guarded expression. Nicolette took her husband's hand and looked up into his face, her gray eyes alight. The power of the attraction between them hit Alistair hard, much harder than he had prepared himself for. He felt as if a hand reached into his chest and squeezed his heart in a tight fist.

So this was Nicolette in love. She had never looked at Alistair that way, as if he were an adored and adoring god.

Regret washed over him at what he had lost. No. He forced himself to admit the truth of it. He had never possessed Nicolette's heart to lose it. And that was his own fault. If he had asked Nicolette to marry him long ago, before the war, she might have said yes. She might now have looked on him, if not with this adoration, then with affection. With love. But he had been mired in the foolishness that a drop of black blood rendered a woman unfit to be a gentleman's wife. He didn't deserve Nicolette. He never had.

"Alistair reads, Finn! He'll talk books with you all day long." Nicolette looked back at Alistair, laughing. "I can't keep up with all the books my husband reads, Alistair. I need help."

Her appeal warmed him. The grip around his heart eased. She did care for him, a little, and that was all he had a right to expect.

Perhaps the three of them could be friends. He thought he could do that, be friends with Nicolette's husband, as long as he could be her friend.

"Are you fond of French drama, Mr. McKee?" Alistair said.

"Molière, yes! And Racine."

Nicolette guided Finn and Alistair to the courtyard where she had sangria cooling in a terracotta pitcher. She poured them each a glass, and as the sun lit on the golden wine, she remembered Alistair's purse of gold, still nestled under Maman's cactus. She'd have it for him, next time he called.

Pleased to have him restored to her, she sat with Finn on the cedar bench as he and Alistair enthusiastically recalled productions they'd seen of *Tartuffe*.

She looked from one man to the other as they moved on to Shakespeare and Marlowe. Alistair looked very fine in his dove gray suit. Her husband smelled of turpentine, and a speckle of green paint adorned his cheek. But Finn's brown eyes sparkled at finding a kindred soul, a man who read Molière and liked to talk books.

Sitting close to Finn on the bench, Nicolette felt the warmth of his long leg against hers. She opened her hand and he took it, readily, without pausing in his conversation. In that absent, intimate way of his, he ran his thumb over the back of her hand.

Nicolette leaned back and closed her eyes, listening to the music of her husband's voice. She smiled to herself. Life was overwhelmingly, astonishingly wonderful.

THE END

BONUS SECTION

Read on for the first three chapters of
Gretchen Craig's new novel —

Tansy

Tansy

Chapter One

For weeks, before she slept, Tansy Bouvier imagined herself dancing with an elegant, handsome man whose gaze promised love and forbidden pleasures — only to waken later in a tangle of sweaty sheets, shaken by dreams of dancers whirling around her, herself in an over-lit circle, alone, isolated, and unwanted.

But this was not a dream. The dreaded moment was upon her, the moment she had prepared for all her life, and she must smile. Maman gave her elbow a pinch, a final warning to sparkle. Tansy raised her chin and followed her into the famous Blue Ribbon Ballroom.

Droplets of fear trickled down her spine as she fought both the dread and the foolish romanticizing of what was essentially an evening of business. A beginning, not an end, she whispered to herself. Time to forget girlhood dreams, time to forget Christophe Desmarais. This night, she entered the world of plaçage in which a woman's *raison d'être* was to please a man, a very wealthy man. In return, she gained everything – riches, security, status.

In spite of the fluttering in her stomach, she found herself captivated by the glamour of the ballroom. Gas lamps glowed like yellow moons between the French doors, and crystal teardrops in the chandeliers sparkled like ice in sunshine. And the music. Tansy's chest lifted at the power and fire of a full orchestra, strings and reeds and percussion propelling the dancers around the floor.

Maman chose a prominent, imminently visible position near the upper curve of the ball room to display Tansy and her charms. Tansy's task tonight was to make a splash, to outshine every other girl who'd entered the game earlier in the season. No, she thought. Not a game. Tonight, Tansy would meet her fate: luxury or destitution, security or whoredom.

What if none of the gentlemen wanted her? What if none of them even noticed her? What then?

"Smile," Maman hissed from the corner of her mouth.

"I am smiling," Tansy replied through wooden lips.

"That is not a smile. Look like you're glad to be here. Watch the dancers."

White men in stiff collars wove intricate steps and turns through the line of women, every one of whom wore a festive tignon over her hair. Tansy squinted her eyes so as to make the dancers and the chandeliers a blur of lights and swirling colors. Such a grand, beautiful sight, as if the most renowned ballroom in New Orleans were not the scene of business and barter.

She had known this night must come, and had imagined the men as leering and brash. Instead they seemed aloof and slightly bored. The young women, though, were as she expected. They wore masks with bright smiles and welcoming, deceiving eyes that promised gaiety and delight. She was meant to do the same.

"Loosen your grip on that fan," Maman whispered. "It is not a sword to be brandished at the enemy."

Tansy swallowed and opened the fan with cold, stiff fingers. She spied her friend Martine on the dance floor, vibrant in a red velvet gown. How splendid she looked in the red tignon wrapped in intricate folds around her head. She laughed, her eyes sparkling as her partner leaned in to speak into her ear. Martine had already been to several balls and had regaled Tansy with tales of handsome gentlemen who whispered love and promises as they twirled her around the ballroom. She was having a grand time waiting for the right protector to offer for her, but Martine had a boldness, a carelessness Tansy could not match. And Martine had never been kissed by Christophe Desmarais.

Tansy glanced again at her own yellow silk, the neckline cut so deep she felt indecent. If Martine was a vibrant scarlet tanager, she felt herself to be a mere mockingbird masquerading as a canary. She touched her matching tignon, terrified it might slip on her head. "I'm too conspicuous in this dress," she whispered to her mother.

"Nonsense. No other girl here can wear yellow like you can."

A Creole gentleman, dark haired, dark eyed, no doubt very charming, bowed to Maman. "Madame Bouvier."

Tansy breathed out in relief. She might feel conspicuous, but at least she was not invisible. The gentleman was tall and handsome, his nose straight and long, his brow rather noble. For a moment, she let herself believe this handsome man would fall in love with her, and she with him, and they would dance and laugh and feel drunk with love, together, forever. She wanted to believe it.

He murmured something polite, and Maman inclined her head. Maman knew every gentleman in New Orleans and the status of his bank account. Tansy's foolish moment passed. She was not here to begin a grand love affair. Love had nothing to do with it. The gentleman delivered the merest glance at Tansy and then turned back to Maman, the accepted code, she supposed for May I have your daughter for the rest of her life?

Maman nodded her approval. He bowed to Tansy. "May I have the honor of this dance, Mademoiselle?"

With a curious feeling of detachment, she accepted his arm and followed him onto the dance floor. It was only a dance. She liked to dance. She'd let the music carry her.

The gentleman wore an expertly tailored coat of deep maroon paired with gray satin knee breeches. He did look very fine, but more to the point, very prosperous. He smiled at her. "Lovely evening."

I mean you no harm she interpreted. *See how nicely I smile? See how I have not once gazed at your plunging neckline, eyeing the wares?*

"Yes," she managed to say. "Lovely weather." The man must be thirty at least. His hand was smooth as a girl's, and as cold as her own.

The dance led them near the orchestra's platform. Tansy darted a glance at Christophe, sitting among the violinists. Oh God, he was watching her. Her stomach dropped and heat rushed to her face. For the rest of the dance, she focused a frozen gaze on her partner's ear, and if he said anything else, she did not note it.

At the end of the set, the gentleman returned her to Maman, tossed a bow at her and went in search of more pleasing company. Maman scowled. "If you don't stop acting like a dry stick, I will take you home this instant."

Like the puppet she felt herself to be, she loosened her shoulders, unclenched her teeth, and obeyed. No dry sticks allowed. She would be a willow branch, graceful, pliable. Yes, that was her. Pliant Tansy Marie Bouvier, a willow to be bent to fit her destiny.

Tansy had a moment to collect herself as another Creole gentleman bent over Maman's hand and made the customary flattering remarks. He seemed pleasant, not inclined to devour young women at their first balls. He smiled. No, no fangs, no sharpened canines.

"Monsieur Valcourt, my daughter, Tansy Marie."

He was of medium height, medium build, medium dark hair and medium brown eyes. Not handsome, not ugly. Maman raised an eyebrow. Such a wealth of information in that eyebrow: this man is rich, this man is a catch, and if you know what's good for you, you'll make him fall in love with you.

"Mademoiselle, will you dance?"

Squaring her shoulders, she followed him onto the dance floor.

Tansy's resolve to ignore Christophe faltered and her eyes found him again. His focus was on the music, his brow creased in concentration. She knew men didn't set so much store in a kiss as women, but she would never forget it. She gave herself a mental shake. It was because of that kiss that her mother had dragged her here, two weeks before her seventeenth birthday, to ensure they both understood that Christophe, a mere fiddler, could not afford a beautiful canary like Tansy Marie Bouvier.

Monsieur Valcourt's attention seemed to be on the music, his gaze primarily directed over her shoulder as he moved her through the steps. He danced well. No red gleaming eyes, no clawed fingers. She liked the fact that he didn't try to charm her, nor did he seem to expect her to dazzle him.

They joined hands as they moved into a turn. Her cold fingers warmed in his palm, and his assumption of connection, of ease in their touch loosened her reserve. A comfortable man, this Monsieur Valcourt.

An older gentleman circled through the line to partner Tansy with a turn through the dance. He leered at her décolletage, yellow teeth on display, and he held his mouth slightly open with the tip of his tongue visible. The thought of his tobacco stained fingers in intimate contact with her skin sent a shiver of revulsion through her.

Or else, she remembered her mother's threat. *Find a protector, or else face a life of penury, a few years in a brothel until your looks fade, and then what, eh?*

The dance moved on and Monsieur Valcourt reappeared at her side. When he took her hand with no leer, no meaningful squeeze of her fingers, she breathed in freely for the first time all evening. The music ended. He bestowed on her an open, guileless smile that warmed his brown eyes.

Yes, she could live with this man. She didn't need to survey, and be surveyed by, a dozen or two other gentlemen. And if Maman was right, that her looks would assure her any man she chose, then she would as soon choose this one and have it done with. He seemed nice. They would likely have a family together. They would be happy enough.

She allowed herself one last glimpse of Christophe among the violinists. He met her gaze over his bow, and for a moment her vision tunneled so that all around him was hazy darkness, Christophe himself bathed in light. She closed her eyes and turned away.

Perhaps no woman could choose her own fate, but she would take control of what she could. She would be the placée of Monsieur Valere Valcourt. Tansy opened her eyes and bestowed on Monsieur Valcourt her most dazzling smile.

Chapter Two
Five years later

Tansy danced with Annabelle's Monsieur Duval, he of the yellow teeth and dandruff-dusted shoulders. Her friend had skin two shades darker than her own and her wide nose reflected her African heritage, so of course Annabelle had not been able to attract the most desirable of protectors. Even so, she reported her patron kept her in comfort, never beat her, and came to her bed no more than once a week. He'd given her two wonderful children of whom he seemed fond, and she found her life reasonably happy. For that, Tansy smiled at him as he led her around the dance floor.

The new placées-to-be danced all around her, dewy-eyed, round-chinned, and thrilled to be attended to by handsome, wealthy gentlemen. She spied one, however, who was as tense as Tansy had been at her first ball. And now she was at ease here in the Blue Ribbon ballroom, a woman more than twenty, a woman with a child.

The orchestra took a break. Monsieur Duval returned to Annabelle, and Tansy joined Christophe where he leaned against a column, the picture of languid ease. He dressed as all the musicians did, but on him the black jacket and white linen looked dangerous, the light in his roving black eyes distinctly carnal. She'd noticed more than one young woman eyeing him from behind their fans. But of course, as a man of color, however light, he was admitted here only as a musician.

Christophe handed her his glass of punch and nodded toward her dance partner. "You've made that old coot a happy man tonight."

"Maurice? He is an old coot, but a nice one." She finished his punch and handed him the glass, accidentally touching his fingers. Her breath hitched. They never touched, not since the night before her come-out in this very room. Trying to appear unfazed, she slowly fanned away the warmth in her face.

She eyed Christophe's scraped knuckles. "I see you've been brawling again."

He grinned. "Me? A shining example of virtue for all my students?"

She shook her head. "If they knew you were a brawler, they'd worship your very shadow."

"Don't tell, though. Their mamans and papas would not be well pleased. Have you noticed the Russians?"

"Is that what they are? I'd love to hear them speak."

He gestured for her to precede him. "Then allow me to introduce you."

"You've met them?"

"My legendary fame as a poker player has earned me an invitation to their table after the ball."

"I suppose you will show them no mercy."

With a wicked glint in his eye, he gave her a malicious smirk. "I will not."

They strolled toward the Russian delegation, Christophe's hands behind his back, a foot or more of space between them. She was well aware he took pains not to touch her. It was right that he do so. She belonged to Valere, after all.

"And where is your beloved paramour tonight?" he said.

Tansy stiffened at the slight curl in Christophe's lip. It was a game he played, trying to goad her into defending Valere, but she'd recently begun experimenting with goading remarks of her own.

"He's at the society ball across the alleyway, of course, with his cousins and friends. With the other *gentlemen*." She gave him a withering glance from head to toe to indicate how far he was from the status of *gentleman*.

Christophe chuckled. "Well done. You'll overcome your regrettable affliction yet."

She was indeed afflicted with an intransigent case of niceness, as Christophe called it. What he meant, she supposed, was that she was dull. Even so, the two of them were, she and Christophe — what were they? Attached, she supposed. Closer in taste and temperament than even she and Martine. They understood each other.

They split to walk around a cluster of people drinking punch. When they rejoined, Tansy fanned her face and looked about with an air of disinterest. "Valere courts a Miss Abigail, I believe."

"Miss Windsor? My fiddle and I played at her birthday ball in January. Pretty girl."

Tansy tilted her chin and looked down her nose at him.

"Forgive me. I have erred. I meant to report that the girl has buck teeth, a flat chest, and mousy hair."

"Indeed you should." Tansy drew her fan briskly through her left hand, in the language of fans an indication that she detested him with all her heart.

Christophe threw his head back in a laugh. He nodded toward the arched doorway. "And here is the gentleman in question."

The slight ache of tension behind her eyes eased as Valere Valcourt leisurely made his way around the dancers, the hundreds of candles in the overhead chandeliers casting a gentle glow on his wavy brown hair. Descended from a disgraced French nobleman who'd been exiled to the wilds of Louisiana a century ago, Valere represented the quintessential Creole, privileged, entitled, at ease in his world.

Christophe slipped away. He had, as far as Tansy could remember, never actually been in Valere's presence.

Valere stopped to talk to Monsieur DuMaine, a man whom Tansy knew to be searching for his fourth placée, having tired of the others. Though he must be very rich indeed to have paid the penalties for breaking three contracts, he epitomized the most dangerous sort of protector in the world of plaçage. There could be no security in an alliance with a man of his reputation.

Martine, clad in her signature red, strolled past the two men, gently fluttering her fan in signal to Monsieur DuMaine. So Martine vied to be number four in this man's serial harem? Tansy did not like the idea of her friend allying herself with such a man. Tansy was no green girl, and the man was handsome, but really – didn't she understand he'd gone through three women in only five years?

Tansy watched Martine's little drama, worried at her friend's lack of judgment, but she was amused, too. Du Maine's eyes tracked Martine as she rolled her hips, touched a hand to her elaborate tignon to call attention to her slender neck, then made her way around the dancers toward the balcony. A scarlet tanager among wrens, she turned at the exit, raised her fan in her right hand to cover the lower part of her face, and flashed dark eyes at DuMaine. Mouth slightly open, he nodded vaguely toward Valere and strode away in pursuit. Tansy nearly laughed aloud at the man's haste.

Valere caught her eye across the room and smiled as he came to her. She put away her nagging jealousy over Miss Abigail Windsor. She had always known he would marry. He needed heirs, legitimate sons. His marriage didn't mean he would abandon her and their son. Valere's own father had raised his legitimate family with his very proper white wife, and yet had remained attached to the same placée for twenty years. She and Valere and Alain were a family now, regardless of when he married.

"Here you are," he said.

"Good evening, Valere." She smiled for him. She always smiled for him.

He stood at ease by her side, surveying the ball room, his glance falling on the group of large, bearish men in their rather rustic fashions.

"Do you see we have Russians here tonight?" she asked. "I would love to hear them speak, wouldn't you? And don't you suppose those heavy beards are hot? I don't imagine they're accustomed to our humidity."

"Russians, are they?"

And that was as much interest in Russians as she could elicit from him. So many other things she would like to talk about. Did the Society ladies dance until they glowed with perspiration? Had Valere danced all evening with Miss Abigail? Did they dance well together? But of course she could not speak of his other life.

"Shall we dance?" he said.

As Valere guided her around the dance floor, she yielded herself to the music, her mind adrift in the flowing colors of the violin, the oboe, the bassoon.

At the end of the number, Valere whispered in her ear. "Let's go home."

Tansy's lingering anxiety vanished. At least for tonight, Valere desired her, not the pale-faced Abigail Windsor.

Tansy reached for the blanket and pulled it over Valere's bare chest. In an hour or two, he'd get up to dress, then he'd leave her for his townhouse. In the morning, Alain would not even know his father had been there unless she told him. Valere took their son for granted, as he did so much in his life, but he was a good man.

Tansy lay a light kiss on his jaw and got up. She lit a candle, wrapped herself in her robe, and settled into the overstuffed chair with her book. This one was about Spaniards discovering the new world. How she would like to have been there when Columbus first made landfall, thinking he was in India. And found all those Indians! She stifled the laugh burbling up at the linguistic absurdity. She was just getting to the part where Cortés discovered the great city cut through with canals.

"Come back to bed and keep me warm." Valere's voice was muffled in his pillow. She blew out her candle and slid in beside him. "Cold feet! Woman, what have you been doing?"

She stuck one cold foot between his shins. "Reading. Did you know the Aztecs built a city very much like Venice? Canals through and around. And like New Orleans, the water table was so high, they practically lived in the marsh. I suppose it's even hotter in Mexico, though."

Valere tossed an arm over her belly. "Why is that?" he mumbled.

She moved her head to see his face on the pillow, but it was too dark to decide if he were teasing her. She suspected he was not. "It is so very much further south, you see."

"Is it?" He shifted to get comfortable. "Go to sleep, Tansy."

Chapter Three

Tansy helped Alain tie his shoes, took his hand, and set out for the Academy. She tried to do all her errands early in the day when she was sure Valere still lay abed in his townhouse and so wouldn't call while she was out. Her first task this morning, to return Christophe's *History of the Americas*.

She and Alain climbed the schoolhouse steps. Too early for the students yet, morning breezes wafted cool air into Christophe's schoolroom. Alain dashed for the resident cat who allowed herself to be caught and petted.

Christophe raised his head and in that one unguarded moment, revealed a depth of pleasure at seeing her that flashed through her with far too much warmth. "Good morning," he said.

"Finished the book." He reached for it with his large, capable hand. That hand had once pressed her body against his. She'd been trimming the jasmine vine that threatened to cover the French doors and he'd stepped into the courtyard. With a gleam in his eye, a glance over his shoulder to check her mother was out of sight, he'd pulled her under the green canopy.

"What are you doing?" she'd whispered.

He caught her in his arms and dared her with his eyes. She could have backed away, like a good girl. But she'd let him pull her close. Let him lean down, the smell of jasmine and Christophe's own scent filling her head. She sighed. He kissed her. His hand traced her backbone till it rested at her waist, and then he pulled her in to his body. When he touched her tongue with his own, her breath caught. When he parted her legs with his knee and deepened the kiss, she completely lost herself in him, in the searing heat of his hand through the back of her dress.

Then Maman had stepped into the courtyard and shrieked as if a tiger mauled her only child.

Tansy jumped back, guilty and ashamed. But Christophe, all the while Maman scolded and railed, ran his thumbnail up her spine and then cupped her bottom and squeezed.

The next night, Maman had presented her at the Blue Ribbon Ball.

Tansy swallowed. She had no business remembering that stolen moment. She belonged to Valere. She was a mother. And Christophe was a respected man, a teacher, a musician. And yes, a gambler who sometimes showed up with a bruise on his chin and a busted knuckle. The two of them were no longer love sick adolescents.

"What did you think of it?" he asked.

"Very sad. The Aztecs losing everything to the Spanish, and then they died from those dreadful plagues." Did Christophe allow himself to think of that kiss? She didn't, she really didn't. She was settled now, and one long-ago kiss didn't mean so very much anyway.

"Not a happy story, no."

"Now I want a book about plagues."

Christophe laughed. "Aren't you the morbid one? Alas, my library is sorely limited." He swiveled his chair and ran his finger along the books shelved behind him. "How about this one?"

She looked at the spine. "*Candide*. What's it about?"

"Where would be the fun if I told you?" Christophe held his arm out. "Alain, come show me your letters."

Alain abandoned the tabby cat and climbed into Christophe's lap. When Alain glanced at her, a secretive smile on his face, Tansy raised her brows in collusion.

He picked up a chalk and laboriously drew an A on Christophe's slate. With his forehead scrunched in concentration, his tongue between his lips, Tansy thought him the most intelligent, handsome boy in New Orleans. He'd practiced his letters for weeks now and was about to astound his friend by writing his entire name.

"ALAIN?" Christophe exclaimed. "You wrote your name! *Tres bien!*"

Christophe hugged him and turned him around on his lap so he could look him in the eye. "You, Alain, are a great scholar."

"*Merci.*" Alain slid off Christophe's lap to pursue the cat.

Tansy sat at a student table and opened *Candide*. Christophe had given her her first book, too. In her last month of pregnancy with Alain, she had lumbered across the Quarter with Maman to visit Christophe's mother. By chance, Christophe had dropped in, a book under his arm. She'd not exchanged a single word with him since that day under the jasmine, but there was no distance between them. They talked and laughed and drank his maman's punch. When he rose to leave, he handed *Frankenstein, the Modern Prometheus* to her and said, "Keep it." And so Tansy read her first book, staying up late into the night, frightened and fascinated.

Christophe came around his desk and sat on a corner to lean over her.

"This one is fiction."

"Is it a love story?"

When she glanced up, Christophe's eyes were on her. Sometimes he focused on her as if she were a puzzle he'd like to solve. Sometimes, like now, she felt he would lift her to her feet and take her across the desk. He wouldn't though. Christophe had never deliberately touched her since their first, their only kiss.

She couldn't meet his eyes when he forgot himself like that. It unsettled her, it hurt her. In another time, another place ... Well. She was spoken for. She was so very fortunate to have a kind, generous patron like Valere. And really, Christophe had no interest in her any more. Just now and then she let herself think he did.

Christophe removed himself to sit behind his desk again, and she breathed more easily. "Not a romance, not like you mean," he said. "But it's fun. It'll make you laugh."

"You don't need it for your students?"

"Those rascals? They're not ready for satire, the little brutes. We're reading a story about a boy and his dog at the moment."

"I want a dog!" Alain said.

"I thought you wanted a cat," Tansy said.

"Maman, I want a dog and a cat."

"We'll ask your father. Perhaps he will allow a kitten."

Alain engrossed himself in the chalk nubs he found on the desks. Christophe's lowered voice barely suppressed his impatience. "Why would Valcourt object to Alain having a pet? Surely that is of no interest to a man who is seldom in the house when Alain is awake?"

When Alain was awake? Tansy's face heated and her shoulders stiffened. She busied herself putting the book in her shopping bag. "He doesn't like surprises, that's all."

She yanked the drawstring on her bag and knotted it too tightly. Christophe thought she was a fool, a childish fool, for deferring to her patron. How could he think that of her when his own mother had been a placée at one time. And yet he made her feel she led a lamentable life. She did not need his disapproval. Maman supplied enough of that for a dozen daughters.

"Alain." She held her hand out. "It's time to go."

"Tansy." She turned toward Christophe, but she still did not look at him. "I beg your pardon."

Now she raised her eyes to his and saw only a mask, rather cold, certainly closed off. "It's nothing. *Adieu*, Christophe. I'll return your book next week."

Christophe sat, elbows on his desk, his eyes closed behind his steepled fingers. Regret scorched him. He'd upset her, again. Her visits every week to borrow a book were too important to him to risk frightening her off, and he'd hurt her. When would he learn to keep his mouth shut? He should know better than to even mention Valcourt. She almost never did.

He rubbed his face. This was an old hurt. He simply had to accept the life she'd chosen. No, that wasn't right, he thought, the bitterness edging back into his mind. She had not chosen. Her mother had done that for her. Tansy had been too young, too immersed in the plaçage culture to see other possibilities for herself.

Estelle had molded her daughter into what every white man seemed to want, a biddable woman. Christophe remembered that day at the lake when they were children. His mother and Tansy's had taken them for an outing and he and Tansy had run wild, darting in and out among the tall pines, shrieking and shouting with abandon. That Tansy had been free and bold and unafraid. She had been herself.

But Estelle suppressed all that joy and used Tansy's inherent sweetness to turn her into a *nice* girl, a biddable girl. Except that one afternoon when he'd caught her under the jasmine vines and kissed her. Tansy had not been sweet or biddable then. She had seized that moment, seized him in a kiss that seared him to his toes.

Christophe ran a hand through his hair. Was she that hot when Valere took her to bed? He shook his head. He had no business thinking of that. Even if Estelle's steady hand propelled her, Tansy had entered into this life with her eyes open.

What added to the bitterness, though, was that he could have supported her from the time he was twenty, a year or so after she'd been taken to the Blue Ribbon. He had already begun investing his poker winnings by then and he'd quickly become a man of property with a growing bank account. He'd never be as rich as Valcourt, but he could keep her and Alain in comfort with his pay as a musician, his salary as a teacher, and his income from the houses he owned in the *Vieux Carré*.

He squeezed his eyes shut. If he'd only had a little more time, been a little older when Estelle sealed Tansy's fate.

He opened his eyes to stare across the room, trying to find the resignation that sustained him. When he'd met her at his mother's that day, her belly full and round, it had been nearly two years since he'd been in the same room with her. Tansy had been radiant. But weren't all women in her condition radiant? Or had she glowed with love for her protector? He hadn't known. And now? She had her fine clothes, her own cottage, a generous allowance. All she need do in return was pretend to adore some fatuous rich man who deluded himself he could buy affection. The muscles in Christophe's jaw bunched. Valere Valcourt was empty, vain, and idle, yet he possessed Tansy Marie Bouvier.

Did she live a lie, pretending to love that ass? Or had she actually developed an affection for him? Christophe hadn't made it out, and it gnawed at him.

The thunder of feet in the hallway announced his pupils had arrived, ready to have their heads stuffed with numbers and letters and facts. He breathed in deeply. When the rascals stormed into the room, he welcomed them with a smile he didn't feel.

You have been reading the first chapters of Gretchen Craig's new novel, *Tansy*. Available soon on Amazon.

Evermore
Questions for Discussion

1. Deborah Ann's father Mr. Presswood signs the oath of loyalty to Mr. Lincoln's government. He feels he must gain the Union's trust enough to continue scheming on behalf of the Confederacy while under Union control, but he feels he has besmirched his honor by shamefully signing his name. Does pragmatism outweigh honor? Are you sympathetic to Mr. Presswood? How do you compare Mr. Presswood with Dix Weber's conduct? Is Nicolette's working with the Union Army also collaboration?

2. Deborah Ann is what they used to call high-strung. What do you think is behind her actions toward Lucinda and the boys? Is she simply spoiled and feels entitled to whatever she wants? Is she temporarily deranged? Do her hormonal difficulties with PMS excuse her actions?

3. Aside from Deborah Ann's rash actions with Lucinda, how do you evaluate her character? What other responses might she have made to learning that her beloved has another woman? What would you be willing to tolerate considering that keeping a placée was an accepted practice among the Creole planters of that time?

4. Marcel has two women, and feels quite justified in keeping both. He doesn't seem to feel the least guilt or uneasiness. His situation is accepted in his Creole culture. What do you make of his sense of morality?

5. Marcel feels he is in an impossible situation when he finds his childhood friend spying for the enemy. If Lieutenant Smythe had not hanged Dix Weber, what would you see as a "good" outcome for Dix and for Marcel? How could it

possibly come out all right? Should Dix accept parole and shamefully sit out the rest of the war to save his life?

6. Alistair Whiteaker is a gentle soul who finds himself in an impossible situation just as Marcel does with Dix. Alistair loves Nicolette. He is responsible for his mother and his younger sister. If he marries Nicolette, his mother will be ostracized, his sister will not find a good match, and his own associates, business and social, will shun him. There is also the real possibility of violence if he should marry Nicolette. What would you have him do? Are your feelings toward him contemptuous or sympathetic?

ABOUT THE AUTHOR

Gretchen Craig's lush, sweeping tales probe the moral dilemmas and raw suffering of people caught in times of great upheaval. Rich in historical detail, her novels test the boundaries of integrity, strength, and love.

Gretchen has lived in the arid prairies of Texas, the cold, beautiful landscapes of Maine, and the humid wetlands of Florida. She now makes her home on the Gulf Coast where the hibiscus and the bougainvillea bloom year round.

Find profiles of each novel at www.gretchencraig.com or find further details at www.amazon.com/author/gretchencraig.

Made in the USA
San Bernardino, CA
16 February 2016